To Bruce Moskowitz,
Thank you for everything.
Sincerely,
Karen Seymour

UNEARTHED

Book 1 of *The Pactem Orbis Legends*

KAREN SEYMOUR

ISBN: 1492747556
ISBN 13: 9781492747550
Library of Congress Control Number: 2013916949
CreateSpace Independent Publishing Platform
North Charleston, South Carolina

To the first author, the foremost in creativity:
All my fountains are in you.

PROLOGUE

G emma Alexandra Pointe is not a fitting name for a warrior, a vigilante, or a mystic.

The name does not lend itself to the conjuring of images, the way other names like Merlin or Frankenstein do.

One would never hear the name and assume it belongs to a powerful person, such as an influential politician or religious leader.

And it *certainly* doesn't sound like the name of a "supernatural"—an angel, a mermaid, or a fairy godmother.

But that's what I am: a supernatural.

It took me a long time to come to terms with what I *am*, probably because I believed my name so aptly identified me for what I *was*: a directionless University of Minnesota junior and the relatively talentless offspring of exceptionally talented but long-deceased parents.

Now that I'm able to access memories prior to the age of twelve, which until recently had been blocked to me, I realize that I was destined for a greater purpose from the beginning.

I should have known all along. My birthmark was too unique, too *particular*, to be the random etchings of nature. Yet I failed to recognize it as anything more, anything that could help me find my way, until Malakai discovered me six months ago and led me down the path that changed my life forever—the path that led to the deaths of twenty-two innocent people in one catastrophic moment.

If anyone ever knew what I did that day to save the others, they would probably call me a hero. If anyone ever knew how I did it, they would probably call me a superhero. But I'm no superhero. I am unqualified for rescuing—as if those I failed aren't evidence enough of that. Anyway, more often than not, I'm the one being rescued.

I regret the loss of the twenty-two. I regret that I didn't solve the puzzle sooner; perhaps everyone would have survived. I regret that I now have countless enemies who will pursue me until I'm dead. And more than anything, I regret losing Jonny.

But I do not regret what I am or the choices I have made. I am an Essen, a living human descendent of an elemental, and one of remaining few. I have inherited gifts of both flesh and mind, as well as the means to harness the forces of earth, air, fire, and water. And I finally know what my purpose is.

I am a light in the dark, a destroyer of evil, a conqueror of enemies, and a beacon of hope in a desolate world.

And my name is Gemma Alexandra Pointe.

PART ONE:
INTO THE MINES

CHAPTER 1

I n my daydreams, I am not afraid of the water.
  In my daydreams, I am not afraid of anything.

But in my fantasies, like in real life, I am restless, always searching for something more, some meaning beyond my current awareness.

I don't know exactly when they started, but by last fall, the daydreams consumed me. I began skipping class, withdrawing to my own hidden spot on the University of Minnesota's Minneapolis campus—a wooded area on the east bank of the Mississippi River—to detach and rest and imagine.

The spot appealed to me because of its seclusion, but also because it was *mine*. It had called to me. I had been drawn to it. I was on my way to Physics recitation one day a month earlier, when, for no understandable reason, I was pulled away from Tate Hall and to the woods. And despite the bustle of activity always present along the running trails of the river, no other soul had ever encroached my sacred space within the circle of oaks.

I went to The Oaks nearly every day after finding it. If the autumn hadn't been so unseasonably warm, and if I hadn't been so incredibly tired every day, I might have attended class more. But though midterms were approaching, the comfort of the leaves-covered clearing beckoned.

Unfortunately, on Tuesday, October 28th, the peace of the place was shattered. The enchantment was broken, and I never daydreamed there again.

It had been quiet on the trails that day. As I made my way to my spot, I wondered if everyone else was too busy studying to enjoy the weather.

The rays of the late afternoon sun slipped through the branches of the naked trees and warmed me. I took off my sweater once I entered the circle and bunched it into a pillow. Mindlessly, I tossed my backpack to the side and sprawled onto the blanketed ground, the fallen leaves crunching in a satisfying way.

Looking up, I admired the way the filtered light painted the trees. When I closed my eyes, the patchwork of light remained.

My mind began drifting almost immediately. The fresh smell of fall was replaced by the scent of salty sea air.

Like always, I was walking along the drift line of a wide, white sandy beach. The ocean was to my right, an overgrown forest far to my left, and massive rocky cliffs in the distance ahead. I pressed forward, uncertain of what I should be looking for, but happy at least for the soft powder squishing through my bare toes with each step.

I was still plodding, certain something would be revealed to me, when I became aware of the ocean speaking to me. Its voice was rhythmic, alluring; it tempted me to enter the water.

Stepping cautiously at first, I waded into the ocean. It was silky and gentle, not gritty and rough like I'd thought it would be. It invited me to keep going, encouraged me to. Sure that my promised prize was waiting beyond the next swell, I moved further and further from shore.

Soon I realized the water was too deep, the waves too high. I tried to swim, but my legs were locked in place by the currents. I knew I was too far from the beach. I would not be able to make it back to shore.

But I was not afraid. In my daydreams, I am never afraid of the water. Instead, I felt an acceptance. I stopped trying to swim, let the next wave crash over me—

"This is no place for sleeping." His voice, forceful and cold, broke into my reverie.

My eyes flew open. He was towering over me, arms crossing his broad and muscled chest. His cropped black hair and his clothing—black utility pants, black work boots, and a form-fitting gray t-shirt—gave him the appearance of a soldier. But his most striking feature, and also his most intimidating, was his eyes. In contrast with his caramel complexion, his eyes were dark green. And filled with disdain.

Adrenaline coursed through me, but I was paralyzed. The abruptness of his intrusion shocked and confused me. I felt embarrassed, disoriented, and violated all at once.

His green eyes flared. "Leave," he said. "Now!"

Further alarmed by his urgency, I was able to react. Without a word, I jumped up, seized my bag and my sweater, and turned to run.

As I did, I saw his eyes register the birthmark on the inside of my right wrist. There was a flash of recognition in them. Then fury.

I had only made it a few steps when he came up behind me, grabbed my arm and twisted it.

"Who put you up to this!" His green eyes were wild now rather than angry, and he rolled my arm further, exposing the café-au-lait symbol on my inner wrist.

I panicked, tried to pull my arm free, but his grip was too strong. "Please," I said, "Please let me go! You're hurting me!" Tears sprang into my eyes.

He released me immediately, seemingly taken aback by my words. I ran away from him as fast as I could, through the woods, towards the river, up the path, back to the campus, not stopping until I was safely concealed by a swarm of other students.

CHAPTER 2

I sat on the marble steps of Walter Library and waited for Jonny to finish class, trying to calm down, trying to make sense of what had happened.

The green-eyed stranger had not wanted me there. Why? At first, he'd been commanding and intense, but not necessarily threatening. When he interrupted my daydream, I'd been extremely startled but not truly afraid. It wasn't until he saw my birthmark and I saw the rage in his eyes that I became frightened.

I rubbed my arm where he'd caught me. It wasn't sore, just red. In that moment when he'd seized me, I had been terrified. His grip felt strong, solid, determined. I doubt I could have struggled to free myself if he hadn't let me go.

Who put you up to this, he'd demanded. Put me up to what?

I looked out at the mall, the tree-lined promenade spread out before me. Students were lounging, studying, and playing Frisbee in the last hour of daylight. I looked at my watch. Jonny would be finishing class soon.

Not soon enough, though. I heard Professor Grayson Dagenais's booming voice before I saw him. I turned. He was coming out of the library, chatting with another faculty member, carrying a stack of books. I stood up, hoping he wouldn't recognize me from class, hoping to leave unnoticed. No such luck.

"Gemma Pointe," he said. He always uses people's full names, but I was surprised he knew mine. There are only two reasons any of my professors ever know me by name. I wondered which reason was his.

He parted ways with his colleague, shifted the pile of books he was carrying, and approached me.

"You missed my class again today, young lady. That's three in a row. You're going to have a very difficult time passing if you keep this up."

I looked down and nodded.

"I expect to see you in class on Thursday. And get the details about the final—I announced them today—from Mr. Jonny Saletto."

So his was the second of the two reasons: my best friend. He associated me with the English department's star student, the legendary *Mr.* Jonny Saletto. I noticed that Professor Dagenais reserved the use of titles for those he considered gifted. I was surprised he didn't call him *Sir* Jonny Saletto.

I mumbled that I would be in class and that I'd follow up with Jonny about what I'd missed. Satisfied, Professor Dagenais marched off.

Moments later, Jonny was walking towards me, looking cool in jeans and a gray hoodie, his backpack casually hanging from one shoulder. As usual, friends from class surrounded him. He broke from them and jogged to where I was standing.

"Why are you covered in leaves?" he asked. He brushed off the back of my t-shirt and started picking leaves from my hair. "Don't tell me. You were napping in the woods again." He rolled his eyes. "You should see someone, Gem. You need to start sleeping at night."

He had a point. For the past month, I'd been having difficulty falling and staying asleep. And when I did manage to sleep, nightmares of water, of moonlit, life-extinguishing black swells, tormented me. Only in my daydreams am I not afraid of the water.

"I know," I said. Sighing, I rubbed my eyes. We started walking towards where Jonny had parked his car. I hated having to be on campus such long days, but carpooling was easier than taking the bus.

"And you need to start going to class." Jonny shook his head at me, his longish brown hair swinging around his face. "I can't keep doing all your homework for you. Prof Dagenais is going to catch on if your essays keep sounding like mine."

"I think he has. He talked to me while I was waiting for you. God, he's an ass."

"He's not an ass, Gemma," Jonny said.

"He called me 'young lady.' Anyway, I only took it *because* you were going to do the homework for me."

"You know, you might learn something if you actually showed up."

I scoffed. "About 'American Nature Writing'?"

"Come on. The guy's brilliant. He's had like ten bestsellers. Besides, you need the English credits."

Ouch. Despite technically being a junior, I still hadn't finished my generals. "Can't you just fill me in on what I missed?"

Jonny smirked. "If you're lucky."

We walked in silence for a while, passing the large-bricked Pillsbury Hall, where my father once taught Geology. Most of the time when a teacher knows my name, it's because he knew my father, Professor David Pointe. Even though he's been gone a long time, I avoid going into Pillsbury Hall. It makes me feel a loss that I can otherwise repress.

Looking into the arched windows of the building, I wished I could remember him. I wished I could remember anything about my life before the accident. But the retrograde amnesia, from which the doctors had originally believed I would quickly recover, was now a permanent part of my life.

Which is why the encounter with the green-eyed stranger was even more perplexing. When he saw my birthmark, it seemed like he recognized it. Did he know me? Was he someone from my past, someone that, for whatever reason, *hated* me?

As we approached Jonny's old, rusted-out, silver sedan, I wanted to tell him about what had happened, but I didn't really know how. Finally I just said, "There was a guy there today. In the woods."

Jonny dug for his car keys and waited for me to go on.

"Jonny, I think he might know me. I think he might be someone from before, someone I should remember. He seemed about our age, maybe a little older, and he… he recognized my birthmark, he asked me about it." I didn't tell Jonny what his question had been.

We got in the car and pulled onto the road, Jonny thoughtfully planning his response.

"Look," he said at last. "I'm not saying this guy *isn't* someone from your past, but I don't want you to be disappointed that he's probably not. More than likely, he was just hitting on you. Just looking for something to talk to you about. Your birthmark is pretty interesting. And guys will try anything to score a conversation with a pretty girl."

Even as Jonny was talking, I dismissed his theory. I knew with one hundred percent certainty that Green Eyes had not been attempting to flirt with me. Though I've never had a boyfriend, I know when I'm getting hit on. But to Jonny I shrugged and said, "Maybe."

As we made our way to the Como Park region of St. Paul, I flipped the radio on to distract me from my thoughts. I turned the dial to 97.1, Cities 97, my favorite station. The song playing was the newest one by a local artist. I like that the station supports local musicians. I've always told Jonny that one day it will be his music coming across the airwaves. One day it will be. But even that thought, pleasant as it was, couldn't displace my thoughts about the encounter I'd had earlier.

Who was he? I looked out the window, only somewhat listening to the music, only partially seeing the houses that I grew up seeing.

Jonny pulled into my driveway. "So. You doing Halloween at The Meet Lab with me on Friday?"

I groaned inwardly. I'm not much for techno clubs, but I'd already told Flash I'd be there. "Yeah, I'm going. I'll have to find a costume this week."

Jonny winked at me. "Wait 'til you see mine."

"Whatever," I said, shaking my head but smiling at him. "See you tomorrow."

I got out of the car and went inside, thinking a little bit about how to get out of the party, but mostly about the green-eyed stranger from the woods.

CHAPTER 3

The Williams house, the only home I remember ever having, is pretty vanilla. Like most of the houses in my neighborhood, it is old and large, made in the days when big families were the norm, and it is settled towards the front of about an acre of land.

My first memory of that place was through the window of my Uncle Dan's pickup, following the hospital part of my recovery. It's brown shingles and reddish brick looked welcoming, if not familiar, as did the kids playing in the yard of the neighboring house, who I later learned were Jonny and his younger sister Lucy.

Aunt Sheri, my dad's sister, and my Uncle Dan have lived in that house since they got married, purchasing it long before they knew they'd only be able to fill it with a single child, my cousin Flash.

No one calls him Benjamin or even Ben. I've been told he's been Flash since he was young, but no one seems to remember why. And though he's five years older than me, he's far less responsible. Nonetheless, he's basically my brother and the person I'm closest to apart from Jonny.

When I first came to live with the three of them, I felt like an outsider despite their best attempts to make me comfortable. It was like living with strangers. Yet over time, they became what they are to me now: my loving family and the best people I know.

When I entered the house, Flash was in the kitchen eating cold pizza, headphones covering his ears. "Hey," I greeted him.

He gave me a nod. Sporting bleach blonde hair frosted with blue tips, a new eyebrow ring to complement the barbell through his lip, and incomplete tattoo sleeves on both arms, Flash is every part expression. It was no surprise to anybody when he began dabbling in beat mixing and turned out being really good at it.

What was a surprise to Aunt Sheri, Uncle Dan, and to some extent me, was that despite his success as DJ Flash, my 25-year-old cousin had no desire to move out. Then again, neither did I. The difference though, at least in my mind, was that I was in school. And Jonny still lived next door.

I passed Flash and went up the stairs to the bedroom I'd been in since I was twelve. Sprawling on my bed, I looked at the ceiling.

Jonny was wrong about the whole he-was-just-hitting-on-you thing. I knew he was. For one thing, Green Eyes had not looked interested in my birthmark; he'd looked furious about it. And for another, his question was accusatory in nature, not flirtatious.

But something else Jonny said had struck me. *Guys will try anything to score a conversation with a pretty girl*, he'd said.

A pretty girl. Did Jonny think I was pretty? In the entire time he and I had been friends, he'd never once made a comment like that. The thought flattered me.

I have never thought of myself as beautiful, or even attractive. Sure, my parents were good-looking, judging from the photographs I have of each of them. My dad, with his sandy blonde hair, suntanned skin, and outdoorsy athleticism, was ruggedly handsome. My mother, tall and slender, had turquoise-blue eyes and light brown hair that fell in loose waves down her back. But despite the appeal they each had, I've always thought that the features I inherited had arranged themselves into plainness.

My eyes, though the same turquoise-blue as my mother's, are not as big as hers were, not as thickly-framed with lashes, and they're muddied by the narrow band of brown that rings my pupil. And while my hair is also long and brown, it lacks the golden hue hers seemed to have. From my father, I inherited a lean build and a tan complexion. I don't know who I got my birthmark from.

Unlike most birthmarks, it is more of a symbol than a spot. It is on the inside of my right wrist, and it has clearly defined lines forming several shapes. There are two circles, one within the other, the larger one fitting snuggly within a diamond and bisected twice—once with a straight vertical line and once with a wavy horizontal line.

Growing up, Jonny used to call it my compass, as if I'd been somehow marked with the tool that could guide me and give me direction. If that were the case, I wouldn't have made it to my junior year in college without knowing yet what to major in.

But Jonny is an idealist. He's the kind of guy girls adore: genuine, supportive, artistic, and even-tempered. He's the kind of guy girls like to be called pretty by. He's the kind of guy girls want to date.

Sometimes Jonny has girlfriends. It has never really bothered me, but I think I bother them. They never seem to last long. It might be hard for other girls to understand our relationship.

Despite how different we are, Jonny and I have been best friends for as long as I can remember. He says it has actually been longer than that. But I count everything with a starting point of eight years ago. When my life started over again.

I closed my eyes, thoughts of Jonny, of Green Eyes, of being called pretty, swirling around in my head until, at some point, I was asleep.

On Friday, October 31, The Meet Lab was a literal zoo.

In keeping with the club's Halloween theme "Wild Night," exotic animals in cages lined the entrance. Snakes, large cats, and brightly colored birds eyed Jonny, Lucy, and me suspiciously as we entered. I felt sorry for them, certain that the thud of the music and the flash of the lights, never mind the small containers, were too vast a departure from their natural surroundings.

The club, nothing more than an old warehouse in Minneapolis on most days, seemed itself alive. Billowing smoke from the stage weaved through a dance floor crawling with people. The heavy scent of sweat, the thick air, the ground slippery with spilled drinks—it all made The Lab an organism bigger than those within it.

Jonny nudged his way to the bar where he ordered two beers, both for himself. I wouldn't technically be old enough to drink until March 25th, and the yellow wristband I'd been given indicated as much.

I shook my head at him as he made his way back to me and Lucy. "Two?"
"What?" he replied. "I'm in character."

Jonny had come to the party dressed as DJ Flash, complete with magnetic jewelry, fake tattoos, and a blonde wig that he'd tipped blue with paint. He looked ridiculous.

Lucy, on the other hand, looked like a sex kitten. Though only eighteen and still a senior in high school, she knocks guys dead with a glance of her pale blue eyes and a flutter of eyelashes. Tonight, wearing a midriff-baring genie costume, she commanded attention.

I most certainly did not, which was okay with me. In the last-minute gypsy costume I'd thrown together, I just hoped to blend into the sea of make-believe.

The three of us waded into the crowd, Jonny straining to see DJ Flash on the raised platform, Lucy searching for her next boyfriend, and me already looking for an excuse to leave.

In the shuffle, I bumped into a tall, handsome black guy. He winked at me. "Watch it, sugar."

Jonny turned to him, saw who it was, and smiled. "What's up, Paul?"

"Hey Flash, what's up?" he said, playing into Jonny's charade. "I like the look."

Flash's oldest friend, the notorious DJ McGregarious, aka Paul McGregor (because no one really wants to call him DJ McGregarious), was dressed as the devil. He talked to Jonny for a while, then winked at me again and prodded me with his pitchfork before moving away.

"Come on," I grumbled. "Is that really necessary?"

Jonny just laughed, motioned to his already-empty beer bottles, and pushed his way back to the bar.

I realized then Lucy had left my side as well, so I stood there alone, surrounded by people collectively throbbing to the pulse of Flash's music. I moved through them, breaking whatever energy they were building, trying to find Jonny at the bar. He wasn't there. I scanned the club, but the kaleidoscope effect of the lights was dizzying, and I couldn't see clearly through the strobes.

As I made my way to a corner of the club, I felt eyes on me. I turned towards the entrance, hoping to catch who was watching me. I glanced past the hulking security guards, took in the confined wild animals again, glimpsed Jonny surrounded by a group of giggling nurses and French maids, and then spotted him.

Standing at the threshold of The Lab, he was not yet obscured by the club's haze. Wearing blue jeans and a leather jacket rather than a costume, his large stature dwarfed the people near him. Though the beams of light from the stage couldn't reach him, the orange glow that shone up from beneath him illuminated his face. He looked every bit as formidable as he had when I saw him in the woods earlier in the week.

And his green eyes were locked on me.

CHAPTER 4

My first instinct was to run, to hide myself in the thick of jumping bodies. Though tucked in a corner, I felt completely exposed. My eyes darted around the club looking for a group of people I could slip into, or any other place that could conceal me.

I looked back towards the entrance, expecting a pursuit, but he had not moved. He just watched me, his jaw set, his expression fixed. His stare was unnerving, but I decided not to run, afraid that if I did, I'd lose him in the crowd and he'd surprise me later.

What the hell is he doing here? I wondered. Something told me he wasn't at The Meet Lab to celebrate Halloween. It was a feeling, a sense of certainty that he was only there because I was. My stomach lurched.

Right then, the orange light that highlighted his face brightened. He looked down at it, then back at me. Very slightly, he shook his head at me. Then he turned quickly towards the entrance and took off through the door.

"What happened to you?" Jonny said as he stumbled towards me sometime later. "You look like you've seen a ghost!" He laughed hysterically at his own Halloween joke. "Come on. Come dance with us!" He grabbed my hand, pulling me out of the corner.

Jonny is a happy drunk. When he drinks, even more than when he is sober, he makes friends with *everybody*. A group of his new friends, males and females alike, waited for him near the edge of the dance floor.

"No, I'm alright," I said, planting my feet. "You go ahead. I'll wait here 'til you and Lucy are ready to go. I'm not in the mood."

Jonny mustered an expression of concern. "What's wrong?"

I shrugged. "Let's talk later, 'kay? It's too loud in here."

"What?" he shouted, smiling. I was not amused. "Okay, for real. I'm here for you. Talk to Jonny." He waved off his friends and sat down on the floor, pulling me down with him. It was sticky and gross, but in his state, Jonny didn't care.

I sighed. "Fine. Here's the thing. You know that guy I told you about on Tuesday? The one from the woods? Well he was here. And it kinda freaked me out is all."

Jonny's eyes widened. "That guy from campus? He was *here*? You're kidding! That is so *spooky!*" His shoulders began to shake, but he was trying his hardest not to laugh. "Of all the parties he could have gone to on Halloween!"

"Never mind," I said, getting up. "I should have known not to talk to you"—I motioned to him on the floor—"like this."

"Like what? Naw, I'm fine. Super, even. Fantastic," he slurred. "I just think it's funny that you saw this guy twice in one week. It's like déjà boo!" And with that, Jonny crumpled into a heap of giggles.

I scanned the club for Lucy, happy to see her walking towards me, trying to shake off an overly attentive werewolf. "Let's go," she mouthed. I nodded and helped Jonny to his feet, more than agreeable to be leaving.

That night, and the two following it, I did not dream of furious waters. For the first time in weeks, I'd been granted a reprieve from the crushing waves. Instead, my subconscious floated images of the green-eyed stranger, sometimes in the woods, sometimes at The Meet Lab, but always surrounded by dancing strobe lights that never touched his caramel skin.

Instead, he was illuminated with a golden brilliance, a warm color that shone from below him.

The dreams were not scary, but nonetheless, I woke up Monday morning, November 3, feeling haunted. The visions lingered in my mind, and I had the uncanny belief that I had not seen Green Eyes for the last time.

I didn't share that thought with Jonny as we drove to school, but I was preoccupied with it. So much so, I almost missed his big news.

"...so I'm not sure what songs I'm going to do yet. I mean, it's a pretty big deal, right? Fervor is packed on Saturday nights. And I have less than a week," Jonny said, pulling his car into a parking spot just north of campus, in an area known as Dinkytown.

"Wow, Jonny. Congratulations. Really. I know you've been wanting to play a show there for a while," I said.

We got out of the car, threw our backpacks over our shoulders, and started walking towards campus. The air was cold, much colder than it had been the week before.

"It just sucks that it's the same day as staff orientation at the park," Jonny said. "I have to work until 5. I'll need to haul ass to get there in time."

"I'm sure you'll be fine," I reassured him.

For the past five winters, Jonny has worked as a snowboard instructor at Board Meeting, a snow park in the west metro. Once the snow starts each year, he works nearly every weekend. From November until March, I don't really see much of him.

We crossed University Ave and were about to head off to our respective classes when Jonny said, "Hey. That guy you were telling me about, the one that was at The Lab. What did he look like again?"

I described the man I'd been seeing in my dreams. "Tall, muscular—just a big guy. He's got tannish skin, and short, dark hair. He's probably a few years older than us. And his eyes are absurdly green. Like they don't go with the rest of him."

"Yeah. That's what I thought you'd said. I can't tell about the eyes, but..." Jonny shifted his backpack to the other shoulder and pointed to the bus stop in front of Folwell Hall. "Is that him?"

I spotted the person Jonny was pointing to. Despite the dark sunglasses and the need for a shave, it was unquestionably the same guy. And he was striding toward us.

"Yeah," I said. "That's him."

Jonny put his hand on my shoulder. "Come on. Let's go see what he wants."

CHAPTER 5

Either because it was a clear, sunny day, or because I had Jonny with me, or both, I had a sense of security when I approached him. Yet he still intimidated me, and with every pace forward, my chest felt tighter and my breathing got shallower.

I stood slightly behind Jonny when we met him on the sidewalk. He looked even bigger than he had in the woods. Jonny, 5'11" and leanly built, was at least five inches shorter than him and probably fifty pounds lighter. But Jonny is nothing if not confident.

"Hey there," he said. "I'm Jonny." He stuck out his hand.

Green Eyes ignored the courtesy and instead gestured towards me. "How long has she had that mark on her wrist?"

Jonny replied, "She was born with it, man. It's a *birth*mark. And her name is Gemma. What's all this about?"

Green Eyes didn't answer him. He turned to me. "Do you believe in coincidences, Gemma?"

I shook my head, though I wasn't sure whether I believed in coincidences or not.

"Good answer." His voice was low and authoritative.

"Look dude," Jonny said. "Is there something we can help you with? Because if not…"

"She needs to come with me," he said.

"Excuse me?" I said, looking to Jonny for help.

"We don't even know you. Why would she go anywhere with you?"

"My name is Malakai Zonn," he said. "And Gemma and I need to talk." He pulled off his leather jacket and pushed up the sleeve of his shirt. "About this."

My breath caught in my throat. On his right forearm, Malakai had a green line art tattoo, one that looked like a simplified version of my birthmark: a circle bisected twice, cut into quadrants by a vertical and a horizontal line.

He pulled off his sunglasses and stared into my eyes. "Why are you surprised, Gemma? Because you haven't seen something like this before, or because you have?"

"I... I don't know what you're talking about," I said. "Why do you have that tattoo?"

Malakai's too-green eyes narrowed in suspicion. "I think you know. And if you don't, you should. In either case, you need to come with me."

"I have to go to class," I said quietly, looking from Malakai's face to his tattoo. The emerald-green tattoo lines appeared dull, faded, as if they'd been inked years ago.

"Fine," he said through gritted teeth. "How can I contact you later?"

"You can't." My words felt more powerful than I did. And judging from the way Malakai bristled after I said them, I had more power than I realized. "I'm not sure what you have to tell me, but whatever it is, you can just tell me here. Now." Out of the corner of my eye, I caught Jonny looking positively gleeful.

"I can't do that. Not with him here," Malakai said, indicating Jonny.

"Well, then, catch you around," I said. I grabbed Jonny's arm and started to walk away.

"Stop." Malakai dug into the pocket of his jacket and pulled out a business card. "Do you know what this is?" Without waiting for me to answer, he said, "It's what I've been giving out to random strangers, to anyone I can, for years." He stuck it in the side pocket of my backpack. "You have no idea what is at stake here. All I need is information—for your sake as well as mine." He leaned down and whispered directly into my ear. "Remember, there are no coincidences. It's your move." Then he turned quickly and walked away.

Jonny and I silently watched Malakai depart, both of us dumbfounded by what had happened. Once he turned the corner of 4th Street and was out of sight, I let out the breath I hadn't realized I was holding.

"Wow…" Jonny breathed. "I'm so sorry I didn't take you seriously. That guy is…"

"Intense," I finished. I put my backpack down and fished out the card that Malakai had slipped into the side pocket.

It was simple white cardstock printed with thick black font. The name MALAKAI ZONN stood in the center, above a Minneapolis-based phone number. I flipped it over. And my knees weakened. Jonny reached out to support me.

We stared at the back of the card. In large letters at the top read the statement: PLEASE CALL IF SEEN. Below it was an exact drawing of my birthmark.

"Holy shit, Gemma," Jonny said. "What in the world do you think this means?"

✳ ✳ ✳

I had no idea what it might mean, but despite my best efforts to clear the whole confusing interaction from my mind, I kept *wondering*. The week was a blur; I moved through each day oblivious to life around me. The sole focus of my thoughts was Malakai and whether or not he'd be waiting around the next corner I turned.

Strangely, though I was worried about him popping up in front of me at any random time, I wasn't really opposed to talking to him. I mean, he hadn't been harsh towards us, just urgent. And cryptic. And slightly paranoid.

When I told Jonny that perhaps I should just call Malakai and clear up whatever misunderstanding there might be about my birthmark, he told me I needed a healthier sense of self-preservation. He asked me to promise that I wouldn't call, and when I wouldn't, he became sullen.

I tried to assure him that after the interaction on Monday morning, I didn't feel threatened by Malakai anymore. After all, I was the one in control. I had the option to call or not call, and I had the right to grant or deny him information. But Jonny wasn't convinced and the truth was, I wasn't myself convinced that he didn't intend me harm. It was just that my curiosity was beginning to outweigh everything else. Everything Malakai had said was eating at me, and I kept replaying his words back in my head. *You have no idea what is at stake here. All I need is information—for your sake as well as mine.*

The underlying message of course was that I could be in some form of danger if I didn't contact him, didn't provide him with the details he was looking for. On the surface, the statement was absurd. But what if? What if I could somehow benefit from the exchange he wanted to have? What harm could there be in a phone call?

Jonny and I had stopped discussing that very question after several strained conversations. By Friday afternoon, we were avoiding talking about anything besides Jonny's show at Fervor. It seemed to be the only topic that didn't end up bringing us to Malakai, and ultimately, frustration.

"I can't believe it's tomorrow already," Jonny said. "I don't even have a set list prepared."

I smiled. "Maybe you should stop pacing my bedroom and get going on it then."

Jonny sat down next to me on my bed, but popped up a second later and started pacing again. "Well, what should I start with? *Centered?*"

It's my favorite of all the songs he's written. He first shared it with me two years ago, just before he started performing publicly. I'd always known how amazingly creative and talented Jonny was, but it was at that moment, listening to the story he was telling with his music, that I realized he was truly gifted. "You know I love that one."

"Do you think it's too slow for an open? I could always do *Shelf Life.*"

"How's that go again?"

He sang the chorus.

When Jonny sings, his voice sounds just like when he talks, but in a designated rhythm and landing on certain notes. It is clear, warm, and passionate. "Oh yeah. That could be good." I leaned back onto my bed. "What about *Something To Hold Onto?*"

Jonny cocked his head at me, his dark hair swinging into his face. "I didn't know you liked it."

I do like it, but even more than that, I like the half-smile Jonny wears when he sings it. Like he knows something the rest of us don't. "Yeah, sure," I said.

Thinking, he walked over to my bookshelf and looked at the baseball-sized boulder opal I kept there, securely displayed in a clear box. He unconsciously picked up the box and gazed out my window.

The opal is my favorite thing, and I don't like anybody, not even Jonny, touching even the case that houses it. It was a gift from my father, a souvenir from the last dig he'd done with his graduate students in Australia one summer. The stone, jagged and dark brown with orange-red flames licking blue-green clouds, feels like a private memento and the only thing that keeps him real for me.

Jonny turned back from the window and put the box back down quickly, realizing what he'd done. "Sorry, Gem." He shoved his hands into the front pocket of his navy blue hoodie.

"Jonny, you're overthinking this. You can play whatever you want, in whatever order, and people will love you."

"And you'll be there?" he asked.

"Nothing could stop me," I said.

CHAPTER 6

As it turned out, something as mundane as lack of transportation could stop me. It was 6:45 on Saturday evening, and Jonny's show at Fervor would start in less than an hour whether I was there or not.

Unfortunately, I'd forgotten to arrange a ride in advance. Jonny was heading to Fervor straight from work, Aunt Sheri and Uncle Dan were out for the evening, and it was too late to take the bus. I walked into the bathroom where Flash was styling his blue spikes and begged him again to drive me.

"For chrissake, Gemma," he said. "This is ridiculous. Get your license." He washed the product from his hands. "And some wheels. I have plans."

Flash was right of course. I knew it was time to get my license and a car, but I'd just never had the desire to drive. Not with such a traumatic accident in my past.

"How'd you overlook such an important detail, anyway?" he asked, walking past me. "Can't you ride with Lucy?"

I shook my head. "Lucy is on a date. They're at dinner, then heading straight there." I was starting to get desperate. "Please, Flash. Jonny's gonna kill me if I'm not there."

"I can't. I told you. Paul and I are spinning a party at Seven Corners tonight. I'm leaving in twenty." He went to his room to finish getting ready.

How could I have been so stupid? I'd been so distracted by thoughts of the mysterious Malakai Zonn that I hadn't paid attention to anything else.

Malakai Zonn. An odd name, attached to an even odder person. A complicated person who, upon first seeing me in the woods, had looked at me with contempt. After seeing my birthmark, he'd become furious. But on Halloween, he'd been impassive—and then departed abruptly. So why, at the U, was it suddenly so important for him to get *information* from me? What could he possibly think I would know? It was almost as if he would do anything to figure out…

An idea occurred to me. Before I could talk myself out of it, I found the business card with his number on it, grabbed my cell phone, and dialed. He answered on the second ring.

"I knew you'd call," he said.

"Look, you need information, right? Well I need a ride to Grand Avenue. Urgently. If you get me there, I'll answer your questions." The words came out in a rush.

"Right now?" Malakai said. "It's not a good time."

"That's the deal. Take it or leave it. You come get me and bring me to Fervor Music Café, and afterwards, I'll tell you what you want to know. This is the only offer you are going to get."

Silence.

Come on, I thought.

"Fine," Malakai said. "Where do you live?"

"2280 McKinley Street. Near Como Park," I said.

Only after I hung up did I question my own judgment in contacting him. But it was too late to back out now.

Malakai pulled up to my house not fifteen minutes later, driving a matte-black sports car that looked entirely too expensive for an evening threatening bad weather. He waited in the car. I threw on a coat and walked outside with Flash right behind me.

"Who is *that?*" Flash said, jaw dropping.

I ignored him and walked to the passenger's side of Malakai's car and got in. It smelled like cigarettes. I coughed slightly.

"Fervor is at Grand Avenue and Avon Street," I said, not looking at Malakai. I focused on keeping my voice even, my expression composed. *Confidence*, I told myself. *Stay in control.*

Without a word, he hit the accelerator. I buckled my seatbelt, suddenly hyperaware of the precariousness of my situation. I had no control at all.

I sat there quietly, trying to observe as much as possible. Three things became apparent to me as we drove. First and most importantly, it seemed that Malakai intended to honor our agreement. He withheld whatever questions he wanted to ask as we made our way to Fervor. Second, Malakai had a death wish. The way he was driving, at speeds way above the posted limits, weaving in and out of traffic, frightened me. And third, Malakai was rich. I mean, filthy, stinking, loaded. The car was one thing, decked out with a sound system and speakers, but there were other clues. Like the designer sunglasses on the dash and latest-release phone in his cup holder. But the dead giveaway was the wads of cash, the thick stacks of hundred dollar bills, stashed in nearly every crevice: tucked above the visor, peaking out from beneath the floor mat, rolled up in the ashtray... Seeing so much money made me uncomfortable. I didn't want to know where it all came from.

I was relieved when we pulled into the parking lot of Fervor Music Café, safely and at 7:26.

I jumped out of the car and hustled towards the entrance.

"Hang on there, Gemma," Malakai said. "We made a deal."

I stopped and turned to him. "Yeah, I said I'd tell you what you wanted to know *afterwards*. After Jonny's performance. Which starts now. So you can either wait here for me, or you can come in. I don't care what you do."

He glared at me. "You aren't leaving my sight until we've had the chance to talk."

"We'll talk," I snapped. "But right now, my best friend expects me to be in there. So it will have to be later." And I walked into Fervor, Malakai on my heels.

As usual for a Saturday evening, the place was packed. The draw of live music and the relaxed atmosphere have made Fervor Music Café a hotspot, particularly among students. And despite its massive size—a two-story amphitheater of sorts, crammed with dark wooden tables—Fervor is cozy. The rich jewel tones of the décor, mostly deep plum with goldenrod and sage-green accents, the aroma of flavored coffee, and the animated chatter of groups of friends contribute to its hominess.

I scanned the crowd, looking for Lucy. I found her sitting at a corner table on the first level, giggling flirtatiously and hanging on the brawny arm of her much-too-old-for-her date. I made my way to them.

"Hi Luce. This seat taken?" I pointed to the extra chair at her table. She looked up, clear blue eyes twinkling.

"Gemma!" she shrieked. "I wasn't sure you were going to make it." She stood up and hugged me. "I saved it for you, but uh, I didn't know you were bringing a… Who's your friend?"

"Um. Malakai, this is Lucy. Lucy, Malakai. And yours?"

Lucy started giggling again. "This is Joshua." She leaned in towards him and playfully jabbed him in the ribs. He grinned broadly and pulled her onto his lap, wrapping her in his arms.

"Looks like you'll have to sit here, doll," he said. "They need your chair."

She giggled again and then said his name slowly, seductively. "Josh-u-a."

I felt awkward, like I was gawking at an intimate moment. Malakai cleared his throat loudly and plopped down on one of the chairs. I took the other one.

"Oh," she said, tearing her eyes from Josh and looking back at Malakai and me. "It's just—Josh is an aspiring magician."

"Okay," I said, unsure of where she was going.

She tossed her hair, and Josh seemed mesmerized by the way it's auburn layers, shiny and straight, cascaded over her shoulders. "Well, before you guys got here, we were trying to figure out his stage name. You know, like 'The Amazing Josh' or 'Josh the Magnificent.' But we just agreed that he should be called 'Josh. Ooh. Aah!'" She said the 'ooh' and the 'aah' with the same wonder that people viewing fireworks collectively murmur them. Lucy became a heap of giggles all over again, and Josh squeezed her tighter, burying his face into her neck.

This is their first date? I thought. I couldn't imagine ever feeling that comfortable with someone I'd just met. I glanced sideways at Malakai, who was surveying the room. Especially not him.

The lights dimmed and the café grew quiet. Jonny stepped into the spotlight, handsomely casual in a charcoal button-up shirt and dark jeans. He slipped on his guitar, a midnight-blue acoustic, and stepped up to the mike. "Hey, everyone. I'm Jonny Saletto. Thanks for coming out tonight. I'm gonna kick it off with a new one. It's called *Unseen Forces*. I hope you like it. Here goes."

Jonny stomped a rhythm and then smoothly brought in the guitar. When he began to sing, he had me, and everyone else in the room from the looks of it, captivated. The melody was light but the lyrics moving, and Jonny's voice was passionate and assured.

> *They say that life happens*
> *In the details*
> *All of the minutes, turning into years*
> *And the water of our lives*
> *Rushes on by*
>
> *Memories keep us afloat*
> *Since they fill up our minds*
> *And life is in the living past*
> *As well as today's details*
>
> *So I will travel forward*
> *Guided by unseen forces*
> *Unsure of their ways*
> *But trusting their aim*
>
> *No one knows the path*
> *Each day will highlight*
> *But the future is waiting*
> *I've made my choice*
> *Guided by unseen forces*
>
> *So I will travel forward*
> *Guided by unseen forces*
> *Unsure of their ways*
> *But trusting their aim*

He let the last note hang in the air while he silenced his guitar with his hand. He pushed back the hair that was hanging in his face. "Thank you." I saw him searching the audience. "I wrote that for my friend, Gemma. Where are you, Gem?"

He spotted me right as he asked the question and flashed me a smile. The expression only lasted a second before it gave way to astonishment.

I had been so captured by Jonny's performance that for a moment, I'd forgotten who was seated next to me. I looked over at Malakai. He was leaning back in his chair, arms crossed, his face unreadable.

The shock of the two of us together at his show seemed to throw Jonny off his game. "Uh," he said into the microphone, all of his previous confidence gone. He pulled a sheet of paper from his back pocket and looked at it. "The next one's called *Holding Pattern*." He shoved the paper back in his jeans and launched into the song, not looking in my direction again.

CHAPTER 7

Looking back now, all these months later, I still feel the burn of shame as I think about that night, especially because of what I chose to do next.

Jonny continued performing, but with a noticeable decline in energy. The guilt I felt knowing I was the reason why was too much. Hadn't he been asking me all week not to call Malakai? 'I just don't trust the guy,' he'd said. And here I show up with him, when I'm supposed to be there only to support Jonny.

A few more songs passed in mediocrity. Certain my presence was distracting Jonny, I leaned over to Malakai. "Take me home." He looked relieved. I turned to Lucy, but she and Josh were making out, so I got up without saying goodbye.

We crossed the room to the door, and though I couldn't be positive because I never took my eyes off my goal, I am pretty sure Jonny saw us leave. His voice caught in the middle of the chorus of *Dark Gray*, and it took him a second to recover. I hoped it would go better once I was gone.

Outside, icy rain had begun to fall. With the temperature dropping quickly, the roads would soon be dangerously slick. I pulled my coat tight around me, nervous for the drive as well as the interrogation.

If I was being honest with myself, I hadn't just left Fervor to give Jonny a better shot at concentrating. That was only part of it. I was also ready to go because the suspense—of not knowing who Malakai was, and not knowing who he thought I was—was killing me.

We got into the car and as Malakai shifted into reverse, I noticed something I hadn't before: a wide, silver ring with a large amber stone on the pointer finger of his right hand. The streetlights shone through the windshield, giving it a faint orange-brown luminescence.

Before I had the opportunity to ask about it, Malakai said, "Jonny knows something. Obviously, you can't have told him much, but he knows something. What have you shared?"

I shook my head at him. "Alright, let's back up. This isn't going to work if you don't give me some idea of what you are talking about."

Malakai kept his eyes on the road. "You were there. His song. *Unseen Forces*, he called it."

"Yeah?"

"Come on. Don't act like you don't know." His tone was challenging but calm.

"I truly *don't* know. So if you want information from me, you are going to have to give me more."

Malakai studied my face. Then he asked something that took me off guard. "That day in the woods, when we first saw each other. You were attracted to me. Weren't you?"

"No," I said a little too quickly. He was undoubtedly good-looking: tall, dark, and powerful, with those unnaturally green eyes.

He rolled his eyes. "Not *attracted*. Pulled. Drawn. If not to me, then at least to the place."

The Oaks had been *my* spot. It had called to me. Bewildered, I nodded.

"You really don't know anything, do you?" Malakai said, his tone less suspicious now. When I didn't reply, he pointed to my wrist. "Do either of your parents have a mark like that?"

"No one has ever mentioned it," I said.

"You don't know?"

I shrugged. "My dad and I were in a car accident when I was twelve. He's dead. And I don't remember anything of my life before I woke up in the hospital eight years ago."

"Where's your mom?" Malakai asked.

"She died having me. I never knew her."

Malakai sighed. Apparently these weren't the answers he was looking for. "Your twenty-first birthday. It's gotta be in, what, March?"

"March 25th," I confirmed. "How'd you know?"

"And Jonny. He's your boyfriend?"

I shook my head.

"Figures," he said.

The mention of Jonny's name stirred up fresh feelings of guilt. I wondered whether his show had gotten better. I stared out the window, at the hopelessly dark night, and felt suddenly very tired. "Look, Malakai—"

"Kai," he interrupted. "Call me Kai."

"Okay. Kai. Here's the thing. I don't know what it is you want to hear, but I don't think I'm who you think I am."

Malakai reached in his coat and pulled out a pack of cigarettes. He lit one and cracked the window, despite the freezing rain. "Smoke?"

"No, yuck," I said. "Hey, you missed the turn. You needed to go right to get to my house."

Malakai kept driving. "Are you sure you don't want one? It might ease your nerves."

"What? No. I'm telling you, you went too far. You need to turn around."

"Suit yourself, then." He put the cigarettes back. "Are you doing okay with the nightmares?"

It was his knowledge of my nightmares, more than anything else, more even than his not turning around, that unnerved me. The only person I'd told about my nightmares was Jonny.

"Take me home now," I demanded. "You've got the wrong person."

"I don't think so," he said. "And even if I do… Well, there's still more we need to discuss."

I crossed my arms and slumped in the seat. Malakai obviously did not intend to take me home until *he* felt the conversation was over. He merged onto 35W heading north and picked up speed, despite the poor visibility and slippery roads. Agitated, I said, "If you aren't going to bring me home, can you at least drive like less of an idiot?"

He finished his cigarette and tossed it out the window. "You should be thanking me. I could have left you to figure it out on your own."

I refused to take the bait. My curiosity had been replaced with a disconcerted anger the moment he'd failed to turn around.

"You're undergoing, Gemma."

I stared out the front window, watching the wiper blades swish back and forth.

"You're an Essen. Like me," he said.

I scoffed, unable to ignore the statement. "What makes you think I'm *anything* like you?"

"Well for one thing, your birthmark." He looked down at his amber ring. It gleamed in the flashes of oncoming headlights and he pondered it momentarily. It was beautiful, as if it were lit from within. "And for another," he said, dark eyelashes framing green eyes that were too intently studying mine. "For another... I'm not dead."

CHAPTER 8

Malakai let the words hang in the air as he turned his attention back to the road. The rain pattered against the car and glimmered with reflected light as it streaked down the windows.

I shook my head. "Dead? Of course you're not dead! Why would you even say that?"

He lit another cigarette. "Being an Essen has certain… implications. Even talking about it with the wrong people can have deadly consequences. And Gemma, you should know: I don't believe there's anyone in your life right now, other than me, who isn't 'the wrong people.' So you shouldn't mention being Essen to anybody. No one. And that"— he pointed to my birthmark—"should always be covered. Don't let anyone see it. It isn't safe."

His words provoked me. Who was *he* to tell me I had 'the wrong people' in my life? I snapped, "What's your problem? Why are you so obsessed with my birthmark?"

Malakai's eyes narrowed. "Because it is not a birthmark, despite your continued insistence that it is. We all have them, always on the inside of the right arm. But yours is an anomaly. *The* anomaly. The symbol I've been trying to find my whole life." He looked over his shoulder and switched lanes. "That symbol is a promise. The link to a better future for the Essen. Only I never expected to find it on… Well. On someone like you." He waved his hand at me dismissively.

The sting of his words, of his disappointment, bothered me more than it should have. He was nobody to me. Why should I care if he was let down, if he had hoped the "symbol" had appeared on someone else, someone better? I felt a tightening in my throat, so I turned and looked out the window without responding.

He continued. "At first we were all looking. For the Link. Then, one by one, they all died or lost faith until I was the only one still searching. Over time, those who were left, the doubters, they began to mock me. They carved the symbol on trees, painted it on rocks... We'd always thought it would be on an inanimate object, never on a person. Let alone an Essen. Especially not an ignorant one.

"Honestly, I couldn't care less that you are one of us. I don't care that you're undergoing and have no understanding of what you are. I'm not the savior type. But if you are the Link..." He took a long drag of his cigarette. "That's what I want to know. Because helping you will benefit me."

I focused on trees lining the highway. They bled into one another, a green-black mass nearly imperceptible against the charcoal night. A trick of the speed and of the steady stream of rain, they locked arms and loomed over us, appearing sinister. The effect was dizzying.

"Gemma, if you know where the weapon is, you *must* give it to me. It's the only reason the Link exists, the only reason *you* exist. To lead me, us—the Essen—to the weapon. We need it. You understand? It's the only reason you have any importance at all. So where is it?"

Tears prickled at the corners of my eyes and I quickly blinked them away. How was it possible for someone I barely knew to make me feel so used? Especially when I had no idea what he was looking to gain. I shook my head without turning towards him.

"You don't say much, do you?" The question was an accusation. He was obviously frustrated. Without warning, he zipped across two lanes of traffic and exited the freeway, pulling into a gas station. "I need to fill up." He nudged my shoulder and held out a hundred dollar bill. "Run in and grab some smokes for me, will you? I'm running low." He named the brand.

I turned and took the bill, grazing Malakai's hand as I did. The metal of his ring was hot, and the amber light that the stone emanated bathed his face in a golden-orange glow. No longer believing that the stone was reflecting light from some external source, I was amazed by the brilliance of the stone's self-illumination. Malakai pulled his hand away with a jerk and launched himself out of the car. I opened the door and stepped out into the hard rain. Who *was* this guy, sending me in to buy his cigarettes for him? I hurried into the store. And who was *I*, complying?

I wandered the aisles for a few minutes, gathering my thoughts and calming my emotions. Malakai was clearly deluded. His conviction that I was an Essen, that I was "the Link," that I had any knowledge whatsoever about a weapon—it all pointed to that fact. And yet... his knowledge of things, true things like my nightmares and the timing of my twenty-first birthday, made me question whether truth could also be hiding elsewhere in his statements. In his mind, could Malakai even distinguish between reality and fiction?

It seemed that Malakai believed I was either withholding information or completely ignorant, both positions equally contemptible in his eyes. Could I convince him that I was not what he wanted me to be? Was I convinced myself?

I paid for Malakai's cigarettes and shoved his change into my jacket pocket. Before getting back into the car, I'd make him promise to drive me straight home. I'd tell him that the Essen, whoever they were, would have to keep looking for their "Link." I'd make him see that whatever weapon he *needed*, I didn't have it or know anything about it.

I stepped out of the store into the rain, but neither Malakai nor his car was where they had been. I jogged around the building, but there was no sign of him. The gas station lot was empty except for a silver pickup at one of the pumps. Disbelief overcame me. He couldn't have ditched me. He just *couldn't* have. I stood there getting pelted by the icy drops.

"You Gemma?" a gruff voice asked from behind me.

I spun around. "Yes."

The man was short and rotund with thick gray hair. He held out a folded piece of paper. "Tall bloke paid me to give this to you." And with that, he walked to his truck, got in, and drove away.

I moved under the gas station's awning and opened the note. Ten words, scribbled as if in haste. I read it three times, becoming more upset each time.

FIND GATE. SEE YOURSELF.
TELL NO ONE. DEADLY CONSEQUENCES.
-KAI

I crumpled the paper, dropped it on the ground, and stomped on it. Hands clenched in frustration, I screamed. When I finished my tantrum, I dug my cell phone out of my pocket and dialed the number of the only person I could bear to share my humiliation with: Flash.

CHAPTER 9

Dreams came on like earthquakes that night: fast, terrorizing, and in waves. Images rippled through my subconscious like tremors, crumbling restfulness like poorly constructed buildings.

I awoke in the gray light of early morning on Sunday, November 9th, sweaty and short of breath. He had been with me. Malakai. We had been running through a dense forest at twilight. We were being chased. I couldn't keep up. Malakai, he was taller than me, had longer legs, was quicker. I called out for him to wait, to help, but he just left me, sacrificed me. Tears filled my eyes, blinded me, and I tripped over a fallen tree. I gasped for air, sheer panic overtaking me, sure that Death would dispatch me at any moment.

The scene changed. I was with Jonny on campus, and he was wearing Malakai's ring, his body and face resplendent in its warm glow. He faced me and put his hand on my shoulder. "You know what you need to do, Gemma." I nodded. "Good," he said. "I know you can do it. Remember, find the gate first. Once you are through it, you will see the weapon. Destroy it. I will be here waiting for you when you are done."

There were more dreams, fragmented images of wrought-iron gates, people with tattoos that matched my birthmark, and hundred dollar bills falling from the sky, but already the images were becoming fuzzy, retreating from my conscious mind, fading into the depths. Shaken, I closed my eyes again hoping a more peaceful sleep would find me. In mere seconds it did.

Later, the light of mid-morning was still gray, though a lighter shade. I sat up in bed and looked out the window. Lazy snow flurries dropped from an overcast sky, landing on surfaces still wet from the previous night's rain.

My head felt hazy and buzzed with static. I shook it, trying to disperse the noise in my ears, but the sound remained. I sighed. Getting up slowly, I thought about the advice Flash had given me as we'd driven home.

If there is one person besides Jonny I can always count on to rescue me from a difficult situation, it's Flash. He arrived at the gas station less than an hour after I called him, hopping out of the car alert with concern. "Are you sure you're okay?" he'd asked. "He didn't hurt you?"

I'd told him I was fine, just exhausted and embarrassed. He opened the car door for me, but before I got in, I retrieved the sodden note from the ground and shoved it in my jacket pocket. A reminder, I thought. A reminder of Malakai's character, should I find myself curious about him again.

At some point in the future, Flash will undoubtedly tease me about the time I got ditched at a gas station in Blaine. ("*Blaine?*" he's said on the phone, as if I'd been stranded on the moon. "What the hell are you doing all the way out in Blaine?") But last night, I knew the delayed but inevitable jokes Flash would make at my expense were the lesser of two evils. There was no way I could have admitted what had happened to Jonny.

I climbed into his car while Flash walked around and sunk into the driver's seat, relieved. "You know, your phone call was the worst buzz kill ever." I stared at him. "Don't worry, I haven't been drinking," he added quickly. "I had to leave Paul manning the party solo. What the fuck happened?"

When we were younger, I had considered Flash my 'brousin.' He was more than my cousin, more like a brother. Despite being several years older than me, and though we often annoyed each other, Flash and I were close. As we made our way home, I'd wanted to tell him everything: about exploiting Malakai's interest in me and using him for a ride, about the conspicuous abundance of money, about the illuminated amber ring. I'd wondered what he'd think about Malakai calling me "an Essen" and "the Link," and whether he'd be disturbed about Malakai's desire for a weapon. But something about my experience with Malakai felt private, personal. His knowledge of my nightmares and the timing of my twenty-first birthday made me feel exposed.

If I shared the details with Flash, it would somehow make it more real, and I just wanted to forget the evening had happened. I wanted to forget about my own foolish lack of judgment. And there was a teeny tiny piece of me that worried about the 'deadly consequences' referenced in the note. So instead, I just told Flash that Malakai turned out to be a giant jackass and left it at that.

We'd spent most of the car ride in silence. We were almost home when Flash asked about Jonny's show at Fervor.

"I left pretty early," I told him, eyes down, ashamed.

"Gemma, you *didn't*. Please tell me you didn't. First you brought a date, and then you didn't even stay for the whole thing?" he chastised. "That's about the worst thing I think I've ever heard." He turned into the driveway. "You've gotta know how Jonny feels about you. Everyone does. What you did, it's just cold. If you don't feel the same way, you should tell him. He deserves to know."

Flash was right. Now, looking out the window, knowing I'd have to face Jonny and explain myself, I felt sick. Jonny was my best friend, the person I cared for more than anybody, but apparently his feelings for me had grown. There were small signs, signs that I'd chosen to ignore or minimize, like his referring to me as pretty two weeks ago. I had been flattered, honored even; but I just wasn't in the same place. He was my best friend, nothing more, nothing less. I wanted him in that role, in my life, forever. Eventually, though, things were bound to change. That's just how life is. He would be graduating in the spring. He'd probably move somewhere to start a career, meet a new best friend, perhaps the love of his life, and maybe even get married. Or he might record an album, explode as a musician, and go on tour. But either way, the cards would definitely be in his hands.

I didn't want him to outgrow me, to move on and leave me behind. As I got dressed and ready for the day, I thought about him, hoped we'd be best friends always, vowed to hang onto that as long as I could. But if there was one thing I knew, one thing life has taught me, it's that people can dissolve from your life as quickly as salt in water, and there's usually nothing you can do about it.

I walked downstairs and slipped on my jacket. If I felt differently about him, I could probably keep him. If there had been any romantic spark at all... But that was not the way I felt. I loved Jonny, but in a proud, faithful, and awe-filled way. His unrestricted talent, his unchecked goodness, his generosity of spirit, it was too much for me. I admired him, sometimes to the point of jealousy. He had become a hero to me. He was my best friend, but also elevated and untouchable. To think he could want more from me was hard to imagine. I was undeserving.

Crossing the lawn, I thought about what I should say. There were no words, but when I got to Jonny's house, I knocked on the door anyway. Knots tightened in my stomach as I waited.

Lucy answered the door. Her cheeks were flushed, causing her freckles to stand out. Despite her worn blue jeans and the casual ponytail that held back her auburn hair, she looked radiant. Blue eyes bright, she said, "Oh. Hi Gemma. I thought you were Joshua."

"Josh again today?" I asked.

"Oh, Gem," she gushed, "I'm pretty sure he's the one." She ushered me in and closed the door. "I'll get Jonny for you."

She left the room, and I waited in the living room. I examined the pictures of Jonny and Lucy as children, the same ones I'd looked at a million times before, mounted on the walls in cherry-stained frames. They smiled back at me innocently, adorably, in every stage of growing up. Wistfully, I thought about the photos of me as a child. They provided evidence that I'd been one, but that was all. My photos didn't hold memories, couldn't stir emotion.

Lucy came back into the room. "He's not here." She shrugged. "I didn't even hear him leave." I thanked her and started towards the door, but she stopped me. "What's up with you and Malakai?"

Her directness caught me off guard. "Nothing. He's just a guy I know."

Lucy raised an eyebrow at me. "Really? Jonny seemed to think otherwise. Anyway, that guy was smoldering. I never thought you'd go for a bad boy. The undercurrent of danger with him… Just be careful, alright?" Then she winked. "But no nice guy will satisfy you the way a heartbreaker can."

She walked me to the door and opened it to find Joshua standing there, ready to knock. He stepped in and took off his jacket revealing a long-sleeved t-shirt that read "FULL OF TRICKS." Lucy greeted him with a long kiss, and I waved my goodbye as I stepped outside. I'd have to try to catch Jonny again later.

✳ ✳ ✳

I lost my nerve, so later never came. We carpooled to campus the next morning without talking, and then back home from it in the afternoon the same way. Every day was like that, and other than our drives to and from school, I never saw him. Jonny, who never skipped class, didn't attend American Nature Writing the entire week. It was up to me to assure a worried Professor Dagenais that *Mr.* Jonny Saletto was fine, just ill, and that he'd be back the following week.

Things had never been so strained between Jonny and me, and by Monday, November 17th, it was really taking its toll on me. I was desperate for things to go back to normal, but I didn't know how to fix it. My days felt lonely. I chatted with casual friends here and there, but the conversations were superficial, and there was an emptiness inside me.

The weather, dreary and oppressive, fit my mood. Even the snow from the week before, which still blanketed the ground due to the recent cold snap, looked dull and dirty. I cursed the bleakness of Minnesota winters as I trudged across the mall from one class to the next.

In my funk, I barely noticed the large wooden pillar fixed to the concrete of the sidewalk that served as an announcement board for students and staff. It was covered in brightly colored papers and advertisements, and I only glanced at it as I walked by.

Something on it caught my eye. I did a double take. It was the heading that drew me in. I moved closer to the document and read it several times before pulling it down, ripping the corners where it had been stapled.

SEE YOURSELF
Hypnotherapy
Are you searching for the keys to your past?
Are you hoping to unlock the door to your future?
Both can be achieved when you SEE YOURSELF more clearly!
"If you are ready to live your best life through
introspective self-assessment, call me."
- GATE DORSUM, Certified Hypnotherapist
*Located at Hennepin Ave & 28th St in Uptown

At the bottom of the page was a phone number and the disclaimer: *Revelations by appointment only*.

Some of the words echoed in my mind, words that I'd read before but hadn't been able to make sense of. I reached into my jacket pocket and felt for the paper I'd kept as a reminder. For more than a week, I'd tried to forget Malakai's note. Unable to throw it away, unable to strike it completely from memory, it pulsed against my consciousness begging me to reread it, to solve the riddle. I had been able to ignore the urges. Until now.

I pulled it out and opened it. The ink had bled when I originally got the paper wet, but the words were still legible: *FIND GATE. SEE YOURSELF.*

Was Malakai's cryptic message a recommendation for *therapy*? He thought *I* was the one who needed professional help? Anger at the slight and opposition to the insinuation rose up inside of me, tangling together into defiant rage.

I shoved both papers into my pocket and stormed forward without looking up. In my fury, I plowed through a group of students.

"Gem," one of them called after me. Jonny.

"What?" I snapped, harsher than I meant to. I turned to face him, but couldn't bring myself to look at him. I clenched my jaw, willing myself not to cry.

Jonny broke from his friends and stood right in front of me, dark blue eyes anxious. "Are you… are you okay?"

"I'm perfect," I said. I felt my chin quiver and looked towards the sky, still avoiding his gaze.

"Come on, what's going on?" He spoke quietly but with true concern.

The stress of nine days without Jonny, combined with my sleep deprivation and the "morning static" that I now woke up to every day, left me choking on my words. Despite my racing thoughts, nothing came out.

"Fine," he said, his tone hardening. "Have it your way."

I lowered my eyes to see him walking away, his brown hair sticking out at odd angles beneath his beanie. "Wait," I said. Jonny stopped, but didn't turn around. I took a deep breath. "Do you think I need therapy?"

I wanted him to come back to me, put his arm around me, and tell me no, of course not. Instead, he looked over his shoulder without facing me and said, "You know what, Gemma? I would have settled for an apology."

Then he rejoined his friends and continued on his way, leaving me standing alone and chagrined underneath the gloomy sky.

CHAPTER 10

"I don't know why I'm here."

I sat in the parlor of Gate Dorsum's small uptown home, perched awkwardly at the edge of his oversized sofa. When I had called to make the appointment, Gate had not asked questions, had not disclosed rates, had not provided details of any kind. I really hadn't offered much information either. I just mentioned that I'd seen his advertisement on campus and asked for a meeting.

We'd agreed to a three o'clock appointment on Thursday afternoon, November 20th, a time that forced me to skip American Nature Writing. Though I was getting perilously close to failing the class, I couldn't bear the thought of sitting mutely next to Jonny like I had earlier in the week. Something had to change, and though I hated Malakai for pointing it out, I realized it might need to be me. If it did, I hoped Gate might be able to help.

The bus ride to Gate's residence, which was also his office, was uneventful, but I was all nerves. Walking up the steps to his tall but narrow house, the uneasiness continued. Now, in his dimly-lit parlor, I felt certain I'd made a mistake.

Though the room was clearly designed with client relaxation in mind, I was highly uncomfortable. The spa-like quality created by the gentle tinkle of piano music, the small corner fountain cycling water, and the rich chocolate color of the walls did not give me peace.

Gate sat across from me in an armchair, observing me thoughtfully. His discerning eyes were a dull gray-green, the distorted color of algae as seen through the glass and water of an aquarium. "Sure you do," he said softly, inclining his head, his salt and pepper hair falling forward. "You're here because you want to know if Malakai is full of crap or not."

I gasped in surprise. "What did he—"

"He sent me this last week," Gate said, holding up a hand-written letter. "He told me that he'd directed you to me, and that I should expect your call."

"Directed?" I said, reaching into my pocket and pulling out the note Malakai had left for me. "You call this directed?"

Gate took the paper and read it, a small smile playing on his lips. "Good Lord," he said quietly, more to himself than to me. "I guess that proves the point." His mossy eyes met mine, and I noticed that behind them, deep sorrow lay buried. "He asked for my help, Gemma, at great personal risk to himself. Malakai wants me to help you access your memories. He paid me a retainer, enough for me to work with you solely for the next six months."

"Why would he... do that?" I asked.

"Because," Gate said, "It's important to him. He wants to understand you."

"Really?" I said, unable to keep the bitterness from my voice. "If understanding me was so important to Malakai, maybe he shouldn't have abandoned me at a gas station two weeks ago, thirty miles from my house."

Gate stroked his goatee, a faraway look in his eyes. "Maybe he didn't abandon you. Maybe he was protecting you. Given his keen interest in you, there is only one reason I think he would have done that. He was being pursued."

I searched Gate's face. "By who?"

His eyebrows furrowed. "By what." He paused. "Make no mistake, Gemma. The Essen have enemies. Theirs will be yours. But not yet." He reached for my right hand. "Now, let me see your notae."

I let him take it, dumbfounded. Something about the way Gate spoke, slow, hushed, and rhythmic, disarmed me. He turned my wrist towards the ceiling and stroked over my birthmark with his thumbs, analyzing it. His touch was gentle, almost fatherly, his tawny skin smooth.

"So strange," he whispered, "to see them together, comprehensively." He released my arm and leaned back into his chair. "You've been experiencing symptoms, too?" Gate asked. "Malakai's letter referenced nightmares, fatigue, and... Gravitation?"

Drawing my knees up to my chest, I shrunk into the couch. "What's that?"

"It's compulsion. The force you feel down here, in your gut, that pulls you forward, towards a person, an object, or location. Towards your destiny." He cocked his head at me. "I think it's how you found me, using only this." He indicated the note Malakai had given me.

Gravitation. So that was what Malakai meant when he asked if I had been attracted to him that day in the woods. "Yes, I have those, uh, symptoms." I played with the ends of my hair. "What's happening to me?"

Gate inhaled deeply. "You're undergoing, Gemma. Malakai was right. Only, this is unheard of. I've never known an Essen who didn't know—"

"Know about what?" I interrupted. "What am I undergoing?"

"Supernaturalization," he said. "You're undergoing supernaturalization. The process of becoming supernatural." He ran his hand through his hair, the wide gold band on his ring finger catching my eye, striking and buttery against his brown skin. Ornately carved with vines, the ring was unique.

"You're telling me I'm becoming supernatural?" I blinked.

"I'm telling you you're undergoing. The process starts six months before an Essen's twenty-first birthday. It's their coming of age, so to speak."

I was acutely aware that Gate used the word 'their' and not 'our.' I leaned in, skeptical. "And Malakai, he's undergoing too?"

"Well, no," Gate faltered. "He should have already... He's twenty-three now, I think. He must have undergone two years ago."

"But you aren't sure." There was an edge to my statement.

He regarded me thoughtfully, as if deciding how much to share. "No, I'm not sure. His letter told me very little about himself, only that he hoped I could work with you, and determine if you are... the Link." A question formed behind his eyes. He hesitated, then: "What is he like? Malakai?"

"You don't know him?" I asked, bewildered.

"He's my nephew," Gate said, sighing. "But this letter"—he gestured to it—"is the only contact I've had from him. It's been eighteen years. He was just a small child when..." He trailed off, his face tightening with emotion.

I didn't know what to say. I felt like I should say something comforting or reassuring, but I've never been good with words. Still, there was something about Gate that reminded me of Uncle Dan, and his confession tugged at me.

Gate stood up. "I'm sorry," he said. "Please excuse me for a moment." And he abruptly left the room.

CHAPTER 11

I waited. For whatever reason, I had warmed up to Gate. He seemed real to me, trustworthy and honest, and I wanted to hear him out. I got up from the couch and wandered the room, noting the many plants placed throughout it. At the opposite corner, there was a wooden desk, a single framed photo on its surface. In the picture, a much younger Gate pushed a little boy on a tire swing while a lovely woman, vastly pregnant, laughed from the sidelines. His expression was pure joy.

Gate, he seemed grounded. His words, so much more than Malakai's, were believable, logical even. Even his statement about undergoing super-naturalization felt acceptable to me. It left me thinking: *Okay, what does that mean exactly? What else do I need to know? What about these enemies I may eventually inherit?*

I sat back down on the couch. Maybe I was being gullible, but Gate had an earnestness to him. If he said I was an Essen, perhaps I was. I didn't know anything about my past, after all, just like I didn't know anything about the Essen.

He came back into the parlor with regained composure. "I apologize," he said. "I should not have been... It's just... I cannot fail in my task. It will be my only opportunity. I must help you recover memories and help Malakai find the portens. Did he tell you about the portens?"

"No," I said. "He told me he is looking for a weapon. That the Link is supposed to know where it is." I shook my head. "I don't know anything about a weapon. Why does he think I should?"

"The weapon is called a portens, but no one is exactly sure what it is. It is said that the portens has the power, is the only tool with the power, to free the Essen. Malakai, he believes that to find the portens, he must first find the Link. That the Link will lead the Essen to the portens. And one will know they've found the Link by the appearance of a 'comprehensive' notae—the symbol on your wrist.

"Malakai thinks you may be the Link, but he cannot bring you to the others until he is certain you can lead them to the portens. His letter informed me that he is… not very respected within the Host. He has been looking for the Link for so long and so intensely, it's become something of a joke to other Essen. He told me about the day he first saw you, that day in the woods. He thought someone was using you to ridicule him, that the symbol on your wrist was a cruel deception. But after being pulled to you by his own Gravitation twice after that initial meeting… Well, a small part of him dares to hope.

"It's a very small part. The rest of him doubts your ability to gain him the portens. He is skeptical because he always believed the Link would be something directional, such as a book, a map, or a landmark. That once he had the Link, finding the portens would be easy. An 'x marks the spot,' if you will. He never expected it to show up on a person. Let alone an Essen who didn't even know she was an Essen. That's never happened before. The Essen always know they are Essen. And the community is small."

It was a lot to take in. I bit my lip, thinking. Could Gate be speaking truth? As inconceivable as everything he shared was, it *felt* true. "Gate…" I started. His name was foreign on my tongue. "Gate, are you an Essen? Who are they?"

Gate smiled, but his expression was somber. "The Essen are people with supernatural abilities, or 'gifts.' They are entirely human, but also supernatural. I am not one, Gemma, but I am safe for you to talk to."

"But how do I know? Who is safe, I mean. Malakai told me that… He said there are implications to being an Essen, that I shouldn't talk about it with anyone." I said, picking up Malakai's note. "What are the deadly consequences?"

Gate's voice was even. "The Essen are prohibited from sharing Essen information with non-Essen. Call it an unforeseen byproduct of supernaturalization. The first Essen learned this the hard way. As soon as the words passed their lips, any acknowledgment of their true identities, they died. Their hearts just stopped beating. These days, no one makes that mistake. The Essen all know the rule. It is programmed in them, trained from youth. Obviously, since you didn't know you were one, Malakai had to warn you."

I hugged my knees to my chest. "I still don't understand. Why wouldn't I know I am an Essen, if all the others do?"

He sighed. "The knowledge may well be trapped in your subconscious. Just as knowledge of the portens' location may be. Malakai sent you to me to verify what he could not. You see," he continued, "I am uniquely qualified to recover lost memories. Malakai knows this because I once offered to do the same for him. And seeing that Malakai is… unavailable for a while, and that there are few people he trusts, he had few options for learning whether you are the Link.

"I hope I can unearth memories about the portens, if you have them. But even if you don't, or if I can't, Malakai thinks your Gravitation may guide you to it, in the same way it led you to Malakai, and then to me. But Gravitation's effectiveness," Gate said, "is like the effectiveness of a magnet. Size and proximity are important. And there's also another factor: training. As we work together, I will help you hone the skill. But Gemma, you must be careful. Gravitation works both ways. While it pulls you closer to your goal, it also pulls your enemies closer to *their* goal: you. The closer you get to Activation, the stronger it gets. You must protect yourself by keeping your birthmark covered at all times. If they see it, if they can confirm it's you that attracted them…" Gate trailed off. Reading the confusion on my face, Gate said, "Activation is the final stage of undergoing, the last step of supernaturalization. It is the stage that starts and ends on your twenty-first birthday. The stage when the Essen enemies become yours."

"How many stages are there?" I asked.

"Three," Gate said. "Gravitation, Affliction, and Activation. Though he has his doubts about you, Malakai thinks my assistance, forbidden as it is, will give the Essen the best shot of finding the portens. And it is critical that it is found. For Malakai's sake. His letter to me, the tone of it, was… desperate. He wants his trials—or his life—to be over."

Gate stared down at the floor. Spinning the ring on his finger, he appeared lost in thought. At that moment, without knowing why, I pitied him. When he looked back up at me, his expression was resolved.

"Your memory block," he said. "Malakai wrote that it was caused by a car accident?"

I nodded.

"And you're sure you want to try to remove the block? My work, regression therapy, it could give you insights into your past, but it can also be traumatic…"

"Yes," I said. "Yes, I want to." I had never been more certain of anything in my life. Though I'd never been hypnotized, it was something I knew I had to do. If I didn't, I'd always wonder what I had missed, what could have been gained. "What do I need to do?"

"I will walk you through it. We'll take it slow, one memory at a time, one per session. Slowly, the wall will come down, brick by brick, over time." Gate met my eyes. "It's possible that certain memories want to be recovered and that those will float more easily to the surface. We'll start there."

Despite having just met Gate, and despite my discomfort when I first entered his parlor, I trusted him completely. Everything he told me was wildly unbelievable, and yet it resonated with me. Until that moment, it was like I'd been wandering through life in darkness. Then suddenly, Gate lit a torch and showed me a path. My instinct told me to follow it, that it was meant for me to walk. I closed my eyes, relaxed onto the couch, certain that my shadowed past was about to be illuminated.

CHAPTER 12

M y recollection of that first hypnosis session with Gate is fuzzy. I remember him telling me about his induction techniques, asking me about my favorite places and colors, instructing me to place my hands palm-down on my knees, and counting backwards from ten several times.

I remember my body, my core and all of my limbs, feeling very heavy, and Gate's voice, soft and cadenced, guiding me deeper and deeper. My visualized self, prompted forward by Gate's suggestions, appeared blurry and cartoonish in my mind.

Blackness surrounded me. I had no concept of time. Gate's statements were my only reality, my only tether to the world. Slowly, the image of myself solidified. Lantern in hand, I wandered into the depths of a cool cave, feeling my way through the murky air.

Gate reinforced my progress, affirming my exploration. I flashed light into the cave's corners, seeing nothing but inky walls. Then the ground sloped downwards, suddenly slick with moisture. Dripping stalactites formed above me, blocking my view. Advancing past them, holding my lantern out in front of me, I found what I was looking for.

A child's room, decorated with white furniture and adorned with daisies. In the twin bed, a girl stared at the ceiling, playing with the ends of her hair. Sitting on the edge of the bed next to her, a handsome man touched her cheek, lines of worry etching his sun-bronzed face.

"I'm sure you'll feel better tomorrow, Gemmy bean," he said. "I know it hurts right now, but the kids who teased you, they don't know you. You are an amazing little person. Know that, and promise me you won't let them get to you."

"But Daddy," the girl said. "They hate me. I don't know how to make them my friends." Small tears slid from her turquoise eyes.

The man stroked her hair. "Do you know why your mother and I named you Gemma?" he said. "Because you are a jewel in the world. You have beauty, so many facets, and depth. You may be shy, but in time, you'll find the right friends. Friends who will appreciate your quiet nature and your curious mind. You have greatness in you. One day, you will know that yourself." He kissed the child's forehead.

The girl, still crying, asked, "How do you know? That I have greatness?"

Chuckling softly, the man shook his head. "Oh Gemmy bean. How could you not? With you, every day is the start of something amazing."

The man tucked her in, turned off the lamp next to the child's bed, and retreated from the room, the whole scene fading into nothingness after him. I turned away, a small itch tickling my throat. I swallowed hard, attempting to force it down. It persisted, growing more bothersome. Lantern in hand, I stumbled up and out of the cave, searching for the exit. I coughed, trying to clear the irritation, but it remained. I coughed again, and again, unable to stop. Tears streamed down my face as the spasm threatened to choke me. I gasped for air, and awoke.

Still coughing, I sat up quickly. Gate placed a hand on my shoulder and handed me a glass of water. I drank it and the coughing subsided. Blinking in the dim light of Gate's parlor, I still felt heavy, almost drug-addled. He handed me a tissue, and I realized my face was wet with tears.

"The therapy part of hypnotherapy," Gate said, subdued.

"What happened?" I asked. My head felt trippy and confused, as if I'd been in the middle of a vivid dream. Had I achieved a memory?

"You broke through, Gemma. You recalled an interaction with your father, one from when you were very young. In sharing it with me, your emotions were unrestrained." He studied me for a moment, his green-gray eyes tender. "After your father turned off the light and left your room, I urged you continue to explore the depths. Your subconscious rejected my guidance. I saw it in your throat, your swallowing. I rephrased the suggestion, hoping we could continue, but you were spent."

"How long was I under?" I felt as though only minutes had passed.

"The better part of an hour. Normally, I'd bring you out at an hour. You happened to be ready to come back sooner this time. How do you feel?"

"Ugh," I responded. A dull headache was beginning to form in the base of my brain, a slow throbbing that nauseated me. I rubbed my neck.

"Your response is completely normal," he said. "Drink plenty of water, and try to rest. It's been an overwhelming session today, I know."

I nodded. "I should probably be going."

"Yes," Gate said. "We'll meet again soon. In the meantime, try to find out as much as possible about your parents, beyond what you already know."

As I made my way out of Gate's home, my mind was mush. If I'd had it together, I would have probed more about the Essen, their enemies, Gravitation training, and the supernatural 'gifts.' But as it was, I could barely function enough to make it to my bus stop.

By the time I got back to campus, my headache was so intense, I had a hard time keeping my eyes open. I stumbled to Jonny's car, aware that I was late and that he'd be waiting for me, annoyed. Only, he wasn't.

I dug my cell phone out of my jacket and texted him. Waiting for his response, I slumped against the car, unable to focus on anything other than the pain.

He didn't write back, but a few minutes later, he found me sitting on the frozen ground, a crumpled heap, holding my throbbing head. Without a word, he put his arm around me, helped me up and into the car, and let me lean against him as he drove home. Through the pulsing ache, my father's words echoed in my head. *You may be shy, but in time, you'll find the right friends.* They rang true now, so many years later, and though I've never been a spiritual person, it was then that I really understood how wholly blessed I was.

CHAPTER 13

When dawn broke on Friday, November 21st, I awoke alert and refreshed, sans static, sans headache, and... *happy*. More than happy. I felt renewed and energetic, expecting the day ahead to be the best one I'd ever had. I rose and dressed quickly, enthusiasm overtaking me.

At first I attributed my joy to the complete rest I'd been able to attain. No nightmares had haunted my slumber, and a full night of undisturbed sleep does me wonders. I'm sure that was part of it, but there was something else. I felt different: healthy, purpose-filled, and whole.

For the first time, I had hope. Years ago, I had given up on ever knowing my past. The effort, all of the medical appointments, laboratory tests, and trial drugs, had been fruitless. But now—a chink in the wall in my mind, a small and inconsequential memory, held the promise of my restoration.

Literally trembling with gratitude, I finished getting ready for school, sure my skin wouldn't be able to contain me for long. There was too much *life* in me. My very soul had been revitalized.

Later, Gate would tell me that I was experiencing what hypnotherapists refer to as a 'hypnosis high.' It was the most powerful and euphoric state I'd even been in. I never wanted it to end. The only thing that mattered to me was prolonging the feeling and ensuring the means to have it again, should it wane.

I didn't know how long it would last, but I was eager to make the most of my day while I had it. Tiptoeing from my bedroom, not wanting to wake anyone, I made my way downstairs and slipped on my winter coat and boots. Outside, the snow crunched beneath my feet as I treaded through it to Jonny's house.

Unconcerned about the early hour, I rang the doorbell, knowing it would be Jonny who would answer. Maggie, Jonny's mom, worked third shift as a nurse in the Emergency Department of Hennepin County Medical Center. She wouldn't be home from the hospital yet. And Lucy, nothing wakes that girl up. Jonny's never had a father. I rang the doorbell again and knocked several times.

A minute later, squinty-eyed and disheveled, he cracked the door and peered outside. Seeing it was me, he opened the door and let me in. Bare-chested and in flannel pajama pants, Jonny looked adorable, like a puppy that had been napping. "Gemma?" he said, rubbing his face, confused. "What's wr—"

Without letting him finish, I threw my arms around his neck and hugged him tightly. His body went rigid with surprise. "I'm so sorry, Jonny," I whispered into his shoulder. "You're my best friend, and for the last two weeks, I've been horrible to you."

Hesitating, he put his arms around me and hugged me back. I melted into him, comforted by his touch.

"I'm sorry," I said again, exhaling into his skin. Goosebumps erupted on his flesh under my breath. "Can you forgive me for messing up? I am so sorry I let you down."

Reaching up, Jonny stroked my hair, tucked a loose strand of it behind my ear, and rested his hand on the back of my neck. He kissed the top of my head and held me for a few minutes like that before pulling away to look into my eyes. "Of course I forgive you, Gemma. You're my best friend too. I could never stay mad at you. I was just... hurt."

Fresh guilt washed over me. "I've no excuse," I said. "I was being selfish. I know you didn't want me to call Malakai"—Jonny's expression darkened when I said his name—"but I was... but I did anyway."

His fingers, callused from years of playing guitar, brushed my cheek. "Didn't it occur to you that he could have been a stalker? That I was worried about you?"

Truthfully, the thought had never occurred to me. Despite my repeated encounters with Malakai, and despite his strange intensity, I never felt harassed. I'd felt a little intimidated, sure, by Malakai's sheer size and his commanding presence, as well as perplexed by the frequency of our 'coincidental' meetings, but I'd been more intrigued than afraid.

Jonny's hand moved down to my chin, lifted it up. "Gemma, you are beautiful, inside and out. And that guy, he is bad news. I know it." His eyes, the deep blue of the ocean at night, were ardent.

"I'm okay, Jonny," I said, trying to sound reassuring. "I'm okay. Nothing happened. Malakai is nobody to me."

As I said the words, I tasted the lie in them. Whatever Malakai was to me, he wasn't nobody. After he'd left me stranded at the gas station, I'd hated him. I'd burned the card with his phone number on it and vowed never to talk to him again, even if he popped into my life at some point in the future. But after talking to Gate yesterday, I wondered what more there might be to him and whether I'd have the chance to find out.

Jonny pulled me into him and held me against his naked chest. Smoothing my hair with his palm, he said, "Let me get dressed. Then I'm taking you to breakfast. We don't have to be on campus for hours."

✳ ✳ ✳

My elation, both from rekindling my friendship with Jonny and as an effect of the hypnosis, lasted the entire weekend and into the next week. Even Aunt Sheri and Uncle Dan, burdened by the long hours demanded of them by their respective careers as a legal secretary and a power generator technician, noticed a change in me.

"That smile looks good on you," Uncle Dan said one evening, winking at me. "Who's the guy?"

A middle-aged hypnotherapist, I thought, chuckling internally. "No guy," I said. "Just happy."

Uncle Dan shrugged. "Good enough for me."

Aunt Sheri hadn't been as easy to convince. Certain that something must have contributed to my high spirits, she found me in my bedroom the following evening, sprawled across my bed studying. "Really, Gemma? Nothing's changed?" Her golden curls bounced as she shook her head. "You're just so cheerful."

"I'm fine, I promise," I said smiling at her. I closed my textbook and sat up. "But, actually, I am hoping you can help me with something. Do you know if either of my parents had any birthmarks? Maybe like mine?"

"David didn't, I can tell you that for sure," she said of her brother. "He was always so proud of yours, so surprised by the order in it."

"And my mother?" I asked.

"We've been over this, sweetie. I never met Lia. She and your dad lived in Arizona until she passed away giving birth to you, and then he moved back home to Minnesota with you when he got the position at the University." She waved her hand. "But it doesn't do to dwell on the past, now does it? You've been in such a great mood. Let's not spoil it with what-might-have-been talk."

My next appointment with Gate was scheduled for Wednesday, November 26th, and I hadn't learned anything new about either of my parents. I hoped he wouldn't be disappointed in me; I was so looking forward to my second hypnotherapy session. And though Gate was the real reason for my new outlook on life, I didn't tell anybody about him. I didn't want to. The hypnotherapy experience had been too personal and the change I was going through, too fresh.

Since Friday morning, when I awoke with newfound joy, my driving desire had been to recover lost memories. Being Essen, understanding Malakai, finding the mysterious portens, none of it mattered to me. Those were distant concepts, unimportant to the present. First and foremost, I cared about forcing down the wall. And if Gate insisted on taking it one memory at a time, one memory per session, I would need to see him every damn day. He was on retainer for me, after all. And I had twelve years' worth of life to unearth from the subterranean tunnels of my mind.

CHAPTER 14

Jonny's forgiveness, it turned out, was contingent on my doing something I'd declined to do several times before. For years he'd been asking me, and for years, I'd told him no, that I wasn't athletic enough. But this time was different.

"You owe me," he'd said as we drove to campus on Wednesday morning. "You left my show only four songs into it, even though you *promised* you'd be there supporting me. So I'm asking you for this instead." His tone had been playful, but I knew he was testing me.

I had no choice. There was only one right answer. "Okay, Jonny. I'll do it." His smile lit up his whole face.

Now on the bus to Uptown, staring out the window at the fluffy flakes dropping from above, I wished for a Thanksgiving heat wave. If the snow all melted tomorrow, it would be impossible to snowboard on Friday, right? But Jonny would be crushed, and I would just have to go with him another time. I sighed and pulled the cord for my stop.

The walk from the bus stop to Gate's house was just a short distance, but by the time I arrived at his door, I was covered in snow. He met me at the threshold, ushered me in, took my coat and hat, and led me into the parlor.

This time, I settled into the couch right away. In the room, and in Gate's presence, I felt secure.

"Tell me about your week," he said, sitting across from me in the armchair. "Have you had any more Gravitational urges? Any nightmares?"

"None," I said. "It's the most amazing thing. I feel incredible."

"Good, that's good," Gate said. "Hypnosis often helps abate the symptoms of undergoing. It may not always work like that, especially as you get closer to Activation, but we'll try."

I frowned. "You mean my nightmares could come back?"

"They *will* come back, Gemma," Gate said. "Gravitation, it's just the first stage. And though the onset of disturbing dreams usually occurs during Gravitation, they intensify in Affliction. As the name suggests, stage two is… highly uncomfortable." He stroked his goatee. "That's when your gifts, usually two or three of them, will start to develop. The evolution of gifts, like the usage of them, is profoundly painful. I'll help however I can, but I won't know how Affliction will present with you until it happens, about three months before your birthday. So for you, it will start around December 25th. Merry Christmas," he said wryly.

"The dreams, they're so awful," I said. "I can't imagine them getting worse. Every night, again and again, the panic, the gasping for air, as waves, hundreds of feet high, hover above me, crash down on me—"

"You always dream of water?" Gate interrupted. When I nodded, he made a note on the legal pad next to him. "Your notae, it's so complex, but I was hoping you'd have a dominant Affiliation within the Host. So the fact that your nightmares center on water, that tells me something."

"What, though? What does it tell you?" I needed as much information as possible if I was going to have to suffer through more of them.

Gate thought for a moment. "The dreams of an undergoing Essen are a lot like the force of Gravitation. They tend to steer you in the direction of your destiny. In your case, water." He paused before going on. "It might not make sense right now, but it will. Eventually. Hopefully before your Activation, if Malakai is released from holding by then."

"Malakai?" I asked. "Where is he?" I didn't want to be surprised by him again, on campus, on the phone, anywhere. Especially not if Jonny was with me.

"He's unavailable, Gemma. I can say no more. It's for him to share, if he wants to. Suffice it to say that he must remain where he is for an uncertain amount of time. And then he will be released." He spun the ornate gold ring around his ring finger, giving the illusion that the vines were growing. He spotted me watching him and stopped. "Habit," he said. "Let's get started, shall we?"

✳ ✳ ✳

I came out of hypnosis more smoothly this time, waking up at Gate's command an hour and ten minutes after our session started. Blinking at him across from me, I said, "I think I fell asleep."

He smiled. "You recovered two memories, Gemma."

"I did? I thought that I was just, well, dreaming. How do I know that what I saw, what I must have shared with you, was real? Couldn't it have been my imagination creating memories, fabricating them?"

"It's possible," Gate said, "but I don't think that's the case. However, I know one way you can be sure." He inclined his head, his salt and pepper hair falling into his face. "Ask him."

"Ask who?" I wondered aloud.

"Think, Gemma. Who was in both memories that could verify the authenticity of them?"

I replayed the scenes back in my mind. It had been summer in both of them, the summer before the accident, I realized. In the first one, everyone was there: Flash, Aunt Sheri, Uncle Dan, Jonny, Lucy, Maggie. Well, not everyone. My father wasn't there. It was the 4th of July, nighttime, and we were all sprawled out on a giant blanket at Como Park staring up at glittery fireworks.

The other scene was less clear in my mind. There were three people sitting around a kitchen table, with what looked like Chinese food cartons spread across it. I was arguing with another girl over something. Was it a fortune cookie? To my left, a boy read a small piece of paper—probably the fortune from his own cookie—and shoved it in his pocket. I asked him to tell me what it said, but he wouldn't.

Gate regarded me expectantly. "You know who it is, Gemma. You called him by name in both memories. And you must still be in contact with him, because in Malakai's letter to me, it was his performance at Fervor that Malakai told me he risked his life to bring you to."

Jonny.

I told Gate I would talk to Jonny, would see if he remembered the events I'd recalled. We set another appointment for the following Monday, and I made my way back to the bus stop in the snow, all the while wondering what Gate had meant about Malakai risking his life by bringing me to Fervor.

CHAPTER 15

"Okay, make sure to bend your knees. Good, you've got it. Now turn towards me, put a little weight on your heels. See, you're turning! We'll just go—"

"Ouwf," I said, falling hard into the snow.

Jonny slid over to where I was lying and bent over me. The sun, sinking to the skyline behind him, gave him a coppery halo. "You caught your edge a bit there."

"Oh really?" I said. "I hadn't realized that." Rolling my eyes, I reached up towards him. Jonny wrapped his mittened hand around my forearm and pulled me to my feet, the board sliding precariously beneath me as he did.

"Chairlifts can be tricky," he said. Smiling, he released my hand. "Ready to go again?"

Thighs and calves aching, I stood motionless. As long as I wasn't moving, I was able to maintain my balance. From the top of the hill, the run looked longer and steeper than it was. I brushed the powder from my coat. "All right," I said.

Catching the weariness in my voice, Jonny said, "You're about done, aren't you?" He popped out of his bindings, and held my arms. "Here, step out."

I stepped off the snowboard and picked it up, glad to be surefooted again. "Holy hell," I said. "My legs *burn*. I can't believe you do this every weekend."

"You get used to it," he said, grabbing his board and strapping it to his backpack. "Anyway, you did great for your first time. Three hours we were out here. Next weekend, maybe we'll try some jumps." He winked at me.

Jonny loves snowboarding. He loves everything about it: the fresh, clean smell of the winter air, the sound of the board cutting through crusty snow, the camaraderie with other boarders, even the technical clothing and gear. But more than anything, he loves riding solo, listening to tunes on headphones held in place by his beanie, and messing around in the park underneath starry skies after everyone else has gone home.

Because he loves it, he wants me to love it. And because I love him, I want to love it, too. But after finally trying it, and in spite of Jonny's instruction and patience, I wasn't sure it would be my thing. "Maybe," I said.

"Come here, I want to show you something," he said. We tromped through the snow across the top of the run, Jonny leading the way. Past all of the slopes and through a wooded area, we arrived at a clearing at the crest of a secluded hill.

He pulled his board from the straps of his backpack, tossed it on the ground, and sat between the bindings, motioning for me to do the same. I did, and together, we watched the sun drop below the horizon, leaving us with a private and unobstructed view of nature's endless color palette.

"Wow," I said. "Now this is my idea of snowboarding." I turned to Jonny. "So I'm forgiven now? Officially?"

He chuckled softly. "Yes, definitely. When you're too sore to get out of bed tomorrow, you'll know it was punishment enough." He pulled his hat off and ran his fingers through his flattened hair. His voice grew quiet and he said, "I owe you an apology too, Gem."

"No," I said. "You didn't do anything wrong. It was my fault. I told you I'd be at your show, and I wasn't."

Jonny fidgeted with the Velcro on his mittens. "I wasn't half as upset about you leaving early as I was that you showed up in the first place, with *Malakai*." He said Malakai's name as though the word tasted bitter. "The truth is, I had no right to be mad at you. I was just... jealous. Because even though I'm not your boyfriend, Gemma, I should be. I want to be. But I never made a move because I thought I had time. And I was afraid that it might ruin what we have. So I didn't tell you, thinking that when the time was right, it would just happen. I took you for granted, Gem, and I'm sorry. You should be able to see whoever you want, and if it is Malakai, and if I'm telling you too late, I understand. I don't own you." He inhaled deeply, holding his breath for a moment before letting it out unevenly. "If anything, you own me."

Oh Jonny, I thought. *Jonny, you are everything to me. But...*

I opened my mouth to speak, but what could I say? Every time I thought of Jonny, I felt warm, happy, and loved. My favorite person in the whole world, Jonny was genuine, funny, attractive, and talented. He would make a perfect boyfriend, and one day, a perfect husband, but... And I realized what the problem was. There was always a 'but.'

"It's okay, Gemma," Jonny said. "You don't have to say anything. I just wanted you to know where I'm at. And tell you that I'm ready. When you are, I'm ready to be more for you, to you. With you." He pulled his knees up and clasped his arms around them, looking into the distance. In profile, his eyelashes were much thicker and longer than I'd ever noticed before. "But please just promise me that you'll let me know if you... if someone else is..." He trailed off.

I closed my eyes, but I could still see him: the strong jawline, flawless complexion, and full lips. He was undeniably handsome, and yet I felt the burning loyalty of friendship rather than the heat of desire. "I promise, Jonny," I said. "I'll tell you. But there's no one else right now."

We sat like that for a while, the evening growing darker, colder, and quieter. I began to shiver.

"Oh, you're freezing," Jonny said, rubbing my arms. "We should head back."

We picked up our boards and started towards the chalet. "Jonny?" I said as we walked. "I think I remembered something. From before the accident. The other day, I remembered it, and I was wondering if, well, since you were in the memory, if you remember it too."

"Oh my gosh, Gemma! That's huge," Jonny said, amazed. "What was it?"

"It was summertime, and I was at your house, I think. You, me, and Lucy, we were at the table, having Chinese, but there were only two fortune cookies. You took one of them, and Lucy and I both wanted the other. I think I ended up letting her have it, because I only wanted it for the fortune anyway.

It turned out to be a stupid proverb, so we threw it in the duck sauce." I shrugged. "You said yours was good though, but you wouldn't let us read it."

A half-smile formed on Jonny's face as he recalled the day. "Yeah, I remember that." His blue eyes, almost black in the evening light, twinkled. "Like it was yesterday."

"Do you remember what your fortune said?"

He laughed. "Yup."

"Well?"

"Well what?"

"What did it *say*?" I asked.

"That's for me to know, isn't it?" he said, jogging ahead of me. "Come on, slowpoke. I'm ready for hot chocolate."

I laughed and hurried after him, relieved that after everything that had happened, things were finally back to normal between us.

CHAPTER 16

For as long as I live, I'll remember the day the static in my head turned into meaning.

It was Wednesday, December 10th, and I was grumpy. I was sitting in a quiet corner of Walter Library, where Jonny would be meeting me after he finished class. We'd planned to study together, but I wasn't in the mood. It's awfully hard to write a ten-page persuasive essay on whether Man is separate from and above Nature, as opposed to simply being part of it, with a head full of static. Yet that was my task.

The term would be concluding in a week and a half, and with any luck, I'd pull off C's in my classes, the exception being Professor Dagenais' American Nature Writing course. Contrary to what people might think based on my study habits, I'm actually a decent test taker. Since the final exams for most of my classes were weighted at fifty percent of the overall grade, I wasn't particularly worried about passing. And passing was my only goal.

Unfortunately, Professor Dagenais, in his infinite wisdom, chose not to give end-of-semester tests. Instead, he felt that learning became "cemented" through the creation of final written projects related to the course material.

I didn't have a philosophical bent about Man's place in nature. Maybe he was at the mercy of it, like the rest of creation. People die in earthquakes, avalanches, fires, and tsunamis every year after all. Then again, maybe Man did have an elevated status above it. We can make snow for our own pleasure, for heaven's sake. Jonny had pointed out the machine to me when we were at the snowboard park. Either way. I just didn't care enough to choose a side and argue the point. And I hadn't read enough of the assigned writings by Aldo Leopold, Henry David Thoreau, or John Muir to draw upon for literary support.

So the essay would have been a struggle anyway, but with the added handicap of "brain buzz," which I'd not-so-affectionately named it, everything I was producing was worthless.

The static in my mind concerned me. It came and went at random, but was typically worse in the mornings and typically better the day or two after hypnotherapy. At first, I tried to ignore it. Eventually it will go away, I thought. But it hadn't yet, and in fact, it was getting worse. When it was present in my head, the intensity of the static, which mostly sounded like a radio stuck between channels, made it difficult for me to concentrate on anything.

I slammed shut my copy of Leopold's *A Sand County Almanac* and put my head down on the book, irritated. Where was a hypnosis high when I needed it?

It had been five days since my most recent hypnotherapy session with Gate, and the pleasurable effects of the hypnosis were not lasting as long. Nor were the sessions as productive. I'd been recalling memories, but they were all simple and inconsequential, and mostly just snippets: me petting a black lab, Flash and Paul playing video games, my dad preparing a lecture.

I'd asked Gate if we could meet more frequently, thinking that if I could meet with him every day, or at least every other day, I might be able to find memories of value more quickly. He'd responded by telling me that he would be available for me any time, day or night, if I needed a resource while undergoing, but that he wouldn't bring me down to look for memories more than once each week. Gate seemed to think that if we took apart the wall in my mind too quickly, I would be left sorting through a pile of mental rubble, unable to distinguish past from present. It was a ridiculous notion and I'd told him so, but he'd held fast to his rule.

I closed my eyes and concentrated on breathing slowly, trying to clear my mind in a meditative manner, the way Gate had advised. Though I had never told him about the static in my mind, the technique was supposed to help with all the symptoms of undergoing, which I was certain "brain buzz" was.

Slowly, the static began to fade away. I was on the verge of drifting to sleep when I heard him.

"Do you think I should bring her to Phoenix?" he asked. His voice was deep and husky, and the question spoken as though it was a secret.

My eyes flew open. *Malakai Zonn.* I jumped up and spun around, sure that he was directly behind me, but he wasn't. I was alone.

Then I heard a different voice, another male's, this one a soft-spoken tenor. "Gemma? Oh man, I don't know. What good do you think it would do?"

Upon hearing my name, I froze. The words echoed in my head. They were talking about me, about Malakai bringing me to Phoenix. And I was hearing them in my mind, not with my ears. *What the hell?*

"You're probably right," Malakai said. "Especially since we still don't know if she's the Link." I heard him sigh heavily. "As soon as I can leave"— his words were lost in static, and I missed several of them—"handle the delivery for me."

"Yeah, okay," the other guy said. "When should I"—there was more static—"the Supernovas?"

And then there was nothing. No voices, no brain buzz, nothing. The library's silence seemed sudden and eerie to me. Heart racing, alert and suspicious, I sat back down.

As soon as I did, the worst pain I've ever felt in my life ripped through my skull, sharp and pulsing. Unable to stop myself, I threw up all over the table, across my notes and my copy of *A Sand County Almanac*. Then I blacked out.

Friends don't clean up each other's vomit. Duties of that nature require a higher level of commitment, or at least a higher *desired* level of commitment.

When Jonny turned twenty-one last August, he'd gone bar-hopping with his buddies and fellow musicians, Devun Drake and Luke Strayton. From what I understand, they'd shown him a great time, too great of a time, and he'd gotten sick in Devun's Toyota. Devun had made him deal with the messes, the ones on himself and in the car, the following morning.

If Jonny hadn't told me about his feelings at the snowboard park, I would have figured it out by the way he took care of me after he found me in the library.

He must have arrived shortly after I became ill. Though I was in and out of consciousness, I do remember him shaking me, asking me if he should take me to the hospital, wiping off my books and clothing, and half-carrying me to the car.

When he got me home, where I am sure I demanded he take me rather than the hospital, his mom was waiting to assess me. Maggie had come over, despite it technically being the middle of her sleep time given her third shift schedule, after Jonny called her on the drive home from campus. Apparently she told him I would be okay with rest, because he helped me wash up and get into bed. Then he waited with me until someone else came home, afraid of leaving me alone.

I slept off and on for the better part of fifteen hours. When I woke up, my brain was filled with buzzing again. Panicked, I called Jonny and told him I wouldn't be going to campus with him that day. Then I called Gate and, stressing the urgency, asked him whether he made house calls.

CHAPTER 17

Gate seemed out of place in my living room. Situated on a plush tan recliner, he looked lankier than he had in the armchair of his own home. He peered at me over the cup of coffee I'd given him, the sage walls of the room bringing out the olivine color in his eyes.

I felt awkward having him in my house, a setting more intimate than our still-somewhat-formal relationship warranted. Though I trusted him, though he'd walked with me into the depths of my mind, I was acutely aware that the boundary that kept us patient and therapist had dissolved. It now felt like our relationship was more, almost a guardianship, and I wasn't sure I was ready for that. I knew I needed his help, his guidance and mentoring, but I've always been an extremely private person.

For that very reason, I'd asked him to come over mid-morning, once everyone else was gone for the day. I don't know how I would have introduced Gate to Uncle Dan, Aunt Sheri, and Flash. As a counselor, a life coach, a friend? I would've had to create a story explaining the visit, because the truth wasn't an option.

The truth. It was absurd, wasn't it? I'd heard voices in my head and then become so desperately ill I thought I was dying. But Gate hadn't thought it was absurd. Ever patient, he'd listened to my description of the static, and of the voices and the pain, with quiet attentiveness.

Forehead creased in contemplation, Gate set down his coffee. "It seems you've reached the onset of Affliction, Gemma. You have begun the second stage of undergoing. And it appears that your first gift will be a gift of the mind."

I raised my chin defensively. "What do you mean, 'of the mind'? Are you saying that it was just in my head, something I imagined? That it wasn't real?"

"No, not at all. That's not what I'm saying. Gifts of the mind are the most powerful." His tone was sincere and reassuring. "They are also the least common, only appearing in those who are keen and adept, strong-willed, and not easily influenced." Gate's mouth quirked into a small smile. "And just because something occurs in your mind, what makes you think it can't be real?"

I rolled my eyes. "You stole that line from *Harry Potter*."

"Dumbledore says something like it in the final book, you're right. It's true enough, though. What you heard in your head… I believe it actually occurred. I think you overheard a conversation that was taking place, at that same time, somewhere else." He cocked his head, pensive. "Almost like you picked up on the frequency of some conversational current."

"You've got to be kidding," I said. "*That's* my supernatural ability? Boundless but random eavesdropping, followed by excruciating pain? God, I'm so lucky I'm an Essen." I felt my cheeks grow hot with my temper.

Unruffled, Gate said, "It's still developing, Gemma. We don't know yet what this gift will become. Once you have Activated, only then will it be set. For now, we need to cultivate what you have."

"Oh yeah? Cultivate constant static and chance conversations? How are we going to do that?" I crossed my arms, defiant.

"I know you're discouraged," Gate said, "but you've only had one episode. You've got three more months of this, three agonizing months if we don't figure out how to manage it." He looked at me pointedly. "Particularly if other gifts begin to develop as well. So please, try to work with me. Here's what I want you to do. You called it 'brain buzz.' Each and every time it starts, give it your full attention. Be deliberate. Visualize a radio dial, and marry the static you hear with the signal setting you see. Then, try to move the dial. Try to change the channel or shut it off. Keep a log of what happens, not just what you hear in your mind, but what happens afterwards. The pain, we need to figure out how to manage that as well."

I threw my hands up in frustration. "Dammit, Gate! That's all you've got for me? I'm just supposed to wait for this to happen again, and then *visualize* a solution? You can't be serious! You have no idea what it was like, how miserable I was, how miserable I still am—"

Gate held up his hand, nodding at me. "I do know, Gemma. I do know, and I'm sorry. I just... I don't have any experience in gifts of the mind. The gifts I've seen, they're corporeal, like superhuman strength or speed, or extrinsic, like the ability to expedite plant growth or generate auroras. The Essen, they are very protective about their gifts. They tend to keep their supernatural abilities secret, even from those closest to them. It's seen as dishonorable to tell and disrespectful to ask. But what I do know, what I'm sure of, is that the human mind is mighty. It has power over the body, over the environment, over reality. Don't forget that. You have untapped potential and fortitude beyond your own understanding. You *will* be able to master this."

Embarrassed by Gate's graciousness in response to my outburst, I shrank into the sofa. My voice was subdued when I said, "Malakai said something about taking me to Phoenix."

"Yes, you mentioned that."

"Why would he want to do that?"

"Because he is bound by duty. He knows he must. He just isn't clear about when."

"But why?" I asked. "What's in Phoenix?"

"Malakai wasn't referring to Phoenix the place. He was referring to Phoenix the person, the current Augur of the Host." Gate's face was unreadable. "At some point, if we discover you are the Link, Malakai will need to bring you before him."

I twirled the ends of my hair, thinking. If I turned out to be anything other than the Link, I'd probably never see Malakai again. His interest was entirely rooted in his desire to find the portens. He'd made it clear that if I wasn't able to help him acquire it, he had little use for me. But the thought didn't bother me—it made me hope I *wasn't* the Link. Malakai was aggravating, and his reappearance in my life would likely destroy my friendship with Jonny.

"I don't want to go anywhere with Malakai," I said. "If we find out I'm the Link, can't you bring me to Phoenix?"

Gate became stern. "I couldn't, but more importantly, I wouldn't. I've told you. I'm not an Essen." He paused, scrutinizing my face. "This isn't about Malakai, is it? This has to do with Jonny."

I looked at my hands. "I need to tell him, Gate. When he found me in the library yesterday…"

"We've been over this. You can't."

"But there must be something I can tell him. I don't want to lie about what's going on. He's going to need an explanation if I keep getting sick."

"All the more reason to work hard to manage your Affliction." Gate said dispassionately.

"Don't give me that bullshit," I said. "You know as well as I do that Jonny, not to mention my *family*, is bound to notice something's up."

Gate folded his hands. "You're right. We should think about getting you accommodations of your own. There's a place in the city, close to campus, so you can minimize your interactions. At least until you're Activated."

I clenched my fists. "Are you kidding me right now? I can't afford an apartment!"

Gate remained frustratingly calm. "I will contact Malakai, ask him to take care of the arrangements for you. Well, until you're able to handle it yourself."

"I am *not* moving to an apartment, especially not one paid for by Malakai. Where the hell does he get all of his money?"

He ignored the question. "You're afraid. That's why you won't leave your family. That's why you want to tell Jonny." He shook his head at me, his brows knitted in disappointment. "You've convinced yourself that Jonny needs to know for his benefit, but that's not the real reason, is it? You want him to know for *you*. You've never done anything on your own, ever. And it scares you."

My face tightened into a scowl. "You don't know anything about me," I said. "Or Jonny. He would want to know—"

"Not if it would kill you to share it," Gate said. "Like it or not, you cannot tell anyone anything about being Essen. Non-Essen are prohibited as confidants."

"You said you aren't Essen," I argued. "Yet here we are."

"Enough, Gemma. I'm not an Essen, but nor am I a non-Essen. Accept that. And accept that this is a road you must take without Jonny." Then he softened slightly, and asked, "Do you love him?"

The question was an arrow to my heart. "Forever and always," I said. "But not in the way he wants me to."

Gate leaned over to me, putting his hand on mine. "It's not your fault. The Essen, they don't love, aren't programmed for love… at least not until after Activation. And even then, many Essen are purpose-driven, called to fulfill a destiny greater than romance." He closed his eyes momentarily, and when he opened them, I saw again the deep sorrow behind his gray-green irises. He squeezed my fingers gently. "Jonny is not your future, Gemma. Your path will lead you away from him. Best that you leave him behind now. If you really care for him, you need to let him go."

My voice came out in a whisper. "I can't. He's my best friend. The only one who really knows me."

He exhaled slowly. "Then you are selfish." He stood up, preparing to leave. In a very low tone, he added, "You can't tell Jonny about your Essen identity. You know that. You won't be able to give him the truth, or valid reasons for things, or… the love he's looking for. So let me ask you, Gemma: Doesn't Jonny deserve more than what you can give him?"

I turned my head away from Gate, numb. He told me to call him, promised to be available if I needed him, and then let himself out of my house.

It's a funny thing, life. A funny, ironic, disheartening thing. All these years, I'd been preparing myself for the moment when Jonny would move on, start a different life, and forget about me. I'd felt sure that the time was coming, that point when he'd realize he was bigger than the life he had currently, better than it. I'd always assumed I'd be left behind, and I'd come to terms with it. But now, in the wake of Gate's speech, I wasn't so sure. Suddenly everything had been turned upside down, flipped inside out, rotated backwards. *I* wouldn't be the one to move on, embrace something else, and leave Jonny behind… would I? The thought was poison in my mind, but I couldn't help wondering—If I did let him go from my life, how long would it take him to forget me?

CHAPTER 18

A dense fog rolled off the water and obscured the terrain. Nonetheless, I sprinted away from the shoreline and into the woods, unseeing, chased by the last rays of daylight.

It was important that I beat nightfall to my goal. Ignoring the sweat dripping down my face, pushing through the ache in my side, I ran as though my life depended on it.

Because my life depended on it.

As I raced further into the forest, the mist hugged the earth, giving me visibility to a clear sky. The final colors of sunset, a neon orange followed by a dark pink and finally a shadowy purple, faded into evening. Against the navy blue, the first star blinked ominously.

I'm not going to make it. Oh God, this is where it ends. Oh God, oh God, oh God.

My breathing became faster and shallower. Hyperventilating, I stumbled and fell to my knees.

And then he was with me. A hulking presence silhouetted by the rising moon.

"Calm down," Malakai said in a low voice. "Gravitation draws them to us. But if it didn't, the racket you're making would."

I put my hand over my mouth, willing myself to stop gasping loudly for air.

"Now get up. This is no time for self-pity." He spoke harshly, intolerant of my terror. "We are wired for survival, not hysteria, and we never give up."

I stood up, dizzy from over-oxygenation. "Kai," I said breathily, "where is your ring?" I wanted to see it. I hoped its incandescence could light our way.

"On a chain around my neck, underneath my shirt. I cannot pull it out. It would give away our position." Malakai paused, scanning the gloom. "We are close. Follow me, and keep up."

Malakai took off and I followed. Dodging wraithlike trees and bushes that entered my sight mere seconds before they entangled me, I attempted to maneuver through the landscape as quietly as Malakai did.

Then I saw it: the faint outline of a looming structure ahead. Our refuge. It was huge and crenellated, like a castle. Adrenaline surged in me, and I increased my speed. I closed the gap between Malakai and myself, passed him, and leapt through an open arch in the stony wall. Lithe and powerful, he launched himself through it immediately after me.

Bent in exhaustion, I glanced back through the archway. Between the fog and the dim light of evening, I saw nothing.

Malakai stepped in front of me. "Never look back, Gemma. Always focus forward." He grabbed my elbow and led me down a corridor illuminated by candled chandeliers.

The hallway was dank and musty and very long. When it ended, it deposited us in a large room, bare except for a gilded throne on a dais, upon which sat a regal-looking man.

Dressed in a cloak and a crown, I knew the man to be Phoenix, the Augur of the Host. I knelt before him. Descending to the floor, Phoenix lifted my chin. I raised my eyes to him, and...

And the vision ended there, in the same place it always did.

I opened my eyes and looked around the library. It was Thursday afternoon, December 18th, and I had been studying for my one remaining final exam when I had drifted into the reverie.

My daydreams of Malakai, like my daydreams of water, were much milder than their nighttime counterparts. In my daydreams, Malakai and I always escaped our pursuers and went together to Phoenix. In my nightmares, we didn't make it to Phoenix—we fell prey to lurking foes before finding asylum.

The new nightmares petrified me. Gate had warned me that they would intensify with Affliction, but I hadn't expected them to be so very real. Every morning when I woke up, the earthy scent of the forest lingered in my nose, the eerie calls of unidentified birds echoed in my ears. And Malakai, the way he fell to the ground every night, the way the flame behind his eyes was extinguished…

I shuddered. The dreams, Gate had told me, were like Gravitation, steering undergoing Essen to their fates. The concept confused and frightened me. Surely the dreams weren't foreshadowing events to come. Some parts of the dreams must be my imagination supplying details, images, and context. But which parts? And what was the 'fate' I was being steered towards?

Malakai was the key. He had to be. He was the common denominator in everything. I still knew very little about him and the Essen, and about myself for the matter. I had so many questions; questions that Gate either couldn't or wouldn't answer. It seemed that Malakai, if and when he eventually reappeared in my life, would have to be the one to supply the information. He was, after all, the only other Essen I knew.

I dreaded the idea of seeing Malakai again, but more than that, I dreaded going through Affliction without more help.

Gate was my only resource, and though he checked in with me daily now that Affliction was underway, I found him to be… insufficient. After the 'advice' he'd given me the previous week, both about my gift and about Jonny, I began to question his wisdom.

Fortunately, there hadn't been more episodes from my 'gift of the mind,' just some minor static. When I had, albeit reluctantly, applied Gate's technique to the buzzing, nothing had happened. The white noise in my mind continued as a low-level drone, an annoying but innocuous-enough backdrop in my life.

So other than the change in my nightmares, the week had been void of activity.

Even my hypnosis sessions had been unremarkable. Since his visit to my home, Gate had taken me under twice. Both times, I had searched the caverns of my psyche without stumbling upon memories of any kind. Deeper and deeper I'd gone until, lost in the vast network of tunnels, my lantern flickered and went out. Panicking in the frigid and pitch black abyss, Gate had had to come down and rescue me.

The fruitless journeys into my subconscious had left me feeling empty. Sitting in the dim light of his parlor, I'd cried.

"Sometimes, Gemma," Gate said in his pacifying and rhythmic voice, "the mind will produce 'blank spaces' right before a breakthrough. It's a shielding mechanism. The mind wants to protect an important memory, one that isn't ready to surface. Do not despair. This is an encouraging sign."

I was not reassured, nor did I achieve hypnosis highs after those sessions. On the contrary: they'd left me wrung out, my energy completely spent.

This, of course, Jonny noticed. How on earth was I going to make it through the next three months of undergoing, constantly distracted by—and miserable from—the nightmares, the development of gifts, and the twitches of impulse I thought might be Gravitation, without giving him some sort of explanation?

I closed my book and abandoned further attempts to study. As I packed my things, I decided that it would probably be wise not to register for spring semester classes. Stage two of undergoing would be hard enough without also having to juggle life as a student.

CHAPTER 19

The party was at Jonny's place and the revelry could be heard throughout the neighborhood. When I stopped over at 10:30, it was with a message from Aunt Sheri to "try to keep it to a dull roar."

I intended to stay for a little while—I was as thrilled as anyone that the semester was finally over—but not the whole frenzied night.

The house was throbbing. Music, heavy with bass, blared from basement, and everywhere swarms of tipsy people mingled. I negotiated my way through them to the kitchen where Jonny was pouring shots for his guests. Coming up behind him, I poked him in the side and said, "Is this what Maggie had in mind when you told her you were having a couple friends over?"

"Gemma!" Jonny raised his arms in surprise. "You're here. Hey everyone, this is my best friend Gemma!" He put one arm around my shoulder and used the other to gesture to the group. "Gemma, everyone."

I blinked. The people in the kitchen were Jonny's buddies Luke and Devun and several folks from our American Nature Writing class. "Jonny, we all know each other."

His eyes widened. "Oh my God, that is so funny!"

I shook my head, smiling. "You're drunk already, aren't you?"

"Nooo," Jonny said, giving the word too many syllables and waving me off. "We were just talking about..." His face went blank.

"Prof Dag's class," a girl named Caitlin supplied.

"Yes, that was it," Jonny said. "You finished, right Gem? Your essay?" He sloppily poured another shot and handed it to me.

"Yeah, thank God." I took the glass but didn't tip it back with everyone else. I wasn't sure what effect, if any, alcohol might have on my symptoms. It wasn't something I wanted to test.

"Hey Jonny, where's your bathroom?" a pretty blonde asked, sticking her head into the kitchen.

"Oh, just through the living room. Here, let me show you," he said, bumping against the doorframe as he left.

I followed him out of the kitchen and wandered the house taking in the scene. People were everywhere: lounging on the furniture, deep in conversation; grouped and laughing in the hallway; dancing in the basement to music mixed by… Paul? I walked to his table.

He smiled and slipped off his headphones as I approached. "Hey girl," he said.

"DJ McGregarious," I said, honoring his DJ persona. "What brings you here?"

Paul shrugged. "Jonny asked." He motioned to the corner. "Check it out." The ever-amorous Lucy was on the loveseat making out fiercely with— yep, it was still him—Joshua. "Didn't she just have braces, like, yesterday?"

I chuckled. "What about you? Flash told me you're settling down. Years of playing the field, and now—something serious?"

"Flash doesn't know what he's talking about," Paul said, but his dark eyes sparkled. "And on a completely unrelated topic, I have other plans for Christmas this year."

I raised an eyebrow. "On an unrelated topic, huh?" For years Paul had spent the holidays—not to mention many non-holidays—with us, due to strained relations with his own family. After so much time together, I tended to think of him as my second 'brousin.'

"Well, you know how it is. Don't want to jinx it." He winked at me. "Kinda like you and Jonny. If you keep it hush-hush, no one can mess it up."

I balked at the insinuation. "There's nothing going on with me and Jonny," I said. "We're just friends."

"Sure. Whatever you say, sugar," he said, putting his headphones back on. He pointed at his equipment and resumed doing his DJ thing.

I went back upstairs musing about Paul. Good for him, finding the right girl. It made me wonder if Flash ever would, especially now that he had lost his wingman. It also made me wonder if *everyone* assumed more about my relationship with Jonny than was true.

"Gemma!" Jonny said, spotting me when I walked into the living room. "Hey, everyone, it's my friend Gemma! Cheers!"

People clapped and drank to my entrance. I leaned over to Luke, one of the few sober-looking people in the place. "Someone collected keys, right?"

Luke bobbed his head. "I'm in charge of the bowl." He took off his Twins ball cap and ran his hand through his sandy blonde hair. "I think a lot of people will be spending the night."

"Oh man," I said, picturing Maggie coming home from work in the morning to random bodies sleeping all over her house. "Jonny's so dead."

But Jonny was also *so* entertaining. Time was a blur as he charmed his way through the night. Good-natured and expressive, he relayed funny stories, did impersonations of professors, and told jokes. I laughed the hours away along with the rest of the crowd, and it wasn't until someone started singing a favorite 'closing time' bar song that I realized how late it had gotten.

I went to Jonny's room and rummaged through the pile of coats on the bed. Moments later, Jonny was beside me looking wobbly. "Leaving so soon?" he asked.

"So soon?" I said, mocking offense. "I stayed way longer than I intended to!" Finding my jacket, I put it on.

He grinned. "That's because you can't get enough of Jonny."

I snorted. "Yeah, that must be it." I don't know why Jonny refers to himself in the third person when he drinks, but it cracks me up.

He laughed too, which threw off his balance. I grabbed his arm as he teetered. At my touch, Jonny's eyes grew serious. "You know I leave Monday, right?"

"I know you leave Monday," I said. Every year, Maggie, Jonny, and Lucy spend Christmas in New York with relatives. "How long will you be gone?"

"A week and a half," Jonny said.

"Well we'll have to exchange Christmas presents when you get back," I said. "I haven't picked yours up yet."

Actually, I was still trying to decide what to give him. We always get each other Christmas presents, usually something small or homemade, like a token of an inside joke or a box of hand-made caramels. This year, though, I was low on ideas.

"Deal," he said. "Yours isn't ready either." His words were slightly slurred.

I shoved the coats to the side of the bed and motioned to it. "Maybe you should sit down. You've had a lot tonight. Want me to get you some water?" I started towards the door, but Jonny captured my hand.

"I'm okay," he said. "Just stay here with me." He pulled me towards him. "It's you we should be worried about."

I touched his flushed cheek. "No, Jonny, I'm good. I didn't have anything to drink."

He squeezed my hand. "I don't mean that." He shifted his weight, searching my face. "It's just, that day at the car with the headache, and then in the library... I want to know you'll be alright. You know, while I'm gone."

I tried to smile reassuringly. "I'm fine, I promise," I said. "Don't worry."

The way Jonny pursed his lips and studied my eyes, I am sure he suspected there was something I wasn't telling him.

Jonny's concern, though endearing, troubled me. To be honest, I was a little relieved he would be out of town for over a week. It bought me some time to figure things out. If I could learn to manage my symptoms effectively, and keep incidents like the one in the library from happening again, then perhaps the suspicion that was building in him would be assuaged.

"I'm fine," I said again. "Really."

"Okay," he said quietly. His fingers moved from my hand to my wrist. Tracing the lines of my birthmark, he asked, almost shyly, "Have you remembered anything else? I mean other than the fortune cookie thing?"

His question, combined with the caress of my wrist, caught me off guard. "A few things," I said. It was pretty much the truth. "Just... flashes of memories. I wasn't even sure the one with the fortune cookie was real. Not until you told me."

He leaned in and whispered in my ear, "Oh it was real. I have proof." His breath felt hot against my neck. "But I can't show you. Not yet. Not until it comes true."

I pulled away slightly, questioning him with my eyes. He didn't actually still have the fortune, did he?

"For me to know," he said, repeating his comment from the snowboard park. He leaned in again, his lips brushing my ear this time as he whispered, "For now anyway." Letting go of my hand, he slipped both arms into my coat and around my waist, drawing me to him.

I tensed as his arms, warm and solid, held me. Looking up into his face, I said in a quiet voice, "Jonny, I think I should go home now. It's late, and you're…" I trailed off.

He tilted his head against mine, inhaling against my hair, breathing me in. "Don't leave yet. Please." There was urgency in Jonny's voice and an undertone of anxiety.

I love Jonny. I could never hurt him. Even though I knew he wanted a different love than I felt, I couldn't ignore his plea. He would take it as rejection. Relaxing into his embrace, I whispered, "Thank you for tonight. I had fun. You have no idea how much I needed it."

His arms tightened around me and he turned his face to look into my eyes. "You have no idea how much I need *you*." He bent his head down, his lips very close to mine. "I don't want to pretend I can just be your friend anymore. It's too hard." His lips grazed mine. "I used to be afraid of ruining what we have." His lips met mine again, lingering a little longer. "But now I'm afraid of never having more." And he kissed me fully and passionately, his mouth warm and tasting of alcohol.

I returned his kiss hesitantly, uncertain about how it would change our relationship. Jonny's embrace, his lips on mine, his hair falling forward against my skin… It all felt comfortable, nice.

Finishing the kiss, Jonny hugged me against him. We stayed like that, me wrapped cozily in Jonny's arms, for several minutes. Then, hearing someone approach, I froze.

"Oh," Paul said, entering the room. "Sorry, guys. I just need to get my"—he pointed to the coats on the bed—"you know." He dug through the pile and grabbed his jacket. "Don't worry, kiddos. Your secret's safe with me." He winked at me, then gave Jonny a nod. "Take it easy, man," he said, and scooted from the room.

I looked into Jonny's deep blue eyes. "I should get going, too."

He nodded but didn't release me. "I know," he said.

"Are you sure I can't do anything for you before I go?" I asked. "Get you water or something? You've had a lot to drink."

He shook his head. "I just want you to stay." Gradually, he lowered his arms from my body. He continued, his tone solemn. "I know you have to leave, but when you do… The one left wondering whether *this* memory was real will be me."

CHAPTER 20

T ime is tricky.

It moves at different speeds, sometimes faster, like it did at Jonny's party, and sometimes slower, like it does waiting for sleep to come, but it always moves forward. As far as humanity is currently aware, there is no going back.

A little more than a month had passed since Gate first told me I was an undergoing Essen, but it felt longer than that. A lot longer. Almost like Gate had been in my life for years.

I had been nervous sitting in Gate's parlor that first time, but what he'd told me about myself *felt* true. My birthmark—my notae—was the mark of the Essen. Gravitation and nightmares were the first symptoms of undergoing. On March 25th, my twenty-first birthday, I would Activate—the final stage of supernaturalization.

Then Affliction started and brought with it the onset of my initial 'gift.' Static and pain were my daily reality. My nightmares, and my daydreams, intensified. And through it all, I was not to talk to anyone about it or I'd die.

So though it was killing me to hide the truth from Jonny, I did. In my heart, I knew I couldn't tell him what I was going through. I knew the 'deadly consequences' were no mere threat. In my *soul*, I knew *all* of it to be true.

But if I hadn't believed what Gate had told me, if I'd had any doubts whatsoever about being an Essen, it wouldn't have been for long. I would have been convinced of my true identity the moment Jonny kissed me.

Jonny is… so wonderful. The kiss itself was amazing. I should have melted into it, melted into him. I should have gotten lost in the moment, been lightheaded, felt my heart race. But what I felt was… contentment. Peacefulness, not passion.

I'm not unaware that Jonny is gorgeous. And sweet. And desirable. There isn't a girl out there who could, or would, resist Jonny's affections. I should have wanted him, from way back when, and felt ecstatic that he now wanted me too. So why didn't I?

Why, in the whole of my remembered life, had I never pursued a boyfriend or even entertained romantic notions of one? The answer, clearer now following Jonny's tender and soft-lipped kiss, was because I was an Essen.

Gate had told me that most Essen are not given to fancies of love; that they aspire to greater ambitions. I didn't know what my own ambitions were—I supposed I might not be called to them until after Activation—but apparently, they did not include romance.

Yet I had kissed Jonny back.

I tried to tell myself that I could grow in love, that I could eventually be for him what he wanted me to be, and that by returning his kiss, I was opening the door to that future. But the stinging truth was, I had kissed him because I was afraid—afraid of the future that might be actualized if I didn't.

A Jonny-less future. A future empty of deep, enduring companionship. A future of isolation. I had kissed Jonny because I feared that by not kissing him, our future together, whether friendship or something more, would eventually be forfeit. And I wasn't able to make that sacrifice.

Then you are selfish.

Gate's words were a dagger that cut me deeper each time I heard them in my head. When he first said them to me, I'd felt certain I wasn't and had never been a selfish person. Introspective, yes. Reserved, sure. But selfish? I didn't understand how, after all the hours of one-on-one time I'd had with Gate, he could have misjudged me so completely.

But now I knew what he meant, and now I knew that it was true.

I am selfish.

I would rather forego Jonny's desire for our future than forsake mine.

I am selfish.

I am selfish and deliberately so. The realization tortured me, but it was too late to change what had happened. It was too late to make a different choice. The path was laid, and I was committed to it.

I was *committed* to it. If Jonny wanted romantic love, then I would try with all my heart to give it to him. Though the returned kiss resulted from selfish motives, it was my intention to fulfill Jonny's hopes too. I *would* grow to love him. It was the only way to redeem myself.

I would not be the one to leave, to calculatedly abandon him or just casually let him go from my life, like Gate had advised. I would stay in Jonny's life, in whatever capacity I could, for as long as he'd let me. If he moved on, like I'd long predicted he would, the choice would be his.

I was committed.

✳ ✳ ✳

My selfishness, it occurred to me, was not limited to my relationship with Jonny. For who knows how long, but especially the past several months, my focus had been on me solely: my troubles, my health, my needs. Nearly every thought—and every resultant action—had centered on me, what I might learn, how I might benefit.

I relied heavily on Aunt Sheri, Uncle Dan, and Flash, in addition to Jonny, for a variety of things. I accepted their generosity of time and energy without outward signs of gratitude and without reciprocating. I hoped they just knew: that I appreciated them, that I loved them, and that they could count on me too.

Only… they never did, I realized. Count on me. Not one of them ever asked me for anything. With the exception of Jonny, who looked to me for occasional support—like being at his show at Fervor—none of them seemed to depend on me.

It was a sobering realization. Redemption, it seemed, required broader action, something that extended beyond being committed to Jonny. It needed to begin with me showing consideration for everyone I cared about. I needed to be thoughtful.

I gave the selection of Christmas gifts extra attention. No more gift cards to restaurants and movie theaters. For Uncle Dan, I tracked down a model of the exact sailboat he hoped to one day buy. For Aunt Sheri, I found a beautiful silk scarf in her favorite combination of colors, indigo and fuchsia. And for Flash, I bought new headphones.

I dipped further into the money my father had left me than I'd ever done before, but it was worth it. The looks on their faces when they opened the presents… I felt certain they knew I loved them.

I got Gate something too, and on Tuesday, December 30th, I brought it with me to my appointment and gave it to him.

"I thought you might like it," I said, feeling bashful. I glanced around the parlor. "It seemed like it would fit with… all the others."

"It does," he said, accepting the plant. "Thank you." He placed the ceramic pot on his desk next to the framed photo and lingered there, touching the fleshy, rounded leaves.

"It's called a Jade."

Gate gave me a small smile, but his eyes were doleful. "Yes it is." He crossed the room and sat in his regular place, motioning for me to join him. "It is also called a friendship tree."

"Oh," I said, feeling the heat of a blush rise in my cheeks. I hadn't realized the plant had symbolism.

A faraway look crossed his face, and he twirled his golden vine ring like he does when he is pensive. "Jade was also my daughter's name. She would have been about your age had she…"

He couldn't bring himself to say the word *lived*, but I knew without him saying it that she was gone. Intuition told me the woman and the little boy from the photo had passed on as well. "I'm sorry" was all I managed to say.

"It was a long time ago," he said, but there was fresh pain, and regret, in his gentle voice. He cleared his throat. "Anyway, thank you again. It was very thoughtful of you."

I nodded, embarrassed. "You're welcome," I mumbled.

Changing the subject, Gate asked, "How was your holiday? Any trouble?"

I shook my head. "I don't know which is worse: an actual episode of Affliction or the apprehension I feel waiting for an episode, knowing another one will be coming."

Gate's gray-green eyes were sympathetic. "But you still have the 'brain buzz' every day? You're trying to work with it?"

I sighed. "Yeah I guess, but... nothing ever happens."

"Something will. It just takes time. I need you to trust the process, Gemma." He paused. "What about Gravitation? Have you felt pulled towards anything?"

"No," I said. "...Well, maybe. I mean there are times when I feel... twinges. But Gate, how do I know if the impulse is gravitation and not, say, a normal human urge? Like sometimes when I'm in class, I have the irresistible urge to get up and leave. Is that Gravitation, or just a typical response to a boring lecture?" I mustered a feeble smile. "The feeling is strong, but not necessarily *compulsion*. Its definitely not as strong as it was the day I first saw Malakai."

Gate's lips twitched with restrained amusement. "I'm thinking the school thing—that's a 'no.' Gravitation will bring you *to* something, not away from something. I know I haven't spent much time on this with you yet, but I promise I will. During our next session, okay? For now, just know that when you get a gravitational urge, you should feel it in your gut, like instinct. It'll be so strong that you have no choice but to follow it. In fact, not following it would be hard. Though," he added, "there are occasions when it is unwise to follow the pull. For example, Malakai was foolish to follow his Gravitation to The Meet Lab, to you, on Halloween night. It was extremely risky."

"The Meet Lab? Why was it risky for him to go there?" I asked.

"It wasn't risky because it was The Meet Lab. It was risky because of the hour. But then, the pull is hard to oppose sometimes." He thoughtfully stroked his goatee. "Like that day you were first pulled to Malakai."

"I was not pulled to *Malakai*," I said defensively, recalling the warm October afternoon. *The spot appealed to me because of its seclusion, but also because it was* mine. *It had called to me.* "It was the place, not the person, that drew me."

"That's a significant distinction." Gate stood abruptly. "The place," he said, "is known to the Essen as 'The Wooded Bridge.'" He crossed the room to his desk and pulled a folded piece of paper from the drawer. "The letter I received from Malakai over the weekend references it." He sat back down across from me. "Here, take a look."

I accepted the paper from him and opened it. As I read it, I was reminded exactly why I wanted nothing to do with Malakai ever again.

CHAPTER 21

He's a complete ass.

Not only was Malakai's message once again hopelessly cryptic, but it was disrespectful of Gate. And it referred to me as worthless.

I read it again, growing more agitated at every word.

> *Gate:*
>
> *Taeo says you have not yet discovered whether Gemma Pointe is the Link. He told me you believe she could be, but that you haven't been able to confirm what or where the portens is.*
>
> *Work faster. There are less than a hundred of us left.*
>
> *The portens is the only thing that matters. We need to know how to obtain it. Without that information, even if this girl is the Link, she is worthless to us.*
>
> *The transcriptions below may help, but protect them. I don't have to tell you what punishments I'll face if it is ever discovered that I gave them to you.*
>
> *I should be out of holding soon. Either Taeo or I will be in touch.*
> *-Kai*

3627 – The Portens

There exists a colored spire
Nestled in the sand.
Housing air and earth and fire
And water, all as planned.

Within its brilliant base,
The symmetry amiss—
A jagged concave space,
Its notability just this:

The gaping hole, a missing piece
Needing to be found.
A portens for a full release,
To which the power's bound.

The forces of the four reside
Inside the stolen mass.
And all who use it shall abide
Effects that come to pass.

3628 – The Link

Comprehensive is the mark,
The one The Link will bear.
A hopeful signal in the dark—
Though searchers should beware.

Seductive is the might
The portens shield contains,
Tempting hearts of right
To launch evil campaigns.

Yet earth and fire, air and water,
Were all for Life designed—
So use the tool, end the slaughter:
It's The Link one needs to find.

Let The Wooded Bridge be tended
Lest The Link remain concealed.
For the war cannot be ended
Until the portens is revealed.

"You're angry," Gate said calmly after I'd finished reading it.

"Well, yeah!" I said, resisting the urge to tear the letter into pieces. Instead, I thrust it back at him. "It's rude. And frankly, not very enlightening." I crossed my arms. "Even if I had the stupid portens, I don't think I'd give it to him. He's a jerk."

Gate observed me, a rueful look on his face. "There is still so much you don't understand. Malakai may lack diplomacy, he may even be abrasive, but I do not believe he is intentionally callous. He is simply focused on his needs, the needs of all the Essen, to the exclusion of everything else—including formalities. I was not affronted by his words, nor should you be." He held the letter out to me. "Read it again. The tone isn't attacking. It's desperate."

I took the letter, examined it, and determined that Gate was giving Malakai too much credit. Malakai still sounded like an ass to me, but rather than tell Gate that, I asked, "What do the poems mean?"

"They are not simple poems," Gate said. "They are visions recorded by Phoenix, the current Augur, the diviner and leader of the Host." He watched me as I studied the lines. "It's interesting, don't you think, that the second of the two visions ties the Link to The Wooded Bridge?"

I nodded silently, processing the information.

"It's another clue," Gate said. "Another clue—in addition to your 'comprehensive mark'—that points to the fact that you really might be the Link." He inhaled deeply. "So Gemma, can you think of something, *anything*, currently in your possession that could be the portens?"

✳ ✳ ✳

To this day, I don't know why Gate phrased his question the way he did. Upon my subsequent reviews of Malakai's letter, I noticed that nowhere did the visions imply that the Link would *have* the portens. The first one didn't even mention the Link at all, and the second one just indicated that the two were somehow connected: that to find the portens, one first had to find the Link.

I also don't know why I lied in answering. Even as I shook my head and told him *no*, that I owned nothing that fit the recorded descriptions, an image remained fixed in my mind.

Gate, who had been perched on the edge of his chair in anticipation, sank back into it, disappointed. "Okay, well, that's okay. I know the visions are vague. We have very little to go on, the same limited information the Essen have had as they've looked." He folded his hands in his lap. "I guess we just keep searching your memories. Ready?"

I wasn't ready. For the first time since my initial hypnosis session, I felt nervous, insecure even. I worried that the image rooted in my brain would be on display to Gate once I was under, and I wasn't ready to share it with him yet. What if it was a false lead? Though I trusted Gate, though I believed I could vet my idea with him, I knew he was obligated to Malakai. And I did *not* trust Malakai.

I settled into the couch as Gate directed my attention to the pendulum swinging slowly from the clock on the wall opposite me. As I focused on it, he encouraged me to breathe deeply, to allow my limbs to become heavy. The rhythm of his voice was calming, and I tried to concentrate on his cadenced words.

"As you relax, your body may feel slightly numb. You are beginning to feel drowsy and sleepy, drowsy and sleepy. You are breathing freely and deeply, freely and deeply. You are becoming even more tired and your whole body is getting heavier. Even your eyelids are feeling heavy. Soon you will no longer be able to keep your eyes open. You are now entirely relaxed. Every part of your body is relaxed..."

I was in a trance, still staring at the pendulum. Gate continued speaking, his words washing over me in waves. Vaguely, I was aware that he had gotten up, had moved closer to me, had lifted one of my arms, had rested his other hand on my shoulder. He leaned over me, looked into my eyes, waited. Then he commanded, "Sleep," slipped his hand away from mine, and guided my head to the arm of the couch.

Instantly, Gemma with the lantern appeared, walking purposefully to a previously unexplored tunnel. Her resolve disconcerted me. Where was she going?

Lying on the couch, I twitched, trying to steer her in another direction.

She would not be deterred. She continued forward, down, down into the recesses of the cave, until she came across Gemma the birthday girl, celebrating age twelve, receiving a gift from her father.

And Gate's voice, coming from somewhere beyond the cavern, reverberated through it, his instruction directed to all three of us, the entire Gemma Trinity.

"Open the present, Gemma, and tell me what is inside."

CHAPTER 22

David Pointe gazed at me from across the patio table, his eyes the dark gray color of a stormy day. "It's okay, Gemma, go ahead and open it." He pushed the cube towards me.

The box was beautifully wrapped in silver paper and adorned with a red bow. "But you already gave me a present," I protested, jingling the charm bracelet on my wrist.

He smiled. "I'm glad you like it. I thought you would."

"Will you bring me a charm back from Australia?" I asked, hopeful.

He laughed. "Oh Lord. Every time I take my grad students to do their field work, I'm going to have to find you a new charm, aren't I?"

"Yep," I said. "It's the least you can do since you are going to be gone *all summer*. Again."

"Hey now," my dad said. "It isn't that bad, is it? Spending the summers with your aunt and uncle? Last summer you had so much fun staying with them, you didn't want to come home. You said the neighbor kids were *so nice*. Aunt Sheri told me you played with them every day."

I scrunched my face at him. "Whatever. Just get me a cool charm."

He ruffled my hair affectionately. "Will do, Gemstone." He pushed the box at me again. "Now open this already, or I'm going to."

I picked up the box—it was heavy—and shook it. He winced and motioned for me to stop.

"Oops, sorry," I said. "Guess it's delicate."

I picked off the bow and stuck it to the table. Then I peeled off each piece of tape, one by one, until the paper fell loose from the clear plastic box. I set it back on the table, admiring its contents.

"It was your mother's," he said. "She left it for you. Her note to me said she wanted you to have it when you were older. I thought twelve was the right age."

I felt sudden tears, hot and prickly, brimming in my eyes. "Then I don't want it."

My dad shot up and hurried to my side. "No, Gemmy bean, no. Don't cry. I didn't mean to upset you." He pulled me from my chair and hugged me. "I'm so sorry. I thought you were ready."

I jerked away. "Ready? How could I be *ready*? She's a horrible person, a terrible human being, and I don't want anything that was ever hers. Ever."

My dad's shoulders sagged. "She wasn't a horrible person, Gemma. I don't know why she left, but I do know she loved you, loved both of us."

The tears spilled onto my cheeks and my lips trembled. "*Good* people don't just *leave* their families. A *good* person doesn't abandon a one-year-old, leaving her to grow up motherless. A *good* mother—" My throat constricted, leaving me choking on the words. Sobbing and coughing, I slumped back into my chair.

Completely deflated now, Dad said, "One day, Gemma, you'll be able to forgive her. And it will free you." He picked up the box gingerly. "I'm going to put this in your room. It was left for you, so if you don't want it, you can dispose of it as you like."

The dejected look on his face shamed me. I tried to apologize, but my throat kept tightening, and I couldn't stop crying and coughing.

Neither could Gemma-with-the-lantern. She was standing at the edge of the patio, convulsing against the black tunnel behind her, the light bobbing with each spasm of coughs.

And neither could Gemma-on-the-couch, who was abruptly back in Gate's presence, gulping air, face wet with tears and sweat.

Gate was with me, stroking my hair, letting me cry against his shoulder the way a father might. Without speaking, he sat next to me on the couch, feeling what I felt, understanding what I now understood.

My mother hadn't died.

She'd left.

Twelve-year-old Gemma had known it, and the knowledge tortured her. The knowledge didn't torture me.

People leave their families all the time, cruel as it is. Parents abandon their children, husbands betray their wives, wives quit their husbands.

No, I wasn't distraught because my mother had deserted me and my dad.

I was anguished because I'd been *lied* to about it, for the better part of a decade, and as recently as the previous month, by the people I trusted most.

Surely my aunt and uncle knew the truth. Surely they could appreciate my wanting to know it. And just as surely, they'd made a *choice*, and ongoing *series* of choices, to keep it from me.

Why? Who else was in on the deception? Was Flash? *Jonny?* And what else that I'd been told about my life was a *lie?*

I withdrew from Gate's touch, from the world, and crumbled into myself, a shaking and devastated heap. Nothing was real, only the taste of salt on my lips and the sound of my ragged breathing. Even my thoughts detached from me, until all that was left of my existence was the broken shell there on the couch.

And Gate stayed with me, wholly present in each moment, caring: Caring that I was hurting, knowing pain of his own, understanding the grief of something lost, offering silent compassion... being a true friend.

Sometime later, after I was completely and utterly drained of emotion, I apologized to Gate for my meltdown, thanked him for his graciousness, and stood to leave.

Gate walked me to the door. "Gemma, please don't apologize. What you learned today... Well, you are right to be upset. We all expect the people we love to be honest with us. Even if the truth is hard to hear." He put his hand on my shoulder. "You've been through a lot in your short life already, especially the last few months, but stay strong. You are not alone."

"Thanks, Gate," I said quietly. I grabbed my coat from the rack and slipped it on. "I guess I'll see you Friday."

"Wait—take this," Gate said, giving me the letter from Malakai. "When you reread it, remember that Malakai is scared. The portens is his only hope." He looked at me earnestly. "I know you know what it is, Gemma. I saw the realization flicker in your eyes. And I understand why you aren't ready to tell me, why you narrated around that detail when you were under. But whatever you saw, whatever your mother left for you in the plastic box—it could mean peoples' lives. I have faith that you will do the right thing."

I bit my lip. "Are you going to tell Malakai?"

"Yes," Gate said. "He expects me to. I have to be honest with him. He's the only family I have left."

His words, spoken with hope and determination rather than self-pity, rang in my ears as I departed. I didn't want Gate to tell Malakai about my memory, but I always knew that when the time came, he would. Gate was loyal to Malakai. Whatever happened eighteen years ago that caused the breach in their relationship was irrelevant. Malakai had asked for help, and Gate desired to answer the call. His loyalty was to his family.

I felt the sharp stab of jealousy in my stomach. My own family had no such loyalty. They had kept the truth from me. If I gathered the courage to confront them about what I'd learned, would they be honest with me? Could *anything* they say truly satisfy me? For the first time ever, I doubted their intentions, their integrity, and their commitment to me as part of the family.

Heavy with sorrow, I trudged to the bus stop wishing I had the energy to be angry.

CHAPTER 23

There were very few things I knew for sure about my past, and now even those were in question. Only one thing was not:

Eight years ago, on the evening of Wednesday, November 29th, my father and I were in an accident that killed us both.

I couldn't remember the accident, but I didn't have to rely on what I'd been told either. I had impartial evidence: copies of the official police report, my medical records, and the printed news story.

The weather conditions were terrible that night—sleet made visibility poor and the roads slick—but we were out driving in them. Then, rounding the curve of a lakeside road, we hit a patch of black ice. The car slid off the road onto the surface of the frozen lake. It came to rest there, but only for a few seconds. According to the testimonials of witnesses, the drivers of two other vehicles, the ice made a violent snapping sound as it cracked under the weight of our car. In the blink of an eye, our car sunk and we were submerged.

We were trapped in the wintry waters for seventeen minutes. Rescue teams pulled us up and attempted to resuscitate us as they brought us to the hospital. We were ventilated with oxygen, but use of the defibrillator proved unsuccessful.

Dr. James Redding, the chief of the hospital's Emergency Department, wrote this in his notes:

11/29, 20:18 – Patients David Pointe, 41, and Gemma Pointe, 12, arrive at the hospital. Body temperatures are 62.8° F and 61.5° F, respectively.

Examination of both patients reveals ice cold and gray skin and completely dilated pupils. They appear to be dead.

Our bodies were frozen, our hearts were not beating, and we had no discernible brain activity, but Dr. Redding believed we were not yet lost. He tried to increase our body temperatures using bypass machines designed to warm our blood outside of our bodies.

Two hours later, our recorded body temperatures were both ninety-seven degrees Fahrenheit, but we still showed no signs of life. Based on the criteria used to determine such things, we were declared dead.

My father remained dead.

I did not.

One hour and thirty-six minutes after I was declared dead: a heartbeat.

It was followed by other heartbeats, slow but steady, and after that, brain activity. Then my lungs and kidneys began to function. Miraculously, I started to heal. For twenty-four days, I was under the close care of medical staff. Then I was discharged with the prognosis that in time, I would make a full recovery.

And I did—with the exception of my memory impairment.

The retrograde amnesia did not affect my remembrance of learned skills or technical facts. It only affected my ability to recall autobiographical information. I did not know the people and places personal to me.

At first I did not ask many questions. I listened, absorbed, tried to understand.

When I eventually did seek answers, I was met with disappointment. No one seemed to know the full circumstances of the accident—where we'd been driving to or from—or why I'd been able to come back while my father had not.

I originally thought I'd been returned to life by a greater power for a specific purpose, as though there was more I was meant to do. Remaining work to be accomplished. And maybe that's true, but as time went on, I adopted a different, more mechanical theory.

Death isn't an event. It's a process.

If conditions are right, the process can be slowed.

Conditions like extreme cold, which can retard cellular degeneration and protect the nervous system from damage if the body is without oxygen for a long period of time.

And *sometimes*, if the conditions are right, the process can even be reversed.

Conditions like those in Dr. Redding's Emergency Department, where brilliant and trained personnel went to heroic lengths and where advanced technologies were understood and available.

The conditions had been right for me. I had been able to move from clinical death back to life because of the conditions.

I held on to this theory for a long time, but something about it nagged at the back of my mind. Why didn't it hold true for my father? Hadn't the conditions, the circumstances of our deaths and revival efforts, been essentially the same?

My questions could not be answered. Death, like life, holds many mysteries. But what I became convinced of was this:

Death is *both* a process *and* an event.

The process relates to the body, and the event relates to the spirit (or the mind, the soul, the essence, or whatever you want to call it).

The death process can be reversed as long as the death event has not yet occurred. The body can, if the conditions are right, be brought back—as long as the spirit has not yet departed.

I believe that my father passed on, his spirit detaching from its vessel, sometime during the resuscitation efforts. For him, bodily death happened secondary to the death event. For him, there could be no movement back from clinical death to life.

But why? *Why* did he choose to loose himself before waiting to discover whether his body could be healed? Why did I choose to stay? Was it a choice at all, or are people just 'released' at the proper moment by a Maker, regardless of the state of our tangible selves?

Anyone who has experienced death, their own or someone else's, knows the futility of asking the *why* questions. The answers don't exist this side of life. Seeking them only leads to bitterness, resentment, and despondency.

But how could I have known that when I was only twelve years old? I had reawakened to a life with no context, no texture, no relationships. I desperately wanted to understand what had happened, whether there was meaning to it, and *why*.

The *why* questions were discouraged from the beginning, at least by Aunt Sheri. She'd shake her blonde curls and say in a warm and loving manner, "Now, now, sweetie. We shouldn't worry about those things, should we? What has been has been. The only thing you need to concern yourself with is moving forward and getting better."

She didn't like family history questions much either, though she was obviously the best resource for them, being my dad's sister. When I'd ask her about my parents, or any part of my past, she'd answer, but always in a curt and matter-of-fact way.

Uncle Dan and Flash were more willing to philosophize with me about the *whys*. Both clever and creative, their responses to my inquiries left me feeling uplifted, like I was a valuable part of the universe.

Sometimes I talked to them about my past, too. While they offered interesting insights and shared occasional anecdotes, they were never able to answer my more detailed questions. For those, I had to go back to Aunt Sheri.

It had been a problem for me then just as it was a problem for me now. Despite her cheerful demeanor and cherub-like appearance, my aunt unnerved me. She can pour on the sugar and be completely dismissive at the same time. Conversationally, she steers away from anything that might be 'unpleasant'—topics like my mother, the accident, or my dad's death—and I've never been able to hold my ground with her.

I didn't want to confront her about why she'd lied to me. I have never been good with conflict. Besides, if history had taught me anything, I'd end up learning nothing and feeling guilty about it. Then again, I *needed* to know the truth, and she was the only person who could give it to me.

My emotions were still too high. In the twenty-four hours since learning about my mother, I hadn't been able to keep my eyes dry. I stayed in my room and avoided my family, telling myself I just needed time. Time to calm down, time to develop a plan for talking to Aunt Sheri.

Time to steel myself for what she might say.

CHAPTER 24

The soft rap on my bedroom door woke me up. I blinked against the pale moonlight that slipped through the space between my curtains and looked at my clock, disoriented. 9:38 PM.

I hadn't intended to fall asleep. Still wearing my jeans and sweatshirt, I rolled across my bedspread and sat up. Paper crinkled underneath me as I did, and I tugged it free. Malakai's letter. I must have drifted off rereading it. It was proving to be a suitable distraction from my sadness. I folded it and set it on the nightstand next to the plastic display case containing my boulder opal.

The knock came again. "Gemma?"

Suddenly alert, I jumped up and swung the door open. "I didn't think you were going to be back until tomorrow!" I threw my arms around Jonny's neck.

I hadn't seen Jonny since the night of his party. We never connected in the three days before he left town. Actually, that had worried me. Was he regretting the kiss? Deliberately avoiding me because he didn't know how to act now?

He tossed his backpack to the ground and hugged me back. "I took a different flight. I hoped you would ring in the New Year with me." He pulled away and peered into my moonlit room at my messy bed. "Unless you already have plans with your pillow?"

"Yeah, yeah. Whatever. I'm lame, bring it on."

Jonny's eyes twinkled. "It's New Year's Eve, Gemma. You're twenty. It's not even ten o'clock. And I just woke you up. You *are* lame."

"It's been a rough couple days," I muttered. Immediately Jonny's forehead creased with concern.

"Are you okay? I tried texting you to see if you were up for going out, but when I didn't hear back..." He shrugged apologetically. "I worried you might be sick. I called Flash and he said you were home, but that everyone else was out. He told me to let myself in through the back."

The back door is always unlocked in case Flash forgets his house key. The practice began after the fifth 3 AM request to let him in.

I shook my head. "No, that's fine. I'm glad you're here. I'm just... I was just tired. Still not sleeping well, I guess. But I'm good."

He looked doubtful. "You're sure? We can just lay low tonight if you aren't up to it..."

"Well what did you have in mind?" I asked. I ran my fingers through my disheveled hair. "I'll need a little time to get ready."

Jonny flashed a smile. "Let's start with presents." He picked up his backpack and walked into my room, flicking the light switch as he passed it. "Don't be mad, but I have two for you this year. Mainly because the first one is the same thing I gave my mom and Lucy and a few other people."

Plopping onto my bed, he drew a gift from his bag. It was small and flat and wrapped in green foil paper. He tossed it to me as I sat next to him.

"A CD?" I guessed.

"Just open it. And don't peel all the tape off." He rolled his eyes. "No one is going to reuse the paper."

I ripped off the wrapping. It was a CD of course. Inserted in the cover of the jewel case was a photograph of Jonny playing his guitar at the edge of a bonfire under a glittering night sky. Printed across the top of it were the words *Like Wildfire*. I flipped it over and looked at the back. There was a list:

Under These Conditions
Never Changing Me
Unseen Forces
Like Wildfire
Dark Gray
Centered
Shelf Life
The Next Day
Holding Pattern
You Have To Know
Something To Hold Onto

"Oh my God, Jonny," I breathed.

"I know," he said, grinning. "I made an album." He looked like he didn't quite believe it himself. "Paul's girlfriend owns a recording studio, did you know? Anyway I got a killer deal. So… there you go."

I opened the case and pulled out the disc. "Can I put it on?"

"If you want." His face reddened slightly. "You've heard most of the songs anyway."

I popped the CD into my laptop and started playing it as the songs downloaded. "This is awesome. The best gift ever. Thank you."

Jonny beamed. "I hope you'll think the *other* gift is the best one ever. But I'm glad you like it. Merry Christmas."

"I do, I love it." Opening my nightstand drawer, I withdrew his present and handed it to him. "Now what I got you is even more appropriate."

It had taken me forever to think of the right gift for Jonny, something that would be meaningful and special. I held my breath as he tore off the paper.

"Oh, thank you!" he said, removing the lid from the box. "A polishing cloth for my guitar." He held up the square swatch of black micro-fiber. He cocked his head at it, his eyebrows knitting together. "Embroidered with little blue flowers?" He turned to me, puzzled.

I felt sheepish. "They're forget-me-nots. That's what they're called. The flowers, I mean." I twisted my fingers together. "It's for when you make it big, because I know you will. You can bring it with you when you tour to… remind you of me."

Jonny clutched the fabric to his chest and closed his eyes. When he opened them, his dark blues were an ocean of tenderness. "Forget-me-nots?" he repeated. "How could I *ever* forget you?" He brought his hand to my cheek. "And even if something does happen with my music—who knows if it will—and I start to travel… You'll never be forgotten. I would be thinking of you, missing you, all the time." He gave me a hopeful half-smile. "That is, unless you decided to come with me. Then I wouldn't have to miss you."

He looked at the cloth again, delicately touching the embroidered corner. His hair fell into his face, and he tucked it behind his ear though it wasn't quite long enough to stay there. It fell forward again, the chestnut strands veiling his eyes. I reached up and lightly tucked them back in place.

"I would go with you," I whispered, because I knew that was what he needed me to say. It was true, though. If he asked me to, I would go with him. Wherever, whenever. I was committed, bound by both selfishness and loyalty.

Loyalty. My confidence in the concept had been shaken, but not by Jonny. In his presence, I became certain he could not have known about my mother. If there was one person in the world who was loyal to me, who would never betray my trust by participating in a lie, it was Jonny.

His eyes, lit with surprise and pleasure, met mine. "Really?" He set the polishing cloth to the side and embraced me. Speaking into my hair, he said, "I was so afraid I screwed everything up at the party. I was a mess. I thought I wrecked our friendship, and I was so embarrassed the next day. I hadn't wanted it to happen like that. I'm so sorry for—"

I didn't let him finish. It was too hard for me to see Jonny filled with such doubt. In a gesture of reassurance, I pressed my mouth to his, letting my fingers slip from his hair to his neck. His muscles loosened as our lips connected, his whole body seeming to sigh with relief.

Relaxing into the kiss, Jonny leaned back on my bed, pulling me with him. Nestled against his side with my hand resting on his chest, I could feel his heartbeat. It encouraged me on. I let my lips slide to his jawline, then his neck. His breath caught as I nuzzled him.

"Gemma?" he said, his voice filled with wonder. "Are we... Am I... Do you want to be..."

In all the years I've known Jonny, he has never been lost for words. It was so incredibly sweet, it made my heart ache. "Shhh," I told him, holding my finger to his lips. "We are. You are. I want to be."

He exhaled completely, staring at the ceiling. Squeezing me to him, he whispered, almost incredulous, "My girl."

Lying next to Jonny, seeing his chest rise and fall rhythmically, I was content. Though I didn't know where the future would take us, in that moment, I felt secure in the knowledge that it would lead us forward together. With my eyes closed, I saw myself in his life, in various scenes, throughout our twenties.

"Gem," he said softly, slipping his arm out from beneath me and sitting up. "Will you open your other present?"

He bent forward, digging another gift from his backpack. It was very small and also wrapped in green foil paper. As I sat up next to him, Jonny handed it to me.

"Really, the CD was perfect," I said. "You didn't have to get me anything else."

Jonny just smiled and watched me unwrap the present. I let the paper fall to the floor and opened the hinged lid of the box. Inside it, gleaming against the black velvet interior, was a pendant on a gold chain.

A boulder opal pendant.

The ironstone was about the size of a quarter and bezel set, with patches of brilliant opal throughout it. I tilted it in the light; the patterns mesmerized me. Flashing a matrix of orange-red and blue-greens, the stone looked like a miniature version of the one encased on my nightstand.

I was speechless.

"A gem for my Gem," Jonny said. He pulled it out of the box and held it up. "Do you like it?"

Dumbfounded, I nodded. He leaned forward, bringing the chain around my neck, and hooked the clasp.

"I know how much you love the one from your dad," Jonny said. "And I wanted you to have something you love that much from me. Something you can keep with you always."

I smoothed the stone with my thumb. "Jonny, it's too much," I managed to say.

"No, Gem, it's not. It's just right." He leaned his forehead against mine. "I hope you'll feel comfortable wearing it."

"I'll never take it off," I promised.

He folded me in his arms and pulled me back across the bed, kissing me, holding me, and talking with me until well after the New Year had begun.

CHAPTER 25

Any of Jonny's previous girlfriends would likely admit that making out with him is not unpleasant. In fact, they'd probably express stronger sentiment than 'not unpleasant.' I myself did not find the experience objectionable. It was nice actually. His lips were soft, his body was warm, and his movements were gentle.

No, I didn't wake up on New Year's Day panicked because I regretted what had happened with Jonny. I woke up panicked because Malakai's note, which had been on my nightstand, was now on my bedroom floor.

Had Jonny disturbed it when he left? I'd fallen asleep in his arms sometime after 3 AM. Vaguely I remembered him kissing my cheek and whispering goodbye, but nothing more. Hopefully he had not noticed the note as he'd departed. It was still folded, which was a good sign. Maybe it was just my own fitful sleeping that had caused the paper to flutter to the carpet.

Last night's dreams, which must have started after Jonny had gone, were even more terrifying than usual. In them, I was prey not only to the mortal enemies of the Essen but also to the Essen themselves. Malakai led them all in stalking me. His green eyes were feral as he captured me and brought me to a rocky basin of emerald water. He carried me into it and lowered me beneath its surface. There he held me until all the fight had left my body.

I shuddered, suddenly chilled. Gate seemed to trust Malakai, but my instinct fired warning that I should not. *The portens is the only thing that matters,* he had written. *We need know how to obtain it. Without that information, even if this girl is the Link, she is worthless to us.*

The portens was all that Malakai cared about and he would stop at nothing to get it. Retrieving Malakai's note from the floor, I reread the visions. Nothing in them screamed "boulder opal," so why was the image so fixed in my mind?

I took the plastic display case from my nightstand and withdrew the opal. The stone could, I supposed, be the "missing piece" of a "colored spire," but in what way could it possibly be a "tool" or a "shield"? It was just a rock, not the weapon Malakai had mentioned. A very beautiful rock, but just a rock nonetheless. There didn't seem to be any "power" bound to it, let alone the "forces" of air, earth, fire and water.

What confused me even more was the fact that both visions, though suggesting the portens could actuate "a full release" (of the Essen?) and could "end the slaughter," actually *cautioned* against locating it, wielding it. Whatever the "effects" that would "come to pass," they couldn't be good if one had to "abide" them.

I rolled the stone between my palms. A part of me didn't believe it could be the mysterious object that Malakai was looking for, but another part of me knew without a doubt that it was. But *why* then did the visions refer to the portens as a "stolen mass"? Was my mother guilty of more than abandonment? Had she also been a *thief*?

Shaking the thought from my head, I put the boulder opal back in its case on my nightstand. I placed Malakai's note in the drawer. Now that Jonny was officially my boyfriend, I would have to be even more careful about my—

Riverview Estates.

As quickly as that, Gravitation had struck. I had to go to Riverview Estates. Immediately.

Everyone who has driven interstate 35W through Minneapolis has seen the ostentatious complex of condominiums known as Riverview Estates. Located near the West Bank of the University of Minnesota campus, the site contains three 39-story buildings, the tallest structures outside of the city's central business district.

All three of the imposing buildings use carbon-fiber panels in their exterior design, giving the complex a posh appeal. While I have never been in the complex, let alone any of the condos, Riverview Estates is well known as the ritziest neighborhood in Minneapolis.

The homes are mostly owned by single young businessmen, wealthy slaves to their enterprises, and many are left unoccupied for long periods of time due to regular travels. As such, the condos feature the highest security possible: voice recognition and retina scan entry, top of the line alarm systems, bullet proof doors and windows, and surely other features not known to nonresidents. These attributes have earned Riverview Estates two popular nicknames: "The Mac Stacks" and "The Fortress in the Sky."

I didn't know a single person in any of the complex's 652 residential units, and yet I was unequivocally drawn to it. I had no idea what I would do when I got there, I just knew I had to go. Apart from the day I first encountered Malakai in the woods, it was the strongest tug of Gravitation I'd felt.

The buses were running less frequently due to the holiday, so I dressed warmly for a potentially lengthy wait. By the time the #3 arrived, I was shivering from the 10° F morning. When it deposited me near my destination forty minutes later, I still had not thawed out.

Walking the remaining blocks to Riverview Estates helped. By the time I stood at the edge of the property, I no longer felt frozen. Still, as I looked up at the towering structures, an icy wave that had nothing to do with the temperature came over me. Something bad had happened here last night.

Trying to seem natural, I walked through the double doors of the middle building, finding myself in its high ceilinged and sparsely furnished lobby. At the center of the room, behind a tall glass desk, stood a thirty-something woman with the name "Vivian" sewn into her blouse. Like the building in which she worked, she seemed very modern: angular and clean, but cold. She swung her shiny black hair over her shoulder and narrowed her canted eyes at me. "Your purpose?"

I crossed the black marble floor. "I'm here to see my..." *Uncle? Brother? Lover?* The correct lie eluded me, but it didn't matter because at that moment, the elevator doors opened. Through them, several authorities emerged, two of them rolling a stretcher. Though the body on the stretcher was covered by a white sheet, the right arm of the deceased was visible, hanging off the side. It was the delicate arm of a woman, a woman with a milky complexion though her skin was now ashen with death. The police wheeled her quickly, roughly even, through the back doors of the building, but not before I glimpsed the simple tattoo on the inside of her forearm: a gray-inked circle with a much smaller circle at its center. The lines appeared sharp and solid on her waxy flesh.

Shocked, I turned back to the Vivian. "What happened?"

She glared at me. "It's police business, not yours. Who did you say you are here to see?"

I shook my head, caught.

Just then a slender young man ran into the lobby from outside. He tore the hat from his white-blonde hair and wrung it in his hands. His light gray eyes were frantic. "Raela, oh my God, where is she?" he asked no one in particular.

Vivian motioned for security guards, who until then I'd not noticed standing in each corner of the lobby, to come deal with me. As they escorted me from the building, I saw Vivian's face soften. She moved around the desk and placed her hand on his shoulder.

"I'm so sorry, Ren—" she began.

"Ren!" interrupted another young man, getting off the elevator. He ran across the lobby to where the two were standing. "It was him, Ren. Alistair saw him leaving the apartment. This morning, right before he found her body." The young man was breathless, his dark eyes rimmed red. "Gate Dorsum killed your sister."

CHAPTER 26

As swiftly as Gravitation had surged into me, it ebbed away, leaving me numb with the shock of what I'd learned. I made my way back home struggling to come up with a logical explanation for the dead woman—the dead Essen?—at Riverview Estates, one that cleared Gate of whatever misunderstanding had taken place.

There was no such explanation. Even if there *was* another Gate Dorsum in the Twin Cities, which I tried to convince myself could be true, what were the chances that he would also be involved with the Essen? And why would I have been drawn to the scene of a crime involving a different Gate Dorsum? No, it had to be my Gate.

But it didn't have to be *murder*, did it? Maybe there had been an accident. Maybe Gate had been framed. Maybe he was acting in self-defense. Maybe—

I felt ill. Pulling the cord for my stop, I got off the bus. Dizzy and weak, I stumbled forward. A frigid wind struck my face, a welcome change from the suffocating air on the bus, and I inhaled shakily.

Gate, he was no killer. With trembling hands, I took my cell phone out and dialed his number. No answer. I left a message for him to call me, trying to sound as casual as possible. Even if he didn't return my call—and I had little hope that he would—I would go to his house tomorrow for our 4:30 PM appointment. Either he would be there or he wouldn't, but at least it would be more information.

Flash was standing in the kitchen when I walked into the house. He folded his arms across his chest and narrowed his eyes at me. "Do you want to tell me the meaning of this?"

I followed his eyes to the enormous vase centered on the kitchen table. The flowers in the vase had long stems and layered petals, like roses, but they were not roses. The petals, bright white with blue stripes running vertically through their centers, were more triangular than those of roses. "They're not mine," I said, indifferent.

"They were delivered this morning," he said. "For you." His blue eyes flared.

"Oh," I said, my tone softening. Jonny was too much. First the necklace, then flowers… I walked to them and breathed in their scent. They smelled both sweet and clean, reminding me vaguely of lilacs.

"Well?" Flash demanded.

"Well what?"

"Why is that asshole sending you flowers?"

"Asshole? I don't know what—"

Reading the confusion on my face, Flash plucked the card from between the blossoms and thrust it at me. "Here."

I took the small square of cream-colored cardstock. On it, written in black ink, was a familiar scrawl bearing a short message, the vagueness of which was also familiar.

Gemma—

Meet me at noon on Thursday, Jan. 8, at the place I first found you.

The flowers: Place them by your bed. Do not change the water. They ease Affliction.

—Kai

"That's the same jerk that ditched you at a gas station, isn't it?" Flash's face tightened. "*Kai?* Why the fuck would he think you'd meet him?"

Suddenly dizzy again, I sunk into a chair and put my head on the table. "What the hell is going on?" I asked, more to myself than to Flash.

"Promise me you aren't going to meet him, Gemma. Promise you'll stay away from that guy."

I folded the note and put it in my pocket, trying to keep my hands from shaking. Flash's jaw was clenched, his posture tense. He was worried about me. I closed my eyes so I wouldn't have to see his reaction to my answer. "I can't promise anything, Flash. I need to lie down. I don't feel well right now."

His voice got louder. "You're not seriously considering *meeting* him, are you? What will you tell your *boyfriend?* Yeah, Jonny stopped by this morning looking for you. He told me the two of you are dat—"

My eyes flew open. "He didn't see the flowers, did he? He didn't read the card?"

Flash glowered. "No. They came after he was here. But I swear to God, Gemma, I'll tell him. If you meet that creep, I'll tell him you went."

I raised my head. "Please—please don't. It'll hurt him. Malakai is nothing to me. But he... I just need some answers. Everything's so screwed up right now. Nothing terrible will happen if I go. For real. It'll just be talking. You can come with if you don't believe me."

As soon as I said the words, I knew I'd made a mistake. I would never be able to explain everything Flash would want to know, and Malakai wouldn't be able to tell me anything if I brought another person along to our meeting. It was bound to be a lose-lose situation. I bit my lip.

"Fine," Flash said. "But this is it. I'll go with you this one time, and I won't tell Jonny." He called over his shoulder as he left the room, "But you should."

* * *

Following that conversation with Flash, I felt even worse than I had leaving Riverview Estates. The anxiety in my chest built throughout the day. By the time I was ready for bed, my heart was pounding so rapidly I thought something might be seriously wrong.

I tried to distract myself with music, but even the attention-worthy tunes played by Cities 97 couldn't keep my eyes from wandering to the vase of flowers on my desk. Instead I picked up a novel, but after reading the same page at least seven times—none of the words were registering in my brain—I turned off my light and hoped morning would arrive swiftly.

Darkness did not come with the flip of the switch.

An eerie black light-type glow remained, bathing my belongings in a faint purplish glow.

The light emanated from the flowers, their white petals now luminously violet. Like the phosphorescent algae of the ocean, their beauty was both enchanting and enigmatic.

But even more curious than the flowers was the other object in my room that had suddenly begun glowing. I wandered to my nightstand and lifted the clear plastic box from its surface, captivated by the mystery. Within the case, my boulder opal was an astounding fluorescent green.

Perplexed, I turned my light back on. Once again, the flowers appeared white and my boulder opal was the same matrix of colors it had always been. I turned off the light, and the glowing resumed.

I chewed my thumbnail contemplating the unnatural neon radiance. It was as if the stone was somehow reacting to the light of the flowers. Holding my breath, I took the box into my closet and shut the door. The purplish glow was completely cut off, and the closet was pitch black—no fluorescent green coming from the boulder opal. I exhaled slowly. When I cracked the door open and placed the stone in the sliver of light, it shone green.

What the hell is going on? I asked myself for the second time that day.

CHAPTER 27

I'm not going to lie—all of the glowing freaked me out a bit. It made the task of falling asleep pretty difficult. I finally placed both items, the vase of flowers and the case containing my boulder opal, on the floor of my closet and shut the door.

For the first time in months, sleep met me somewhere in a black abyss, an empty place void of dreams. It was like heaven. I woke up on Friday morning flooded with a certain peacefulness.

They ease Affliction, Kai had written of the flowers. Damn right they do, I thought cheerfully. I went to my closet and pulled the vase out, setting it back on my desk. The flowers—their effect was so peculiar. I touched the silky petals, admiring the electric blue stipe down their centers. Even the static in my mind was lessened, like someone had turned the volume down on the imaginary radio that Gate had asked me to visualize.

Gate. At his name, my heart was suddenly heavy, as though filled with lead. It sank deeper in my chest as I remembered hearing his name spoken at Riverview Estates, spoken in the context of murder.

There was no way. I pictured him as I'd always seen him: In jeans and a flannel shirt, sitting across from me with an intent gaze, his mossy eyes compassionate but somber. Stroking his salt and pepper goatee, his tawny face lined in thought. Twisting the leafy golden ring around his long fingers.

Despite his height and broadness, he'd had a gentleness about him that made him seem smaller, more approachable. His presence was calming and his voice soothing, even when he said things I didn't want to hear. Gate, who I'd come to think of as a guardian and a friend, was clean. He had to be.

I would go to my appointment later in the day and he'd tell me how everything had been a colossal case of mistaken identity. He would chuckle quietly at my concern and then proceed with my hypnosis. Nothing will have changed.

In an effort to prove that to myself, I practiced what Gate had taught me, the technique he'd given me for 'honing' my gift. For the first time, I really concentrated, setting aside my doubt and putting all of my energy into the work, as though the trueness of Gate's innocence was tied to the strength of my efforts.

For whatever reason, the radio my mind conjured was antique. Made of walnut wood, the companion radio was cathedral style and about a foot tall. The speaker, covered with a tan fabric, comprised the center of the radio, while two dials, an analog tuner and a volume control, sat at opposite sides of the base. The relic rested on an old English drop leaf writing desk in a room with saffron flocked wallpaper.

I turned the knob slowly, watching the gradual movement of the needle across the FM radio band and listening hard for anything beyond the random crackling. At one point, I thought I heard the hushed sounds of whispers floating through the static, but I couldn't be sure. Reaching the end of the band, the higher FM frequencies, I paused and strained to find meaning in the noise. Nothing. Then—as I was about to abandon the exercise—I heard it. A musical rising and falling of tones in an odd rhythm, drifting towards me like the sound of distant wind chimes through a gale.

The crystal notes tinkled against my mind, remote but real. I waited, hoping for more. The musicality continued, a curtain of sound through which no meaning emerged. I hesitated a moment longer, then pressed the switch to turn the radio off.

All was silence. I looked around my bedroom, uncertain. The buzzing was gone. My head was quiet. On top of that, there was no pain.

I smiled to myself. It was a small success, turning off the static, but a success nonetheless. I couldn't wait to tell Gate.

✳ ✳ ✳

By the time I arrived at Gate's place, right at 4:30 PM, the sun was low in the pearl-gray sky. I stood on his doorstep, waiting for him to respond to my knock, convinced he would welcome me in from the cold as he usually did, with an affable smile.

Several minutes passed. Several minutes had never passed before.

Still I waited. I stared at the front door, willing Gate to come open it.

The sun sank to the horizon, but though the sky darkened, no lights flickered on in the house. My shoulders slumped.

I *needed* Gate. He was my only connection to the Essen, my only help for undergoing. He couldn't be gone. He couldn't have left me to figure everything out on my own. He *couldn't* have.

I leaned my head against the door, allowing the fierce chill of it to seep through my winter hat. I rested my hand on the doorknob. What if it was open? Would I go in? What would I look for? More than anything in that moment, I wanted to see for myself that Gate wasn't home. I twisted the handle.

"Hello there," a gruff voice called from behind me.

I wheeled around, startled. A stocky, fortyish man, of Greek or Italian descent judging by his coloring, was looking up at me from the bottom of Gate's front steps. His expression was not unfriendly, but nor was it warm. "I uh, I was just—" I stammered.

"I'm Detective Jack Tommegren." He flashed a badge at me and then stuffed it back into the pocket of his navy blue parka. "I'd like to ask you a few questions. Can you please come with me?"

Nodding, I followed the officer away from the house. "What is this about, Officer?" I asked, trying to sound as though I had no idea what might be going on. I felt jittery, like some crime *I* had committed was about to be discovered.

The detective led me to an unmarked Ford sedan, parked on the opposite side of Hennepin Avenue. He got in the driver's seat and pushed the passenger door open for me from the inside. The leather seat was freezing, and even in the car, I could see my breath. My body began shivering, though I'm not sure it was from the cold.

"I'm trying to locate the owner of that property," he said, finally answering my question. He set a digital recording device on the dashboard. "I'd like to get a statement from you. Are you okay with that? Good. First, tell me your name."

"Gemma," I said timidly. "Gemma Pointe."

"Okay, Gemma. What brought you here today? Why were you knocking on the door of that house?"

"I… I had an appointment," I said. "With Gate Dorsum. He's my… therapist." I don't know why I left the *hypno* part of the word off of hypno-therapist. Somehow it seemed less embarrassing to me. "It was scheduled for 4:30 today." I looked at the clock in the car's console. 4:39 PM.

"When was the last time you spoke with him?" he asked.

"Monday," I responded. "I came by to give him a Christmas present." For whatever reason, I didn't want the officer to know I was a two-therapy-appointments-per-week type of girl.

Detective Tommegren made a note on a small lined pad. "And how would you characterize your relationship with Gate?"

"He's a… friend, I guess. I met him in November, after I saw a flyer at the U advertising his business." I shifted my position in the seat. "I'm just going through some stuff," I added. "He's been helping me sort it out."

Thankfully, the officer wasn't interested in those details. He continued, "Do you know Gate well? Where he hangs out, who his friends and family are, anything like that?"

I stared through the glass of the front window, realizing how little I actually knew about Gate. "We never really talked much about him," I said. "That's the nature of therapy, I guess. The conversations tend to be pretty one-sided." I gave him a rueful look.

In truth, I didn't know much about Gate's personal life with certainty—other than he had a daughter, Jade, who was no longer alive, and a nephew, Malakai, with whom he hadn't been in contact until recently. I didn't offer up either tidbit, afraid it might lead to questions about the Essen, questions I couldn't answer.

The detective rubbed the back of his neck. "Are you aware of any connection between Gate and a woman named Raela Celere?"

"No." His brown eyes probed for more, and I shrugged. "He never mentioned her."

"Alright then." He handed me his business card. "Thank you for your time, Gemma. If you hear from Gate or have any other information about his whereabouts, please call me." He shut off the recorder.

"Okay," I said, pressing the door of the car open. "Um, Detective Tommegren? Is Gate... in trouble?"

He nodded once. "You may want to do yourself a favor and find a new therapist."

I got out of the car slowly, the reality of his response gripping me. So it was true. Gate was wanted for questioning, or maybe as a suspect, in the death of Raela Celere. And now he was missing, probably running, making the possibility of his innocence doubtful. An overwhelming despondency, a ragged sort of ache, filled my chest as I shuffled down the path to my bus stop. I had never felt so alone. Everything felt gloomy. Even the sky of early evening, without the diffused rays of the winter sun, was now the dull, dark gray color of titanium. It was oppressive, like it always seemed to be lately.

"Hey!" The detective called after me. I stopped, but didn't turn around immediately, afraid he would notice the tears gathering in my eyes. The door of his car slammed, and I heard him hurry toward me, his steps crunching against the frosty sidewalk. "Who are you?"

I spun to look at him, confused and alarmed. He had sunglasses on now, and his mouth was set in a hard line. "Excuse me? I'm Gemma Pointe. You just recorded—"

He was in front of me in seconds. "Not. Your. Name. Your *identity*." His tone was harsh, his manner of speaking somewhat staccato. He grabbed my right wrist and in a swift motion, forced up the sleeve of my coat. Seeing my birthmark, he dropped my arm. "You bear all four," he said with venom. "You are unique, but still *one of them*. Beware, Essen. You are not yet the enemy of God. But if you choose to become so, you will attract quadruple the attention. Including mine, undivided. Make the wrong choice, Essen, and yours will be the most offensive existence on earth. Make the wrong choice, and it will be my greatest honor to annihilate you."

And he turned on heel and stalked away, leaving me staring open-mouthed after him.

CHAPTER 28

The detective's words were a blow to me. Until that moment, I believed the Essen and non-Essen worlds were completely separate, that the boundaries that kept the factions divided were fixed and impassable. Until that moment, everything had fit neatly into distinct pockets of information—Essen and non-Essen.

Even as I stood there watching him retreat back to his car, my mind reeled, desperately trying to process his message. But though my thoughts were racing, they were jumbled. Nothing was making sense. In my head, the data had been compartmentalized. So where did Detective Tommegren fit? He wasn't an Essen—he'd made it clear he despised them—but nor could he be otherwise since he was talking about them.

If I'd been able to get my wits about me, I might have followed him back to his car, tried to understand what he meant. But my body felt rigid, my feet frozen in place. The collision of my two realities scared me, and I couldn't grasp the overlap. There shouldn't be an overlap. Who could have a foot in both worlds?

Gate could, I realized. Gate had admitted he wasn't an Essen, but he knew of their existence. He lived in the intersection of that Venn diagram, the one where Essen and non-Essen prevailed in different circles, and if *he* could… Maybe others could as well? How had I failed to realize there might be others like him?

The bus stopped for me and I boarded, still rocked by what the detective had said. *You are not yet the enemy of God. But if you choose to become so…* I sat at the front, feeling like the wind had been knocked from me. How could one *choose* to become the enemy of God? How could *I*? *Why* would I?

My phone dinged, startling me. I pulled it from my coat pocket and saw Jonny's text: *Where r u? Come over for pizza & movie? Also, mom wants to meet my new g/f. ;-)*

His note, simple as it was, shook me almost as much as the detective's words. Reading them, I realized my mistake. I had been trying to keep one foot in each world, too. But it wasn't a position I could maintain. Eventually, I would be pulled away, my tether to my non-Essen life broken by the final stage of undergoing. Eventually? No, not eventually. In less than three months. On my twenty-first birthday, I would Activate. I would become unequivocally Essen. Like it or not, my feet would both be anchored in the same circle as the others who had been supernaturalized.

How long could I keep Jonny in my life if I was *lying* to him at every turn? I had told Gate that I needed to tell Jonny the truth, and he'd blasted me, telling me I was selfish, that I'd never done anything on my own, and that I wanted him to know for my own benefit, not Jonny's. But Gate had also said: *We all expect the people we love to be honest with us. Even if the truth is hard to hear.*

Jonny loved me. He expected me to be honest with him, the same way I'd expected those I loved to be honest with me. And though I couldn't pretend to know much about God, it seemed logical to think that one way someone might make an enemy of Him would be by lying repeatedly.

Yes, I wanted to tell Jonny the truth for me. Life had become too overwhelming. In the past four days alone, I'd learned my mother had abandoned my father and me, and my remaining family had lied about that fact. I'd learned that my boulder opal had not been a souvenir from my dad, but my mother's parting gift, potentially lifted from rightful owners. I'd learned that the damn thing glowed in the light of bioluminescent flowers. And now, I'd learned that my best resource for working through all of these things, Gate, was a wanted man, implicated in the death of an Essen woman. Who could blame me for wanting a little support?

But I also wanted to tell Jonny for *him*. He deserved the truth, or as much of it as I could give him. I owed him my honesty. I was committed to him, committed to keeping one foot in each circle.

I texted him back. *Be there in 30. We need to talk.*

✳ ✳ ✳

It started slowly, like waves lapping at the edges of my mind. Deliberate the rhythm, gentle the caress, I barely noticed the pulsing tingle as the bus rolled from stop to stop.

In my head, I rehearsed what I wanted to say to Jonny. Maybe I couldn't tell him that I was undergoing, or about being Essen, or about the phases of supernaturalization, but I could give him something. I could tell him about Gate, about my hypnotherapy sessions, and about my interaction with Detective Tommegren—though probably not the part that freaked me out the most. I could also tell him that I'd learned the opal had been my mother's and that she hadn't died when I was a baby, like I'd thought. I could ask him if he—

The pulse was intensifying, becoming a dull throb that momentarily stole my attention.

I glanced at my phone, which displayed Jonny's response to my text: *Do we need to talk?* ☺ *or… Do we need to talk?* ☹

I began typing reassurances but stopped myself. I really didn't know whether he'd take what I had to tell him as "nothing to worry about." After all, it was my intention to meet Malakai as requested on January 8th. And though my interest in him was anything but romantic, I would be hard-pressed to convince Jonny that he represented no threat.

If I told Jonny I planned to meet Malakai, he'd insist on accompanying me, and I couldn't risk that. I needed information, and it was bad enough that Flash would be tagging along. No, I couldn't tell Jonny about the meeting. At best, I would only be able to share that Malakai was Gate's nephew, and that I might run into him from time to time. Then I would try to persuade him that there really *wasn't* anything to worry about.

The throbs encroached on the center of my brain, sharpening. My vision blurred, then went spotty. I closed my eyes.

Maybe it was the shock of my interaction with Detective Tommegren, or maybe it was the culmination of a stressful week, or perhaps it was another episode of Affliction coming on, but I was really starting to feel ill.

I pulled the cord for my stop and departed the bus as the first bout of nausea rolled through me. Steadying myself against the trunk of a large maple tree, I swallowed the mass rising in my throat. I was in no shape for confessing anything to Jonny at the moment. I sent him a text: *Not important. Talk tomorrow. Need to go home. Sleep.*

Between my cold and fumbling fingers and the black spots in my vision, it was all I could manage to write. Hopefully Jonny would understand.

I stepped away from the tree and felt the ground pitch beneath me. It twisted under my feet, the world spun before my eyes, and suddenly I was horizontal on the frozen ground, a full-blown tsunami of pain, solid as stone, keeping me down.

The last thing I remember thinking before losing consciousness was, *Jonny used to call it my compass. If only. I could not be more lost.*

CHAPTER 29

"Gemma, can you hear me? Gemma?"

There was a long pause, and bits of static crackled in the otherwise-silence.

I opened my eyes, straining to make out the red numbers in the darkness. They indicated it was 5:14 AM, and it was only upon seeing them that I became fully aware that I was in my bed.

"Gemma, I know it's a long shot, but if you can hear me…" Then he spoke more quietly, seemingly to himself. "I wish I knew whether you could hear me."

His voice sounded far away, but it held the same warmth, the same even rhythm it always carried. The only difference was the increased urgency in his tone.

"If you are there, Gemma, there's something I need you to do. Please listen closely." Another pause, more static.

I felt caught between sleeping and waking, unsure whether Gate's voice in my mind was a dream or a manifestation of my gift.

"Malakai knows you have the portens. He will try to bring you to Phoenix by way of the Wooded Bridge. When you see him, ask him about that night eighteen years ago. I need to know what he saw. You must do this for me. And tell him I did not kill Raela Celere. Given my history with the Host, he may not believe it, but it is critical you tell him that I…" There was crackling and I missed several of Gate's words. "…Malakai, he is not to be trusted. I don't know what he has planned, but do not part with it willingly. Hide it, keep it safe."

Silence ensued, and I believed that whatever connection I'd been able to achieve with Gate was severed. I shook my head and sat up at the edge of my bed, feeling slightly hung over from the previous evening's episode of Affliction.

"One more thing," Gate said, startling me. "There is more to all of this than I have been able to piece together yet. Do not tell anyone about your gift of the mind. I hope you get this message."

I heard a small *pop*, almost like a bubble bursting.

There's something really unnerving about hearing voices in your head, about the supernatural eavesdropping on others' conversations. But the feeling is exponentially creepier when what is heard is directed to you, meant for you to hear, spoken out loud specifically for your benefit. I shuddered, feeling as though Gate had violated the privacy of my mind. Isn't it the one sacred place each of us has to retreat to?

And yet I was also somewhat relieved to hear his voice, to hear him say he was not responsible for the death of the young Essen woman. Was it true? I couldn't know for sure, but I hoped so.

Where was Gate now? How was he able to reach me?

What he'd shared with me was important. He acknowledged that the Essen might not believe in his innocence because of his past. He wanted me to find out what Malakai remembered about the events that transpired nearly two decades ago. Gate also said that Malakai would *try* to bring me to Phoenix. Was he implying that I should not go? And why, after several previous attempts to persuade me that Malakai was truly not a bad guy, did Gate all the sudden tell me not to trust him? That I should I keep my gift and the portens (for I assumed that was what he was referring to) secret?

In spite of all that information and all my questions, my thoughts zeroed in on one sentence more than the others: *He will try to bring you to Phoenix by way of the Wooded Bridge.*

By way of the Wooded Bridge.

By way of the Wooded *Bridge*.

When Gate introduced me to the name of that spot on campus to which I had initially been called, I didn't give it much thought. It was just a place in the woods after all. Undoubtedly it had some significance to the Essen, but beyond the vision recorded by Phoenix suggesting that the Link would be found there, I wasn't sure exactly how much.

Now something clicked in my brain. Bridges connect things. They offer passage from one location to the next. How could my spot, that clearing between the oaks on the East Bank of the U of M campus, be a *bridge*? A bridge to *where*?

I got up from my bed, completely awake as a result of Gate's communication, and padded over to my desk. On its surface, the flowers from Malakai were still fragrant and blossoming. *They ease Affliction*, he had written. I touched the silky white petals, and as I suspected, the remaining lethargy and achiness in my body ebbed away.

I should carry one of these with me at all times, I thought, pulling a flower from the bouquet. But as soon as the stem was clear of the water, the whole flower dried up and turned to powder in my hand, peppering my desk as it slipped between my fingers.

It was only then that I noticed the two envelopes resting at the vase's base. Both were addressed to me. One was large, cream-colored, and embossed with the University of Minnesota logo, and the other was greeting card-sized and lavender.

The smaller one was from Jonny—I recognized the flourished script that was his handwriting—so I opened it first.

The card was sweet and simple, depicting a sketched teddy bear pushing a wheelbarrow overflowing with roses. On the front of the card were the words, *If I had a rose for every time I thought of you today...* And on the inside, *I'd need a truck!*

Underneath it, he'd written:

> *Wonderful Gemma,*
> *Please feel better soon. Text me when you wake up. I want to hang out!*
> *Love, Jonny*

I chuckled to myself, set the card next to the flowers, and picked up the envelope from the U. Flipping it over to place my finger underneath the flap, I spotted another message from Jonny.

> *Gem,*
>
> *Went to campus to pick up my final essay from Prof. Dag. He asked me to deliver yours to you as well. Don't know what you wrote, but I'm very curious! He told me, well, you'll see what he told me. Apparently, he wrote it directly on your paper. Okay. Text me when you wake up!*
> *Love, Jonny*

I ripped the envelope open and saw a bold "C" scrawled across the top of the page, along with the score "74."

Hmph, I thought, leafing through my essay to see where he'd written comments. On the final page, in a very neat hand, he'd given the following feedback:

> *Ms. Gemma Pointe,*

So I've been granted the honorific 'Ms.,' I mused.

> *I must convey my sincerest disappointment regarding the obvious lack of research and analysis that went into the crafting of this course culmination essay. Your casual and sparse references to the assigned readings reflect a certain complacency about your educational performance.*
>
> *However, I must also tell you that though I seriously doubt you actually read most of the passages you cited, I was supremely impressed with the creativity of your content.*
>
> *In my fourteen years teaching American Nature Writing, I have never received an essay response quite like yours.*
>
> *I've read well-written essays that have persuaded me to believe that Man is separate from, and therefore above, Nature. I've also received carefully researched*

papers that have convinced me that Man is undeniably part of, and subject to, Nature. I've even had the pleasure of reading very clever final exams, like the one submitted by Mr. Jonny Saletto, that maintains Man can be both separate from and part of nature, depending on the circumstances.

But your radical assertion—that "Man" is a misnomer because it encompasses two different sects of human beings, one that is above and separate from Nature, and one that part of and subject to Nature—was new to me. I found it genuinely entertaining.

True, your essay was not the thoughtfully constructed and thoroughly supported argument that I had hoped for, and true, it was more fantasy than philosophy, but the imagination you displayed in developing your (albeit science-fiction-laced) thesis, not to mention your strong command of the written word, made your paper worthy of a 74.

It also made you eligible for the invitation-only honors course that I am teaching this spring semester, "Storytelling in the Twenty-First Century." I strongly encourage you to register for it.

Best Regards,
Grayson Dagenais

At the bottom of the page, he had written a special code that served as the registration permission.

It was the most flattering "C" I'd ever received.

I wasn't used to praise from my teachers, especially not one as esteemed as Professor Dagenais, and his approval of my "imagination" honored me. I suddenly found myself considering spring classes, despite my previous decision to take the semester off.

Truth be told, I didn't really think I was all that creative, so I felt slightly guilty receiving the compliment. My idea for my essay stemmed from my knowledge of the Essen, nothing more. Though I didn't call them by name in my essay, I alluded to a sect of 'Man' that was gifted with certain powers to command Nature, such as the 'ability to expedite plant growth' or 'generate auroras.' I used specific examples that Gate had shared with me when he had told me about "extrinsic gifts."

Gate.

I felt a pressing melancholy in my chest. What happened with him? Would I ever see him or be able to learn from him again?

Filled with such a spectrum of emotions, I was surprised I could also feel hungry. I texted Jonny, who I knew would want to hear from me right away. *Awake? Breakfast?*

He wrote back almost immediately. *Yes. Give me 15. Feeling better?*

Me: *Yes. Thx. Will meet you at your car.*

Jonny: *K. BTW, interesting flowers on your desk. ???*

Shit. I assumed that my aunt, uncle, or cousin had placed those envelopes on my desk, not Jonny himself. Now that he'd seen the bouquet, I'd be forced to tell him who sent them to me. When a person is committed, she doesn't lie to her boyfriend. She might omit things that could lead to her death, but she doesn't outright lie. Shit, shit, shit.

I washed up, changed clothes, and made my way downstairs, silently practicing the speech I'd deliver to Jonny. In the kitchen, Uncle Dan sat at the table reading the news and spooning up healthy amounts of oatmeal. As I entered the room, he looked up, a morsel dropping from the utensil and dribbling down the front of his sweatshirt and landing on his jeans.

"Well doesn't that just figure," he grumbled, wiping his clothes with a napkin. "Where are you off to so early?" he asked, still cleaning himself.

"Breakfast. Jonny," I said, hoping to keep the conversation short.

"Are you sure that's a good idea? Maybe you should rest a bit longer. You fell pretty hard, you know."

I stopped and looked at him. "What?"

"You're just lucky Lucy spotted you. Her new guy was driving her home, and she saw you get off the bus and slip on the ice. She said you tried to catch yourself by grabbing a tree, but you went down, knocked your head on the sidewalk. Quite the concussion you received." He ran his hands over the newspaper, flattening it. "Of course, it took Jonny all of twenty seconds to run to the bus stop and carry you home." Yawning, he said, "And I've had the fun job of waking you up every hour like they say you're supposed to with bumps to the head."

By my blank expression, I'm guessing Uncle Dan knew I didn't remember any of that.

"But I suppose you should just as soon get some food in your system," he continued. "Jonny will keep his eye on you. Probably too close of an eye. That young man is pretty serious about you these days."

There was a question in his statement, but I didn't take the bait. Instead I glanced at the paper. "Anything interesting in there today?"

He started to speak, but I cut him off mid-response. "Oh my God!" I said, snatching up the pages and scanning the story that caught my attention. I sank into the chair, staring at the photograph.

"What, did you know him?" he asked, looking across the table at the picture.

"I just met him yesterday," I mumbled. I read the article again.

OFFICER DIES DURING INVESTIGATION
by Jennifer Harstad

MINNEAPOLIS – While on duty yesterday evening in Uptown, Detective Jack Tommegren died suddenly of a heart attack, according to a statement issued by the Minneapolis Police Department.

Jonathan "Jack" Tommegren, 44, was working surveillance on Hennepin Avenue near 28th St when the incident took place at about 5:05 p.m.

Tommegren, who collapsed in front of a group of pedestrians, was taken by ambulance to Hennepin County Medical Center in Minneapolis, where he was later pronounced dead.

Tommegren was a father and husband, and served as an officer and a detective during his 22-year tenure. He was also a veteran of the U.S. Marine Corps.

The police department is working with Tommegren's family on funeral arrangements, which are still pending.

I bit my lip, trying to understand what I'd read. If it was true that Detective Tommegren had died around 5 last night, then it had happened only moments after he had collected my statement.

"Can I keep this?" I asked, trying not to show how much the article had disturbed me.

Uncle Dan nodded, and judging from the sympathy in his brown eyes, he'd seen more in my reaction than I'd wanted to show. In a low voice, he said, "You know, I'm here for you if you ever want to talk."

"I know," I said.

"About anything, I mean."

"Okay, Uncle Dan. Thanks," I said, tucking the page under my arm and turning to leave the kitchen.

"Even your mother."

I stopped in the doorway and faced him again.

"You've been wanting to ask," he said. "So there's your opening. Whenever you're ready. We'll talk." He got up from the table and kissed my forehead. "Say hi to Jonny for me, and have a good breakfast." Then he went back to the table to finish his oatmeal, leaving me to wonder how he could possibly have known.

CHAPTER 30

The world dazzled me as I stepped out my front door, cloaked as it was in silver and black. An ivory moon, gleaming against the velvet canvas of the still-dark sky, gave light to the spiraling and sparkling snow that seemed to be dropping straight from space, like twinkling stars themselves were sprinkling the earth.

All was still, giving the moment a timeless feel. It was as though that part of the morning existed outside of reality, outside of the difficult decisions I would too soon need to make.

I wanted to live there forever, in that soundless and wondrous moment, watching my breath rise towards the heavens. In those fleeting seconds, feeling outside of time and circumstances, I could imagine things different than I knew them to be. I could imagine my mother out there somewhere, still alive and wanting to meet me. I could imagine marrying Jonny, growing old with him. I could imagine a simple life, one where I would not be called to do more than I thought I could. I could buy into fairytales, even my own fairytale, one in which my heart would not end up broken.

But my heart, like the ice underneath my dad's car more than eight years ago, was destined to crack. I knew the peace that moment lent me could not last; it wasn't meant to.

I believe that every person has some degree of intuition that influences his or her choices and actions. Though each of us acknowledges it to varying degrees, its presence is as constant as it is unexplainable, providing precise but unpredictable favors of insight.

Intuition was a fire within me that morning. The knowledge that the day would be one of life-altering choices, one of *consequence*, burned inside me. I did not feel ready.

But when is *anyone* ready, really and truly ready, to walk into one of life's storms?

Like most people, I would have preferred to stay comfortable, to stand safely at the edge of the downpour waiting for rainbows. I had no desire to enter the torrential chaos, especially because I knew I would never be able to explain why to the person who mattered most to me.

Intuition told me that I would enter the tempest, though, for reasons still unknown to me. It told me that the enigmatic Malakai, as mysterious as he seemed to be wealthy, was at the center of it. It also told me that even if I weathered the storm, even if I remained standing after the violence had desisted, I'd lose my best friend in the process.

That's the problem with intuition. It endows awareness of *effects*, but not causes. I was cognizant, in my spirit if not my brain, of certain outcomes; but I was not able to perceive what choices made could alter those outcomes. Intuition imparts knowledge, but not wisdom.

Outside of time, I could thwart intuition. Outside of time, the outcomes that seemed predestined would never come to be. Standing on the threshold in the bitter cold, I desperately wanted to remain outside of time, even if it my body had to freeze along with the moment.

I still remember how it felt to wait there, weighed down by emotion, watching Jonny scraping the windshield of his car with his back to me. He was my perfect match, even if he wasn't the ardent affair of my heart. And yet I knew I'd betray him.

Pulling my hood up over my head, I treaded delicately across the crystalline blanket that covered the expanse between Jonny's house and mine, unwilling to disturb the glittering brilliance of it, trying to keep the moment, and my world, pristinely preserved for eternity.

PART TWO: TUNNELING FORTH

CHAPTER 31

*B*eware, *Essen. You are not yet the enemy of God. But if you choose to become so, you will attract quadruple the attention. Including mine, undivided. Make the wrong choice, Essen, and yours will be the most offensive existence on earth. Make the wrong choice, and it will be my greatest honor to annihilate you.*

Detective Tommegren's threat floated back to the surface of my thoughts, even as I tried to convince Jonny that everything was fine.

Tommegren was dead, so his words were now empty. But *why* was he dead, expiring only minutes after conveying his warning? Malakai had said, nearly two months ago already: *Remember, there are no coincidences. It's your move.*

It was my move again.

The Essen enemies were becoming mine, as Gate had predicted, and apparently Tommegren had been one of them. If Gravitation was going to be bringing more of them my way, I needed to be prepared. Who were they, why did they hate the Essen, and how could I protect myself?

I couldn't wait passively for the answers. I needed to act. I needed to launch an investigation of my own.

The urgency to do so made me restless. I folded my legs beneath me in the booth, playing with the sugar packets as Jonny continued talking between bites of pancakes.

"They're just freaky, you know? I mean, what kind of flowers *glow in the dark*? What do you think he did to make them light up like that?" He searched my face earnestly.

Apart from checking to see if I was okay, the flowers were what Jonny had asked about first. He'd been going on about them pretty much since we'd left his house.

I spent most of the drive to Perkins Restaurant explaining that Malakai had sent me the flowers, and no, I hadn't seen him since early November. Yes, he had been kind of a jerk that day. Sure, the flowers might be a gesture of apology. No, they didn't come with a request for a second date. Yes, it was weird that they made my boulder opal look neon green. No, I don't know why they did that.

Jonny had been more upset that I hadn't *told* him I'd gotten flowers from Malakai than he was that I received them in the first place. Though he was still a little wary about Malakai's intentions and confused about the gesture, he seemed confident in his formalized role of boyfriend. I no longer sensed any self-doubt or jealousy.

As we sat there working on our breakfasts, I tried to steer the conversation away from the flowers, telling him as much as I could about everything else. For the most part, it was easier than I had expected it to be. Jonny makes communicating simple. He listens well and asks perceptive questions, responding without judging or lecturing.

He didn't question my decision to meet with Gate, despite Gate being Malakai's uncle, and he seemed genuinely happy about the progress we'd made breaking down my mental wall together. His surprise at the boulder opal being a gift from my mother, rather than my father, was evident; I could tell he was wondering if it, and consequently my necklace, would mean as much to me in light of the discovery.

I reassured him that I still loved my new pendant, and I held it between my fingers as I shared the revelation about my mother's leaving. He said he'd only ever known what I'd known, that she died when I was a baby, but encouraged me to talk to my aunt and uncle, believing there had to be a reasonable explanation.

Gate's disappearance seemed a bit more difficult for Jonny to process. Though it's not in his nature to be skeptical, it was like he somehow knew there was more I wasn't telling him. But my visit to The Mac Stacks, my knowledge of Raela Celere's murder, and even my interaction with Detective

Tommegren and his subsequent passing, had to remain unshared. It was just too risky.

So with nothing else forthcoming, he shrugged, accepted what I had told him, and went back to speculating, with increasing perplexity, about the flowers.

"They're just not *natural*. What if he treated them with some toxic chemical?"

I sighed, setting down my fork. "Really, Jonny. You're being ridiculous. There's nothing to worry about. I'm sure they're just a novelty, the latest gimmick in the flower industry." I doubted it—they had purple luminescence *and* an eerie but positive effect on the pain of Affliction—but *maybe* it was true.

"But where do you think he got them? I've never seen anything like them. I wonder what they're called. I wonder if you'll have a chance to ask him. Do you think he'll try to contact you again?"

"Would it bother you if he did?" I asked, trying to sound casual.

Jonny hesitated. "Well, I'm guessing he's not going to be your new best friend or anything, but… It still weirds me out, the tattoo he had, and how he acted about your birthmark." He paused to let me respond. When I didn't, he said, "But maybe, if you did see him, he could tell you where Gate went and when he'll be back. Then you could, you know, keep remembering stuff."

The thought had occurred to me too. But if Malakai couldn't be trusted, as Gate had cautioned, then what could he tell me that I could believe? I started shredding the sugar packets. I needed to get to the bottom of things. Today.

Jonny reached for my hands. "Hey. Why so fidgety?"

A plan was developing in my head, one that excited and scared me. But there was a balance I needed to strike, a balance between how much I could say and remain alive and how much I could keep to myself and remain with Jonny. The key was to be honest but vague, to answer his question without inviting more.

"I just don't want you to be late," I fibbed. "What time do you have to be to the Park again? Nine?" What can I say? I'm no conversational wizard.

He nodded and gulped the last of his orange juice. "Come on, let's go," he said, leaving cash on the table.

I couldn't wait for Jonny to drop me off at home and be on his way to Board Meeting. My plan was simple but I was ready to carry it out, certain it would lead me to answers.

Jonny had a knowing look in his eyes as we said goodbye that morning. He hugged me tightly and said, "Be safe today." It was as though some notion of danger had taken root in him. But flashes of intuition, I suppose, though inexplicable in nature, are not limited to supernaturals.

"Don't be silly," I said, getting out of the car. "I'm always safe."

As Jonny drove away in the direction of his work, I hoped that would prove true.

CHAPTER 32

As luck would have it, Saturday, January 3rd, was the coldest day of the season up to that point. Though the actual temperature was only four degrees Fahrenheit—not really *that* bad—the wind was fierce and relentless, making it feel sixteen below.

A less resolved individual might have abandoned the plan and waited for a different day, but not me. I was determined to get answers.

I was determined, but not stupid. Having spent all but the first year of my life in Minnesota, and having survived a winter accident, I knew well the risks of hypothermia and cold-weather exposure.

The plan required me to endure the elements, which I was not equipped to do. I didn't have the technical clothing that Jonny had for staying warm during long days on the hill. But Lucy did.

An avid snowboarder herself, Lucy had everything from moisture-wicking thermal undergarments to waterproof outerwear. And though she was shorter and slimmer than me, I knew her gear would fit. Snowboard apparel is not particularly formfitting.

Lucy was still in her pajamas when she answered the door, looking drowsy but nonetheless beautiful. "Yeah, sure, you can borrow them," she said after I made my request. "Come on in while I get it all together for you."

She entered a deep closet adjacent to the entryway, disappearing from view. "Yeah, the winter coat you normally wear is not gonna cut it today," I heard her say while rummaging through boxes. "You're staying local then?

You should try that new place, Digs. I hear it's a pretty good hill for the Cities." When she emerged, she was holding a huge nylon duffle bag stuffed with pants, shirts, socks, mittens, hats, scarves, and jackets that were all designed for layering.

"Thanks, Luce," I said, taking the bag from her. "Sorry I woke you."

She yawned loudly. "It's no big deal. I'm glad you're feeling better. You spilled hard last night." Then, as if struck by some brilliant idea, she said, "Hey, you and Jonny should double with Joshua and me sometime. It would be super fun."

"Yeah, maybe," I said noncommittally. "How're things going with Josh?"

A dreamy look crossed Lucy's face and she wrapped herself in her arms. "So, so good. He's perfect. I'm going to marry him someday. I just know it."

I was fairly sure she'd said the same thing about her previous three boyfriends, but I let it slide.

"Anyway," she went on, "I'm *so glad* you and Jonny finally got together. He's been on cloud nine since Thursday… I was like, it's about time! But it was bound to happen sooner or later. Jonny wouldn't miss the chance to date you. You're exactly his type!"

"Oh?" I asked, slightly surprised. "What type is that?"

Lucy waved her hand nonchalantly. "You know… the kind of girl who has to be taken care of. One in need of rescuing. A perpetual 'damsel in distress,' if you want to think of it that way."

I felt my face fall. "I'm not like that…"

Lucy smiled. "Oh, please. I can't count how many times Jonny has saved you from some type of drama." She rolled her eyes. "You are *totally* like that."

Her words hurt my feelings. I know she didn't mean them to, but they did. I pursed my lips.

"No, it's not a bad thing!" she said, reading my expression. "It's exactly what Jonny needs! He's a protector-type. Rescuing you all the time, like carrying you home from the bus stop last night, it makes him feel like a hero. He *wants* to be there for you. It's all good. Really."

I folded my arms. It was *not* 'all good.' The type of person she was describing was a *victim*—someone constantly in the throes of circumstance, someone powerless to help herself. Was that really how people saw me? Was that really how I *was*?

"I didn't mean anything by it, Gemma," Lucy said, backpedalling. "Jonny really loves you, exactly how you are. He's just always been drawn to people who need a little extra help. It's how he's wired. Why do you think he still lives at home? It's because he's afraid to leave mom alone, afraid that our dad will come back after all these years and beat up on her again. He hasn't come around since we were little, but Jonny's instinct is to protect. He wants to make sure we'll be okay, just like he wants to make sure you'll be okay. That's all I was trying to say.

"But I know he thinks you're beautiful and smart and caring and thoughtful, too. And those things are *also* his type. Okay?"

I met Lucy's pale blue eyes and nodded. She put her arms around me in a bear hug, wished me a good day, and reminded me of the invitation for a double date. Then I thanked her and trudged across the snow between her house and mine, no longer caring whether I shattered the shimmering surface.

Be safe today, Jonny had said.

I was an idiot. He hadn't been having some sort of sixth sense about my plan. It was just his subtle way of letting me know he was out of pocket for the day, that he wouldn't be around to save me if I ran into trouble.

I'm always safe, I'd responded. How laughable.

I sighed heavily into my scarf, and looked up at the naked limbs of the oak trees. What was I doing here? What had I expected to find?

The sun moved lazily across the sky in a low arc, deceptive in its brightness. As the hours wore on, the day had grown clearer as well as colder. I found myself wishing for any modicum of warmth, even if it meant the snow had to start again.

I shifted in the tree stand I'd taken from Uncle Dan's long-forgotten hunting stuff that was stashed in the basement. It had been surprisingly easy to put together, especially because I set it up relatively low to the ground, climbing only about twelve feet into the oak.

In the hours I sat there waiting for something to happen, I started to doubt the brilliance of my plan. It was too cold for surveillance work. Lucy's snowboarding clothes were top of the line, but I was still freezing. I started to feel sleepy. I knew the danger of feeling sleepy. My eyes closed slowly in what I promised myself was only an extended blink.

I forced them open. It was time to go. If I didn't move my body now, I might end up unable to. I tightened my backpack around me and shimmied down the oak, leaving the tree stand where it was.

"I was wondering how long you were going to stay up there," a small voice said.

Startled, I missed the branch to which I'd meant to drop. Instead, I fell the remaining four feet to the ground, landing roughly on my feet.

Turning quickly, I faced a boy stepping into the clearing. He was no more than ten or eleven, his pale skin pink from the wind. Platinum hair protruded from the hood of his white parka, and his clear blue eyes, bright with attention, studied me.

"How long have you been here?" I asked, alarmed.

"I have been with you all this time," he replied calmly. His manner of speaking was formal, giving the impression of wisdom way beyond his years.

"You've been *watching* me? Why?"

"Why indeed?" he answered. "Were you not, these many hours, attempting to do the same thing to us?"

I looked from the boy to the woods. Were there others out there, hidden in the shadows of the trees?

"You need not worry, Gemma Pointe," the boy said. "I am alone, and I am here to help you." He held out a mittened hand, as if to shake mine. The gesture looked strange, too mature for his petite frame.

I stepped forward, cautiously taking his hand. "Who are you?"

"My name is Erec Medeis," he said. "Though to most I am known only as Echo."

"How do you know my name?"

"I know much about you. I know that Malakai discovered you in this very place. I know you have the mark of the four. I know you have a unique gift, and another on the way. I know you have questions that need answering."

I pulled my hand away from him, spooked.

He looked amused. "Knowing the lives and gifts of others is *my* gift."

"But... You're too young for gifts. Aren't you?"

He smiled a sweet and delicate smile. "You are a clever girl." He looked up at the branches of the trees. "That is why you are here, though, is it not? Because you are clever. Clever enough to realize the bridge must connect places together, and that others may come here to cross it. You wish to meet those others, those people like you."

His insight into my plan unnerved me. I began shivering. "Are you... like me? Are you an..." I couldn't bring myself to say the word, for fear that I might fall down dead on the spot. What if he wasn't?

"An Essen?" Echo supplied. He took off his left mitten and pushed up the right sleeve of his parka. On the inside of his forearm was a simple circle, outlined in black ink. He stepped forward. "I can help you, Gemma. I have wanted to help you for quite some time now, but I could not reach you. I needed you to meet me here, which now you have finally done."

"If you wanted to help me," I began, suspicion coloring my words, "why didn't you reveal yourself sooner? Why did you let me sit here all day, freezing?"

His blue eyes, so filled with the innocence of youth, looked apologetic. "I had to evaluate your commitment. I needed to know you were sincere in your quest for answers. If I was going to give you support, I had to know you would appreciate it. If I was to give you guidance, I needed to believe you would accept it.

"Your determination to remain here in the cold suggests you are desperate enough to entertain any advice—even that conveyed by a child."

I narrowed my eyes. "And what advice would that be?"

Echo's face was solemn. "Meet Kai as he has requested. Arrive here, next Thursday, and he will give you the answers you desire. But do not return to this place again until that time. It is critical that you remain undiscovered by others, at least until—"

"But I've *already* been discovered by others," I interrupted. "I need answers *now*."

His white-blonde eyebrows furrowed. "Who else knows about you?"

"A man—last night. He saw my birthmark, called me an 'Essen.' He said something about... annihilating me if I make the wrong choice. And then this morning, I found out he's dead. He died of a heart attack, right after threatening me."

Echo's breath caught.

"Please," I pleaded, stepping towards him. "I know it's not a coincidence. Tell me what all this about. Tell me what's going on."

He shook his head. "Kai will explain everything on Thursday. In the meantime, stay away from people, Gemma. Between the hours of dusk and dawn, stay away from all people. Do not wander into the company of others while the earth is yet in shadow."

"What do you mean? *Why?*" I demanded. "It's not even *possible*. You know that, right? The earth is 'in shadow' for about sixteen hours a day right now!"

Echo blinked. "It might be difficult, yes, but I would not advise it were it not necessary."

"You're serious, then."

"It is a serious matter. While you are not presently at risk—the enemy cannot harm you until you are Activated—it seems from what you've just told me that your friends and family are. If you care for them, for anybody, keep yourself isolated between sundown and daybreak."

I glanced at the sun, which was sinking steadily in the afternoon sky. "Between sundown and daybreak. So you're telling me that in about an hour, I need to be home and I need to stay there until first light tomorrow?"

"Not just home," Echo corrected. "That will not keep your loved ones safe. You need to be *alone*."

A chill ran up my spine that had nothing to do with the biting wind. "Who *are* these people? They would pursue me, even though they can't hurt me—at least not for a few more months?"

"They are the Dothen, and they are not people, not exactly. They are hunters; their sole purpose is to find and vanquish the Essen. They are driven by the belief that the world must be restored to order, and that *they* have been commissioned by God to do this work. To restore order, the Essen must cease to be. The Dothen, they are *programmed* to stalk you. They are programmed to stalk all of us. Gravitation gives them the method, and nighttime gives them the means. Heed my advice: Detach yourself from company in the sunless hours, lest you jeopardize the lives of others."

He began to retreat once more to the shadows, but I lunged toward him and grabbed his sleeve. "Wait!" I said. "What do these hunters look like? How could they hurt my family? What can I do to defend against them?"

Echo tried to pull his arm away, but I held tight waiting for his answer. "There *is* no defense! You will not know they are there until it is too late. They are sneaky, taking others' forms. Now please, let me go. I need to get back to—" He stopped abruptly, his eyes widening as they registered on something behind me.

CHAPTER 33

"**D**o not move, except to release the boy," said a voice from behind me. Despite the low tone in which they were spoken, the words carried the weight of authority.

I released Echo's arm. He met my eyes, but his face was unreadable. He shuffled back several steps.

"Now slowly, very slowly, turn around." There was a smoky quality to her voice.

I raised my arms in a show of innocence and faced her.

She stood at the edge of the clearing with her hands at her sides, eyeing me coolly. Wearing clothing that suggested she valued function over fashion—a gunmetal-gray utility coat and pants that looked as though they were made of canvas, both exhibiting a multitude of pockets—her posture was not relaxed, nor was it rigid. It was catlike, poised for pouncing should the need arise. About her hatless head, long strands of coppery hair whipped like tendrils of fire. She looked wild; though she appeared about my age, height, and build, I had no doubt she could kick my ass without effort. Her black combat boots seemed made for doing so. She narrowed her almond-shaped brown eyes. "If you so much as twitch a muscle, you're toast. You hear me?"

I opened my mouth and shut it again. I heard her, but words failed me. Filled with trepidation, I managed to nod my head. I hoped she wouldn't notice my shivering.

She turned her focus to Echo. "Did she hurt you?"

Echo moved across the clearing and placed himself in front of her. "I am unharmed. Stand down, Rori. She is no threat."

Rori pushed him aside and strode towards me. "I'll decide that for myself." Stopping inches from my face, her stare bored into me. I lowered my eyes, embarrassed by her scrutiny. "Look at me," she demanded. I did, though my chin remained tucked defensively in my scarf.

It was several long minutes before she backed away and said to Echo, "Her irises are strange, both brown and blue, but not distorted by evil."

"The day has only begun to wane," Echo replied. "She could not be—"

"I know, okay?" Rori said. "I just—"

"Besides, she cannot be taken," Echo interrupted.

Rori's eyebrows shot up in surprise. "She's...?"

"An Essen, yes. Her name is Gemma Pointe. Until recently, she was naïve to her identity. However, she is now undergoing and requires assistance."

"So you decided to abandon your post! Rather than notify a Keeper?"

"I am a keeper," Echo said.

"You're *bridge*-keeper, Echo. Mind your role. You know how Phoenix feels about bridge security. Bad things happen when bridge-keepers neglect—"

"In no way did I neglect my duties," he interjected. "This errand, this brief crossing to address Gemma, was *assigned* to me *by* a Keeper. I promised that if I could reach her, I would."

"Oh yeah? *Who* did you promise?" Rori asked.

Echo faltered. "It was... I just..." He sighed. "Kai. I promised Kai."

"You promised *Malakai*? Let me tell you something, kid. That guy's a loose cannon. Go on, continue listening to him and see what happens. You'll wind up dead for sure, just like anyone he's been charged with Keeping. He can't even protect *himself* for—"

"Stop," Echo said, inclining his head towards me. "I am not unfamiliar with your opinion of Kai, but allow Gemma to form her own judgment, for he desires to claim her for Keeping as well."

Rori's jaw dropped. "When did this happen? Why hasn't he brought her forward? Never before has an Essen been discovered this side of the bridge, and he *delays*? He sends *you* to—" She stopped abruptly, searching Echo's face. "What duty did he send you to perform, exactly?"

"Mine is an errand of secrecy," Echo said.

"Well then you failed, didn't you?" Rori said, turning her attention to me once more. "You. Gemma. Answer the question. What did Echo tell you?"

The entire time they were bickering, I had been focused on keeping my body from shaking too much while also trying to retain their words. Now I looked from Rori's face to Echo's, unsure of how to answer. Who should I align myself with? The strange child who was sent by Malakai or the pushy girl who openly disliked him?

"Speak," Rori said.

I wasn't sure how I felt about Echo yet, but I wasn't ready to trust Rori either. "He hadn't gotten that far," I said. "He just told me his name and that he wanted to help me. But before he said anything else, he must have heard you coming because he started to leave. I tried to make him stay. Then you got here." I attempted a shrug of indifference, but it was lost in my shivering.

From behind Rori, Echo gave me a barely perceptible nod. He placed a mitten on Rori's arm and said, "It is time. I must return. Others are also requesting passage and will soon arrive. Allow Gemma to depart. She is nearly frozen, and only Malakai can satisfy you with an explanation anyway. You know where to find him."

Rori rolled her eyes. "Of course I do. He's *always* there, isn't he?"

"Gemma," Echo said, moving directly in front of me, "I daresay our paths will cross once more very soon." He lowered his voice to a whisper, scarcely audible above the wind, and added, "We will meet again on Thursday. Until then, heed my advice."

Then he and Rori walked together to the edge of the clearing and waited for me to leave.

The sun was just dropping below the horizon by the time I arrived at home, and I wasted no time getting into my room and barricading myself behind the door with my desk chair, nightstand, and a box of books. I stripped off Lucy's clothing and climbed into my bed, on which I'd piled a mountain of extra blankets.

My muscles were still trembling, partly from the cold, but also with fear. As my flesh began to thaw, it also became extremely itchy. I scratched my thighs and hips and chest and back, digging my fingernails as much as I dared into my numb-feeling skin. The physical sensation of it occupied my mind for a while; but try as I might, there was no escaping Echo's words. They were like the current of a river, guiding my thoughts from below the surface.

Buried beneath the covers, I willed myself to stop shaking. My body did not obey. Though the itching was subsiding, my shivering was growing more and more violent. I tucked myself into a tight ball and forced my thoughts away from the faceless hunters against whom there was no hope of defense.

I steered my brain towards Jonny, sweet Jonny, who had been out on the hill today, also suffering in the cold. Had he spent the day giving snowboarding lessons to groups of kids? Did he feel as exhausted by his time outdoors as I did by mine? He would be home from work soon. Would he understand if I said I was too drained to hang out tonight?

I hugged myself tighter within my cocoon of quilts. What if he just stopped by? How could I explain, through the door, that for his own safety, I could never see him again between dusk and dawn?

He'd think I was crazy, that I was having some form of psychological response to my traumatic past. He'd want to *help* me. But there was no saving me now. I was broken, destined to be supernatural and hunted forever. The only thing left to do was protect those I loved. Without telling them anything.

I had to pull away. Disappear. I had to hope to be forgotten.

It was me the Dothen were after. Gravitation was bringing them to me, even as I burrowed deeper into my blankets. Echo had told me that I would not know they had arrived until it was too late. They take others' forms, he'd said.

Shape shifters? I thought to myself. The idea of being hunted by someone that looked like Jonny, or Flash, or anyone else I knew and loved horrified me. How would I ever know if the person with me was genuine or an imposter?

Thursday could not come soon enough. If Malakai was the one with all the answers, then I would *make* him tell me everything. I would beg, plead, even threaten him if it came to that. I couldn't live like this, not knowing what I was up against or how to protect myself and others. I couldn't continue to obey without understanding. I needed the *reasons* for the rules, I needed to know the *whys* behind the whats. I couldn't *live* like this.

I wondered if Rori, who seemed as certain of where to find Malakai as she was exasperated by it, was getting her answers at this very moment. I felt resentment pooling within me. Why was there so much secrecy? Why was Malakai, who supposedly wanted to be my "Keeper," blowing me off? Why had he allowed Gate and Echo to provide me with information that he should have given me himself?

As I thought about it, my resentment grew into a deep and thorough anger, displacing my fear. My life was *normal* before Malakai. It was boring. It was safe. Then he came along and ruined everything.

My muscles began to relax, the trembling slowing and then stopping, as I channeled my energy into faulting Malakai. Oh, I would meet him on Thursday at the Wooded Bridge. I'd meet him and give him a piece of my mind. Then I'd make him tell me everything.

Everything. Where was Gate? What had happened eighteen years ago between the two of them? Why had Detective Tommegren died? What happened to Raela Celere? How could the Dothen bring harm to my family and what could be done to protect them?

The crystalline morning seemed like a dream now. Gate's intrusion on my sleep, the notes from Jonny and Professor Dagenais, my conversation with Uncle Dan in the kitchen—they were so far away.

The peace of the morning hadn't been meant to last, and it didn't. Intuition had told me that the day would be one of life-altering choices, one of *consequence*, and it had been. So though it was only early evening, I succumbed to fatigue and drifted into a turbulent slumber. I could not have known that the real life-altering choice, the one my intuition had truly been warning me about, was on the waking end of sleep.

CHAPTER 34

I dreamt of the Wooded Bridge, a rickety brown thing made of ancient lumber. As I began across it, I looked down at the mighty Mississippi gliding along beneath me. When I was about halfway to the other bank, I saw a huge swell rising upstream. I began to run, but the water moved swiftly. Before I could reach the end, the rogue wave was swallowing the bridge. I gripped the wooden handrails but I knew the bridge would not be able to withstand the force of the river. Within a breath, the whole structure collapsed, taking me with it.

My body was screaming for oxygen, but I couldn't fight my way back to the surface. Broken beams pummeled me as they sank, and I thrashed about in my panic, knowing that this time, no one would save me.

I was crying when I woke up, crying and sucking air and sweating from the mound of blankets on top of me. I shoved them off and sat up, feeling totally and utterly defeated. Though I wiped the tears from my face, a new stream of them spilled from my eyes. Loneliness settled in me as I thought about my remaining hours of isolation.

It was quarter to midnight and I had been asleep for several hours. Though the dawn was still eons from breaking, I knew there was no way I would be able to fall back asleep.

On my nightstand, my phone flashed a text from Jonny, sent at 6:35 PM: *Dearest Gem—Heading to Luke's for a while. See you tomorrow? Love ya!*

Thinking of him, I found myself clasping my opal pendant. I really was so lucky to have him in my life. How would I ever be able to explain my seclusion going forward? How would I be able to explain it to anybody?

With an ear to my bedroom door, I listened for movement. Nothing. Aunt Sheri and Uncle Dan must have turned in already, and as it was Saturday night, Flash wouldn't be home until at least three o'clock. I moved my nightstand, chair, and books, and crept from my bedroom with the sole objective of finding some food.

I made my way downstairs carefully. On the third step, I heard a creaking noise from above. Freezing against the wall, I waited. When no other sounds ensued, I lowered myself to the next step. *Just the house settling*, I thought. *Nothing to worry about*, I told myself. As I descended the remaining stairs, I strained to hear anything beyond the beating of my own heart. Then I hurried silently towards the kitchen.

Echo had terrified me, as much by what he didn't say as by what he did. The vagueness in his counsel left me to imagine the various ways the Dothen might appear and bring doom to family. My adrenaline spiked at every sound, and I quickly decided to grab something simple and transport it back to my room to eat once I had barricaded myself in again.

Ever so quietly, I opened the fridge and spied a block of cheese and an apple. I snatched them out and made my way to the pantry, from which I pulled a sleeve of crackers.

I shut the pantry door and turned. In front of me, dressed in an oversized sweatshirt and flannel pants, stood a scruffy-looking Uncle Dan. I squeaked and drew back, dropping everything that I was holding.

Uncle Dan chuckled. "I'm sorry I startled you," he said. "I heard you get up, and once I was awake, I felt hungry too." He stooped to pick up the food, grabbed a paring knife from the drawer, and brought it all to the table.

"Pull up a chair," he said as he began to slice the apple.

Warily, I sat down opposite him and watched with vigilance as he handled the knife. Under normal circumstances, the slicing of an apple is a harmless enough activity, but now, in light of Echo's warning, I would have preferred to eat the apple whole.

"Here," he said, thrusting some of the apple toward me. I recoiled.

Uncle Dan frowned. "I'd ask you what's gotten into you lately, but I'm afraid I know." He sighed and set down the knife. "I'm so sorry, Gemma. Your aunt and I, we thought we were doing what was right. It was never our intention to hurt you." He reached his hand across the table, but I maintained my distance. His brown eyes filled with sadness. "The things we kept from you, it was for your own good. Well, that's what we thought then. But now… I realize we were wrong. I just wish you had come to us right away. I would have explained why we did what we did."

"Then explain now," I said somewhat coldly. "Start at the beginning, and be specific."

He ran his hands over his bald head in a very characteristic manner. If this was an Uncle Dan imposter, he was skilled at impersonation. But if this was an imposter, his response would give him away. I hoped.

"You were only twelve when David died," he said. "When we brought you home after the accident, you didn't know who you were, let alone who we were. You had a tenuous grasp of reality, and we feared that if you knew the truth about your health, you'd lose hope."

"What truth?" I asked, my tone softening a little.

"That your memory wasn't ever going to come back. The doctors, they told us that the trauma you had suffered, it was too much. They said the part of your brain that housed your memories had been damaged so severely that… Well, it was unlikely you would ever really recall your past. I remember it like it was yesterday. 'Do not cling to hope,' they advised us, 'but do not discourage hope either. Gemma needs to feel hope for her physical recovery, even if it won't improve her amnesia.'

"So, supported in our choice by hospital staff, we told you that any day, your memory would return. It was only a matter of time, we told you. But in our hearts, we knew the chances of you ever remembering were slim, if chances existed at all. We truly believed you would never know your father, yourself, or your life prior to the accident. It was like a reset button had been pressed.

"Your aunt and I, we saw it as an opportunity. We made a decision to free you from the part of your past that had caused your pain. We thought it was the best gift we could give you. Your mother's leaving, it had always hurt you, and you had never really been able to let go of it. So we told you she had passed on.

"There were times when I thought we *should* tell you the truth. After all, what if your mother tried to come back and find you after all these years? We never knew what became of her after she left, and that worried us. So we hired a private investigator only to find out she'd been murdered—robbed and stabbed in New York City—less than a year after she'd gone.

"It didn't make sense to tell you the truth after that. There was no way you'd ever find out, we thought. But here we are. You did find out. And now I realize how foolish the whole thing was. Gemma, I'm so sorry. How long have you known?" Uncle Dan's forehead creased as he waited for my response.

"About a week," I said. "I remembered my dad telling me how she…" I paused, figuring out how much I should say. Though this certainly was the one and only Uncle Dan, the details were just too personal. "We talked about her leaving."

"Your memory is back?" he asked.

"No. I've only remembered a few things. So… is there anything else you need to tell me?" I couldn't keep the insinuation out of the question.

Uncle Dan shook his head. "No, Gemma, I promise. Everything else about your past, everything we've told you, is the truth."

"You didn't deliberately leave anything out?"

His brows furrowed. "What do you mean?"

I sighed, disappointed. I couldn't tell him what I meant. Instead I asked, "How did you know? That I'd found out about my mom?"

He looked embarrassed. "You talked about it in your sleep all last night. Every time I went in to check on you to make sure you didn't have a concussion, you were mumbling about your mother leaving, about your family lying to you, about not being able to trust us. It was the most ashamed I've ever felt." Leaning forward across the table, he looked into my eyes. "Will you ever be able to forgive us, Gemma?"

His gaze was warm but anxious. I took in his expression, earnest and humbled and loving, and I started to answer. Before I could utter a single word, though, his face slackened and his eyes went vacant. The emotions I'd seen in his features disappeared, leaving me the object of a blank stare.

Alarmed, I leapt up, knocking over the chair. The clatter of it was a cacophony in the otherwise silent house.

As I watched, Uncle Dan's pupils contracted in his irises and began to drop within the brown of them. They settled at the bottom, the small black circles fixing themselves to the lower edge of his irises.

I screamed.

Uncle Dan stood up, his motions jerky. "We have—locked on you. You cannot hide. From us." The words came out in an oddly staccato rhythm.

He advanced towards me, and I pressed myself into the corner, unable to escape. "This will be your last—warning. Choose wisely, Essen. Or next time, you are mine."

And then Uncle Dan's pupils returned to center, and he swayed there for what seemed like an eternity before collapsing to the floor.

He remained there unmoving, and I knew without getting any closer that I was looking at his corpse.

CHAPTER 35

Aunt Sheri was in the kitchen, cradling Uncle Dan's head, screaming at me to call 911. The operator was talking to me, but I don't know what either of us said. The medics and officers arrived, a swarm of people in the kitchen. They asked me questions. I am not sure how I responded.

They were putting Uncle Dan on a stretcher, rolling him into the ambulance. Aunt Sheri was with him in the back. I stood in the driveway without shoes. Someone offered to take me to the hospital to meet my family. *No, no, no, I can't*, I said. I watched them all leave.

Jonny got home from Luke's as the flashing lights pulled away. He saw me and was running to me wild-eyed, dashing across the land that separated our driveways.

As he got closer, I realized that *it was my fault*. Uncle Dan, lying on the floor, eyes open but unseeing... *it was because of me*. I darted in the house, up the stairs, and into my room, slamming the door. Barricade restored, I ignored Jonny's pleas to let him in.

He was knocking and knocking, asking me to talk to him. I shouted at him to go away, told him it was for his own good. He wouldn't listen; he stayed on the other side of the door. Frustrated, I threw a book. It flew out of my hand and shattered the vase of flowers. Water and shards of glass were everywhere. The flowers became piles of ash where they landed.

"Don't you get it?" I sobbed. "I'm cursed! Please, please, leave me!"

A squeak of the floorboard told me he was going. I wailed hearing him leave, as anguished by his departure as I was by his presence.

My weeping was loud and bitter and filled with regret. I don't know for how long I cried, but my throat ached from the work of it.

At some point, I was spent. My breathing slowed and I grew quiet. And then I heard him.

From outside my door, he hummed a sorrowful melody, strumming his guitar lightly. The music was unrehearsed, but all the more soothing for its rawness. He repeated the song over and over, letting the sound of it float to me. Then he was singing softly, his voice steady and pacifying.

I closed my eyes and let him sing me to dawn.

I kept him out until well after the sun had risen. When I finally opened the door, he was sitting on the floor, looking as rough as I felt. Without a word, he got up and embraced me tightly.

In Jonny's arms, I found rest. I didn't offer an explanation for my behavior, and he didn't demand one. We just made our way through the shards of glass and puddles of water to my bed and fell into it. I tucked myself against him and we both slept until early afternoon, when Aunt Sheri and Flash woke us.

Between sobs, Aunt Sheri told us Uncle Dan had died of a ruptured brain aneurysm. Flash stood behind Aunt Sheri with his hand on her shoulder, silent tears falling down his cheeks.

All four of us grieved together. We held each other and cried but none of us were comforted. For me especially, there could be no consolation, for my grief was also infused with guilt.

I did not go with Aunt Sheri and Flash to make the arrangements that afternoon. I stayed in my room the entire day, letting Jonny stroke my hair and whisper solaces. But as nightfall approached, I began to panic. Convincing Jonny that I needed time alone to grieve, he left. And I was by myself to withstand the darkness once more.

I barely slept that night, or any night that week. When I did manage to sleep, nightmares of an unparalleled intensity plagued me. Without the flowers to lessen the symptoms of Affliction, the static in my head was almost unbearable too. I tried to use the technique Gate taught me, but when the antique radio in my mind was ineffective, I smashed it against a wall, leaving it broken on the floor like the flower vase.

It was one of the darkest periods of my life. Poisoned by the secret that I was responsible for Uncle Dan's death, I grew despondent. I don't know how it happened, but I *knew* it was my fault. So I stayed in my room, even during the day. I only left the house once, to attend the funeral.

Everyone handles loss differently. Aunt Sheri surrounded herself with others; the house was filled with people who I could hear talking consolingly and moving about on the floor below. Flash focused on his music. In the basement, mixing beats with Paul, he got through the days. For my part, I let people believe I had to manage my grief in seclusion, though I would have preferred company.

I would have preferred Jonny. I couldn't risk it though, so I kept him at a distance, telling him that I needed space. He said he understood, but of course he didn't. No one did. Self-pity joined sadness, anger, and guilt, and they jumbled inside of me, making me feel volatile.

But even though he didn't understand what I was going through, he understood *me*. The gift he gave me on Wednesday afternoon made that clear. He stopped by on his way to work, promising me he would only stay a minute. He handed me a bag stuffed with tissue paper, kissed me on the cheek, and told me to text him later.

Only after he left did I look in the bag. I pulled out the card first and read it:

> *Dear Gemma,*
> *I know you need me to respect your grieving process, but I miss you so much. You are my best friend and I hate that you are hurting. I love you. I hope these gifts bring you peace.*
> *Yours Forever, Jonny*

I reached into the bag and pulled out two items: one was a CD on which Jonny had written the words, "Gemma's Lullaby." When I listened to it later, I recognized it as the song he'd played outside my door the night Uncle Dan died.

The other item was a leather-bound journal, debossed with my initials. Inside the cover, Jonny had written, *The soul would have no rainbow if the eye had no tear. May writing be your therapy, as it is for me.*

I started writing, filling the pages with my thoughts, my fears, and my memories of Uncle Dan. Page by page, the darkness began to recede. My heart felt lighter, and then, for the first time in four days, I began to hope.

Somehow, despite my best efforts to push him away, Jonny had rescued me again.

CHAPTER 36

When the day broke on Thursday, January 8th, I was still furiously trying to do justice to the memory of Uncle Dan. Having written all night, I had recorded much: the way he looked, the phrases he used, his mannerisms, and how he dressed. I wrote about our relationship and how it had grown from awkward and uncomfortable, when I first came to live with him and Aunt Sheri, to warm and easy. I jotted anecdotes and made notes about some of the times we had together.

I desperately wanted to capture who he was, but in everything I recorded, something was missing. I felt insufficient, like I didn't have the skill to preserve him on paper the way I wanted.

Still, there was something about the act of writing that cleansed my spirit. The physicality of using pen and paper, of writing until my hand throbbed, of trying to keep him alive in my heart... brought *me* back to life. So powerful was the experience that I seriously considered taking Professor Dagenais' writing course. Then I registered for it. I hadn't intended to go to school spring semester, but the idea of taking a composition class *felt* right. The recounting of Uncle Dan's life deserved a higher level of ability than I was currently able to lend to the task.

I loved my Uncle Dan. He had been a *good* man, and writing helped me honor him. It helped me begin healing. But the healing was—and it would always be—incomplete. I could recover from the loss, but not the guilt. No amount of regret, remorse, or repentance would be able to bring him back, and his untimely death was *my fault*. No, writing could not remedy that hurt. It could not release me from the mistake that would always be mine. It could not grant me the forgiveness that my soul longed for.

What writing could do, though, was give me clarity. Clarity about what had taken place, what my choices now were, and how to move forward. Through writing, I became convinced of two things.

First, the Dothen were not shape shifters. When Echo had told me, "They are sneaky, taking others' forms," I had assumed they took on the physical appearance of other people. But after seeing Uncle Dan's... demise, I realized what Echo had actually meant. The Dothen quite literally take others' forms, like unholy viruses seizing the bodies of existing people. They were beings of a spiritual nature, demons maybe, with the ability to steal hosts, rendering them dead after the incident.

Second, it didn't appear a Dothen could do this to an Essen. For whatever reason, it seemed an Essen could not be attacked in this manner. In order to communicate with or harm an Essen, a Dothen would have to find a host in that proximity. And after nightfall, those people would typically be those closest to the Essen—family and friends.

Typically, but not always. That wasn't the case for Detective Tommegren, whose death was also my fault. A Dothen had taken his body and then left him for dead as well. I threw up into my wastebasket when I made this connection.

I had the blood of two men on my hands. Why hadn't Gate or Echo or Malakai *told* me what would happen? How could they let such horrors come to pass? All three of them were as guilty as I was. Guiltier, even, for they had known what could occur. They should have told me what I needed to do to keep everyone safe, but they didn't.

My outrage grew. In a few hours, I would be meeting Malakai at the Wooded Bridge. I had no idea what I would do when I saw him, but I did know this: I *hated* him. He was *never* going to get his hands on my boulder opal. If the stone really was the portens—that precious item capable of freeing the Essen—then it was *my* portens. I would not use it to liberate him from whatever prison held him. If I was to be a prisoner of my guilt, then he deserved his captivity too.

✳ ✳ ✳

Sunrise was my bedtime lately, but I didn't dare sleep. Weary as I was, I stayed awake by writing and pounding coffee until, around 11:15 AM, I snuck out of the house to catch the bus.

I wasn't as stealthy as I thought. Before I even got to the end of the driveway, Flash had followed me out the door. "Hey," he called to me, still pulling on his coat. "I said I'd go with you." His voice sounded husky, like he had just woken up.

I turned to face him. He was unshaven, his hair was flat, and his jeans had obviously spent several days in a crumpled ball on the floor. I thought he probably looked better than I did. "It's okay," I mumbled as he approached. "You don't have to."

"No," he said. "*You* don't have to. Why are you going, Gemma? With everything that's happened this week…" Flash searched my face. "You've stayed in your room, you've avoided mom and me and even Jonny. But *this* guy—you wanna talk to *him*? Why? What is he to you?"

Unlike the last time we talked about Malakai, there was no judgment in Flash's questions. He did not seem disapproving; he just genuinely wanted to understand. "I don't know," I whispered, staring at my boots. "I just have to do this."

"Then I do too," he said. "Come on, get in the car."

I made no attempt to argue. When Flash made up his mind about something, he couldn't be persuaded otherwise. And truthfully, I was relieved to have him with me. I was outraged with Malakai, but also terrified of meeting him.

"Where are we going?" he asked as we pulled onto the street.

"U of M. East Bank," I said, trying to keep my voice even. If he noticed my nerves, he pretended not to.

We drove all the way to campus without saying much. It wasn't until after we had parked and were walking to that place among the oaks that Flash said, "I just can't believe he's really gone, you know?"

"I know," I said. "I can't either."

"It was just so sudden. We had no warning." He stared straight ahead, rather than looking at me. "I just wish I'd had a chance to say goodbye."

"I'm so sorry, Flash," I said, feeling my face tighten with emotion.

He inhaled deeply, holding his breath for a moment before responding. "He was a father to us both," he said. "I'm sorry too, Gemma."

We walked for a while in silence, listening to the snow crunch beneath our boots on the frozen sidewalk. It was the only sound, and it seemed eerily loud on the deserted campus.

Then Flash said, "Do you think he can see us now? Do you think he knows…" His voice cracked slightly on the word *knows*.

"He knows you loved him," I said.

He pursed his lips and nodded, his chin quivering slightly.

We were both blinking back tears as we left the path, Flash following me into the woods.

We arrived at the spot where I first encountered Malakai but no one was there. Flash's eyes still glistened, and I hugged him. "I'm sorry," I said again. He had no idea how sorry I was, how heavy my burden.

He wiped his eyes and cleared his throat. "So where is this guy anyway? He couldn't have met you at a restaurant or something? It's fucking cold out."

"I'm here," Malakai said gruffly, moving into the clearing. He was even bigger than I remembered him being, and more forbidding. Flanking him were Rori and another man about his age. The other man was also tall, though not quite as broad, with a bearded face and a charcoal-colored pageboy hat, from which hung a light brown ponytail. All three were dressed in the same gunmetal-gray utility clothing and black boots that I'd seen previously on Rori.

As they came forward, I sensed danger. I found myself grabbing Flash's arm and drawing him back. They exchanged glances with one another, and then, as swiftly as wolves, rushed us. Rori restrained me while the bearded man attacked Flash, stabbing the needle of a syringe into his neck. Flash instantly went limp in his arms.

"Flash!" I howled, battling Rori's hold. I stomped her shins and threw elbows as violently as I could until she loosened her grip enough for me to pull free. As I broke away, Malakai crossed in front of me. "Get out of my way!" I said, trying to get to Flash.

"You should have come alone," Malakai said, leaning over me, blocking me. "You know the risks. He was a liability."

I clenched my teeth, balled my hands into fists, and felt every ounce of anger erupt through me as I punched one of Malakai's too-green eyes.

"Oh my God, I love this girl!" Rori said, bursting into laughter.

Malakai glared at her and then at me. "Listen," he said, rubbing his eye. "Flash is—"

"No, you listen!" I yelled. "I hate you! My uncle is dead because of you!" I swung at him again, but he blocked it.

"Fine," he said. "We can play it like that." He pulled another syringe out of his coat pocket.

I didn't hesitate. I flew from him and into the woods, moving as quickly as I could through the snow.

He caught up to me easily, tackling me into the ground. His massive body was on top of me, crushing me. I tried to scream, but his enormous weight had forced the air from me. "It didn't have to be like this," he said. Then I felt the sting of the needle as it pierced my neck.

CHAPTER 37

I was cozy, lying there in the sand. Without opening my eyes, I knew the sun was high and bright in the cloudless sky. Its gentle rays kissed my skin, thawing me. I stirred and felt the powder shift beneath me. It was fine, like dust. I spread my fingers into it, letting its silkiness cover my hands.

This is a dream.

The sea was louder than it normally was in my dreams. The sound of it—*whoosh, crash, whoosh, crash*—was so close. If I extended my fingers just a bit more, I might touch a wave. It would be magical. I smiled, stretching out my arms, filling my lungs with salty air, lingering in that state between sleep and waking.

Something is wrong.

I didn't dream, not like that, with sensations of softness and warmth and beauty. I never woke up slowly, basking in pleasant remnants of thought. No, my dreams were of a darker, more horrifying nature, and when I was mercifully jolted from them, it was sudden and definitive.

Reluctantly, I opened my eyes.

The landscape before me was breathtaking. Turquoise water extended as far as the eye could see. Closer to shore, white-capped waves threw themselves forward and then retreated, beckoning to me. I pushed myself up, anxious to bathe in the surf.

Only then did it register that I was dressed in a winter coat, mittens, hat, and boots. Almost unconsciously, I touched my neck. There was a small scab where the needle had entered. Alarmed and confused, I shuffled backwards in the sand, scanning my surroundings. Down the beach, several miles away, magnificent cliffs. Behind me, a dense forest of leafy trees. And at the edge of it, a small wooden beach house.

I've seen this place before.

In my daydreams, the ocean called to me. It lured me from shore, assuring me of a prize that existed just over the next swell. But the sea is as deceitful as it is eager. I turned my back to it, trying to ignore its whispers.

As I stood there, Echo emerged from the beach house. He was wearing plaid swim trunks and an orange t-shirt that made his skin and hair look even whiter. He squinted as his eyes adjusted and slipped on a pair of sandals. Then he slung a cloth sack over his shoulder and began making his way to me.

He stepped calculatedly but clumsily through the sand, and I could see at once why: both of his legs were badly disfigured, and one of them was inches shorter than the other. When I encountered him before in his snow gear, his disability escaped my notice.

"You have many questions," he said when he was within a few yards. "I will endeavor to answer them. But first, I expect you will feel more comfortable if you change your attire." He held out the sack. "These garments are from Rori's collection. They should fit you nicely."

I accepted the bag and withdrew its contents, sage-green hiking shorts, a white tank top, and flip flops.

"The Axis is unoccupied at the moment," he said, indicating the beach house. "You may leave your cold-weather apparel in the wardrobe. I shall wait here for you." He lowered himself to the sand and stared out at the sea.

I was struck again by the formality of his diction and the maturity of his mannerisms. Something about the way he presented himself disarmed me, put me at ease even. *What a strange child*, I thought as I wandered up to the house.

Inside, the structure was not partitioned into rooms. Rather, it was one great room filled with mismatched sofas, chairs, and ottomans. Lining the walls were various sets of shoes, boots, and sandals. At the far end stood a large wooden wardrobe inside of which hung insulated utility clothing like those I'd seen on Malakai and his counterparts. I took off my coat and hung it in the wardrobe, along with the rest of my clothing, and redressed quickly in the items lent to me by Rori.

Echo was still gazing at the ocean when I returned to him. He didn't face me when he said, "I do not like secrets. In my life, too much has been hidden from me. Too much will always be hidden from me. Are there not enough mysteries in the universe, enough truths concealed in the folds of time? Must we seek to shroud information from one another as well?" He picked up a small seashell and threw it into the water. "Were it possible, all people would be forthcoming, all things transparent."

I sat next to Echo in the sand but did not speak.

"Today," he continued, "I am relieved of my burden. Though I do not fault Kai for his secrecy—his reasons are justified—and though I do not resent my involvement, I am glad it is nearly over."

I picked up a shell of my own and rolled it between my hands. There was still a very dreamlike quality about things, but the shell felt smooth, solid, and *real*.

Echo turned to me. "He is not worthy of your hate, you know."

I released the stone in a half-hearted toss and watched it drop into the crest of a wave. "My uncle is dead," I said. "He should still be alive. He *would* be if Malakai, or you, or somebody, had just… cared." I felt the heat rise in my cheeks. "But Malakai only wants the portens. He's using me."

Echo put his small hand on my arm. "I am sorry about your uncle, Gemma. It is my fault; I should have told you everything about the Dothen. I let my commitment to Kai get in the way of helping you. I prioritized his secret over your family's safety. And to what end? Kai's secret was still exposed—you were discovered by another Essen—and your uncle was also lost. I failed you both." He shook his head. "Do not condemn Kai for the wrongs *I* have committed."

"Why do you defend him?" I said, yanking my arm away. "He could have told me back in November! I haven't heard from him in *months*. He disappeared from the face of the earth while I had to endure the pain of Affliction, the fear of nameless enemies, and the guilt of my uncle's death, all of it, *alone*. He abandoned me to Gate, an alleged murderer, and to *you*, a child who—"

"Abandoned you?" Echo interjected. "Surely, you cannot believe that! He nearly *died* that night he was with you. For sixty excruciating days, he has been confined to the Mederium, recovering! And the whole while, he kept your existence a secret, even from other Essen, in order to *protect* you. Then finally, after two months in recovery, he was released this morning. And what did you do? You sent him back there for more healing!"

I punched him in the face, I thought. *Good. Serves him right for—*

"Where is Flash?" I demanded as images of the morning came flooding back to me.

"He is at the Somnus—the sleeping quarters. Taeo carried him there, and he and Rori are watching over him. Should he waken, additional serum will be administered. Do not be concerned. Tomorrow, he will remember today as a dream."

"Then it is not a dream?" I said, not trusting my senses.

"No," Echo replied. "Though your confusion is understandable. The serum is Phoenix's specialty. It makes the division between dreams and reality fuzzy, and you were injected with it as well."

I touched my neck again, feeling the puncture in my skin. "The bastard stabbed me with a needle," I said.

"Would you have gone with him willingly?"

"No," I admitted.

"Then he was right to act in the manner that he did. It was imperative that you come here today." There was urgency in Echo's clear blue eyes.

"Why?" I asked.

"Because, as I told you, I do not like secrets. Now that Kai has been released and can bring you forward himself, this secret, the secret of your existence, can finally be revealed. Before Phoenix, he will commit himself as your Keeper, and only afterwards will he allow your notae to be observed by other Essen.

"His claim of you is a protection, Gemma, for it grants him alone responsibility for your undergoing. This is important, as there is one who would seek to exploit you. I know not who it is—the person is but a wraith in my mind—but I am certain it is not Kai. Allow him to become your Keeper, and he will divulge every secret of this place to you." He stared out at the sea again. "And there are many."

"Echo?" I asked, following his gaze to the water. "What is this place? Where are we?"

His face took on a solemn expression, and he recited a poem:

"This place is our heaven, but also our hell.
This place is our haven, but also our cell.
An earthly asylum, away from their reach,
A dreary confinement, here on the beach."

He dug his fingers into the sand. "What I would not give to see the mountains one day." He sighed and faced me once more. "We are on Salvos, a small island in the Atlantic. It is our only sanctuary on Earth, accessible solely via the Wooded Bridge. Here, we are safe from the Dothen. Here, we remain caged." Echo pursed his lips into a sad little smile. "Welcome to your new home, Gemma. Your beautiful, tropical cage."

CHAPTER 38

A knot tightened in my stomach. "You're not implying... I'm not trapped here, am I?"

Echo did not respond immediately. He picked up a handful of beach and let it slip through his fingers, his expression pensive. "Yes and no," he said at length. "As bridge-keeper, I cannot, without cause, deny you passage. Should you wish to traverse the Wooded Bridge, you need only ask and I will open it for you. It is your prerogative to come and go from this island as you see fit." He paused. "On the other hand, you are bound to this place—not by me or Malakai, but by your own Essen identity. Like all of us, you will come to depend on Salvos for refuge and resources, and like all of us, you will resent your dependency. A will to survive and a sense of duty will drive you here, but a desire for freedom and a hunger for *life* will make you deplore it. You will be trapped here as a matter of choice, but it will be a cage nonetheless. Until such time when things change, this is the plight of the Essen. None of us can be both safe and free."

My mouth went dry. "So every night to avoid the Dothen... we just flee? There must be some way to fight them. The Essen—"

"—Have been hunted by the Dothen for millennia, Gemma. There is no angle you could consider, no plot you could form, no attack you could strategize, that has not already failed. Across the generations, thousands have perished daring to think as you do now. No hope of thwarting the Dothen has ever existed." Echo leaned forward, his eyes probing. "That is, unless there really is a portens."

The eagerness in his face reminded me that he was yet a child. "I don't know, Echo. I really don't."

His mouth twisted into a frown of disappointment. "But you *are* the Link, are you not?"

I shrugged. "Gate believes that I am."

Echo cringed. "You would do well to avoid using the name Gate Dorsum while you are here. He is despised by all within the Host. Though I have never met him, though he has not stepped foot on Salvos for nearly two decades, I am familiar with his legacy. Most heinous was his crime."

"Please," I said. "What did he do? Tell me what happened eighteen years ago."

He shook his head. "I will not speak of it. For that account, you must appeal to Kai."

"Then take me to him." I was filled with urgency, suddenly convinced that Gate's story would help me understand my own.

"Are you certain you are ready?" Echo asked. "Will you restrain yourself to hear what he would say, or is there a probability of you striking him again? Can you promise you will do him no harm?" There was genuine concern in Echo's eyes.

"You can't be serious," I said, huffing. "You've seen Malakai, right? You know he's got at least a hundred pounds on me. Cut me some slack. I got a lucky punch in."

Echo stared at me, waiting.

"Okay, I promise," I said.

"Good," he responded, getting to his feet with effort. "Follow me, then." He made his way to the firmer sand at the water's edge and began walking along it towards the cliffs.

✳ ✳ ✳

Echo informed me that the Mederium, where Malakai had gone, was at the top of the cliffs. We trekked along the beach for what felt like hours, but the rock face did not seem to get any closer.

It occurred to me that if Malakai had made this same journey to the cliffs, he had either done it with great speed or had a substantial head start because he was not visible in the distance.

"How long was I out, Echo?" I asked.

He shot me a knowing look. "Much less time than expected. The serum typically affects people for a half-day or more. You were under its influence for less than twenty minutes. Kai asked me to keep an eye on you, but it was his intention to return to you before you awoke. I knew I should have told him to wait. It was only a matter of time before your second gift began developing."

I stopped walking. "My second gift?"

"Knowing the lives and gifts of others is *my* gift," he said to me for a second time.

"Then can you tell me more about mine?" I asked. "What are they supposed to do?"

"They are still taking shape, both your gift of the mind and this, your corporeal gift. They will not be fixed until Activation, so I am disinclined to divulge what I have seen. The gifts may yet change." He smiled at me. "I can tell you this, though: It is rare to have a gift of the mind, and virtually unheard of to have both a gift of the mind *and* a corporeal gift. Protect them well; speak of them to no one."

A breeze ruffled my hair and I pushed the loose strands from my face. "You will protect them too?"

"An Essen's gifts are personal. I only discuss them if asked, and only with the individual to whom they belong. I would never tell Kai or anyone else what I have seen of your gifts, nor would I share with you the nature of theirs."

We continued along the beach making our way north. Gradually, the sand became grainier and small stones dotted the shoreline. As the rockiness of the terrain increased, our pace slowed. Echo maneuvered with care but did not appear to grow weary. Still, I became concerned for him.

"Are you okay?" I asked him.

If my question offended him, he did not let on. "I have made this journey many times," he responded. "It is challenging for me, but not overly difficult. In any case, once we reach the cliffs, you will proceed without me. I must remain within range of the Axis, and the Mederium is beyond the acceptable radius. My chief responsibility is and always has been to ensure safe passage across the bridge." Echo clambered between several boulders and then waited for me to do the same. Ahead, the cliffs loomed majestically.

"You can ask me, you know," Echo said. "I can see the questions forming in your mind. You want to know about the bridge—what it is, where it is, how it works."

I nodded, unsettled by Echo's ability to read me.

"The bridge is a bridge," he said. "Nothing more, nothing less. Like all bridges, it serves as a shortcut between two points—in this case, the woods of the East Bank and the beach of Salvos—allowing for travel that would otherwise be impeded. The Wooded Bridge is similar to a drawbridge in which access can be permitted or prevented through certain actions, like the lowering or raising of the deck. In the case of our bridge, it can be either open or closed, but in the case of our bridge, it is nearly always closed. I only open it upon request and even then only once I confirm that approach is secure."

"The approach?" I asked.

"The entrance," he replied. "One may cross to the opposite end of the bridge from either side, but extra attention is given to the East Bank approach. I will not open the bridge if non-Essen are present, unless they have been injected with serum, nor will I allow passage if night has fallen."

I thought back to my initial encounter with Malakai. *This is no place for sleeping*, he had said. *Leave. Now!* he'd commanded. "So if non-Essen are present, or if night has fallen..."

"If people are present, it is up to the Essen to scare them away. Once that has been accomplished, I will open the bridge. But if night has fallen... I will not. Opening the bridge becomes too risky once Dothen are about. If an Essen has not crossed by sunset, he or she must resort to the established contingency plan."

We arrived at the base of the cliff, and Echo tilted his head back taking it in.

"What plan?" I asked, staring up at the striated formations. He walked forward, and I followed him towards a narrow opening in the rock face. At the threshold, he turned and looked at me evenly. "What contingency plan, Echo?"

"Retreat," he said. "Retreat to the Riverview Estates, and try to avoid becoming Dothen prey." He pointed through the opening. "This footpath will lead you to a set of stairs. Take them to the top, then follow the trail of Amaranth—small magenta flowers—to the Mederium. There you will find Kai." He inclined his head to me. "Now I must take my leave."

The idea of continuing on without Echo made me nervous, and I hesitated. "Are there others up there? Will Malakai be alone?" The idea of facing Malakai one-on-one gave me jitters.

Echo placed a reassuring hand on my arm. "You need not fear him, Gemma. He is direct and intense and pursues that which he wants, but he means you no harm. As it happens, though, he is not alone. He is with my sister. Go now. The truth awaits."

I thanked him for his help, took a deep breath of ocean air, and, filled with both resolve and timidity, stepped through the opening in the cliff.

CHAPTER 39

The ground beneath my feet was solid, but I had the sensation of float-ing. On both sides of me, craggy walls reached towards the heavens, their striations pointing, it seemed, onward and upward. I followed them forward across a length of narrow, stony floor until, at my right, an expanse of steeply ladder-like stairs stood yawning.

Looking up at them, I became overwhelmed. I was not and had never been an athlete, and this climb would demand everything I had. I mustered my energy, placed my sandaled foot on the first step, and began.

Deprived of my guide, I felt hyperaware of my surroundings. Far above me, wispy clouds swept across the visible slice of blue sky. Hidden from the sun, the stairway was shadowed and chilly. I touched the walls as I ascended, letting their rough and sturdy matter anchor me in the present.

It was surreal. My feet treaded up crumbling white stairs, made of what I thought to be limestone. The smell of the rock, chalky and earthy, brought to mind my father. It wasn't a specific memory; rather it was a simple notion of him, a gentle nudge at the fringe of my consciousness.

The thought of my father, as well as the physical exertion of the climb, took the tension from my chest. My muscles, already loose from the long walk along the beach, fired again and again, contracting with each step, until they began to burn and eventually shake. My breathing was ragged and la-bored, but I didn't stop.

I worked steadily, pushing myself one step at a time. The heart-pumping task required all of my effort, leaving no room for distracted or anxious thoughts. I focused on moving and breathing, moving and breathing, moving and breathing.

The closer I got to the top of the cliff, the faster I climbed. Despite muscle fatigue and just all-around exhaustion from not having slept, despite lack of food, and despite the prospect of being with Malakai once I reached the summit, I was motivated by the idea of finishing.

I clambered over the last step and collapsed, sweating and heaving, onto the path that was lined, as Echo had said it would be, with beautiful purple-red flowers. I let their fragrance wash over me, a heady, musky scent, and closed my eyes. I felt intoxicated: dizzy, dehydrated, and as though my surroundings were distorted.

Lying flat against the cool rock, I spun. I gritted my teeth and waited for the sensation to pass. My thoughts turned, unconsciously, to Jonny. Jonny, my friend; Jonny, my rescuer; Jonny, my hero.

Jonny, my love.

What is love, if not the most humbling of emotions? Who is love, if not he who consumes every thought? Where is love, if not in the mind and body of she who is loyal, she who is committed?

I ached to have him scoop me up and hold me until the spinning stopped. So what if mine wasn't a fervent love? It was love nonetheless. Wasn't I entitled to that? Didn't I deserve to be part of whatever type of love I had the capacity for?

Even as I tried to persuade myself that what I was doing—leading Jonny on, letting him believe I loved him the way he loved me—was justifiable, I knew it wasn't. Jonny deserved more than me, more than this. I pressed my eyes closed but felt the burn of tears that seeped from them anyway. I would have to tell him. When I returned, I would tell him.

I didn't want to get up. I didn't want to see Malakai, or go through more Affliction, or remember that Uncle Dan was really dead. I didn't want to go on into a future where I would have to say goodbye to Jonny.

Somehow, though, I found the strength to stagger to my feet. I did not venture too close to the brink but I peered over the side, watching the whitecaps dance far below. Along the beach, the small dot that was Echo traveled south, illuminated by the descending sun.

If not for Echo's tiny form, already so far away, I would have thought again that I had wandered into a dream. Here, high above the shore, I felt lonely and insignificant, paralyzed by the view. The curve of the earth, covered by ocean, filled my vision. The enormousness of the world was incomprehensible, as was my purpose in it. But purpose there had to be.

There *had* to be. I turned my back to the water, squinted into the light, and followed the Amaranth-lined trail west across the gray-white rock and into a cluster of trees that comprised the outskirt of the forest.

The trees were like none I had ever seen. Their trunks were smooth, covered by waxy-looking bark that was the same color as fresh asparagus. Stemming from their thin branches, veiny leaves sought the sun.

I hiked among them along the gradually descending footpath. The landscape was foreign but friendly, becoming lusher and less severe as I traveled deeper into the woods. As I roamed further from the sea, fluty calls of unseen birds replaced the sound of crashing ocean waves.

Still I followed the flowers until, deep in the territory of the trees, the path disappeared beneath the sea of Amaranth that overtook it. I waded across the bed of flowers, attempting to follow the trail that was now hidden from me. Tiptoeing through them, doing my best to avoid trampling their fragile forms, I noticed two large boulders in the distance, set side by side, like the markers of an entrance. I made my way to them.

Each rock was over ten feet tall and at least half as wide. They were deep, too, forming something rather like a hallway. I walked through.

On the other side of the boulders, a rocky basin dipped into the earth, holding a circular pool of teal water. The pool was wide and undoubtedly deep, judging from the vastly darker center, and it was identical to the one I'd seen in my nightmare. Within it, treading water easily and causing small emerald ripples in the surface, was Malakai.

He had his back to me. Streaks of sunlight shone through overhangs of trees, gleaming on his wet, caramel skin, making it appear as if he were dipped in gold. He shook his head, and diamond-like droplets flew from his short, dark hair. Though most of his body was submerged, his broad shoulders and muscled upper back were visible, flexing and relaxing as he sculled the water.

I stepped forward, watching him. Two lines of words fluttered across his skin as he moved, a tattoo that stretched from his left shoulder, across his traps and the back of his neck, to the right. The letters were large, block-print, and a dark, fern green. *I am the master of my fate, I am the captain of my soul.*

The words rang familiar. They were lines from a poem, but it took me a minute to place them. Then it came to me: *Invictus*, by William Ernest Henley. Jonny had written an essay on it the previous year for one of his lit classes.

Invictus. What did it mean? I tried to remember what Jonny had told me. He had liked the poem, that much I recalled. I crept forward, straining to make out the image beneath the words, and hoping to escape Malakai's notice.

My presence was detected, but not by Malakai. A girl, appearing to be about Echo's age, emerged from behind a boulder on the other side of the pool, and scanned the area where I stood. I froze.

She had an olive complexion, a long plait of black hair, and bottomless brown eyes that were wide and alert but obviously sightless. Still, she knew I was there. Gliding gracefully to the rim of the pool, she sat down, her knee-length lavender sundress billowing slightly as she did. She dangled her legs into the water and said to Malakai, "Gemma does not hate you. I know she told you she does, but there is no hate about her. She is surrounded almost entirely by the greens and blues of fear and sadness." She inclined her head to me. "Hello, Gemma."

Malakai spun in the water, surprise taking over his features. "Gemma!" he said. "You're awake."

Obviously, I retorted silently, wiping my forearm across my head. I felt vulnerable standing there, all dirty and sweaty, with his green eyes on me.

Malakai swam to the edge of the pool and hoisted himself out, his navy board shorts dripping. He reached for a towel that had been flung across the branch of a nearby tree and began to pat himself dry. As he did so, the girl got up from where she was sitting, walked the perimeter of the pool, and stood in front of me.

"Echo told me about you." Her voice was like honey.

"Echo is... your brother?" I asked, keeping an eye on Malakai.

"Echo is my twin," she said matter-of-factly. She stuck out her hand in a formal greeting that mirrored Echo's. "My name is—"

"Eclipse!" Malakai called to her, slinging the towel across his shoulders. "Where'd you put my shoes?"

She smiled apologetically, a rosy flush rising in her cheeks, and darted away into the woods.

Malakai grumbled, a low sound that seemed to vibrate in his chest. "She's forever hiding my stuff. We used to play this game, but now—it's just annoying." He reached for a pack of cigarettes and a matchbook that was tucked in the V of two tree branches. Lighting one, inhaling deeply, he surveyed me. "You look terrible," he said. "All haggard and grimy."

I should have said, *Really? I don't look fantastic after getting stabbed in the neck and drugged? I don't look exceptional after hiking along the beach and up a cliff for miles and miles?* At the time, though, all I said was, "Whatever."

He flicked his cigarette and said, "Echo brought you to the stairs, I take it." The corner of his mouth quirked up a little. It might have been amusement, but I wasn't sure. "Maybe you should have a swim," he suggested. "You know. Refresh yourself." He toed the green-blue water.

"I don't have—"

"You don't need a suit," he said. I could feel the horrified expression taking over my face, and he added, "Don't flatter yourself. I meant you could just wear what you've got on. Rori has other clothes you can change into later."

I glanced longingly at the water, imagining the silky feel as I slid through it. Like the ocean, it called to me, but like the ocean, its power was too great. I sensed magic within it, supernatural properties beyond my understanding. Shaking my head, fearful of what the pool contained, I stepped back.

"Suit yourself, princess." He moved closer to me, and, with mere feet between us, I became embarrassed by the proximity of his half-naked body. I diverted my eyes from his brawny chest and sculpted abs, but it was a mistake. In lowering my gaze, I found myself glimpsing a bulge in his low-riding board shorts, and looked up instead, feeling heat color my neck and face.

Malakai's face was serious, his angular jaw set. Narrowing his eyes, he said in a low voice, "Let's be honest with each other, Gemma. Let's be honest about what we want from one another."

I met his eyes, for the first time noticing that tiny flecks of brown speckled the green. There was no trace of the blow I'd landed. "I already know you want the portens," I said.

"And to claim you for Keeping," he agreed soberly. "And you, what do you want?"

I gritted my teeth, reluctant to admit that I wanted anything from Malakai. Even though I needed information he had, I was resistant to forming any sort of relationship with him.

He smiled tightly. "Don't forget, it was *you* who met *me* at the Wooded Bridge. You came because you wanted something from me, not just to tell me to get lost. So be honest with yourself, if not with me."

I made no reply. *Malakai, he is not to be trusted*, Gate had warned.

He took another drag from his cigarette and said, "They say quiet people have the busiest minds." When even that didn't elicit a response from me, he said, "Do you have it with you? The portens?"

"No," I said. "It is hidden. Tucked away. Safe."

Malakai didn't bother to veil his skepticism. "If I possessed something that precious"—his eyes wandered down to the amber ring on his right hand—"I'd keep it with me at all times." He paused, staring at me. Then: "Tell me what you want, Gemma."

He wasn't going to let it drop. "Alright," I said, getting agitated. "You know what I want? I want to *understand*. I want to know who the Essen and the Dothen *really* are, who *you* really are, and Echo, and Eclipse, and Phoenix, and *Gate*! I want to know what happened to Gate, where he is. I want to know what happened eighteen years ago too, what he did that was so horrible, all of it." I felt my throat constricting as emotion crept into my words. Malakai opened his mouth to speak, but I cut him off, my thoughts gathering momentum. "I want to know what my part is in all of this, why I am the way I am, and why my uncle had to die." Angry tears gathered in my eyes and threatened to fall, but I continued. "Why did he have to die? Why do any of us have to die? Why are we being hunted? *That's* what I want," I pleaded in spite of myself. "I want to know *why*."

Malakai's expression remained stony and unsympathetic, but his tone lost its patronizing edge as he said, "Then you want to know about the *Pactem Orbis*. The so-called 'Covenant of the World.' You want the context, the reasons, the legends." His eyes swept to the left where Eclipse was returning with his shoes. "Fine. But know this: they're only legends. The truth is lost somewhere among them, distorted by time and the omissions and exaggerations of Record-keepers." He accepted his sandals from the girl, slipped them on, and said, "Thanks, kid." Then he walked to the other side of the pool, past the boulder and into the trees, and called back to me, "You coming or what?"

CHAPTER 40

Malakai didn't stop to wait for me, and I had to jog to catch up. The path was narrow, allowing only for single-file movement, so I had the misfortune of staring at his brawny, tattooed back as we walked. His huge frame and the dense bushes through which the path ran blocked my view of what might lie ahead, leaving me with little to do but examine Malakai's ink.

The image that had been drawn on Malakai's even, golden-brown skin, the one I hadn't been able to make out when he was in the pool, was that of an immense deciduous tree. The base of the trunk began at his hips and grew up his back, culminating in a canopy that extended across both shoulder blades. The level of detail in the tattoo was incredible. The breadth of the roots, the coarseness of the bark, the serration of the leaves—they were all depicted with the greatest of precision. It was truly a work of art, and I would have admired it if its beauty had not been marred by the inclusion of one other element: a giant axe lodged in the core of the trunk.

The blade of the axe was disproportionately large and imbedded in what I imagined was the tree's central nervous system. Fluid resembling blood streamed from the tree's wound, giving the design a macabre effect. I shuddered at its violent symbolism.

Paired with the disturbing image, the words *I am the master of my fate, I am the captain of my soul* troubled me. What did he mean by it?

Clearing my throat, I said in what I hoped was a casual, semi-interested tone, "I never figured you to be a poetry kind of person."

Without so much as a glance back at me, he replied, "And I never figured you to be a Link kind of person. But here I am with poetry on my back, and there you are with the mark of the Link on your wrist."

His response, really more of a jab than anything, shut me down. I continued to follow him but focused my attention on the bushes to my right and left rather than on him.

They were laden with small scarlet berries that looked like miniature cherries. Upon seeing them, as if on cue, my stomach growled. My mouth suddenly felt parched as well. I plucked a berry from the bush as we walked, motivated by hunger and thirst, intending to determine its edibility.

Hearing the *snap* of the bush as it released the fruit, Malakai whirled around, dropping his cigarette to the ground, and swatted the berry from my hands. He rubbed my fingers vigorously between his, as if to rid my skin of any remnant of berry juice.

His fingertips and palms were rough, and so was his touch. He turned my hands over inspecting them, and, satisfied that they appeared to be okay, dropped them unceremoniously. "The first thing I need to teach you once I'm your Keeper is how to not be a putz."

"I wasn't going to eat it!" I insisted. "I was just—"

"It's poisonous," he said. "The skin, the juice, all of it. If you hold one too long, the natural acids from the Necis berry will seep into your flesh and burn it away, down to the bone. Don't. Touch. Them."

"Well thanks for telling me," I said, indignant.

"I just did." He turned from me and began along the path again.

"At least tell me where we're going," I demanded. "I'm beat. I can't do another hike. I need food, water." I hadn't wanted Malakai to see further weakness in me, but my thirst was almost unbearable.

"You can make it," he said dispassionately. "We're almost there—the Aerarium. You can get something to drink from Phoenix when we arrive."

I had no choice but to simply march on, following the bleeding tree.

Olfaction is tied more closely to memory than any other of the human senses. Scientists believe the proximity of the olfactory nerve to the amygdala, the area of the brain that is connected to the experience of emotion as well as emotional memory, helps explain why. In fact, they are distanced by a mere two synapses (the regions in the brain where nerve impulses are transmitted). Additionally, only three synapses separate the olfactory nerve from the hippocampus, which is responsible for associative learning.

Research studies have concluded that when these areas of the brain responsible for memory are damaged, an individual's ability to identify smells is typically impacted as well. This is because one must remember having smelled a scent before—in connection with visual information that occurred at the same time—in order to associate a scent with an object.

So "The Day of the Bouquet," as it later became known, was momentous. Only nine days after the accident that killed my father, I awoke to the scent of roses. I could smell them but not see them. Stuck in the bed of my charming gray-white hospital room, I rang for a nurse. When he arrived, I asked him where the roses were.

"You can smell them? You know what they are?" he asked, lowering the flowers from the shelf behind my bed. His surprise gave way to excitement and soon the discovery, which seemed to enthuse all of my medical staff equally, inspired a revised memory-recovery treatment plan.

Thereafter, as part of the ongoing therapy designed to rehabilitate me from the accident, I spent thirty minutes each day with a specialist who exposed me to an assortment of scents, each in isolation, in hopes that I would be able to both identify the scent and remember a circumstance in which I'd encountered it before. During these sessions, aromas would waft towards me via a small fan. They were common scents, like mint, cinnamon, orange, and pine, and in most cases, I knew them. I was never able to determine from where, though.

It was my lack of success in those sessions, as well as in my other treatments, that I suppose led to the prognosis that my memory impairment was permanent. Nothing, not even my mysteriously unharmed sense of smell, had sparked a memory. Until now.

The whiff caught me off guard and I halted. The fragrance was unmistakable. *Cedar.* Though the woodsy scent was one I'd encountered on many occasions since "The Day of the Bouquet," it was this time, lumbering along behind Malakai, that triggered the memory.

Perhaps my work with Gate had somehow made my mind more malleable, enabling memories, to use his words, to "float more easily to the surface." Regardless, it was the first time I had ever recalled any pre-accident event without Gate's help.

Aunt Sheri opened the cedar chest at the foot of her bed, releasing its distinctive aroma. From it, she lifted a thick handmade quilt and handed it to me. It too smelled like the earthy wood from which it was withdrawn.

"Just lay this over the comforter, sweetie," she said. "It's a cold one tonight."

"Do I have to go to bed now? Can't we do just one more?" I begged.

Aunt Sheri laughed and tossed her head back, her blonde curls bouncing across her shoulders. "Okay, one more. But then you have to go to sleep. Your dad will be back from his trip tomorrow, and I don't want you overtired. He'll think we let you stay up late every night!" She sat down on the bed and motioned for me to sit next to her. "Here you go:

I'm in your future and in your past,
I am very real but rarely last.
In the darkness, I abound
But in the daylight, I'm seldom found.
No one knows why I exist
But until you stir, I persist."

"What does abound mean?" I asked.

"It means there's plenty of something."

I thought for a moment. "Um. Repeat it?"

She did, and then said, "This one stumped me the first time I heard it. Do you need a hint?"

Shaking my head, I said, "I think I know the answer. It's just… it can't be that easy, can it?"

Aunt Sheri raised a perfectly groomed golden eyebrow at me. "Well then. Tell me. And say it boldly. If something is worth stating, it's worth stating with confidence."

"It's dreams," I said trying to convey my certainty in spite of my quiet voice. "That's the answer: dreams."

"Very good," Aunt Sheri said, smiling broadly.

"I like riddles," I said. "They are like my dad's work. The answers are always there, and they always make sense, but sometimes it takes a bit of digging to uncover them."

She gave me a quizzical look. "Did David tell you that? That solving riddles and studying Geology are alike in that way?"

I shrugged. "Well… no. But they're the same, aren't they? Brain teasers?"

Aunt Sheri's crystal blue eyes searched mine. "I love the way your ten-year-old mind works. You are very creative, you know that?"

"What do you mean?" I asked. Her comment confused me. I didn't draw or paint or do anything else artistic; I didn't arrange music or play any instruments; I wasn't particularly imaginative or good at storytelling.

"Creativity isn't just about expression and originality," she said. "It's about how you think, about being able to associate things—seemingly unconnected things—in your mind. …Things like riddles and your father's research." She hugged me. "Your father is a man of adventure, Gemma, no doubt about that. But I have a feeling any discoveries he might make about the world will pale in comparison to the ones you will make. You have a natural talent for both understanding problems and seeing solutions. It's your gift." She stood. "Come now. Time for bed. If you want to stay here again this summer, we need to prove we can manage winter break."

I knew from the stories my aunt and uncle shared that my father had traveled frequently and that I had always stayed with them when he was doing fieldwork. What I had failed to realize, though, was the amount of mothering my aunt had taken on in this arrangement. When I thought of her, I tended to think of her as critical and disapproving, not as loving or affirming. But here she was in my memory praising me and complimenting me.

Of course, I've always been good at puzzles—any and all kinds of puzzles. Her acknowledgment of that was less meaningful than her assessment as to why. Creativity. Seeing beyond the differences of things and pulling out the likenesses. Drawing conclusions after extracting distilled information. Finding common denominators.

Her definition of creativity resonated with me. It implied that I was both investigative and capable. As I trekked along behind Malakai, the memory lent me confidence. This giant in front of me, he was just another riddle. He had clues and an answer. I smiled to myself, suddenly certain that I was resourceful enough and talented enough to solve him. And once I did, I would be able to identify both the problems and the solutions of the rest of my situation as well.

Thank you, Aunt Sheri, I mused.

Malakai stopped abruptly in front of me, and I nearly ran headfirst into his poetry-stamped shoulders. Standing beneath a great stone archway, he announced, "We'll cut through here."

I looked up at the rock. Carved into the stone were the words *Solve et Coagula*. "Latin," I whispered.

"Yes," Malakai responded. "It means dissolve and coagulate. Break down and solidify. Destroy and recreate. However you want to think of it. It was the motto of the Fathers." He walked through the entrance.

Together, the impressive structure and the arcane phrase were awe-inspiring. Standing beneath the archway, I felt as though ancient history was somehow meeting me in the present. It was magnificent. It was marvelous. It was *nothing* compared to the majesty I beheld upon crossing the threshold.

CHAPTER 41

I stepped through the archway and into a glorious and expansive nature-made chamber. Slabs of stone jutted from the earth creating walls and corridors; canopies of trees provided a sheltering ceiling. Under my feet, the earth itself was flat and even, as though each extraneous rock had been plucked from the ground and relocated, and the remaining dirt treaded upon uniformly for centuries.

More striking than the chamber itself, though, was the room's adornments. Fastened to the surfaces of the stone walls were hundreds or perhaps thousands of tablets, green glass tablets, each measuring approximately one square foot. They lined the walls, rows upon rows of them, all of them with beveled edges, causing me to question whether I'd slipped into the interior of a perfectly faceted and enormous emerald.

"What is this place?" I wondered breathlessly. Stray beams of light penetrated the leafy ceiling, spotlighting random tablets. I was mesmerized. I ran my fingers across the surface of one of the tablets. It was etched with foreign letters and symbols. Greek, maybe.

"We are in the Tabularium," Malakai said from behind me. "The Hall of Tablets. The Archives. It has many names, but it is and has always been the workplace of the Record-keepers."

I turned to face him. "What are they Records of?"

"Essen exploits. Augur prophecies. Myths, legends. Some actual history, I assume."

"You assume?"

"Well I can only account for the English Records. I don't read Latin, Greek, Aramaic, Italian, or any of the other languages in which the Records have been written over the millennia. Do you? I didn't think so. None of the living Essen can read them. Maybe at one time we were a race of scholars, but now… Those of us that are left are less concerned with learning about history and more concerned with making it."

"What do you mean?" I asked. "These tablets could contain information, valuable clues—"

"You see those Records?" Malakai pointed to the end of the chamber, at a wall perpendicular to the one I'd been admiring. "Those are the 641 Records that have been written in English. Less than half of them are what I would consider *modern* English. And every single one of them is in verse. They are cryptic, coded, and confusing. Like every Essen, I have spent *my life* trying to glean meaning from those Records. Which, I'm sorry to say, has been enlightening about four percent of the time and either frustrating or dull the rest. So don't waltz in here, *princess*, and try to convince me that I need to learn the other eleven languages the Records have been written in so that I can die trying to make sense of the other 2,987 tablets." He peered up at the sky. "Come on. We have less than an hour until the Host starts to arrive."

He led me through the Tabularium in what felt like both a random and deliberate manner. The chamber was a labyrinth, and we weaved around the smooth rock walls until I was no longer certain from which direction we'd entered. As we walked, I couldn't take my eyes off the walls, so bejeweled were they. The beauty of them, but also the depth of history they represented, amazed me.

And then we arrived at a dead end. The stone slab in front of us was taller than the others, seemingly the perimeter of the space. "Now what?" I asked.

Malakai ignored my question and moved to the wall. Then he turned to the right and slid behind it disappearing from view.

Bewildered, I hurried forward. Drawing nearer, I realized that what had appeared to be a dead end was in fact two overlapping walls. I slipped between them and hastened after Malakai, finding him nearby, his gaze transfixed at an opening in the earth.

The cave's entrance, nothing more than a wide and rocky hole in the ground, flickered with an amber radiance. I peered into the pit, noting the wooden ladder that clung to its side. Far below, I reasoned, was a well-lit cavern.

"Ladies first," said Malakai.

"Not on your life," I replied.

He rolled his eyes and lowered himself into the hole, the tree on his back arching and bowing as he moved, as though it were being tossed about by an unseen tornado.

"Wait," I said. "What's down there?"

He squinted up at me. "All of my favorite things." He began climbing down the ladder, and then paused to look up at me again. "Oh, and Phoenix." Then he continued his descent.

I briefly lingered there at the surface before muttering a curse and placing my foot on the first rung of the ladder. Down I went, twenty feet, thirty feet, forty, the golden glow growing brighter until my foot found a solid platform rather than wood.

It was a massive cavern indeed, illuminated by cylindrical vials of blazing yellow-orange liquid that were fixed to the walls as torches might have been in days gone by. The walls themselves were golden, as were the floor and ceiling, and gilded shelves lined them. Every surface reflected the warm light, and I had to shield my eyes from the brightness.

When my eyes adjusted, I saw that the shelves were crammed with objects of two varieties: flasks and bottles of every shape and size, filled to the brims with mysterious fluids, and mounds of shiny metal bars, stacked haphazardly.

I gasped and snatched a gold brick from the top of one of the piles. "Malakai!" I exclaimed, scanning the enormous room for him. "Are these solid? Are these real?"

He was rushing into the deepest part of the cavern. "You've got to be kidding me!" he said. "No. No, no, no, no. No! Not today!" He darted to an elevated working table—one that had a large ceramic bowl, like a water bath, resting in its surface—and bent down. Only then did I see the pathetic figure of a man slumped on the ground against the table leg.

"Wake up, you asshole!" Malakai yelled, shaking the man's shoulders. His head rolled on his neck, but he did not awaken. Malakai swore under his breath and released the man, letting him fall against the cavern wall. He stood up and leaned over the table, placing a finger into the bowl of liquid in its center. Licking his finger, he swore, shoved the lifeless man's body, swore again, and began rummaging through the bottles and flasks on the shelf nearest him.

I gingerly set the bar back in its place and maintained what I hoped was a safe distance. Malakai was obviously pissed off, and I didn't want to say or do anything that might further provoke him.

He continued combing the shelves, pushing bottles aside, examining others, becoming increasingly agitated until, after several minutes, he found what he was looking for. Taking the blue bottle from the shelf, he held it up to read the markings, withdrew the cork, and poured its contents into a clear beaker that was sitting on the table.

The liquid was brown and dull, like a flat cola. He took a swig and then brought the beaker to me. "The *Consociare*," he said, placing it in my hand.

Parched as I was, I hesitated. "What is it?"

"The *Consociare*," he repeated. "That's what it's called."

I sniffed at the fluid, and it burned my nostrils. "Alcohol?"

"There might be a little something in there," he said, "for preservation or whatever. But it's mostly syrup concocted from various plants' juices. It's a rejuvenation elixir." He glanced towards the man on the floor who was still motionless. "Drink it."

I lifted the glass to my lips. The elixir tasted both gritty and spicy.

"Stop!" a voice shrieked from behind me. Rori leapt from the ladder, skipping the last few rungs, landing lightly on the platform. She flew across the room to me and knocked the beaker out of my hand. It shattered on the cavern floor, splashing my legs with brown liquid.

I raised my arms in defense, fearing another attack. She grabbed my wrist and held it in front of Malakai. "What *is* this, Kai? What the hell is *this*, you jerk? You rotten, selfish *liar!* You told me she was Affiliation Terran!"

Kai stepped forward, prying my wrist from Rori's grasp. "Yeah, well, it appears that someone else told you otherwise. Thanks a lot, mate," he said to the man coming down the ladder.

"What?" Taeo said, shaking his brown ponytail. "You made me swear not to tell anyone until we got her to Salvos. We're here, dude." He hopped from the last rung. "And that woman"—he winked playfully at Rori—"is a fireball. A vixen. She's wily. I didn't have much choice."

Rori glared at him. "You are *not* off the hook, Mattaeo Fide. Don't you dare play the hero, like telling me now, *months* after you yourself found out, is okay. I'm your *girlfr*—"

"Rori," Malakai interrupted, his voice low and calm. "It's done already."

"No." she said. "No, I don't believe you. She didn't drink any." Rori narrowed her eyes at me. "You didn't swallow any of that elixir, did you?"

I stammered.

"Did you drink any or not?" she demanded.

"I did," I said.

"Did Kai drink first? Well, did he?"

"Yes," I said. It came out as a plea.

Malakai smirked. "Done and done, Rori."

Rori threw up her arms in disgust. "Well congratu-fucking-lations then. Don't get her killed, you careless jackass."

Taeo touched her shoulder. "Enough with the name-calling, Rori. You may be my girl, but Kai is my best friend. Besides, who else believed the Link existed? Who else trusted enough to keep looking? Only Kai." He tipped his head to me. "She may not *solely* be Affiliation Terran, but she is in part, and as far as I'm concerned, she's always been his to Keep."

"But he had no right," Rori argued, somewhat subdued, her attention now on the man heaped in the corner. "He stole the elixir. He obviously wasn't awarded it. And the girl—he didn't even give her a choice." Her brows knitted in concern as she once again faced Taeo. Her expression made me feel anxious.

"A choice?" I asked. "What choice?"

Rori pitied me, I could see it in her eyes. "A choice in your union," she said. "In the matter of your binding." She shook her head. "But now it's done. Malakai's your Keeper, you're his Kept. That's what the elixir does. Until you are Activated, you're bound to him, and he to you. You'll rely on him, and he'll take responsibility for you. He'll care for you and keep you safe, like he cares for himself and keeps himself safe." She snorted. "That's the kicker, though, isn't it?"

Malakai met Taeo's eyes and pursed his lips. Then he grabbed the blue bottle from the table, stoppered it, and placed it back on the shelf.

"So…" Taeo began, eyeing the man slumped against the table leg. "You couldn't have, ya know, gotten approval. You just…?"

"Yes," Malakai said. "I just. I couldn't ask permission, so I'll have to ask forgiveness." He nudged the sleeping man with his foot. "If he ever comes around."

"What's he on?" Taeo asked.

"Some potent shit," Malakai said, dipping his finger into the concave center of table once more. His lips curled up into a mischievous grin. "Want some?"

"All of Phoenix's stuff is potent," Rori muttered. "That's why he's spent half his life unconscious." She yanked Taeo's hand as he stepped forward. "Don't even think about it."

"Naw, man," Taeo said. "Maybe later. You up for catching a wave or two tonight?" He slung his arm over Rori's shoulder and steered her to the ladder.

"Yeah, alright," Kai said.

Rori started climbing. After she had disappeared from view, Taeo lowered his voice and said, "Bring the sauce. I'm in." Then he chased after her.

It was the first time I'd seen Malakai look truly pleased.

CHAPTER 42

I wasn't drunk or high after drinking the elixir, but I was definitely affected. It hit me sometime after Rori and Taeo exited the cavern. My vision became spotty and my heart raced. Beads of sweat formed on my skin.

Was it a reaction to the elixir? Or were exhaustion, dehydration, and shock finally taking their toll on my body? At some point, Malakai noticed my condition and gave me a flask of water and a granola bar. I ate and I drank, but still the world went black.

Shades of dark blue filled my vision. I shifted on the mattress and blinked into the night. A full moon, visible through the sheer material of the tent, cast eerie shadows that deepened the blue to black in places.

I sat up. The tent was big, containing two full-sized beds, and high-ceilinged, with long wooden posts over which the fabric screen hung. Across from me, sleeping soundly, was Flash.

Next to my bed, on an ornately carved table, was a vase of glowing flowers identical to the ones I'd been given the week before. A glass of water was there also, and a small dish filled with nuts and dried fruit.

Without a watch or my cell phone, which I realized was still in my coat pocket back in Echo's cabin on the beach, I had to guess at the time. The evenness of the sky's inky color, the position of the moon high above me,

200

and the presence of so many glittering stars, made me believe it was after midnight. But even if it wasn't that late, I knew I'd been out for hours.

When Flash and I had left the house that morning, we had done so without explanation. No one knew where we were going or when to expect us back. Aunt Sheri and Jonny were both undoubtedly worried. I needed to send them messages.

Flash's phone wasn't in his coat or on the table next to him. I rolled him over, muttering for him to stay asleep, and reached into the pocket of his jeans. Bingo. I withdrew his phone, but too late. His eyes fluttered open.

"Gemma?" he said.

"Shh," I said. "Go back to sleep."

"Where are we? Why did you take my phone?" He raised his head; his blonde-blue hair was flattened to his scalp.

"We're at a party," I said. "You had too much to drink. My phone is dead, so I'm using yours to call for a ride home."

This he seemed to find plausible. He put his head back on the pillow and closed his eyes. I stood still, waiting. When he didn't move again, I stole from the tent.

It was uncannily quiet. Scores of tents, similar to the one I'd been in, stretched across the wooded camp. The lightweight fabrics—chiffon, lace, silks, and sheer crepes—afforded little privacy, and through them I could discern the silhouettes of dozens of sleeping Essen.

I held up Flash's phone, trying for a signal. Nothing. Tiptoeing between the tents, hoping to achieve at least a few bars, I heard it: *the ocean*. Its voice was rhythmic, alluring; it tempted me to enter the water.

Compelled to answer its call, I wandered through the sleeping quarters, or the Somnus as Echo had called it, and onto the beach.

My breath caught.

The cove onto which I'd stumbled was less an inlet of the sea and more a treasury of the earth. Swaying on the surface of the water, filling the entire circular recess, were innumerable flower heads, their white and blue petals radiating purple light into the darkness.

The forest from which I'd emerged was not to be outdone. Crooked pinstripes of fluorescent green painted the trees, giving them an incredible strobe-like appearance.

"There's really nothing like it, is there?"

I recognized Rori's smoky voice at once, though I didn't immediately see her.

"It's the best light show nature has to offer." She got up from her place in the sand, throwing off the shadows that hid her. "I could stare at it all night."

She approached me, her movements steady and graceful. "We call the flowers 'Supernovas' because of their brightness, but the Records name them 'Salubris.' They are said to be the Merlas' answer to their sisters' Amaranths. But that, like the *Pactem Orbis*, is mythology. The real reason they glow is simple science. Bioluminescence. A chemical reaction in the flowers releases energy in the form of UV rays."

"And the trees?" I asked. "Also bioluminescence?"

"Oh no," she said. "They have a splendor of their own." She moved to the nearest tree and motioned me to join her. "These green streaks are just the tree's sap. It's clear in normal circumstances, but it does contain something called green fluorescent protein. It fluoresces when exposed to ultraviolet light."

"So without the flowers…"

"We wouldn't see the sap."

Rori turned back to the water. "But the flowers and the tree sap have properties more spectacular than their ability to glow," she said. "As I'm sure you already know."

"What do you mean?"

Her answer held a hint of skepticism. "Taeo told me he delivered Supernovas to you last week. So you know they take away the pain of Affliction. Or didn't you notice the difference? And the tree sap, didn't that come up when he told you about the legends?"

She meant Malakai. She practically spat the word *he*.

"He hasn't—"

"The tree sap," Rori interrupted, her obvious distaste for Malakai spurring her on, "is an excellent sealant. It's not even noticeable when it dries and hardens. We apply it to a ton of things, to protect them from the elements. In the beginning, though, it was used differently. It was applied in a thin coat to repositories of energy, to contain it. At least, that's the lore. I'm not sure I buy it, because the sealant dissolves easily enough in saltwater, so—" She stopped abruptly, alarmed by the look on my face. "Are you okay?"

I was not okay. I was charged with excitement by the puzzle piece that had just clicked into place. "What time is it?" I asked. "When can I cross the bridge? When can I go home?"

"Echo opens the bridge when the sun has risen on the other end. Just before 8 AM your time, 10 AM here. That's about nine hours from now. Why? What's wrong?"

"My aunt and my boyfriend"—Rori's eyebrows shot up on the word boyfriend—"don't know I'm here," I said. I held up Flash's cell phone. "I was going to text them so they wouldn't worry, but I don't have any signal."

"You wouldn't," Rori said. "Too much supernatural interference. You'll need a new phone, one built to work on Salvos. One like mine," she pulled it from her back pocket. "Here, go ahead."

Thanking her, I began typing messages to Aunt Sheri and Jonny. But my mind was already elsewhere. It was at home in my bedroom, preparing to dissolve the sealant from my boulder opal.

CHAPTER 43

Nature, not the sea, was calling now, and that was a call I had to answer immediately.

Rori and I backtracked through the woods until we came out on a different beach, one bare before the ocean, one unprotected from the savage surf. She pointed out the shack that served as the facilities, and I went there straightaway.

When I came out, Rori was sitting on a broad platform at the shoreline watching the tiny forms of far-off surfers as they carved moonlit waves. Even in the low light of nighttime, even at a distance, the muscle tone of her body was visible. She looked tough, solid. Yet strands of coppery hair, lifted by the salty breeze, danced on her shoulders, softening her appearance. She was untamed but beautiful, strong and self-sufficient but feminine. I felt a twinge of envy.

I waded through the sand and sat down next to her on what turned out to be the broad stump of a felled tree. At one time, the tree must have stood several stories high; its base was yards across.

It didn't make sense to me, a colossal tree growing companionless on the beach, but then, I supposed, neither did bioluminescent flowers and fluorescent tree sap.

"I'm sorry you weren't well today," Rori said without turning to look at me. "I know how much it sucks, being sick like that. We all do."

I didn't respond. What was there to say?

"Are you feeling better now?" she asked.

"A bit," I said. "At least I'm not seeing spots anymore. Is that stuff I drank... Does it have this effect on everybody?"

She looked confused. "The *Consociare*? No. No, it's doesn't have any effect. Not on anybody. It's one of the few that doesn't. It wasn't the elixir that made you sick. You had an episode."

"Affliction?"

"What else?"

"Ugh," I groaned. "I can't wait for this to all be over."

"No doubt. It was the worst three months of my life." She shot me a sideways glance. "Sorry."

"How did you get through it?"

"Honestly? I worked out. I ran, I swam, I hiked the god-awful cliffs. Everyday, all day. It was the only thing that seemed to help. I don't know why. Maybe it was the release of endorphins, but when I pushed myself physically, the symptoms went away."

"And... everyone else? That's what they did too?"

Rori laughed. "Not remotely. Your boy Malakai out there"—she gestured to one of the riders—"just drank himself to oblivion every night. Got bent out of his mind on Phoenix's painkiller elixirs. And when Taeo started Affliction a month later, Kai got him obliterated too. Let's hope that's not how he 'helps' you."

"They're not...bent... right now, are they?"

"Are you kidding? Malakai is a dolt, but even he isn't *that* stupid. He's irresponsible and daft and I'm pretty sure he would rather die than live, but he's not outright suicidal. And surfing at night, elevated on elixirs, would be suicide. No, they're saving their 'sauce' for later." Her jaw tightened with contempt. "Gemma, I really feel very sorry for you. Malakai, he's got to be the worst Keeper you could have been bound to. He's the only one of us who's lived through *four* Dothen attacks, which might sound impressive except that it means he's put himself in a position where he *could* be attacked *four* times. It's like he *thrives* on it, like it's a game. And okay, fine, if he wants to play it like that, if he thinks he's invincible because of that silly little trinket ring he wears, whatever. But he involves Taeo, he involves him *every time*, and that's what I can't stand." Her eyes landed on her boyfriend as he paddled at the crest of a wave. "He's too good for a best friend like Kai. He deserves better."

She watched him ride across the water, and there was such tenderness—no, *love*—in her expression that I had to ask:

"How did it happen? You and Taeo. I thought the Essen…"

"What? That we don't fall in love, get married, have kids? Of course we do. It's just… different for us. It doesn't happen gradually over time. For those of us called to that path, it's kind of… explosive. It hits us like an anvil from the sky sometime after Activation. It's just dormant until then." A small smile played on her lips as she remembered.

"Taeo claimed me for Keeping. I couldn't understand why. He's a couple years older than me, and Affiliation Arith. He seemed nice enough, though, and he promised to work with me every day, helping me to develop my gifts, so I picked him to Keep me. I grew to trust him. I mean completely and entirely. And then, shortly after my Activation, I saw him, and it was like I'd never seen him before.

"That's what he had hoped for. He had been hoping for it since the day *he* Activated, the day he realized he was in love with me. So it worked out for us. It doesn't always work out, but sometimes… sometimes the Keeper-Kept relationship turns into more. Sometimes that's the Keeper's plan, but sometimes it's just what happens when you are bound to each other for a few months. You can't help but become attached."

I spotted Malakai, all bulk and height, cutting across the water on his board. My stomach dropped.

Rori followed my gaze. "Oh, hey now, Gemma. Don't you worry. I hardly think you and Kai… Well, we both know why he claimed you, and it's not love. He's chasing your portens, not your heart." She sighed. "He made that pretty clear this evening."

Had it been possible for my stomach to sink further, it would have. "What did he do? What happened?"

She winced. "He basically promised the Essen… Well, he told them the portens was as good as found. He announced it to all of us, the entire Host, Phoenix too, while you were asleep. He said our days of being hunted by the Dothen are nearly over.

"No one believed him, of course. He's gained a reputation in his years of obsessing over the Link. But then Taeo came forward, and Echo. Even I admitted that I'd seen your mark. Soon everyone was treating Kai like some goddamn hero, like he's going to single-handedly take out the Dothen just by using this portens that no one has ever seen. No offense." She looked at her hands. "The thing is, I don't think it can be done. Portens or no portens, I don't think we will ever be free of them. And you know what? I'm okay with that. I have a good life. I'm happy. Yeah there are rules to follow, but aren't there always?"

I tried to keep the skepticism out of my voice. "That's not how most Essen feel though, is it? *They* aren't happy with the way things are, are they?" I felt more like them than like Rori. How could I make peace with a life of persecution? A half-life filled with nocturnal enemies who would hunt me forever?

Rori shook her head. "No. Most of them are scared or angry or both. And now that they know you, the Link, are real… they will be impatient. I'm worried. If you can't or won't help them in a relatively short timeframe, I fear they will turn on you."

"Who will?" I asked.

She shrugged. "Whoever's left."

The Host, Rori told me, consisted of ninety-three Essen. Ninety-three Essen, broken into four sects, called Affiliations: Terran, Iro, Merla, and Arith. Each Essen was marked with the notae of his or her Affiliation, always on the inside of the right arm. Rori's notae, a reddish-brown circle sitting snugly within a diamond, sat in the crook of her elbow. "Affiliation Iro," she said.

My notae was an anomaly because it combined all four Affiliations' symbols into one 'comprehensive' mark. Something like it had never been seen before, and though Record 3628 referenced its existence, most of the Essen didn't expect it to be revealed in their lifetime, if at all. Its placement on a human was never even considered. According to Rori, even the children produced by parents of differing Affiliations were born with the mark of only one of their parents.

Affiliations, she told me, were of greater importance in the days when the Host numbered in the thousands. In present times, however, given the ever-diminishing size of group, there was little-to-no distinction between the sects, except in matters of Keeping.

Though it wasn't strictly followed—Rori herself was Kept by Taeo, an Affiliation Arith, after all—it was generally accepted that undergoing Essen be claimed by Keepers of their own Affiliation. The reasons for this were many, not least among them was a better understanding of the undergoing's developing gifts, which tended to be similar between Affiliation members. Since I bore the notae of all Affiliations, I could technically have been claimed by, and could have selected as my Keeper, anyone within the Host.

"You should have had a choice, you know," Rori said, completely fired up. She flung herself across the top of the tree stump and stared at the endless glittering sky. "You should have been brought to Phoenix, because that's what's supposed to happen with the undergoing, and then Phoenix would have presented you to the Host, asking who would claim you. Then, if multiple Keepers came forward, you would have been asked which person you wanted as your Keeper. After that, Phoenix would have *awarded* the *Consociare* to you as a pair.

"It's so wrong, the way it happened. Kai must've known you wouldn't pick him. He couldn't bear the thought of someone else claiming you and beating him to the portens—and the glory.

"Hell, I would have claimed you myself—and I'm pretty sure I'm the only one who doesn't give a damn about the portens—but Malakai told me you were Affiliation Terran, and even though you don't look it, I believed him. And Taeo and The Anchored Set, the only three other people who knew otherwise, never told me the truth."

"The Anchored Set?" I asked.

"Echo and Eclipse," she said. "Those freaky-ass twins."

"That's not very nice," I said quietly.

"What?" she said. "I can't help it. They creep me out."

At least she was honest. "Why? They're just kids."

"Well, sure, that's what they look like. I guess that's what I'd think too if I'd just met them. But they're not."

"They're not what? Kids?" The notion was ludicrous.

Rori sat up. In the moonlight, I saw myself reflected in her dark brown eyes. "How old do you think they are?" she asked.

"I dunno. Ten or eleven maybe."

"Exactly. That's what I thought when they first came to us." She leaned in, lowering her voice. "*Six years ago.*"

"What, you mean—"

"They don't seem to age. But even aside from that, they're strange. You've spoken to them. They don't talk like children, they know too much. And their marks are incomplete. They each have a circle as their notae, a black circle, but nothing more. No mother symbol, no Affiliation."

Rori's gaze floated skywards, as if the mystery of the twins was somehow connected to the mystery of the cosmos.

"It was Malakai who found them," she said. "When he was seventeen. Then, like now, Echo was crippled and Eclipse was blind. Kai said they were disoriented and terrified, holding tight to each other's hands as they wandered through the forest. He asked them who they were, where they came from, how they got on the island, how they became injured, all that stuff, but the only things they knew were their names, Erec and Eren Medeis, and that they were twins.

"Before he did anything else, he brought them to the Mederium. Believing the pool would heal their conditions, he carried both children into the water and swam with them. It was a decent thing to do—the only decent thing he's ever done, as far as I can tell—but it didn't work.

"So, he brought them to Phoenix, and Phoenix made them part of the Host, giving them assignments like he does for the rest of the us. He made Echo the bridge-keeper and Eclipse the Mederium-keeper, because it aligned with their abilities and gifts. And they've been part of our dwindling group, as well as Malakai loyalists, ever since." Her attention shifted back to the surfers.

I thought about what she'd told me about Echo and Eclipse, about Malakai, about the flowers and the tree sap, about everything. It was all too much for my overloaded mind to comprehend. *But they're just riddles*, I told myself. *Riddles that can be solved—one at a time.*

CHAPTER 44

If not for Rori's company, the night might never have ended. As it was, the hours dragged on, resulting mainly from my desire to get home to work with my boulder opal. But her companionship, and her willingness to talk with me about everything and anything Essen, helped ease my anxiousness.

In spite of her intense dislike for Malakai, or perhaps because of it, I found myself becoming very fond of Rori. We reclined across the top of the tree stump, sharing stories and counting shooting stars. She was waiting for Taeo. I was waiting for morning.

It was still, by Rori's reckoning, a few hours before sunrise when the small group of surfers, five of them in total, waded from the water looking exhausted. In addition to Malakai and Taeo, there was a slender boy with white-blonde hair, a husky carrot-top, and what appeared to be a bald-headed walking tattoo. I'd seen the fair one and the redhead at Riverview Estates the morning of Raela's death. Rori said their names were Ren and Shea, and she introduced "the guy wrapped in art" as Alistair.

They gathered around a fire pit further down the beach, which until then had escaped my notice, and began coaxing flames from it. From somewhere nearby, they withdrew various bottles and began tipping them back.

Rori stood up. "You can come with me, but be prepared for a firestorm of questions if you do. Everyone will want to know about the portens. Hell, I'm sure someone would have woken you to ask about it, but Kai promised to beat anyone who bothered you before morning. I guess that's one benefit of having a brute for a Keeper."

I glanced at the merry-makers next to the fire, celebrating the freedom they believed was imminent. Theirs was a party I felt disinclined to join.

"Uh, I think I'll just…" I motioned in what I thought was the direction of the Somnus.

"Alright, but be careful," she said. "It's tricky navigating the woods at night. All the rocks sticking up randomly and whatnot."

I nodded and headed off, weighing everything Rori had told me. Her words had triggered thoughts, new and exciting thoughts but also frightening thoughts, some of them connected directly to what she had said and some not even loosely so. They swirled within me like spinning galaxies, but from the spiraling chaos emerged two ideas of potentially life-changing significance. My heart pounded with anticipation as I found my way back to the Somnus, grabbed the vase of flowers from my tent, and ventured once more into the night.

I held the flowers up like a torch and walked cautiously between fluorescing trees. Their purplish glow penetrated the darkness in a wide radius, and as I crept forward, it reached into black places and threw off the inky cloaks revealing rocks, trees, and bushes. Though this made it easier—no, possible—to find a path through the woods, it made me feel vulnerable, for I too was without the cloak of darkness.

My arm shook with fatigue and I switched the flowers to my left hand. The vase was large, made of glass or crystal, and it was half-full with water. After carrying it for what was surely an hour or more, it had become very heavy. I wanted to take the flowers out and leave the vase behind, but it wasn't an option. The one blossom I had tried it with had disintegrated the moment its stem left the water.

In the violet circle of light, the landscape grew increasingly rocky. I was getting close. *It's working*, I thought. *I can't believe it's really working.* Feeling a rush of nervous excitement, I pushed on, impelled by the pulse of energy in my gut.

When I'd set out from the tent, I didn't know if I'd be able to find the Mederium on my own, particularly with only the light from the flowers and the moon to guide me. I had no knowledge of the island's size or geography, or even my current position on it. I hadn't been conscious when Malakai brought me to the Somnus, and had I been, I doubt I would have seen more than his tree-covered back anyway. Regardless, I needed to try.

If I had asked, Rori might have shown me the way. It was her account of Malakai's swim with Echo and Eclipse that had sparked the idea, after all. I just wanted directions, though, not an audience, and if I had asked her, she might have become too interested in my purpose. My purpose was personal. I didn't need anyone to witness my attempt, to share in my success or console me in failure.

So I'd gone into the woods by myself, employing the only resources I had: the flowers and my radio. Yes, *that* radio.

Almost a full week had passed since I'd successfully turned off the polished, antique radio, the one Gate had asked me to visualize. I'd felt proud of my work with it, at least until it failed me following Uncle Dan's death and I smashed it against the wall. Since that time, the radio had been reconstructed, but I had pushed it to a tight little corner in the back of my mind and forgot about it. There it remained, a phantom tool in my head, available but abandoned.

The radio was symbolic, of course. It was the simple instrument Gate had chosen to represent my gift, the tangible object he selected to help me grasp the concept of gift "management." I don't think Gate intended me to use it forever. I think he designed the exercise to help me hone my skills, and though I'd originally thought the whole thing was absurd, it had actually worked. I'd been able to turn the radio off, and with it, the brain buzz.

I could *manage* my gift. I had turned it off, and since I could turn it off… Didn't it stand to reason that I would be able to turn it back on? And if I could do *that*, wasn't it likely that I'd be able to find new channels, and eventually, home in on whichever conversational frequency I liked?

Even more exciting than that realization was this one: If an Essen's *gifts* could be managed, couldn't she also manage the *other* aspects of her undergoing? Couldn't she turn off nightmares and dispel or at least minimize the pain of Affliction? Couldn't she turn *on* Gravitation?

Gate had told me, back in our initial meeting, that Gravitation was like a magnet, pulling one forward. He said that the proximity of an Essen to the object emitting the pull and the size of the object were important, but that training was also a factor.

Training.

He had promised to work with me on honing my skills related to Gravitation, too. *During our next session*, he'd said. Truthfully, I hadn't given it much thought, occupied as my mind had been with everything else. But when I did give it thought, when the idea of managing, or maybe even manipulating, Gravitation surfaced—I knew that it, like my Mederium theory, needed to be tested.

It would have been prudent, of course, to wait until daybreak. Navigating anyplace, especially someplace unfamiliar, can be downright dangerous in the dark. But soon the night would vanish, and with it my privacy. This was something I needed to do alone. Besides, I was on to something revelatory. Two ideas, two *theories*, awaited validation. And when has prudence ever preceded revelation?

Feeling like a target centered within the violet ball of light, I had entered the woods warily. Licking my lips, I mustered my energy and called the radio forth, drawing it from the recesses of my mind, and turned it on. Symbolic though it was, it proved to be a suitable device for the work I was doing. With the tuner dial, I explored the frequency band for gravitational 'pulses.' When I felt the rhythm of the Mederium, rapid but faint, I used the volume knob to increase the amplitude.

It was easier than I'd expected it to be, locking onto the Mederium and letting Gravitation bring me forth. It had taken concentration to find it, sure, but once I did, I felt unstoppable. My theory had proven true. Gravitation, like gifts, *could* be managed. Pride surged within me.

In those darkest hours before dawn, creeping ever closer to that mysterious emerald pool, I was afraid. A knot of apprehension formed in my gut and throbbed alongside the gravitational pulse.

I could see them now, the boulders that marked the entrance. The pulsing quickened, confirming I had nearly arrived. I walked between them, holding my breath.

The pool was before me, a rocky basin filled with calm teal water that seemed almost black under the starry sky. Now I would discover if my second theory would prove true. Now I would learn whether the Mederium really did have the ability to heal—perhaps even damaged memories.

CHAPTER 45

The young woman staring back at me did not look hopeful. She looked scared. Though her turquoise-blue eyes held mine in a steady, determined gaze, her body betrayed her. It was the rise and fall of her chest revealing her shallow breathing and the clenching and unclenching of her slender hands that gave her away.

She shook her arms at her sides and flipped her long brown hair over her shoulder. Pursing her lips, she leaned closer, determined to appear confident. She still looked frightened.

Standing at the edge of the pool, I kicked at the water, scattering the image. Before she could form in front of me once more, I stepped away from the rippling surface. I would not let fear make this decision for me.

The Mederium intimidated me. The supernatural energy it contained was almost palpable. But that's not why I hesitated.

For the first time in my life, I wasn't sure I wanted my memory back. If I stepped into the jewel-colored water, and if it healed me like I thought it could, I'd *remember*. I'd remember the happy times and the disappointing ones. I'd know my childhood achievements and frustrations. I'd recall moments of anguish and serenity. In my mind's eye, I'd see my father and maybe even my mother. And, after the initial flood of emotion that came with remembering subsided, I'd *know*.

I'd know who my father really was, not just the stories I'd been told. I'd know where we were going the night of the accident. I'd know if anybody had ever told me about my identity as an Essen or as the Link. I'd find the answers to my current questions, or if not the answers, then at least some clues.

Remembering and *knowing* were potentially wonderful. On the other hand, I'd had eight years to build things up in my mind, eight years to romanticize my father and my childhood. What if they were somehow less than I'd imagined it to be? What if there were horrors in my past that, like the true prognosis of my amnesia, my family had deceived me about? What if, upon unearthing my childhood, I discovered terrible secrets, traumatic or shameful in nature?

I was losing my nerve. I had to stop analyzing the possibilities. The more I thought about the decision, the more fear entered the equation. I was alone at the Mederium. It was now or never.

I scanned the woods carefully before kicking off my sandals and stripping down to my undergarments. In my rush to conceal myself beneath the teal waters, I stumbled over a jagged rock, the sharp point of which sliced my right foot from toe to heel, and fell to the ground.

Lying flat on my back against the rocky earth, my immediate concern was less about the searing pain in the arch of my foot and more about my near-nakedness. Embarrassed by my tumble despite my isolation, I hopped up quickly, bent on hiding myself in the pool.

Bad idea. My injured foot screamed with pain as I landed on it, the cut ripping wider and deeper. I howled in agony. Biting my lip to keep from further yelping or cursing, I sat back down and assessed my wound.

It was a ragged gash, spreading apart the shreds of my serrated flesh. It would be impossible to walk on. By the light of the flowers, which I'd placed against one of the entrance boulders, I found the offending rock and hurled it into the woods in frustration. Then I crawled on my hands and knees to the pool and sat at the edge. Slowly, I lowered my foot into the water.

It was warmer than I'd expected it to be, almost bath-like in temperature, and silky. Upon breaking the surface of the water, my leg stirred up powdery white minerals as fine as talc that clung to my skin and gave the water a milky-green appearance. I circled my foot, watching the pearly clouds swirl around it. When I stopped, the minerals settled on my skin once more.

I had expected my wound to sting as I soaked it. Instead, I felt a pleasant tingling sensation throughout my leg as the chalky particles covered it and wrapped themselves tightly across it like a bandage. Gradually I became aware of increasing pressure on my skin, the gentle touch of the water becoming a tender caress and then a rolling massage.

It was heaven. I dropped my other leg, which had been tucked under me, into the water as well. The opaque substance frosted it too, and I breathed deeply, enjoying the pressure it applied up and down my calves, ankles, and toes. There was nothing like it in any spa on earth, I was sure. Relishing the feeling, I relaxed into the moment, allowing myself to briefly forget my true purpose in coming.

After a time, I brought my legs out of the water and inspected them. The gash on my right foot had been mended, the flesh knitted together beneath a barely perceptible scar. I prodded it with my finger and felt no pain at all. The small scrapes and bruises I'd acquired on my hike up the cliff the previous day were gone too. My legs, glistening with green-blue droplets, looked flawless. *Some pool*, I mused, sliding from the side into the water.

At once the floury minerals collected around me, covering my body. Like thousands of tiny but firm hands, they rubbed the achiness and fatigue from my muscles and smoothed and polished my skin. I had never felt more refreshed, healthy, and whole than I did right then.

Before I could talk myself out of it, I drew in a big breath, sunk beneath the surface, and let the powder settle around my head. The familiar kneading pressure formed around my face, neck, and scalp, and I remained under, luxuriating in the feeling, until I was desperate for air.

I came up blinking water from my eyes. Tiny beads of it sparkled in my lashes, making the rocky basin look bedazzled with rhinestones. I rubbed my eyes and smoothed my hair back from my face, feeling better than I'd ever felt, ever.

…Or at least, it was the best I'd felt in the past eight years. I tried to remember a time beyond that, but the wall that blocked my memory still stood. It hadn't worked. I was disappointed, but not as much as I thought I'd be. Instead, I felt a twinge of relief.

Exhaling fully, I stretched across the water, letting the comforting pressure of the supernatural energy surround me. It was peaceful, lying on my back in the calm pool under the twinkling sky. Had it really been only five days since Uncle Dan's passing? Though my insides still ached with loss, it felt so far away. I tried to imagine my desk at home and the items atop it: the note from Professor Dagenais, the card and the journal from Jonny, my laptop. Now, after spending less than a day on Salvos, *those* were the things that didn't seem real. *Everything* felt far away—the frigid Minnesota air, the sunless days trapped beneath a dome of gray, the slushy waits at the bus stop... *My life* felt far away. As I floated on my back drinking in the stillness of the night, it struck me that the circles of my Venn diagram were also floating further apart. Soon they wouldn't intersect at all. Soon Jonny and I would exist in separate, disconnected worlds. And for the first time, it was an idea I could accept.

Maybe it was the soothing effect of the Mederium, but when I thought of Jonny and I drifting apart, I didn't have the tension in my chest like I normally did. We were on different paths, and that was okay. We would both be okay.

I closed my eyes and sunk into the water, letting it cover my face. The minerals no longer attached themselves to my skin, but I still felt the rolling massage of the pool currents as they stroked my head and body. I could have stayed there forever. I probably would have, except—

"What are you doing? Get out! Get out now!"

Malakai was screaming at me from the edge of the pool, his face twisted and panicked.

Confused and alarmed, I swam hastily to the side and climbed out. "What? What's wrong?" I said, standing dripping in front of him.

The terrified expression on his face transformed into a wicked grin and he looked my body up and down. "Nothing's wrong," he said, circling me. "Not a single thing is wrong." He stopped when he was in front of me once more and thumbed over his shoulder at my clothes. "I just knew you were without those."

"Wha—?" I stammered, feeling the heat rise in my neck and cheeks.

Malakai raised an eyebrow at me. "Hey, just because I'm not interested in *love* doesn't mean I don't like to—"

"Just stop. Stop right there," I said, diving for my clothes. "Don't look at me. Turn around."

Malakai turned lazily away. "Whatever."

I kept my eyes on him as I hurriedly dressed. "Why are you here, anyway?"

"Because I'm your Keeper, and you were hurt or in trouble. I could feel it, just like you'll feel it when it happens to me. Through the elixir, we are bound to one another, compelled to find each other in times of need." He glanced over his shoulder and, seeing I was clothed, faced me. "But by the time I got here, you no longer needed help."

I glared at him. "I cut my foot, that's all, but I'm fine now. So no need to stare at my chest."

"You're chest really isn't all that impressive. Besides, I was looking at your necklace. It's the more interesting of the two. Where did you get it?"

Unconsciously, my hand touched the boulder opal at my throat. "Can't you just go away? I was having a perfectly nice bath until you got here. I don't need your protection."

His green eyes grew serious. "You might have before your swim was done. It's dangerous to use the Mederium at night, without Eclipse to monitor the energies. She's the only one who can read them as they cycle through, and sometimes… Sometimes they aren't as friendly as you found them to be tonight."

He stepped forward and the smell of alcohol wafted towards me. Lowering his voice, he said, "It didn't work, did it?"

"Are you drunk?" I asked, my words colored with disgust.

He smirked. "Probably, but I can't feel it over the elevation. You want some?" He pulled a small, metal flask from the waist of his board shorts and offered it to me. I shook my head and he shrugged. "You're missing out. Anyway, the pool—it healed your foot, but not your memory. Right?"

I nodded.

"That's what I thought. The Mederium only works on certain things. It doesn't cure old injuries, it doesn't help emotional pain, and it doesn't heal most types of deliberate, self-imposed wounds. Thank God for that, or my ink would be all scarred over. Oh, and it doesn't help with any of the stages of undergoing. Actually, amplifies the pains of Affliction or Activation. So yeah, it's just great. Full of restrictions and conditions, like everything we have." Malakai folded his arms across his chest in irritation.

His t-shirt tightened across his popping pectorals. I tore my eyes from them and swallowed. He really was one big dude. How could *anything* think to attack him? He looked indestructible. What had been done to him that he'd been confined to the Mederium for *sixty days*? If the same thing had been done to someone else, would they have survived?

"Rori said… I heard her tell Echo you spend a lot of time here. She seemed to think too much time."

"If you haven't noticed, Rori doesn't like me much," he said flatly. "Of course she thinks I'm here too much. To her, everything I do is wrong."

"But is it true? Are you here a lot? Have you really escaped the Dothen four times?"

He looked at the water, thoughtful. "It's the only time I feel alive."

Was he being deliberately evasive? *When* did he feel most alive—during his close calls with the Dothen or during his recoveries at the Mederium? I opened my mouth to ask, but he cut me off.

"Let's go. It's almost daybreak, and the Host will be looking for you. I need to fill you in before they all find out just how little you know. It's a reflection on me if you remain totally ignorant." Then he walked to the entrance boulders, picked up my vase of flowers, and started off into the woods, just like he had before. At least this time he was wearing a shirt.

CHAPTER 46

I stayed close to Malakai, mainly to keep within the circle of flower-light. "Where are we going?" I asked as we tramped east across the Amaranth-covered trail. "To the cliffs?"

"To the cliffs," he answered without further explanation.

He moved along the ascending footpath swiftly, as if to discourage further conversation. It wasn't until we reached the edge of the forest and found Phoenix passed out atop a flat, gray-white boulder that Malakai spoke again.

"What an asshole," he said, shaking his head.

It *was* a disappointing sight. When Gate first told me about Phoenix, the Augur of the Host, I'd imagined him with a cloak, a crown, and a scepter. He'd sat regal on a golden throne and offered wisdom and direction to the Essen. In my daydreams, I'd knelt before him, presenting myself humbly, seeking his approval. This was not that man.

This man had a crumpled look about him that made him seem older than the forty-something he probably was. His clothes were wrinkled, his graying rust-colored hair was disheveled, and his freckled skin hung slack on his face and body like any muscle he'd once possessed had been magically removed from beneath it. He was snoring, and as he exhaled, I caught a whiff of his scent: a noxious combination of ammonia, orange juice, and body odor. I took a step back, disgusted.

"Our fearless leader," Malakai said, turning his back on Phoenix. "And the first and only Augur to fail at Record-keeping." His deep voice held shame and resignation, in addition to contempt. "Pathetic."

"Why is he... like that?" I said, unable to mask my repulsion.

Malakai started up the path again. "He lost hope, I guess. I don't really know. He's been a junkie as long as I can remember."

"When you say junkie..."

"Yeah, I mean elixirs," he said. "He experiments with new combinations nearly every day. Then he passes out under the stars, elevated beyond the moon, nearly every night."

I bit my lip.

"Don't even think it, Gemma." Malakai stopped and faced me. "I'm not like that. I'm not like *him*. I like to have a good time—and hitting elevation *is* fun, you'll see—but that's it. I'm not like Phoenix." He glanced back at the boulder. "Phoenix is... obsessed. There's nothing in this world for him except his *art*. He doesn't interact with the Host, he doesn't give us Records, and he never leaves the island. He just wants to be left alone to 'work.' But it's at the expense of his actual *job*. He should be having one or two visions each year and recording them on the tablets. Every Augur since 63 AD, when the first Vision was recorded, has given us one or two each year. Every Augur *except* Phoenix. He gave us two—3627 and 3628, the two Gate told me you've seen—right away, and then... nothing. We think it's his overuse of elixirs. No visions, no Records, no direction. We've basically been leaderless since Kerithe died and he became Augur eighteen years ago.

"I used to believe in him," Malakai went on. "I used to believe in him years ago when he told the Host he was on to something big. An invincibility elixir, he said. 'Once I've got it,' he told us, 'we won't need to find the Link. We won't even need the Mederium.' And he basically asked the whole Host to leave him the hell alone so he could focus on his task.

"But creating elixirs, no matter how useful they might be, isn't the Augur's job. The Augur is supposed to use the gift of Foresight, secure visions, and record them. It's the Augur's job to assign keepership based on each Essen's gifts, which we divulge to him in secret after Activation. It's his job to give us guidance... and hope." Malakai's jaw tightened. "It's been a long while since the Host has had any hope."

He began walking toward the top of the cliffs once more and I followed him silently.

It was the most he'd ever said to me at one time. Compelled to convince me he was nothing like Phoenix, he had been real with me. In that moment of realness, when he was so appalled by Phoenix and the thought of being compared to him, Malakai became less of a riddle and more of a human being with actual feelings. He, like all of the other Essen from the sounds of it, was just a person in search of hope.

I took a steadying breath before I voiced my question. "Just how long has it been, Malakai? ...Eighteen years? What happened that shattered everyone's hope?"

Our path flattened as we arrived at the top of the cliff. Malakai set the flowers down and walked to the rocky ledge. He stared out over the water for so long I didn't think he intended to answer me.

"On Salvos," he began, "everyone has a job. It's a task or a person for which we have responsibility. Every Essen is a keeper of something or someone, and every job is important. The Augur, who is technically the Host-keeper as well as our Record-keeper, is responsible for assigning jobs that align with our gifts—which is why we tell him what they are after Activation.

"We have a treasure-keeper, the person responsible for selling our gold, exchanging money, and managing our bank accounts; a pantry-keeper, who keeps our food and water stores full at the Axis; a communication-keeper, who is so gifted with technology that she's built phones to withstand the island's supernatural energy. There's even a closet-keeper to manage the island's bathroom situation.

"Then there are those of us who are Keepers, capital K. We are the Activated Essen responsible for raising the children orphaned by Dothen attacks. We get them to Riverview each morning to meet with their tutors, and we make sure they return to Salvos well before sundown. Right now, there are seventeen of them, ranging in age from four to twenty. All Keepers are responsible for all kids; we don't claim them for personal Keeping until they begin undergoing. There are currently forty-two Keepers, which means we aren't very busy.

"Most of us have two or more jobs. In addition to being a Keeper, I'm also a time-keeper. It means I am responsible for investigating and studying the

Dothen, and for trying to find their weaknesses. The role allows me to cross the bridge at any time, even at night. Taeo and I are the only time-keepers."

Malakai sat down on the edge of the cliff and let his legs dangle over the side. The sky was lightening at the horizon; soon the first rays of daylight would stretch across the sea. I carefully lowered myself next to him.

"The only Essen who don't have jobs are children, those not-yet-Activated. Echo and Eclipse are the sole exceptions, mainly because they aren't like the others. They already have gifts. We call them the Anchored Set because they can't go further from the island than the other side of the bridge. No one knows why. Anyway, they were bored out of their minds. They needed jobs.

"Some Essen take their jobs very seriously. Some, like Phoenix, less so. There are repercussions for failing at your job, of course, ranging from losing the Host's respect to losing your friends to the enemy, but still it happens. That's what happened eighteen years ago, Gemma. Our bridge-keeper left his post to *take a nap*. He overslept, and he wasn't there to open the bridge before sundown. The Dothen got them. We lost thirteen Essen that night, including my parents, and Kerithe, who was the Augur at that time.

"The bridge-keeper was Gate Dorsum. His family was also killed in that attack, including his kids. The Dothen never kill the not-yet-Activated, but Éoin and Jade, they were clinging to Tathra, Gate's wife. When the Dothen depleted her, they died too.

"I was there, on the wrong side of the bridge when it happened, but I don't remember anything of that night. I was only five years old. And I was the only survivor.

"The incident destroyed the Host. Families were shattered, trust was shattered, Gate himself was shattered. We were fragmented, leaderless, and uncertain what to do. And then the gift of Foresight transitioned Phoenix— no one was more surprised than him, I'm told—and he became Kerithe's successor. As the new Augur, he demanded that Gate De-Activate. I think it was a mutual decision. But that was really the only thing he ever did, other than give us Records 3627 and 3628. It was obvious he had no natural talent for leading. The Host fell apart.

"Everyone had loved Kerithe. She was young when she became Augur, only twenty-two, and she'd only been in the role four years before she died, but she was strong and bold and smart and decisive. After her, Phoenix was the ultimate letdown. The right successor could have united us in hope, but not Phoenix. How can someone who is himself too afraid to leave the island inspire hope in others?"

My heart felt heavy. I looked down at my notae, the comprehensive mark of the Link. "And now… you would have them put their hope in me? I know Gate told you I have the portens, but I'm not even sure how to use it."

"I wouldn't have them put their hope in *you*," he said. "I'd have them put their hope in *me*. I found you, didn't I? It was through *my* talents, *my* abilities, and *my* perseverance that you are finally here. And it will be *my* skills, *my* knowledge, and *my* daring that figures out the portens. You just need to give it to me." He flashed me a humorless smile. "Don't worry, princess. If I can't figure it out, I'll give it back to you. And if I can't figure it out, if this one last hope of freedom proves false, I'll finally quit."

He didn't mean he would quit trying. He didn't even mean he'd De-Activate, like Gate had, whatever that meant. If the portens didn't work, if he no longer had any hope—he planned to quit life. The image of his tattooed back floated into my mind. *I'm the master of my fate, I'm the captain of my soul*, it read.

Surprised by the dark nature of his confession, my response came out as a whisper. "Why should I give it to you? Why do you think you're the only one who can figure it out?"

He threw his arms up, and I startled. We were too close to thin air for such sudden movements. "Really, Gemma?" he said. "Come on. No one else has studied the Records to the extent I have. No one. No other Essen understands the risks as well as I do—you know, the *all-who-use-it-shall-abide-effects-that-come-to-pass* business from the vision—and no one else is willing to take those risks. But more than any of that, and I can't stress this enough, there is no one else I trust—except for Taeo, and believe me, he would never want the responsibility of it—to use the portens *for the benefit of us all*."

I said nothing and watched the sun slide up from behind the water. In spite of everything Malakai had told me, my thoughts had settled on Gate. He was no murderer, I was sure. What happened eighteen years ago was a horrible accident, one for which he had undoubtedly suffered the most of anyone. And there was more to the story, there had to be. Why else was he so anxious to find out exactly what Malakai, his nephew and the only survivor of the attack, could remember? What else had happened that night? I clutched my pendant, deep in thought.

Gate was my ally, the one person I could trust. I believed him when he told me he had not killed Raela Celere, but it was no accident she was dead. Someone had framed him. Why? Had they really wanted Raela dead, or did they just want Gate out of the picture and on the run?

"Well," Malakai said impatiently. "Are you going to give me the portens?"

What I needed more than anything was another message from Gate, one explaining *why* he thought Malakai shouldn't be trusted. He was my Keeper. Who else could I turn to for help?

"No," I said quietly. "At least… not yet."

He blinked. "You don't trust me."

"I barely know you, Kai."

A tiny smile played at his lips. "That's the first time you've called me 'Kai' rather than Malakai. Maybe you know me more than you realize."

"I doubt it," I said, feeling a little sheepish.

"So you won't give it to me?" he pressed.

"No," I said.

He searched my eyes. "But you will if I can get you to trust me."

I shook my head, but I think it lacked conviction. If I *could* trust Malakai… Who knew how things might play out?

He sighed heavily, a long and drawn-out exhale. Leaning forward, he squinted into the rising sun, his expression contemplative. He looked statuesque as the brazen beams landed on his golden-brown skin.

Then Malakai pushed off the ledge and dropped from the cliff.

CHAPTER 47

I shrieked and hastily pulled my legs up, scooting back across the rocky surface before jumping to my feet. There I stood, several feet from the edge, paralyzed. Heart racing, I tried to move my feet but they were frozen in place. My shaking hands tightened into fits, and it took everything I had to force myself to inch forward.

Swallowing hard, I peered over the edge.

"You're a jackass, Malakai Zonn!" I screamed at the figure below me. He was standing on a slab of stone that projected out from the cliff and made a wide shelf about ten feet below. I hadn't seen it before because when faced with heights, I never look directly down.

He laughed, which more than doubled my rage. I stomped towards the stairs, fuming.

"Where are you going?" he called up to me.

"Back to the Axis," I hollered back, "to wait for the bridge to open!"

But when I reached the crumbling white stairs, I couldn't bring myself to descend them. I was beyond angry with Malakai, but something held me back. I sat on the top step and seethed.

Eventually I calmed down. Gritting my teeth, I went back to the edge and found Malakai lying on the shelf below, apparently napping. Sensing my presence, one eye popped open.

"I knew you'd be back," he said.

"What are you doing?" I asked, irritated.

"Waiting for you, princess. Climb down." He rolled over to his stomach and did a perfect push-up before getting to his feet.

I folded my arms. "Yeah, right."

"I thought you wanted to *understand*. I thought you wanted to know who the Essen and the Dothen *really* are," he said, mocking me. "If that's really what you want, you need to climb down. Now."

I eyed him suspiciously. "If I do, you'll tell me about… about the *Pactem Orbis*? The so-called 'Covenant of the World?'" I said, quoting him.

"Well I didn't bring you here to romance you with the sunrise, if that's what you were thinking. Climb down." He pointed at some crevices that were supposed to serve as hand- and footholds.

"Why don't you climb back up and tell me up here?"

"Look—it's not that hard." He wedged his foot into one of the cracks and stuck his hands in another, raising himself off the platform. "See?"

"Sure, if you have eight hundred pounds of muscle."

Malakai rolled his eyes. "My God, you're helpless." He climbed higher until his chest was even with the top of the cliff and then held himself away from it. "Lie down on your stomach," he instructed. "Bend at the waist and let your legs come down over the side. I'll get your feet into place, and we'll go from there."

Every fiber in my body quivered with dread as I positioned myself according to Malakai's coaching. Too late did I realize that my rear was basically in his face. I pushed the thought from my mind and focused on keeping my hands and feet where Malakai was placing them. Slowly, we moved down the rock face. His chest pressed against my back, but it only gave me a small amount of comfort. Limb by limb, he guided me lower until finally I felt him step onto the landing. He wrapped his arms around my waist and plucked me from the wall, setting me down in front of him.

Immediately I flattened myself against the rock, arms and legs trembling.

"Nice to see you have nerves of steel," Malakai commented, taking in my condition. "That'll be handy during a Dothen attack."

He began walking along the shelf, which extended north along the cliff for approximately thirty feet. Looking over his shoulder to make sure I was following him, he said, "You have a decent body, but it wouldn't kill you to get stronger, you know."

I ignored this remark and crept along the wall behind him.

"I'm just sayin'. Speed, strength, agility. They could be the difference between life and death." He stopped at the end of the platform and faced me. "You'll need to start training. You're already years behind."

He didn't expand on this. Instead, he felt the surface of the wall and, finding what he was looking for, jammed his fingers into a narrow fissure and slid open a stone door. He moved through it and disappeared into the cliff.

"Watch yourself," he said as I stepped through the opening.

The morning sun flooded the space, which reminded me of an animal den. It was little more than a hollowed out part of the cliff, and its ceiling was so low Malakai had to stoop. There was nothing remarkable about the place at all.

Malakai sat down and leaned against the wall, his legs stretched out before him. "Have a seat, princess. This is gonna take a while."

I was annoyed. "Why are we down here? There's nothing to see. If we're just going to sit around and talk, we could have done that at the top."

Malakai put a finger to his lips and pointed up.

At first, I didn't hear anything. Then—voices. They sounded distant and muffled but became louder and clearer as their owners drew nearer.

"I knew they'd come looking for you," Malakai whispered. "They want to see if you're really the Link. Are you ready to face them all?" When I didn't respond, he clasped his fingers behind his head and said, "You're welcome."

I waited several minutes until I heard the search party move on. "Won't they find us down here?" I asked in hushed tones.

"No. No one knows about this place but me and Taeo. And I suppose now Rori," Kai added irritably, "since he tells her everything these days. Anyway, we found it when we were fourteen and we never told anybody. Salvos isn't all that big—you can walk its perimeter in a day—so privacy is hard to come by. It's our own, and I want to keep it that way." He looked at me pointedly, as if *I* had anybody to tell. "We call it 'the Nest.'"

He closed his eyes for a moment. "Man, I'm beat. I should've joined you in the pool instead of scaring you out of it... It helps," he mumbled in explanation, "but only for a little while. We still need sleep, though less of it. Maybe four hours a day to feel fully refreshed versus eight."

Four hours of sleep, I thought longingly. Even if I had no other reason to visit the Mederium every day, that would be enough. I could do with fewer nightmare-plagued hours each night.

Malakai opened his eyes. As if reading my thoughts, he said, "The dreams will stop when you're a full-fledged supernatural. After Activation."

"When I'm a full-fledged supernatural," I repeated, feeling subdued. I slid down the sidewall and stuck my legs out perpendicular to his. "So I won't be tormented by nightmares anymore, I'll just be hunted by supernatural enemies. Great."

"Don't call them supernatural," Malakai said, green eyes flashing. "That term is reserved for us. The *Essen* are supernatural, above nature. We have gifts outside the scope of natural law. We have access to supernatural resources. We undoubtedly have supernatural origins, though they're probably not as the legends portray them. But our enemies are *not* supernatural. They are the lowest, vilest, basest creatures to inhabit this world. Yes, they are also outside the scope of natural law, but they are *below* it. We are hunted, Gemma, by *sub*natural enemies. Don't ever forget that."

"But what *are* they?" I twisted a few strands of hair between my fingers anxiously.

"They are spirit beings with no physical forms of their own. They exist solely to eradicate Essen, who they believe are *un*natural. They don't see us existing outside of nature... They see us in opposition with it. We go *against* nature, according to the Dothen. We shouldn't exist. And though we keep to ourselves and don't engage with the rest of the world, they see us as a threat. They mean to destroy us, every last one of us. To do so would be to restore natural order. That's what they think."

"So they just... wait? They just wait for Essen to be out after dark? Then they kill us? How?"

Malakai pulled a pack of cigarettes and a book of matches out of the side pocket of his board shorts. "You ever heard the term 'incubus'?"

"Yes..." I said.

"It's not what you think. An incubus isn't a demon rapist that descends upon sleeping women. It's a spirit being that *violates* a human by entering his or her body, displacing the soul. Over time, the definition of incubus became distorted due to the loose translation of *violate* to *rape*. The point is, the Dothen 'take' bodies, filling them up with their own energy and ousting the life-force of the Taken. They can only do this at night; I don't know why. They are the original incubi."

He lit his cigarette and took a drag, letting the smoke out slowly. "From what I can tell, they don't take a body for any reason other than to threaten or kill an Essen, and they only do it if the body is already near or with the Essen. They can't take us directly—maybe we have no souls to displace, who knows—and they can't harm us in their spirit forms, so finding a body is their only option. But I don't think they like being in people. They aren't particularly adept at manipulating the human form, even after doing it for thousands of years, and I think it takes a lot of energy for them to animate otherwise dead flesh. So they allow Gravitation to pull them to an Essen before taking someone. Which is why it's important, if you are on the wrong side of the bridge after hours, to be *alone*. Not just for your safety, but for the sake of those who might otherwise be taken."

"And the Taken…" I began, looking at my hands, "Do they ever survive?" Fresh guilt washed over me as I thought of my uncle. If only I had listened to Echo and stayed in my bedroom. Maybe my door would have been enough of a barrier.

Malakai's voice softened slightly. "The Taken never survive. Once a Dothen takes a body, once a person's soul has left its vessel… they're gone. That person is dead. And when the Dothen vacate the body, they leave it damaged. The death usually ends up looking like a heart attack or a stroke… or a brain aneurysm." He met my eyes. "I'm sorry about your uncle, Gemma. The Dothen don't normally lock on the not-yet-Activated. I hadn't considered that you might be different, that Gravitation might pull them to you more forcefully since you're the Link."

His apology caught me off guard and for the second time that morning, Malakai seemed like a real person. I felt emotion rising in my chest.

Looking away quickly, I asked, "So what happens if they get you?"

Malakai finished his cigarette and pressed it into the floor. "They kill you, but not with weapons or tools. They do it flesh-to-flesh, and it starts with a touch. In that contact, they steal your time. Then they hold on until you're depleted, until your time has literally run out and your body has become dust. If you can break the contact, if you've only been tagged before getting away, then the Mederium can restore you. But… it's difficult to escape. The Dothen are strong. It doesn't matter what body they take, their power isn't of the body. I've seen an adult Essen die at the hands of a Taken child. So my recommendation is to get across the bridge before sundown. And if there's ever a time you can't, you'd better be fast. And strong. And agile."

As he spoke, I realized that my chances of surviving as an Activated Essen were nil if I didn't make it back to Salvos every night. Speed, strength, and agility were not traits I possessed.

Picking at my fingernails, I said, "So… that's why you're the only one who's lived through four Dothen attacks. You're the only one who's strong enough and quick enough to escape after being tagged."

Kai's face was unreadable.

"And suppose I wanted to… you know, improve *my* chances…" My words came out reluctantly. It was humbling acknowledging my deficiencies.

"Then you would need to be fitter," Malakai replied matter-of-factly. "You would need to commit to training. Hard. Everyday. With me."

I tried to keep the suspicion out of my voice. "You want to train with me?"

"I don't *want* to train with you. You're not exactly my ideal workout partner. But I'm your Keeper, remember? I'm responsible for you. It's my job to make sure you're as prepared as possible for life after Activation. It's my *job* to train you. Despite what Rori may have told you when you were talking to her last night, I do take my job seriously."

Malakai's emphasis on the word *job* stung. I had no delusions about our quid pro quo relationship—he wanted the portens and I wanted help with undergoing—but he made no pretense about what an *obligation* I was.

"Yeah, well, you volunteered for this *job*," I snapped. "You made it so no one else could even *apply* for the job. And if you really took it that seriously, I wouldn't still be wondering what the hell the *Pactem Orbis* is, would I?"

"Whoa," Malakai said, holding up his hands. "Easy, princess. I was getting to that." Then he smirked and added, "If you always rile up this easily, I'm going to have a fun couple of months."

CHAPTER 48

I folded my arms. "Well? What is it?"

Malakai swung his legs in and faced me squarely. "The *Pactem Orbis* is a fable. A myth. A story fabricated to explain the circumstances of our existence. It's the starting point, the foundation for all other Essen legends. It means 'Covenant of the World,' and it's the agreement that supposedly resulted in the Essen race.

"I grew up hearing the *Pactem Orbis* legends the way other kids grew up hearing Bible stories. They had Jonah and the Whale, David and Goliath, Noah and the Ark; I had Nalera's Method, Mace and Inra, and Amiah and the Amulet.

"The legends were presented as fact, and like everyone, I believed them. That is, until I got older and noticed one fundamental flaw in the main tale: *motivation.*"

He rubbed at his jawline, which was peppered with stubble. "A covenant only makes sense if both parties have something to gain, if they both stand to benefit from making the agreement. In our story, that's not the case. The advantages are clearly one-sided. Unless I'm missing something, it's unlikely that a covenant was ever formed."

He stopped and tilted his head, listening for sounds above us. Satisfied no one was coming, he went on. "Look, there's probably *some* truth to the stories, and you can decide for yourself what you want to believe, but like I said before, meaning gets distorted when certain details are omitted. And motivation is a pretty key detail, in my opinion. So for me, it's hard to say what parts of the legends are authentic."

In my mind, I saw the Tabularium, its walls lined with thousands of emerald tablets, the oldest of which was dated 63 AD. Surely the Records contained details of historical accuracy, or at least significance, that could confirm or invalidate the legends.

At the risk of antagonizing him, I said, "Don't you think... Isn't it possible that the missing details are on the plaques in the Archives? That the ancient Records could hold—"

"Hold the keys to our past?" Malakai cut in. "And our present and future? You think?" He let out a snort of derision. "Look princess, you really don't get it, do you? The Records are our only real resource for understanding *anything* about the Essen race. *I* know that, but I've had my hands full with the English ones. If you want to tackle the others, be my guest. Really. I'll wait here." He paused dramatically. "No? Well, whenever you feel like accepting that challenge, you go right ahead. I can't wait to hear what you come up with, what you unearth to enlighten all of Essen-kind. But until then, here's what we'll keep telling our children:

"In the first century, the world was ruled by Rome. The Roman Empire extended from England to Africa, as far west as Spain and all the way to Syria in the east."

He sounded bored as he began, like he'd either heard or told this tale hundreds of times.

"The Roman Emperors of the day wanted more, though: more power, more influence, more veneration, more assets. Each ruled with a hunger for total supremacy and a lust to surpass his predecessor in eminence. So it was with Nero, who took the throne in 54 AD.

"Nero wanted to reign forever, to be the last and best emperor of Rome, whose kingdom would never end. He obsessed over this goal, convinced of the inevitability of it, but was unclear about how to make it so. And then he learned of a Greek apothecary named Jasten.

"Jasten was gifted at formulating liquid medicines for the sick and dying that could restore them to full health. He created elixirs for nearly every ailment, and his accomplishments gained him much attention, including Nero's.

"In a manner of utmost secrecy, Nero summoned Jasten to his palace and charged him with developing an elixir that would prolong his life indefinitely, an immortality elixir. An Elixir of Life."

Malakai's voice, though lacking in intonation, was deep and clear and strong. It had an even rhythm and it resonated in his chest such that I could almost feel the air around us vibrating. I leaned in, anxious to learn more.

"Accomplished and skillful though he was, Jasten doubted the possibility of such a solution. Still, he was in no position to refuse the will of Nero, so he began his assigned work. He was given one year and the undivided support of thirteen of Nero's personal, on-staff alchemists to complete the task.

"Days went by, weeks turned into months, but Jasten was unable to make the solution. As the year marker approached, he became desperate. Nero was notorious for intolerance, and Jasten knew that the deadline was a literal one. Should he fail to produce a working Elixir, his death would be horrible and brutal and certain.

"On the eve of what was likely to be his death, he called upon the cosmos for help. Four spirits of nature came to him, four females each representing their own domain. Terran was of the land, Merla was of the sea, Arith was of the wind, and Iro was of the flame. They told him they would make a covenant with him, freeing him of the injustice of his situation. They promised him—and the other alchemists, who would also otherwise meet their ends—a secret place to hide, a remote land protected from every type of threat. They brought them here to Salvos, and then they bestowed gifts: Merla and her sisters, who were most concerned with health and wellness, gave them the Mederium; Arith's sect, who valued wisdom and truth, gave them the Tabularium; Iro and her women, who loved power and passion, gave them the ability to make elixirs of all types—though not one for immortality—and the ability to make gold from any other metals; and Terran, she and her sisters, who prized strength and independence above all, gave them the bridges.

"To formalize the covenant, which they called the *Pactem Orbis*, the twenty-eight spirit-women—seven from each domain—laid with the alchemists, two to a man, every night for a month."

I snickered at this new plot development. Malakai's point was now well taken. This was no symbiotic relationship arising from respective needs. The covenant sounded less like an agreement and more like a concocted story, derived, most likely, from the fantasies of a man.

Malakai cleared his throat and went on.

"All of the women conceived and bore children. The babies were marked with what was dubbed a *notae*, a symbol representing their mother's domain, on the inside of the right arm. These children, the product of the union between the alchemists and the spirit-women, were the first supernaturals—the first Essen. We are their descendants. We bear the notaes of our mother lines, the domain which is dominant in our blood."

Malakai paused and held out his arm, again showing me his notae, a circle quartered by perpendicular lines. "Mother Terran," he said, "or as we call it now, Affiliation Terran."

"The children were also endowed with remarkable talents, which presented at Activation, the onset of adulthood, following a six month period of development—what we know as undergoing. One of them also received a gift of Foresight in addition to other gifts, making him the first Augur and the leader of the Host. And if that's where the story ended, everything would be all well and good. But we both know it's not."

Malakai pursed his lips. "There were some unforeseen byproducts of the *Pactem Orbis*. For unknown reasons, the spirit-women were no longer able to influence their natural domains, and the elements of earth, water, air, and fire persisted ungoverned. The Essen were not able to speak of their Essen identity with anyone not of the Host because in doing so, they'd die. But the worst consequence of the covenant was the persecution by the Dothen, the spirit-men who were supposedly ordained to put an end to all supernaturals."

I leaned back, realizing that the story had concluded and that my posture had tensed with the telling of it. I met Malakai's too-green eyes.

"Is that how it happened?" he said. "I don't know. Maybe some of it's true. Maybe very little of it is. Does it matter? We know who and what we are, if not why, and it's our reality to deal with. We have Salvos, we have bridges, we have Records; we've got gold and elixirs and the Mederium. We have an Augur and our Affiliations and gifts. And we also have enemies. We know the parameters of our existence, the rules we have to live by. We know the things that matter.

"It doesn't matter how we came to be. It only matters that we *are*. I don't study the Records because I am desperate to know *why*. The *why* isn't relevant to our current situation. I study the Records because I want to know *how*—how to be rid of the Dothen once and for all. The answer is in the visions, I know it is, especially 3627 and 3628. I just need to work it out. Before we lose any more people."

Malakai's low voice held the ownership and determination of a natural-born leader. If he had been even slightly likable, if he wasn't so cold and arrogant and condescending, he probably could have generated followers to his cause. Sitting across from him, I saw his posture stiffen with resolve. It said that he would be *damned* if the Host dipped below ninety-three Essen.

Sympathy tugged inside of me. "Does it happen often?" I asked quietly. "Losing Essen to the Dothen?"

Malakai gave me an even look. He didn't respond immediately; instead, he clenched his jaw, as if deciding how much he wanted to say.

"It's not the Dothen that are killing us, Gemma. I mean, it is but it isn't. On average, the Dothen deplete one Essen every other year. Think about it, how hard is it to cross the bridge before sundown? We know we are safe on Salvos. We know how to follow the rules. No, we aren't dying out because of Dothen attacks. It's the *fear* of Dothen attacks that's killing us—the fear and the inconvenience of our lifestyle. People just don't want to deal with it. They don't want to raise kids who will have to deal with it. So they don't. They opt out."

I gasped. "You don't mean… they don't commit suicide, do they?"

When he responded, Malakai sounded bitter. "Some do, but no, that's not what I meant." He sighed and looked past the stony doorway to the sea. "I guess you were going to find out sooner or later. Gemma, there's a reason the Dothen don't hunt children, the not-yet-Activated. It's because they'd rather we go extinct on our own. They know that each Essen has a *choice*. We can choose *not* to be supernatural. Beginning with Activation, on our birthdays each year, we can choose the life of a De-A. *You* can choose the life of a De-A."

A De-A. A Deactivated Essen, I realized suddenly. Like Gate.

"I told you we lost thirteen Essen the night Gate failed as bridge-keeper. It was bad, but not as bad as the thirty-four we lost to De-Activation in the year that followed. They'd had enough, they wanted out. They made the choice to De-A. Just like you can."

I covered my mouth, scarcely daring to believe what I was hearing. "And if I De-A, everything would go back to normal?" I asked. "I would be just me again?"

"Yes," he said. "But the decision is permanent, and it can only be made after Activation, and only on your birthday. That's it, that's when it has to be done. If you don't do it on your birthday, you have to wait a full year before you'll have the opportunity again."

Malakai continued talking, but I didn't hear him. I was distracted by the image that had popped into my head. I saw the circles of that Venn diagram again and they were still drifting apart, but this time I was standing in the same one as Jonny, waving as the other floated away. I already knew what my choice would be. In less than three months, I would have my life back.

CHAPTER 49

"You've decided, then," Malakai said. His words betrayed no emotion. "It's written all over your face. You intend to De-A immediately after Activation."

I raised my chin defensively. "Wouldn't you?"

"Obviously not," he said flatly.

"Why, though?" I asked. It seemed like such a simple matter. "Why would you choose to live this life? Why would anybody? Is it the gold? What good is an unlimited amount of money if you aren't free?"

Malakai's eyes darkened. "Boy, you really are a princess. How *glorious* it must be to be *you*, to have been privileged to grow up not knowing who you really are. What an unburdened life it must have been, being raised away from Salvos, oblivious to the struggles of our people." His voice was venomous. "It's not about the gold. It never has been. It's not about the elixirs or the Mederium or even the supernatural gifts. It's about *integrity*. Those of us who remain do so because it's *who we are*. Unlike your situation, there is no alternate life for us. Our family is *Essen*, our friends are *Essen*. Our *life* is Essen. To De-A would be to renounce everything we've known, everything we *are*. I will not change who I am just because it might be easier. I will not give in based on Dothen persecution. For me, it's this life or none. I don't want to be a De-A, surviving in the world as someone less than I am meant to be. I want to *win*. And as long as the portens is out there, that just might be possible."

I stared at the ground feeling ashamed. "I'm sorry," I mumbled. "I didn't think about it like that."

"Well think about it like that," Malakai said. "And think about it like this: De-A's are still bound to the rules of covenant. They can't tell non-Essen about us. Also, on top of giving up supernatural gifts, money, and access to Salvos, the De-As also give up the race. They are forbidden from making contact with any other Essen. It goes both ways. If anyone were to discover that I'd found Gate and asked for his help… I'd be on the run, too, hiding from the covenant-keepers.

"I suppose none of this matters to you, though. You're not giving anything up to De-A, not really. You've only known you're true identity for a couple months. It'd be easy to turn your back on a race you didn't feel part of. You'd be giving up more to stay Activated, wouldn't you? You'd be giving up Jonny."

I opened my mouth to speak, but Malakai interrupted.

"Don't get me wrong. I truly don't give a damn what you decide to do, but if you've made up your mind already, I think you're a fool. Jonny doesn't define you. *That*"—he pointed to my notae—"is what defines you. That and your gifts. Once you're Activated and your gifts have solidified, we'll see how easy it is for you to dismiss your true identity and take up the normal, boring life of a De-A."

I bit my lip, gazing down at the light brown lines of my birthmark. It no longer looked like a compass to me, now that I could see the domain symbols within it. Like all notaes, its core was a circle, and like Rori's, the core was encompassed by a diamond. Affiliation Iro. I noted the smaller circle centered with the core one and remembered seeing it on Taeo. Rori told me he was Affiliation Arith. In Malakai's notae, the notae of Affiliation Terran, the circle was bisected twice—though in mine, the horizontal line was wavy rather than straight, which most likely matched that of Affiliation Merla.

How had I come to have all four domains in one notae? How had I come to be the Link? Was it really the mark of my destiny? Was I really supposed to wield the portens for the benefit of the Essen race? *My* race?

No. I knew who I was. Malakai was trying to manipulate me. I held my head up, defiant.

"I'm *not* a fool," I said. "I know who I am. This"—I held my wrist up—"doesn't define me. Jonny doesn't define me. My choices and my actions define me, and they're *my* choices and actions, not yours. *I* will choose what to do with the portens, and *I* will decide whether or not to De-A."

Malakai gave me an approving look. "Well. You have some strength in you after all." He paused to listen, cocking his head to the left, then continued. "You're right. It is your decision whether or not to De-A. And like I said before, I couldn't care less what you decide. You know why? Because regardless of your choice, you *don't* get to decide what will be done with the portens. On that account, Gemma, you're wrong. Even if you decide to hide it away, *I* have decided to find it and use it for its intended purpose, and my will is stronger than your will."

He stood up abruptly and moved to the opening. "Someone's coming."

I got to my feet and watched Malakai lean out the entrance of our hideout. He turned back to me. "It's Taeo."

A moment later Taeo popped into the small cliff dwelling, and though he wasn't as big as Malakai, his presence crowded the space.

"I thought this is where you'd be," he said more to Kai than to me. "Hey man, I hate to interrupt, but we've got a little bit of a situation."

"What's that?" he asked, eyes narrowing.

"That guy, the blue-haired one Gemma brought with her to the Wooded Bridge yesterday…" He ran his hand through his long brown hair. "Yeah, um. He's gone."

✳ ✳ ✳

University of Minnesota students who enter their junior year without a declared major are encouraged to take an aptitude test. In addition to aptitude tests, other assessments are also available; surveys measuring everything from personality type, cognitive style, psychological preferences, natural strengths, predictable behavioral traits, decision-making defaults, and hard-wired values.

In September, I took a variety of these tests. I learned that I'm an introvert (Really? Who knew?) who tends to lean on intuition as much as, if not more than, logic when making decisions. I learned that I prefer structure and consistency in my life, and that I embrace routine over change. In terms of strengths, I am steady and analytical. I tend to process information linearly. My skills are more quantitative and less verbal. I typically respond to stress and conflict by withdrawing rather than pushing back.

This information was supposed to help me determine a career path. Though I did meet with my advisor to review the synthesized data, I left her office still uncertain about what to do with my life.

It wasn't time wasted, though. I learned something valuable: People with my personality profile are sometimes seen as weak. Because we are programmed to retreat rather than charge, because we withhold our opinions rather than spouting them, we are susceptible to bullying.

I myself have never been bullied. More often than not, I'm just ignored. But just because I tend to keep my views to myself doesn't mean I don't have any. I am not weak, and I will not be bullied. Especially not by my Keeper.

When Malakai followed Taeo out onto the rocky ledge and ordered me to stay put, I refused. He spun on me, demanding I remain in the cliff dwelling. I told him that Flash was my cousin and if he was missing, I would not be left hiding while others went looking for him. In this matter, I informed him cheekily, my will was stronger than his will.

He turned away quickly, but not before I caught his lips twitching into a smile.

Without further argument, the three of us climbed back to the top of the cliffs, first Taeo, then me, then Kai. I accepted the help of both of them, Taeo from above, Kai from below, as I made my way up.

At the top, Taeo told us that Rori had already formed a small search party that was focusing on the north and west areas of the island, the land surrounding the Somnus and the Trifarium (which I discovered was the combined name for the Tabularium, the Mederium, and the Aerarium—the underground cave that served as the treasury by housing the gold and the elixirs). The three of us, then, would be scouring the south and east parts of Salvos.

I was not looking forward to another long hike, and to my surprise and relief, we didn't have one. Our journey to the Axis region of the island was condensed due to the presence of a shortcut, another mysterious bridge that linked the cliffs to the beach cabin.

The approach to the bridge was barely noticeable, but once Taeo pointed it out, I saw it. Next to a large boulder at the top of the cliff, the air shimmered like it does above the surface of a road on a very hot day. We walked through it.

It was my first time crossing a bridge, at least while conscious, and the experience was wondrous. Blinking lights filled my vision reminding me of fireflies dancing on a summer evening. My skin tingled as if kissed by a menthol-infused breeze. I felt energized but also very relaxed and at ease. It only lasted a moment, and then it was over.

We were standing in the woods. From our position amongst the trees, I could just make out the back of Echo's beach cabin.

"Hey!" I squawked.

"What's your problem?" Malakai said.

"I just realized… When I woke up yesterday… Why did Echo walk me along the beach to the base of the cliffs? Why did he have me climb the endless stairs? He could have just…" I gestured to the bridge.

Malakai chuckled at my indignation. "I guess he thought you weren't ready to see me yet. He thought you needed time." He shrugged, looking me up and down. "Or exercise." He winked at Taeo and tromped ahead of us towards the beach.

Taeo smiled ruefully. "I know he's a bit abrasive, but don't take it personally. He's like that with pretty much everyone. He's really not that bad once you get to know him."

"I don't think he wants people to get to know him," I grumbled.

He scratched at his light brown beard. "Yeah. Well. He's lost more than most."

We walked to the edge of the forest, but before we left its cover, Taeo held out an arm and stopped me. His gray-blue eyes settled on my face. "We do need to find Flash, but there's no way to avoid doing this first."

"Doing what?" I said.

He pointed at a throng of people standing near the Axis. "It's past 10 AM. The bridge is open. They're not waiting to cross. They're waiting for *you*."

"They knew I'd be here?"

"I guess they figured you'd take the bridge at some point today."

It was a huge group of people. Had *everyone* in the Host come to meet me? My pulse quickened and I began to sweat. I have never enjoyed being the center of attention.

I cast a glance at Malakai, who was making his way to the crowd. He turned to us and motioned us forward. Taeo gave me an encouraging nod.

Taking a steadying breath, I walked out of the woods, onto the beach, and into the lives of ninety-three expectant Essen.

CHAPTER 50

Meeting the Host was the closest I think I'll ever come to knowing what it feels like to be a movie star. As we approached, Taeo walked next to me with a hand on my back, assuring me of his presence like a bodyguard, or a big brother, or a respectable Keeper, might have done.

They watched me approach with rapt attention, and I gaped back at them, trying to project more confidence than I felt. From a distance, I could see people whispering. Though I couldn't hear them, I knew what they must be asking each other. *Is that her? Is she the Link? Where's the portens?*

According to Rori, Malakai had told the Host that the portens was as good as found. He'd told them that their days of being hunted were almost over. As I drew nearer, I could see the hope in their respective faces, the eager light of anticipation behind their eyes. The crowd itself seemed to quiver with barely-contained enthusiasm.

It terrified me.

There were so many people, all of them looking at me, looking *to* me. Malakai, who had stopped in front of the Host, was watching me too. Arms crossed, expression inscrutable, he waited for Taeo and me to arrive by his side. When we did, Taeo dropped his hand from my back and stood, protective and reassuring, behind me.

The whispering fell off. The group seemed to collectively cease breathing. My eyes swept across the sea of faces, and for an endless moment, we stared at each other. I licked my lips, which suddenly felt very dry.

They were a varied bunch, ranging in height, build, age, and coloring. Men, women, and children craned their necks to get a better view of me, and the younger ones shoved to the front like they were watching a parade.

Then, like a storm that follows an eerie calm, the crowd erupted into pandemonium. People threw themselves at me, grabbing me, hugging me, touching my notae. They cheered, they wept, they hollered questions.

"Do you have the portens?"

"How will it destroy the Dothen?"

"When will we be *free*?"

Some thrust gifts, cards, and flowers into my hands, while others tossed them at my feet. Faces flashed in front of me as people pressed forward, jostling one another out of the way.

Malakai and Taeo encircled me with their arms, endeavoring to shield me from the barrage of attention, but still the Host swarmed into me. In an attempt to restore order, Kai barked for people to back off, but it wasn't until Eclipse got knocked to the sand and nearly trampled that Kai's voice became truly menacing.

"Enough!" he shouted, scooping her petite frame from the beach and setting her gently on her feet next to him. "What is wrong with you people!" he said as the masses began to recede. Holding Eclipse by the shoulders, he said, "You okay, kid?"

She nodded solemnly and looked in my direction. "I'm okay, but Gemma is rattled."

He regarded me and then surveyed the group. To the entire lot of them, he said, "For years you've told me the Link isn't real, the portens isn't real. You've discredited and scorned me, assuring me that Records 3627 and 3628 were the absurd ramblings of the worst Augur the Host has ever had. And maybe Phoenix is, but those visions weren't. I deciphered them and found Gemma—but not until last night, when I told you she was here, and not until today, when you saw her with your own eyes, did you *believe*." Kai grabbed my right wrist and raised it, displaying my notae to the crowd. "Yes, she's real, and yes, it's exciting. Freedom is near! But don't be a bunch of idiots. Gemma and I have *months* of work to do before the 'full release' that's referenced in 3627. As her Keeper, I need to train her, teach her, and help her develop her gifts. I don't expect we'll know everything we need to know about the portens until her Activation." He glowered at the group, cracking his knuckles. "I've got a lot to cover with Gemma, and I don't want a lot of distractions. So starting tonight, if you see us around, clear off."

Charming, I thought, watching the Host deflate as Malakai punctured their metaphorical bubble. His speech, far from winning people over, seemed to demoralize them. Though I understood his intentions—he was trying to buy us both time and privacy until my birthday—his delivery lacked diplomatic finesse. It was no wonder he was, as Gate had put it, not very respected within the Host.

As I took in their reddening faces, it occurred to me that it would be in my own best interest to do some damage control. Though I hated public speaking, Malakai had left me no choice. If I stood back and said nothing, I was sending the Host a message: that Kai was not only my Keeper, but also my captain. I needed to show them—and Kai—that I could make decisions for myself and that I would not be easily exploited. At the same time, I knew it would be unwise to discount anything Malakai had said. For both of our sakes, he and I needed to appear aligned.

I cleared my throat loudly, swallowing my nerves, and stepped forward. Malakai raised an eyebrow at me and stretched out his arm as if to say, *You think you can do better? By all means, give it a try.*

"Um," I began as I spotted Rori and a few others, one of whom was burdened with the unconscious body of my cousin on his shoulder, now standing at the back of the crowd. "Um," I repeated, dropping my gaze to the collection of presents at my feet.

"Thank you," I said somewhat quietly, finally finding my words. Raising my head to the Host, I said it again, more clearly. "Thank you all. ...For these gifts and for receiving me so... heartily... I don't know if Malakai already told you, but even though I have this"—I raised my wrist to them once more—"I never knew it meant anything. I didn't know who I was or that was I was part of... something more... until he found me and brought me here, to you."

I paused, taking a deep breath. "I was raised across the bridge, by my aunt and uncle. My parents are dead and I can't remember them, so I really don't know if they were Essen or not, but something tells me they weren't. I'm not sure why I have this notae, or how I came to be the Link, but I want to know the answers as much as all of you do. Like Malakai said, there's a lot of work to be done to get me up to speed. I have so much to learn.

"To be honest with you, this life, the only one all of you have ever known—it frightens me. It's difficult and restrictive. I believe it frightens you too, which is why you waited here for me today. And I understand what you want from me."

I caught myself before I said more, before I misled them with a lie or promised them something I wouldn't be able to give.

"I understand what you want from me," I repeated. "And I want you to understand what I want from you. I'll need time and space to figure things out. I want your support and your patience as I train with my Keeper. I'm not saying I'll be completely inaccessible, but I have less than three months until Activation, and based on what he's told me, I'm already *years* behind." A few people tittered as they recognized Malakai in my words. A glance in his direction told me he was not amused.

"Anyway," I went on, scooping up some of the cards and a vase of Supernova flowers at my feet, "thank you again. I, uh… I have to cross the bridge today to take care of some stuff, but I'll be back tonight."

I didn't know what else to say. Nobody moved, and I stood there awkwardly, waiting for them to realize they could leave. Finally Malakai spoke up.

"You heard the lady," he growled. "Go about your business."

Slowly the Host began to disperse. Several of them disappeared in front of the Axis, taking the bridge to the Minneapolis East Bank, and others made their way into the woods or down the beach. As they departed, I remembered Echo's comment and wondered who among them would seek to exploit me. No one stood out as more threatening or more desperate than the rest… They had *all* seemed rather tough, every single one of them firm and displaying hard lines of muscle. Even the smallest children, who should have had softness about them, seemed *fit*.

So it was with the girl who remained behind, the last remnant of the crowd. She came forward timidly, her big turquoise eyes filled with awe as she approached me.

"Gemma?" she squeaked.

"Yes," I said, smiling at her. "What's your name?"

"Hannah," she said, lowering her eyes bashfully. Her long lashes brushed her cheeks.

"How old are you, Hannah?"

"Seven," she said. "I'm Affiliation Merla." She kicked at the sand.

She reminded me of a younger version of myself, the self I'd seen in my very first hypnotherapy session with Gate in which I'd gotten tucked into bed by my father.

"Will you play with me?" she said, still not looking at me.

"Oh," I said, watching as Malakai and Taeo joined Rori's group at the entrance of Echo's cabin. The man holding Flash lowered him to the sand. "I can't today, sweetie. I have to go home."

Hannah met my eyes. "Isn't this your home?"

I cringed inwardly. "Well... I guess I have two homes. I have to go to the other one today to tell my family I'm okay. If I don't, they'll be worried."

"But..." She looked forlorn. "If you leave, I'll be worried."

"Why, sweetie? You know I'll be back tonight, right? I have to come back. We all do."

Her bottom lip began to tremble. "People *have* to come back, but not everyone *does*." A breeze blew wisps of her soft brown hair into her face and she brushed it back.

Lost for words, I set the cards and the flowers down and gave her a reassuring hug.

"I made this for you," she said, pulling away and withdrawing a folded paper from her pocket.

"Thank you," I said, taking it from her.

"Don't open it," she said, her cheeks flushing pink. "Look at it later."

"Okay," I said. "Later."

"Gemma?"

"Yes, Hannah?"

Her small face grew even more serious. "I'm glad it was Kai who found you. He's the best one. Just don't get lost again."

I told her I wouldn't, and as I made my way to the Axis laden with cards, gifts, and flowers, I felt something stirring in my heart, something that felt a bit like regret.

CHAPTER 51

Hannah had drawn, in colored pencil, a picture of me standing next to Malakai. In her sketch, he was two times taller than me and his amber ring was bigger than my head. I chuckled to myself. Underneath the drawing, she had written in large, uneven letters, "To Jema. The Portins-Keeper. Hero of the Essen."

I folded it and tucked it back into my coat pocket. Stealing a peek at Flash, who was out cold on the cramped back seat of the sports car, I then turned to Malakai.

"Where did they find him?" I asked.

"Wandering along the beach," he said. "He was very confused. He said he was thirsty, which was lucky because Rori didn't have anymore of the *Dormit* in concentrated serum form, only in drinkable elixir form."

He accelerated and shifted, and I grabbed at my seat. Kai was still driving too fast for my tastes, but anything slower, he informed me, was wasting daylight.

He was right.

By the time we'd changed into our winter gear, gathered up my gifts and my cousin, and crossed the Wooded Bridge, it was after 9 AM (11 on Salvos). We'd walked as swiftly as possible along East River Road, Malakai carrying a limp and lifeless-looking Flash over his shoulder, me holding a vase of flowers and a canvas bag full of cards and presents, and both of us ignoring the inquisitive looks of strangers. We made quick work of loading his car, which he'd left parked behind the campus hospital, and of buckling Flash into the back, but still the minutes ticked away.

Sunset was in less than eight hours. Feeling fidgety, I took Hannah's drawing from my pocket once more. "Did you see what Hannah gave me?"

Kai grinned. "No, but last night she asked me what you look like. She drew a picture of you?"

"She drew a picture of *us*," I corrected, holding it up so he could steal a glimpse while driving.

"She's a sweet girl," he said softly, looking back at the road. He still wore a faint smile, but his green eyes had lost their light.

"You worry about her," I observed.

"*She* worries about *us*," he said. "Everyday, she worries. She won't even cross the bridge for tutoring with the other kids."

"Is she...?" I wasn't sure how to ask if she was one of the seventeen children currently under the charge of the Keepers.

"She's orphaned, if that's what you're wondering."

"But she's taken care of," I said, thinking of the forty-two Activated Essen responsible for bringing up the parentless.

"That's the problem with our Keeper system, Gemma. Hannah is everyone's responsibility. Which is another way of saying she's no one's." His voice was flat, but his hands tightened around the steering wheel as he spoke. It was the system in which he himself had grown up, I remembered.

"Well, she told me you're the best one," I said, trying to lighten the mood.

He shook his head but seemed pleased. "It's only because she thinks she doesn't have to worry about me. She calls me 'unconquerable.' All the kids do. It's because I have this." He lifted his hand, showing me the ring on his pointer finger. "I found it on Salvos when I was searching for that stupid colored spire that 3627 references. There's no spire on the island, I've looked everywhere," he added as an aside. "Anyway, they think the ring protects me, and I let them think that. All it really does is tell me when a Dothen has locked on me, when he's close enough to deplete me and is just waiting for a body to take."

Eyeing the wide silver band and the large amber stone, I said, "Did you happen to find any others? Maybe in a lady's size?" I tried to sound like I was joking.

In his deep timbre, he said humorlessly, "Now what would your boyfriend say if I gave you a ring? In any case, I don't have another. I find a lot of things—I have a knack for finding things—but I've only ever found one Dothen Detector ring."

"Is there any other way to know if a Dothen is close?"

He shrugged. "I've heard dogs can sense them. I've never tried it. No one I know has, either. Frankly, we're not sure if dogs can be taken, and I wouldn't like my chances if they could be. Dogs are fast."

I waited for him to say, *And strong. And agile*, but he didn't, his attention once more on the road. I sighed, smoothing Hannah's drawing across my lap. "Were Hannah's parents depleted?"

"Yes. Last year. They are the Host's most recent losses… well, except for Raela."

"Raela Celere," I said.

Malakai's eyebrows shot up. "You know?"

"I was supposed to meet with Gate last week, but when I showed up, a detective was there instead. He said he was looking for Gate, that Gate was wanted for questioning in connection with her murder."

"I see," Kai said.

"He didn't do it, Kai. Gate didn't kill that girl."

His face was impassive. "What makes you so sure?"

"I just… feel it. I know I haven't known Gate long, but he's innocent, I'm just *sure*. He's not a murderer." Malakai made no response, so I asked, "You don't think he did it, do you?"

"It doesn't really matter what I think. He was the last person seen with her, and the circumstances of her death… Well, they're beyond suspicious. She was poisoned, Gemma. The wine she'd drunk, it was laced with Necis juice. There were two glasses, but the other was untouched. If Gate didn't know the wine was poisoned, wouldn't he have drunk it as well? And then there's the obvious: Gate fled the scene while she was yet writhing on the floor. Alistair saw him take off. All the evidence points to him. Phoenix has every covenant-keeper—our version of law enforcement—trying to find him."

"But *you* don't think he did it, do you?" I said, reading between the lines.

Malakai turned into my neighborhood. A moment later he said, "My problem with pinning Raela's death on Gate at this point is the same problem I have with accepting the story of the *Pactem Orbis*. There's no apparent motivation. Gate had no reason to kill that girl. She was only twenty-one—she'd just Activated a few weeks ago—which means she was a toddler when Gate De-A'ed. He would barely have known her. It doesn't make any sense to me."

I thought of Gate's somber mossy eyes and the way they'd shined when he'd said, *Jade was also my daughter's name. She would have been about your age...*

"He didn't do it," I said again. "He wanted me to tell you that."

This surprised him. "You've spoken to him since it happened?"

"Well... He left me a message," I replied vaguely. Hurrying past this statement, hoping to avoid questions about it, I said, "He also said I should ask you about that night eighteen years ago, the night of that Dothen attack." I searched Kai's face. "He wants to know what you *saw*."

He gave a sharp grunt of exasperation. "He asked me that in his letter. When I wrote back, I *told* him: I saw the Dothen take a group of joggers and then deplete my parents and the others right in front of me. I saw the terror in their faces as the life got drained from them. Only after they crumbled to dust did I see the Taken drop, one by one all around me, as the Dothen discarded their bodies."

The lack of emotion in his account told me he'd recited it many times over the years.

"Gate insists I saw more," he went on. "He said that the day after it happened, when I was back on Salvos, I went to him and told him I needed to tell him something, something I'd seen. Apparently I started to tell him, but we got interrupted and I never got the chance to finish. When he tracked me down later that day to ask me about it, I told him I had no idea what he was talking about. To this day, I have *no idea* what he's talking about.

"He believes I may have blocked it—that whatever it is I saw is buried in the depths of my mind. He thinks the memory's there, waiting to be retrieved, and he thinks it's of critical importance. It's why he became a hypnotist. He wants to take me under, have me explore that night."

Malakai shuddered, revealing his true feelings on the matter. "As if I'd ever want to relive that. It was worse than being tagged myself."

He pulled into my driveway. "Gate's message—what else did it say?"

I looked at my hands, avoiding Kai's probing green eyes.

"Gemma… Tell me what else it said," he demanded, shutting off the car and facing me.

"There was nothing else," I said.

"You're a terrible liar," he said. "Tell me the truth."

Deciding it was a battle I wouldn't be able to win, I blurted, "He warned me not to trust you, not to give you the portens."

Kai crossed his arms. "You're wrong."

"What?"

"Gate didn't say that. He wouldn't have said that. Recheck your message. He knows I'm the only person you *should* trust."

He spoke with such certainty that I found myself questioning what Gate had really said. The message had woken me, after all. Maybe I'd missed something, maybe I *had* misunderstood.

"I'm just telling you what I heard." I reached for the door handle, but before I pushed it open, Kai caught my shoulder.

"Hey," he said. "What's your plan?"

"What do you mean?"

"You can't just walk into your house and act like nothing's happened. What's your story? How're you going to explain everything? We've already determined that you're a terrible liar. You need to have a plan, some answer for last night. And tonight. And every night for the foreseeable future."

"Only until March 25th," I said pointedly. I glanced over my shoulder at Flash. "It's fine. I'll think of something."

"In the next ten seconds?" he asked, looking at my house.

I followed his gaze. My Aunt Sheri had thrown open the door and was waiting, arms folded across her chest, in the entryway. Hovering behind her, forehead creased with worry, was Jonny.

I ignored Kai's comment and opened the car door.

"Do I need to pick you up tonight or are you going to meet me at the bridge?" he asked.

I sighed. "Pick me up, I guess. I don't want to waste my time sitting on the bus."

He looked at his cell phone. "I'll be back in six hours, then. At 4 PM. Sunset is at 4:51 today. That should give us plenty of time."

We got out of the car and Kai began to wriggle Flash out of the back seat.

I gathered up everything I'd been given, nestling the vase of flowers into the crook of my arm. "Where are you going now?"

"You're not the only one with a home this side of the bridge," he said. "I'm beat. I'm going to my place to sleep for a few hours. That reminds me…" He took his wallet from the back pocket of his pants and withdrew a plain white plastic card. "This is the key to your condo. Don't lose it."

"You got me a condo?" I said, bewildered.

He scoffed. "*I* didn't get you a condo. You're entitled to one. Undergoing Essen all get their own pads."

I flipped the card over. It was unmarked. "Where?"

"Riverview Estates, the complex we own. We built it years ago. It's private housing, just for Essen. We lock it down to outsiders every night at sunset and we don't open it until sunrise. I don't recommend staying there overnight—it was designed as a last resort—but some people do." He hoisted Flash out of the car and onto his shoulder. "Go see Vivian this week. She's the non-Essen we've hired to manage the property. She knows nothing about us, by the way, just that the building must be secure from outsiders, including herself, after hours. She'll get your security protocols established."

I tucked the card into the canvas bag with my gifts, well aware that my aunt and Jonny were watching my every move.

"Tonight I'll give you your bankcards," Kai continued in a lowered voice as I led him up the walkway to my house. "The funds are unlimited; they all just link to our master account, which contains literally billions. The treasure-keeper, Puck, handles our finances, but you should know he doesn't pay much attention to purchases under a hundred grand. You want a car? Feel free to buy one. Oh, one other thing"—Flash's head rolled across Kai's back as he stopped and dug in his coat pocket—"this is from Kelby, our contact-keeper." He handed me a cell phone. "It'll work on Salvos. Every Essen's number is already programmed in it."

I placed the phone in the canvas bag, too.

Aunt Sheri held the door open as we entered the house, her pale blue eyes blazing. Without a word to either of them, I set down my load and directed Malakai to Flash's bedroom so he could do the same. It wasn't until he'd brought Flash through the living room, up the stairs, and out of sight, that I turned to my aunt and Jonny.

Aunt Sheri's cheeks were flushed with anger, but before I had the chance to say anything to her, Jonny caught me in a bone-crushing embrace. I prolonged the hug, my racing mind formulating some type of plan.

CHAPTER 52

I prolonged the hug, my heart suddenly full to bursting.

Standing there with Jonny's body pressed to mine, feeling his arms wrapped tightly around me, I realized I'd *missed* him. I'd missed him not just while I was on Salvos, but for all the months of my undergoing, all the months I'd been consumed with everything *me*. I'd missed the things about him that I'd stopped noticing: the sparkle in his dark blue eyes, the lightness of his laugh, the bluesy sound of his voice. How could I have ever thought I'd be okay without him?

I'd seen Jonny on Wednesday, but it felt like a lifetime ago. I had been a different Gemma then, a Gemma who'd wanted to remain committed to him but who was despairingly resigned to our Venn diagram circles floating away from each other. Now, knowing there was light at the end of my undergoing tunnel, my commitment was renewed. In less than three months, I'd have no other competing priorities; I would be solely his. I squeezed him back, closing my eyes against his shoulder.

I didn't have a plan, but my mind was no longer racing. Somehow everything would be okay. With Jonny in my life, everything would always be okay.

Even as he stroked my hair and asked in whispered tones whether I was all right, Aunt Sheri began blasting me for my 'complete disregard for other people.'

"It's only been three days, *three days*, since your uncle's funeral," she admonished. "You decide to just disappear without telling anyone? I might have

257

expected something like this from Flash, but from you? It's inconsiderate, Gemma! I have enough to worry about without dealing with this too! You'd think one of you would've had the decency to call and let me know where you were, but no, all I got was this ridiculous text message in the middle of the night from an unknown number."

She waved her phone in my face, displaying the message I'd sent to both her and Jonny: *This is Gemma. Using friend's phone, mine is dead. Flash and I are at a party. All's okay. Be home in the AM.*

I pulled away from Jonny and opened my mouth to respond, but she cut me off. "I don't want to hear it, Gemma. I don't want to hear, 'But I'm almost twenty-one. I can do what I want, I'm an adult.' You're living here, and you'll have some respect." Her voice cracked. "It's been a rough week for all of us, and we've all done what we've had to do to cope, but I don't want it happening again. Staying out all night getting wasted is not going to bring Dan back." Tears filled her eyes and she paused to dab at them, but when she spoke again, her words were emotionless. "He's been gone a week now. We all just need to move on."

It was in that moment, watching my aunt trying to regain composure, that I finally began to understand her. In all my years of asking questions, of wanting to know about my parents and my past, she'd been dismissive. Always, she'd responded, *Now, now, sweetie, we mustn't worry about things we can't change*, and with a toss of her blonde curls, she'd changed the subject. It had never crossed my mind that it was her *own* pain, her *own* loss, which prevented her from remembering the past. She was so afraid of living in it, of getting stuck in it, of being perpetually miserable, that she didn't even dare to pay the past a visit. It wasn't about me at all. It was about her missing her brother, and now her husband. She wanted to bury the pain and the loss. She wanted to minimize her suffering. She just wanted to move on.

I wanted to throw my arms around her and comfort her as she tried to mask her grief. I wanted to tell her I understood and reassure her that it was okay to mourn. I wanted to remind her that it only *had* been one week, and that moving on didn't need to mean forgetting.

I didn't do any of those things. If our relationship had been warmer, more like it had been pre-accident, back when we'd played at riddles, I might have. We just weren't that close anymore. Instead, I mumbled a weak apology.

She still looked agitated but was unwilling to talk about it anymore. Her arms dropped from her chest and she stepped back, sniffing. "Well. Don't leave your friend lingering on the stairs. Introduce him."

Jonny raised an eyebrow at me as I motioned Kai forward. To Aunt Sheri, I said, "This is Malakai Zonn. I met him at school last fall." It wasn't a lie, exactly. We had been on campus the first time we'd crossed paths.

Malakai stuck out his hand to my aunt and said, "Flash'll be okay. He just needs to sleep it off." Then he turned to Jonny and simply said, "Jonny."

"Malakai," Jonny responded. His eyes narrowed and he said, "So you just happened to be at the same party as Flash and Gemma."

"No, not at all," Kai said. "It was *my* party."

Jonny looked affronted and I shot Malakai a warning glance.

"Which was why I couldn't bring them home until the morning," Kai went on. "I had to wait until everyone else had cleared out." There was an awkward pause, and then Kai rolled his shoulders back and said to me, "Well, I'm gonna take off."

"Thank you for giving them a ride," Aunt Sheri said as he pushed open the door, "and for bringing Flash up to his room."

"Yeah, sure," Kai said. "Hey Gemma, tell Flash I took his keys when he passed out. Tell him I'll have Taeo drive his car back over when I come to pick you up this afternoon. I'll see you at four. Be ready to go."

Jonny nearly convulsed. "What?"

Kai's eyes slid to me. "You mean you didn't tell them yet?"

He knew I hadn't told them anything. He'd stood on the stairs listening to the whole interaction.

Taking my silence as an invitation to proceed with whatever story he'd concocted, he said, "Gemma's going to be working security at the building my family owns, Riverview Estates. Video surveillance, mostly. Night shift."

"The Mac Stacks?" Jonny asked, confused.

"The Fortress in the Sky," Malakai confirmed.

Aunt Sheri turned to me. "You got a job? Why? Did you run out of the money David left you?"

I stammered my way through an explanation that I thought would allay suspicion, something about Uncle Dan's death making me feel like I needed to contribute more. I told my aunt and Jonny that I'd met some of Kai's family at the party, and that they'd taken pity on me and offered me an overnight position.

"So like I said, I'll pick you up at four," Malakai said. With that, he exited the house.

Jonny seemed less than thrilled as he watched Malakai get in his matte black sports car and drive away. Rubbing his neck, he said, "So I guess he's part of our circle now. Is that it?"

Aunt Sheri looked between Jonny and me and then shuffled away, obviously loath to get in the middle of whatever this was going to be. There was no argument, though. When she had gone, I flung myself at Jonny and held him tightly, partly to reassure him but also to conceal my smile in his neck.

I knew he was upset and that it would bother him to see the grin spreading across my face, but I couldn't help it. Jonny had said 'I guess he's part of our circle now,' and it reminded me of the image that had popped into my head back on Salvos, the image of Jonny and me standing together in the same Venn diagram circle, waving as the other floated away. He'd called it *our circle*, and even though he didn't mean it the way I thought of it, I still took his saying it as a very good sign.

✳ ✳ ✳

All in all, things with Jonny could have gone better. Malakai was right. I should have had a plan.

Nothing much was said as we went up the stairs to my room, me carrying the canvas bag and Jonny grudgingly carrying the vase of flowers. Once the door was shut though, and we were sitting together on my bed, Jonny let loose.

"What the hell, Gemma," he said in a hurt voice. "You shut me out all week and then you go to a party? *His* party?"

I tried to convince him that Malakai and Flash had met on Halloween and that it was Flash, not me, who had gotten the invitation. Flash had just dragged me along to get my spirits up.

Jonny wasn't buying it.

"He's into you, Gem. I mean, come on. He got you more of those freaky glowing flowers—and you accepted them. Don't you know what kind of signal that sends?"

I bit my lip. The Supernova flowers sat on my desk in full bloom. I had known it would be risky to bring them home with me, but I needed them.

"He gave the flowers to both Flash and me," I said. "You know… for our loss." I placed my hand over Jonny's. "He wasn't making a move, I promise. He was just being nice."

Jonny looked skeptical. "What about that bag full of presents and cards?"

To this I had no response. Instead of making up a story, I just said, "Those aren't from him." I touched the pendant at my throat. "You have nothing to worry about. Please trust me. Everyone—Malakai included—knows I'm yours."

Jonny's expression softened. "I'm sorry," he said. "I guess I just missed you this week."

"I missed you too," I said. "And I'm sorry for pushing you away. I was just… dealing with everything."

"I know," he said. He leaned forward and tucked a strand of hair behind my ear. "But you know I'm always here for you, right?"

"I know, Jonny," I said, meeting his eyes.

"If you ever need me for anything… even a ride to work…" He tilted his head at me as though trying to figure things out.

"Okay," I said quietly.

"I could even take you today. I'm supposed to be at Board Meeting at three, but I can call and tell them I'll be late…"

I lifted my hand to Jonny's cheek. "I don't want you to blow off work. I'll be fine. Really. Kai already said he'd pick me up before our shift."

Jonny's face fell. "*Kai?* When did he become *Kai?* I didn't know the two of you were so close."

"We're not *close*," I said, "but after talking with him last night, I guess I don't *hate* him. He's not ever going to be my favorite person, but he's not *all* bad." I shrugged one shoulder. "Actually, I think the two of you might even get along. You know, if you got to know each other. He's into poetry, I found out. He's got lines from that poem you studied last year... *Invictus*, I think it's called... tattooed across his upper back—"

"You saw his upper back?" Jonny interrupted.

"What? No! Well, I mean I did, but just because he was walking around with his shirt off, not because... Look, it was out there for everyone to see, it wasn't like I... you know..."

Jonny put his head in his hands. "You're killing me, Gemma."

"All I meant to say was that he likes the same poem as you."

He raised his head and stared at me. "A guy like that, walking around half-naked, and you're telling me all you noticed was his tattoo."

This was getting very out of hand. I flopped back against my pillow, feeling tired. "You're being totally unreasonable. He isn't—"

"Oh, I'm being unreasonable? Let's recap, shall well? First he was stalking you, showing up wherever you were. Then he gives you flowers twice in as many weeks. Then he—"

I held up a hand. "Stop. Just stop, Jonny. This insecurity thing—it isn't you."

He looked as though I'd slapped him in the face. "Maybe I wouldn't be jealous if I knew you were leveling with me. You're not, though. You're being evasive, and that's not you either."

He pursed his lips, waiting for me to say something, but words didn't come.

"Maybe I should just go then," he said.

I didn't want him to go. I just wanted him to be the fun-loving, light-hearted Jonny that I'd come to depend on for stability.

"Do what you want," I said, feeling edgy from all the questions. "I'm going to take a shower."

I got up from my bed and opened the door to find Flash poised to knock. He looked groggy and disheveled.

Blinking, he said, "Gemma? We hung out last night, right? Can you shed some light on what the hell happened to me?" He traced his fingers over the puncture marks at his throat, his face screwed up in thought. "Was I involved in some sort of vampire LARP thing?"

"LARP thing?" Jonny said, standing up.

"Live action role-play," I said. "No, Flash. It was just a party."

Flash ran his hand through his short blonde-blue hair. "Well what the fuck is up with these holes in my neck?"

I tried to look perplexed.

Shaking his head, he said, "And I had the funkiest dreams. There was this girl with super short bleach-blonde hair and tattoos all over, but she was still totally hot, and we were laughing... Then I was standing on a beach and I was so thirsty..."

He turned and walked back down the hall, still mumbling about his dream. I followed him until I got to the bathroom, and without a glance back at Jonny, I shut and locked the door.

I stood in the hot water for a very long time trying to wash away the guilt. I didn't mean to snap at Jonny, but I'd felt cornered. I didn't know how to answer his questions, and I hated lying. If only I could convince him to trust me, to accept that there were things I couldn't tell him. If only he could bear with me for three more months... Then we could get on with our lives and pretend this rough patch had never happened.

By the time I toweled off, dressed, and returned to my room, Jonny was gone. He had left me a note, though, a short message scribbled on a post-it. It read:

> *I found this downstairs when I opened the door to leave. You must've dropped it coming in.*
>
> *Who are the Essen, Gemma?*
> *I need you to be straight with me. I really do miss you.*
>
> *Jonny*

My stomach dropped as his words sank in and as my brain registered to what the post-it had been attached. It was Hannah's drawing, her picture of Malakai and me that had been labeled, "To Jema. The Portins-Keeper. Hero of the Essen."

CHAPTER 53

I had been anxious to examine my boulder opal from the moment I suspected it was covered with a sealant, but now that I was alone and at liberty to do so, I couldn't. There was something I had to do first, something that was just as important, and even more urgent. I had to respond to Jonny.

Jonny is one of the most self-assured people I've ever met. He's talented, funny, kind, smart, charming, and handsome... and he knows it. Not that he's arrogant—I've never seen him be anything but gracious about his good fortune—but he *is* confident.

The self-doubt he displayed whenever Malakai entered the picture wasn't a matter of insecurity, and it had been unfair of me to contend that it was. Jonny's not stupid. He could see there was more to my relationship with Malakai than I was letting on. He knew I was hiding something. What else was he to conclude except that I was being unfaithful?

I had to set things right. This was not going to be the beginning of the end for us. Not now, not when I was so close to getting my life back.

It took me five attempts and almost two hours to come up with a response I felt was adequate. When I was done, I set down my pen and read what I'd written.

Dear Jonny,

You know I've never been very good at saying what's on my mind. I have a hard time opening up about my feelings. It's always been okay though, because you can read me better than anyone. You get me, and I'm glad that you do.

But after all these years, I decided I owe it to you to actually tell you what you mean to me. You deserve to hear it straight from my lips… or, since I'm too timid to do this in person, straight from my pen.

I'm not sure that I'm any better at writing how I feel than I am at speaking it. Professor Dagenais told me I have a "strong command of the written word," but I find that hard to believe. Either way, I discovered that writing is a useful way to sort things out (thanks to the journal you gave me on Wednesday), so please just forgive my lack of eloquence as you read on. Finding the exact right words has always been your thing, not mine.

Actually, there're a lot of things that I would call "yours, not mine": popularity, charisma, musicality, optimism, passion… You are an amazing person, Jonny, and I'm sometimes astonished that you love me.

Of course you know I love you, too. It's more than that, though. I adore you, Jonny. I'm so grateful to have you in my life and so afraid of losing you from it. I never want to face a future that you're not in.

I should have told you that this morning. I should have reassured you that I would never do anything to jeopardize the future for us. I should have convinced you that Malakai is no threat.

He's no threat, Jonny. I need you to trust me in this. I know things might not make sense to you, the things I do and the reasons I do them, but don't give up on me. It's a selfish thing to ask, I know, especially when I don't have the answers to all of your questions, but I'm asking it anyway. Please trust me.

I'll come by tomorrow morning after work, probably around nine. I hope you'll have forgiven me for... everything.

I love you.
Right now. All along. Forevermore.

- Gem

I jotted the phone number for my new, Salvos-friendly cell at the bottom of the page, along with a post-script that told Jonny I'd been issued a "work phone" that he could call at any time. I tucked the letter into an envelope, licked it closed, and set it on my desk on top of Hannah's drawing.

I felt better having written the letter. I hoped Jonny would feel better reading it, even though it failed to answer his question: *Who are the Essen, Gemma?*

It was a question I'd actually considered answering as I wrote my letter. Yes, I was aware of the 'deadly consequences.' Malakai warned me back in November that sharing Essen information with non-Essen would kill me, and Gate had confirmed it. Yet Jonny had found out—there was his post-it, clearly referencing the Essen—so maybe, since he already knew...

Then the worst thought entered my head. If Jonny knew, then was the person who had 'told' him already gone? Panicked, I picked up my new cell-phone and made a call.

"What, you missed me already?" Kai answered sleepily.

"Kai, I need your help," I said, unable to keep the dread out of my voice.

Sounding alert now, he said, "What's going on?"

"I need you to find out if Hannah's okay."

"Hang on," he said without further questions. A minute later he was back on the line. "She's fine. I texted Echo and he said she's with him right now at the Axis."

I breathed a huge sigh of relief.

"What's this about, Gemma?" he asked.

I explained about Jonny finding Hannah's drawing and about my fear that she had, albeit inadvertently, exposed Jonny to Essen information and... died.

The line became quiet. "If I were you," he said at length, "I'd be a bit more careful about what I leave lying around."

"But maybe there aren't really any deadly consequences," I said, feeling hopeful.

"Or maybe there are, but the sharing has to be intentional," he said. "Or more specific than just the word *Essen*. I don't know, but I can personally tell you—the consequences are real. I've read enough Records to know that." He yawned loudly. "But just in case you're thinking of testing how much you can say, maybe you should tell me what and where the portens is. You know, in case you die."

"I'm not going to *die*," I said, "I know I can't tell Jonny the truth." I huffed loudly. "I wish you hadn't thrown me into a web of lies, though."

"What, the job thing? You didn't have a plan. I was doing you a favor."

"Some favor," I grumbled.

"Some gratitude," he said. "Look, unless there's someone else you think you killed, I'd like to go back to sleep."

"Whatever. I'll see you in two hours."

"Get some rest, too," he instructed. "Tonight's training is going to kick your ass."

I was about to ask Malakai what the point of training me at all was, given that he knew it was my intention to De-A, but he ended the call.

A moment later I got a text message from him: *Forgot to ask. Where's Flash's car?*

Feeling irritated, my reply was a bit cross. *Find it the same way you made me find Gate: Use the force, Luke.*

Snarky shrew, he wrote back.

✳ ✳ ✳

There was no time for a nap. I brought the vase of Supernova flowers to the bathroom and held it over the sink while I pulled all but one of the stems from the water. The ashy mess created by the disintegrating flowers covered the counter, but it was easier to clean there than it would have been in my room. Dipping my finger into it and licking at the water, I confirmed what I had supposed: It was saltwater.

I carried the vase back to my bedroom and placed it on the floor of my closet. Then I grabbed my boulder opal out of its display case and brought it into my closet as well, shutting the door behind me. The single flower glowed violet, and in its light, my opal fluoresced green.

By removing most of the bouquet, there was enough room in the vase for the stone. But by keeping one of the flowers, I'd be able to see when the otherwise-clear sealant had entirely dissolved. Holding my breath, I plunked the opal into the vase.

Immediately the opal was effervescing. Soon the water had become so fizzy that I could barely make out its outline, let alone its green hue. Small bubbles rose to the surface, misting my face as they popped.

It took several minutes, but then the fizzing stopped. I peered into the vase at my opal. There was no trace of the neon green color on it anywhere, and through the water, it looked just as it always had when it was sitting in its display case on my bookshelf.

I reached into the vase and seized the stone. When I withdrew it, I noticed something remarkable.

The colors were moving.

It wasn't a trick of the light, like sometimes happens with opals. A matrix of colors flashing across one another is normal. A vibrant swirling of colors like the dance of vast and brilliant clouds of cosmic dust is not normal.

I held the stone in my palm, mesmerized by its beauty. Indigo and aquamarine, fuchsia and garnet, saffron and tangerine, they all curled around one another, curled and melted and blended, like paint whirling across the canvas of some strangely animated artwork.

It truly was a thing of grandeur. I opened my closet and moved across my room to the window, wanting to view it in full light. It made me breathless.

I literally could not catch my breath. I tried inhaling deeply, but the more air I tried to take in, the less oxygen I seemed to have. My mouth became dry and then so did my eyes and throat. I began coughing and gasping for air simultaneously.

I tried to drop the stone, but it was stuck to my hand, frozen to my skin. I could hear the crackling of my palm where the flesh was crystalizing. It was as though the stone was drawing the heat from my body, pulling it from further and further up my arm.

My legs began shaking and then so did the rest of my body. I was gulping air in shallow and ragged breaths between coughs. My insides felt as though they were being wrung out, like the moisture was somehow being extracted from my very cells. Then my legs gave out completely.

As they buckled, I threw out my hands to catch myself. I landed hard on all fours, the impact knocking loose the opal. It flew across the floor and under my bed. As soon as it left my hand, my lungs filled with air. Tears gathered in my eyes and spilled down my cheeks.

Holy hell, I thought, bringing myself to sitting position. I leaned back against the wall and waited for my muscle spasms to stop. Maybe I could be persuaded to part with the portens after all.

CHAPTER 54

The new cellphone was ringing and I should have known it was Malakai before I even glanced at the screen. He had programmed his own ringtone, a song that included the lyrics "you got what I need."

I shakily pushed myself up from the floor and answered his call.

"Can't a guy get any sleep?" he said.

"You called me," I retorted, still feeling breathless.

"Because something happened. I felt it; it woke me up. What happened?"

I looked at the broken flesh on my hand. My skin burned where the heat was returning. Feeling weak, I sat down on my bed.

"Gemma, answer me."

Too lightheaded to come up with an excuse and certain that Malakai would see right through one anyway, I said, "It's dangerous, Kai. It—it's not safe."

His voice became quiet. "You tried to use the portens?"

I couldn't bring myself to respond. I felt foolish.

"But you're okay, yeah?"

"I think I'll live," I said, struggling to speak normally. My lungs ached with each breath.

"You're in pain."

"Yes," I said, suppressing a cough.

He sighed. "Hang tight. I'll come get you. We need to get you to the Mederium." I heard him moving about, and then he said, "Where's the portens now?"

It was still under my bed, and there it would remain. I wasn't about to touch it again or allow anyone else to go near it. Its power was destructive.

"Fine, don't tell me." He muttered under his breath that I was also *a* pain. "Have you gone through your presents yet?" he asked.

"No."

"Do that while you're waiting for me. Find the long cylindrical gift and open it. It's from Taeo—a canister of *Restas*, a low-grade painkiller elixir. He put it in your stack while you were changing." He paused while I rifled through the canvas bag. "See it? Drink a few ounces. It'll help until you're back in the pool. I'll see you in a bit."

I hung up and stared at the metal container. The last time I drank something that Kai said would 'help,' I'd ended up bound to him as his Kept.

But this is from Taeo, I told myself, unscrewing the cap. I sniffed the liquid, which smelled like it was infused with lemons and cucumbers. *Taeo is all right, isn't he?* Truthfully, I had no idea whether Taeo was all right, but as he was Rori's boyfriend, I was inclined to believe he was. On the other hand, I argued with myself, he was best friends with Kai, and at the moment, that seemed like a huge strike against him.

I set the canister down on my nightstand. Still feeling awful, I decided to go through the other gifts and the cards before making a decision about the *Restas*.

The presents were ridiculous. Each one I opened seemed more elaborate than the last. In addition to the elixir from Taeo, there were gold-foil packages filled with fine candies and nuts, miniature felt-lined boxes containing exquisite jewelry and polished gems, an eight-sided bluish-purple stone that looked like a small paperweight, dried flowers pressed between thin sleeves of hardened tree sap, and an snowflake-shaped ornament of carved wood.

The cards were equally overdone. Though most of them appeared to have been made by children, they were each and every one stuffed with wads of hundred dollar bills. I must have had at least twenty thousand dollars spread across my bed.

I sensed that these gifts were mere trinkets to my Essen counterparts, and that the cash I'd been given was as pennies to the average non-Essen, but I felt even sicker after going through the canvas bag than I had before. Were the presents simple gestures of welcome for the long-awaited Link, or were they more like a bribe, an advance payment made for the use of the portens?

My stomach was queasy. If Malakai had really promised the Host that freedom was around the corner, then this outpouring was surely a result of the latter. A mass rose in my throat and threatened to spill from me. I swallowed it down and spotted the painkiller elixir on my nightstand. Throwing caution to the wind, I drank several large gulps of *Restas* directly from the container and hoped it would take effect quickly.

✳ ✳ ✳

The *Restas* did little but make me drowsy. Still feeling shaky and ill, all I wanted to do was crawl into bed. Instead, to keep myself from dozing, I put away the gifts and money and then repacked the canvas bag with workout clothes, tennis shoes, a swimsuit, and a towel—everything I thought I might need for the evening. Then I lay down and fell asleep anyway.

At half-past three, Aunt Sheri knocked on my bedroom door and announced tersely that Malakai had arrived to bring me to work. "He's thirty minutes early," she said in a manner that sounded somewhere between approval and annoyance.

My legs felt wobbly as I made my way downstairs with the bag slung over my shoulder.

Kai was standing in the entryway waiting for me. A moment later, Taeo joined him, holding out Flash's car keys to Aunt Sheri as he walked into the house. She thanked him and then the three of us left, piling into Kai's car. I took the backseat, given that Taeo was only slightly smaller than Kai.

"Wait!" I said as Kai backed out of the driveway. I dug the letter I'd written for Jonny out of my bag. "I have to leave this for Jonny."

Kai and Taeo exchanged glances, but Kai stopped the car and Taeo got out, allowing me to clamber from the backseat. I jogged up to Jonny's house and rang the bell. Lucy answered the door, draped in the beefy arms of Joshua, who was standing behind her wearing a t-shirt that read, "PREPARE TO BE AMAZED."

She looked flushed, like I'd just interrupted a hot and heavy makeout session, but she took the letter, promising to give it to Jonny when he was home from work. But before she closed the door, she spotted Kai waiting in his car.

"Malakai again, Gemma?" She narrowed her eyes, tapping the letter against her palm. "This isn't a breakup note, is it?"

"No, nothing like that," I said. "Just make sure Jonny gets it, okay?"

Lucy seemed like she wanted to ask several more questions, but as Josh had begun kissing her neck and running his hands along the waistband of her low-rise jeans, she just said, "Okay, I will," and shut the door.

I walked back to the car, hoping that Lucy hadn't already cast the letter aside, forgetting about her promise once the amorous activity resumed.

"You didn't do anything stupid, did you?" Kai said to me as Taeo got out and helped me climb into the back of the car once more.

Taeo shook his head at Kai. "You'll have to excuse him," he said to me as he settled into the front. "He gets crabby when he doesn't get enough sleep. Or when he hasn't eaten. Or when he doesn't get his own way. Actually, he's like this pretty much all the time, so never mind." Then he winked at me and turned back to Kai. "I'm sure Gemma has not done anything stupid. Lay off her already. Don't you know you'd catch more flies with honey than vinegar?"

"I don't want flies," Kai said, reversing into the street. "I want the portens, and I can't have Gemma telling her boyfriend all about the Essen and dying on me until I know where it is."

"I'm sure she didn't tell her boyfriend anything. Did you, Gemma?" He gave me another wink. "See, Kai? She's a smart girl. She knows the rules. And anyway, you might have better luck getting her to share the portens with you if you tried being, you know, *nice*. Here, I'll show you." He took off his pageboy hat and let his long hair fall about his face. With genuine concern in his gray-blue eyes, he said, "How ya feeling, Gemma? Kai told me you tried… Well anyway, did the *Restas* help?"

I told him it hadn't done much of anything but make me sleepy.

"Really?" he said, looking perplexed. "It didn't take away the pain?"

"No," I said, trying to ignore the throbbing in my hand and arm.

He scratched at his beard. "Man, that sucks. The *Restas* is normally very effective... for Affliction and everything else." He shrugged. "At least Eclipse'll have you good as new in no time."

Taeo smiled at me and then looked at Kai. "See? *Nice.*"

Kai ignored him and lit a cigarette. My lungs, which were still aching from my bout with the portens, couldn't handle the smoke. I choked on the fumes.

"Come on, man. Put it out," Taeo said. "She's sick, all right?"

Silently, Kai stubbed out the cigarette.

"Why do you smoke anyway?" I said as my coughing subsided. "Doesn't it fly in the face of being fast and strong and agile or whatever?"

Kai and Taeo looked at each other, their unspoken exchange heavy with meaning.

To me, Kai said, "Everyone has a vice, Gemma. Even me, though I know it must be hard to believe."

Taeo snorted. "Yes, you're so perfect in every other way."

"Well you're vice is probably going to kill you," I said matter-of-factly.

Kai eyed me through the rearview mirror. "When you saw the Host this morning, how many elderly Essen did you see? None, right? That's because, in spite of the Mederium, those of us who don't De-A tend to die before old age... and not of lung cancer."

"Maybe you'd have a better chance of living longer if you weren't undermining all your so-called training with cigarettes," I muttered.

"*Damn*," Taeo said, trying to keep the laughter out of his voice.

"It's not my training you should be worried about right now," Kai said. "It's yours. From tonight forward until your Activation, this is our agenda: combat training in the evening; recovery at the Mederium and dinner; sleep for four hours; fitness training in the morning; recovery at the Mederium and breakfast; and then gifts honing with Echo followed by Records-study at the Tabularium. Your training concludes sunrise Minnesota-time each day.

"The daylight hours are yours. Do what you want, I don't really care, just stay out of trouble. You can go back to your aunt's house, catch up on sleep, hang out with Jonny, whatever. But when you're on Salvos, your schedule, like you yourself, is mine to Keep."

I slumped back against my seat. "Why bother?" I grumbled. "You know I've already decided. What's the point in training me when—"

"Yes, *I* know, and yes, Taeo knows, but beyond us, and maybe Rori"—Kai shot Taeo an even look—"the assumption is that you will remain an Activated Essen. You're the Link! The Host would never believe their quote-unquote savior would abandon them. If they found out that's exactly what you're planning to do, they'd view you as the worst kind of traitor. I *have* to train you, not just because I'm your Keeper and the *Consociare* compels me to, but because if I *don't*, they'll know what you've decided too, and that would be bad for both of us."

Taeo faced me. In a gentle voice, he said, "Like it or not, Gemma, the Host has expectations—both of you as the Link, and of Kai as your Keeper. We expect the portens. Maybe you think that's unfair, but isn't it just as unfair for you to withhold it? We need it for our survival, and if you're going to De-A, you've got no reason to keep it. Besides, the sooner you hand it over, the sooner you can end the charade that you're in this for the long haul. You won't have to train or study. You can just bide your time until your birthday."

I looked at the disfigured flesh of my hand. "And what if I can't?" I said quietly. "What if I can't hand it over?"

"Can't?" said Kai. "Or won't?"

Taeo pursed his lips. "You can't have it both ways, Gemma. You can't De-A *and* keep the portens. If you do, you'll lose one enemy but gain another. The Dothen would stop hunting you, but the Essen would start. It wouldn't end until you'd given up the weapon."

I folded my arms and looked out the window at the passing snow banks. Why shouldn't I let the Essen have the boulder opal? It had lost its sentimental value once I'd learned it was from my mother rather than my father, and heaven knew I wasn't likely to touch it ever again. It obviously meant more to them than it did to me, and if I gave it up, I could stop pretending I planned to remain Activated. It would be so easy. I could just pass it off to Malakai and let him bear the burden of learning how to use it.

Why *shouldn't* I? In the back of my mind, Gate's warning nagged at me. He'd told me not to trust Malakai, not to part with the portens willingly. But where was Gate now? All he'd given me was some broken instructions about…

A thought struck me. Gate's message to me had been *broken*, interrupted by moments of static. The static had obscured Gate's message, and because of it, I had missed several of his words.

Something Kai had said earlier that morning resurfaced. In telling me about the *Pactem Orbis*, he'd said that the omission of certain details distorts meaning. Were the words that had been lost in the crackling transmission of Gate's message *important* words? Were they significant words, the omission of which had distorted the message's overall meaning?

Based on Malakai's reaction when I repeated what Gate had said, maybe they were. He'd been adamant that I was mistaken, that Gate would never have told me not to trust him.

But how could I know? Gate was off the grid and I'd received no other communications from him, so how could I know what he'd meant for me to hear? How could I know if I should trust Malakai? How could I know whether or not I should give up the portens?

I sighed inwardly, knowing I wouldn't feel comfortable giving Kai the portens until I could determine if there was more to Gate's message. And until that time, I would have to train and study and act as though I wasn't intending to De-A.

Of course, if March 25th arrived without my drawing additional meaning from Gate's message, I would have to hand over the portens anyway, whether I was comfortable with it or not. Taeo was right. If I didn't, the Host would come for it, and wasn't the point of leaving the Essen world behind... to leave the Essen world behind?

My words came out soft when I finally responded. "The Host won't have to hunt me down, Taeo. It won't come to that."

"Damn right it won't," Kai muttered without turning to face me. "How could it, when my will is so much stronger than yours?"

CHAPTER 55

Night had fallen on Salvos and I stood beneath the ever-darkening sky at the edge of the Mederium. Eclipse circled me, moving deftly for someone without sight. It was her process, Malakai had explained, to read the life-force of the injured prior to granting immersion in the pool. So I waited, allowing her searching brown eyes to finish assessing my wounds.

She addressed me directly when she was finished, telling me that the internal damage I'd sustained was like none she'd seen before. She said it looked as though various aspects of my health had been *consumed*, and that the reduced levels of water, salt, and oxygen in my cells, combined with my lowered body temperature, would require a minimum of two hours of healing.

Malakai was markedly interested in Eclipse's evaluation. I could almost see his mind processing her words, marrying them with the lines of Record 3627. He wanted to know how the portens worked, and since I didn't know and hadn't given him the opportunity to analyze it for himself (which he so sullenly reminded me), he had to try to work it out on his own. He reclined against the large entrance boulder as I entered the pool, reciting in a murmured voice the lines: *The forces of the four reside / Inside the stolen mass, / And all who use it shall abide / Effects that come to pass.*

Eclipse sat down at the edge of the pool, dangling her feet in it. She glanced at Malakai and then spoke to me in a lowered voice, as though worried about breaking his train of thought.

"He's been all scarlets and ochres as long as I've known him. This is the first time I've seen him plum, and it's because of you." Her expression was a mixture of admiration and envy.

I followed her gaze to Malakai. His eyes were closed and he appeared to be very deep in thought, but he looked the same to me.

As if reading my thoughts, she said, "I cannot see the way others can. My eyes do not work, but still people appear in my mind. They are black silhouettes, surrounded by the full spectrum of color."

Like a solar eclipse, I realized.

"Most people display one or two colors more prominently, depending on their overriding emotions," she went on, playing with the end of her long braid. "And Kai's emotions have been constant for years: anger, which is scarlet, followed distantly by hope, which shows as ochre."

"Then what is plum?" I asked, unable to take my eyes off him.

"Isn't it obvious?" she said.

I shook my head.

"Resolve."

Resolve. Of course it was resolve. Only resolve could replace both his anger and his hope. He didn't need either of them if he was determined to get the portens and *win*.

I looked down into the water, at the chalky minerals covering my body. They worked their magic steadily, their lovely pressure rolling up and down my skin. I took a deep breath and held it, knowing I shouldn't ask.

I couldn't help myself. The question came out in a rush as I exhaled. "What do you see when you look at me?"

Eclipse cocked her head at me. "You truly want to know?"

"Yes," I whispered, despite my apprehension.

"I see fern green, Gemma, the color of terror. I see an overwhelming fear and a longing for safety. I see a desire to hide in the shadows."

I opened my mouth to protest but shut it again. As much as I hated to admit it, she wasn't wrong. Fear *was* my overriding feeling. I was afraid of so much since I'd begun undergoing: pain, change, failure, and loss.

"The fear will go away, Gemma," she said. "If you remain in the shadows, you will find safety, and the fear will leave you. But know this: In the shadows, you can never be great. Only safe."

"What makes you think I want to be great?"

Eclipse smiled knowingly. "We all want greatness. We all want to be somebody, to leave our mark on the world. None of us were meant to exist entirely in the shadows."

"And you think... You think I'm existing in the shadows?"

"It's not what I think. It's what I see. Fern green, a desire to hide in the shadows." She started to say something else but hesitated, bringing her fingertips to the surface of the water. Swirling them around, she said, "That's not all I see."

I waited for her to go on, but she didn't. She gazed down into the water, raking her hand through it again and again. After several minutes, curiosity got the better of me. "What, Eclipse? What else do you see?"

Without raising her face, she said, "Echo and I, we have gifts. Not Essen gifts, but gifts granted to us when we entered the Realm Beyond. Gifts of wisdom and discernment. Echo has knowledge as well. It's not limitless, and he still gets frustrated by that which eludes him, but he knows more than most. As for me, I have... perception. I can see some of what others can't." She lifted her head, her dark eyes reflecting my inquisitive expression. "And I can see your parents, Gemma."

I covered my hand with my mouth. "What do you mean? My parents are dead."

Eclipse nodded once. "Yet I can see them, and in seeing them, I am certain you are their blood... But neither of them bears a notae. Your hunch was right. Your parents were not Essen."

I swam to the edge and touched Eclipse's knee, urgency filling my voice. "Please," I said. "Are they here now? Where do you see them? Can I talk to them?"

Her little form seemed to sag. "I'm sorry, Gemma," she said. "They are not here. They exist elsewhere, and I cannot communicate with them where they are."

I let go of her leg, my shoulders drooping with disappointment. Would I ever figure out how I came to be the Link? Or why the portens was in my possession? I sunk beneath the water, allowing the talc-like particles to roll across my neck and scalp, and reminded myself that after March 25th, none of it would matter.

✳ ✳ ✳

With the exception of visiting Eclipse at the Mederium immediately after arriving on Salvos, my schedule that night was exactly as Malakai had described it. Once Eclipse confirmed I was healed and released me from the pool, he ushered me deep into the woods for combat training.

Taeo and Rori were waiting for us when we arrived at the large, circular clearing. Though it was late, the space was well lit by the pastel glow of hundreds of spherical paper lanterns dangling from overhanging tree branches.

We wasted no time getting started because, as Malakai reminded me, our agenda was packed, and due to my visit to the Mederium, we were already behind schedule. He stood opposite Taeo and indicated that I should face Rori. Then, and for nearly two hours after that, he and Taeo demonstrated various techniques to neutralize threats while Rori partnered with me to emulate the moves.

The training, Taeo told me, was modeled after the combat-defense system used by the Israeli Defense Forces, called Krav Maga. It included boxing, grappling, and street fighting techniques, and had proven effective for escaping the Dothen.

"The Dothen don't seem to feel pain," Kai said, "but they have a hard time operating a broken body. So if you are ever caught, do everything you can to crush, sever, and crack any part of the Taken you can reach."

He wanted me to practice, first on Rori, then on himself, and it became obvious to me why our training was to be followed by another visit to the Mederium. At the end of our session, everyone was injured. My efforts had given Rori a variety of lumps and bruises and had left Malakai with a busted, crooked nose. Taeo was wincing and hobbling from repeatedly being used as a demonstration dummy, and I had a twisted knee and a jammed shoulder.

That was combat training. I hated every minute of it.

Back at the Mederium, Eclipse handed each of us a glass filled with clear liquid which resembled water, except for the miniature multicolored beads that were suspended in it. The tiny pink, blue, and yellow pearls made the *Restoration* elixir look like a confetti-clad party in a cup, but as Rori explained, it was no mere post-training celebration drink. The beads contained various types of proteins, branch chain amino acids, and fast-digesting carbohydrates to support recovery. I drank it down along with everyone else, enjoying the lemon flavor that was released as the bursting beads landed on my tongue.

After our soak in the pool, which was relatively short, we adjourned to our respective tents. The "dinner" Malakai had referenced was waiting on the table next to my bed. Consisting of some sort of jerky and a bowl of granola, it seemed less a dinner than a snack, and I wolfed it down. Then, exhausted, I fell into bed.

The sky was still pitch-dark when Malakai whistled me awake from outside my tent four hours later. A bleary-eyed glance at my phone told me it was 3:30 in the morning and that Jonny had texted. *Got your letter,* his message said. *See you in the morning.*

A pang of worry ran through me as I dressed. Was he still upset with me? The brevity of the text wasn't his typical style. I sat on the edge of the bed and began typing a message in response when Malakai whispered loudly, "What's taking so long? Let's go, princess."

"All right already," I grumbled, setting the phone down. Jonny would be fast asleep right now anyhow. I emerged from the tent, annoyed to find Malakai shirtless once again.

✳ ✳ ✳

A guy like that, walking around half-naked, and you're telling me all you noticed was his tattoo.

Jonny's words rang in my ears and stabbed at my heart. Of course I'd noticed more than the tattoo. How could anyone overlook the rippling muscles that made the tree dance as though by wind?

I desperately wished for Malakai to put on a shirt. His body was a distraction—not because it excited me in any way, but because it was so sculpted, like art. Yes, it was like art. And every time he moved, something new flexed and drew my attention. It was beautiful to look at.

"Focus, Gemma," Malakai repeated. "Don't let your mind wander. Concentrate on what we're doing."

What we were doing was pure torture. After finishing our forty-minute "warm up" run on the beach, we had begun the process of breaking down our muscles. We'd already done pushups, situps, and squats, and now we were doing lunges.

As much as I despised what he had called "fitness training," I didn't dare let up. In everything, Malakai was testing me. He was assessing my strength of body and will, and despite my physical weakness, I would not give him the satisfaction of seeing me quit. I would not break, even if it meant getting right back up and trying again after my body failed. Call it pride, but I had to demonstrate my fortitude. Malakai had to see that my mental discipline was a force to be reckoned with. I couldn't bear him telling me, even once more, how much stronger than mine his will was.

We spent two hours working every muscle in our bodies. Trembling, I collapsed to my knees and threw up on the beach. Then I covered the mess with sand, the fine grains sticking to my sweaty arms and legs, and stood up, ready to prove myself again.

Malakai folded his arms across his bare and glistening chest. "That," he said, "was gross." He shook his head in disgust and said, "Come on, it's time for round three," and I knew he was referring to the Mederium.

CHAPTER 56

'Extensive tear, immediate repair.' That was the Essen fitness training philosophy.

Because of the Mederium's supernatural healing capabilities, broken down muscles could be rebuilt in as little as thirty minutes. This allowed the truly dedicated Essen to train each muscle group two or even three times a day without fatiguing and delivered accelerated results: increased muscle strength and size in a timeframe competitive bodybuilders would kill for.

Of course, the Essen weren't concerned with appearance as much as they were performance. Like Kai, they valued speed and strength and agility. It was ingrained in them from youth. The Essen culture and lifestyle seemed to revolve around it.

It was a matter of survival, but it was also a bit of an addiction. Adults and children alike arose at first light, eager to get a workout in before the bridge opened. Then in the evening, once they were back on Salvos, they'd train again.

All this was explained to me by the blonde-haired, blue-eyed treasure-keeper named Puck who had joined me and Malakai in the pool shortly after we'd arrived. He had boyish good looks, a lean build, and a mischievous twinkle in his eyes, all of which he used to bait me.

Malakai ignored Puck's shameless flirting and showing off, choosing instead to talk with Eclipse. It wasn't until Puck's boisterous chatter turned into a hungry inquiry about the portens that Kai spoke up.

"Time to go, Gemma. You're recovery should be complete. Finish your *Restoration*. Echo's waiting."

I stepped out of the pool and toweled off, amazed at how I felt. *I'm never going to get used to that*, I thought, reflecting on the wonder of the Mederium. My body felt fresh, strong, and healthy. It wasn't sore at all.

We ate a hurried breakfast, which was some sort of dry oat-fruit-nut mixture, and headed off to the Tabularium just as droves of Essen began to arrive at the pool.

"The Mederium is busiest between 7 and 9 AM and between 8 and 10 PM," Kai said as we walked, "so we'll be avoiding it at those times. Your morning workouts will be earlier than everyone else's, and your evening training will be later. I don't have to tell you how disruptive constant interrogations about the portens would be."

Kai's discouragement of my interaction with the Host made me suspicious. Why didn't he want me getting to know other Essen? Was it really a protection for me, or was he protecting his own interests? Was he afraid that if I got too chummy with another member of the Host, I'd either choose *not* to De-A and keep the portens, or choose to give it to someone else instead?

The portens represented—and held—power. Whoever ended up with it would need strength of character. It would have to be someone smart enough to understand it but wise enough to use it discriminately; someone hearty enough to handle it but virtuous enough to withstand corruption.

Was that person Malakai?

Echo believed he was.

Echo, who had been to the mysterious Realm Beyond, whatever that meant, and who had been granted the gifts of wisdom, discernment, and knowledge. Echo, whose knowing eyes belied his youthfulness. Echo, who was studying me with those clear blue eyes right now from beneath the Tabularium's stone archway.

"Good morning," he said to Kai and me.

"Hey, kid," Kai said, ruffling his platinum hair. "Thanks for this."

Echo nodded. "I will return Gemma to the Axis when we have concluded."

"Cool," Kai said, turning to leave. "See you at 9:30, then."

"Wait, where are you going?" I asked.

He arched an eyebrow at me. "Echo is perfectly capable of leading your Records training. And he's the *only* one who can help you develop your gifts. That is, unless you want to tell me about them?"

"I'll tell you mine if you tell me yours," I said.

"Yeah, right." Kai said, rolling his eyes. "Echo, if you need me, I'll be on the beach."

"Fitness training?" Echo asked, shifting weight from his deformed leg.

"Yeah."

"But we already did—" I began.

Kai looked mildly amused. "What we did was for you. It did nothing for me." Then he leaned in and whispered loudly in Echo's ear, "Be careful how hard you push her. She's a puker," and darted off into the woods before I could smack him.

✳ ✳ ✳

The radio crackled in my head, and as I moved the imaginary tuner up and down the FM band, I heard voices I didn't recognize engaged in conversations I didn't understand. And still, at the end of the radio band, floating through the highest frequency setting, was the tinkling sound of wind chimes.

I described what I heard to Echo, but rather than enlightening me as to what it might mean, he just smiled encouragingly. It was maddening, even more so than it had been with Gate, because Echo *knew*.

He knew what my gifts would become but wouldn't tell me. Like a plant that grows sturdier in the wind, he said, so my gifts would grow stronger with adversity—namely, the struggle of puzzling it out.

I applied all of myself to the fruitless task, sure that Echo would report back to Malakai, but felt relieved when we changed focus to Records training.

If it was possible, the Records mesmerized me even more than they had the previous day. Early morning rays shone almost horizontally through the trees, creating long and distorted shadows across the rocky walls and green glass tablets. I wandered between the rows of English Records, reading and absorbing and interpreting.

Studying the Records was my favorite part of the training agenda, partly because it was self-directed (Echo allowed me to read them as I pleased and only commented when I asked questions), and partly because I was *really good* at it.

Now that I knew some of the *Pactem Orbis* legends and had some context for the writings, I found them relatively easy to understand—well, the modern English ones anyway. They were like riddles, and my brain does well with riddles. And the longer I studied them, the more patterns emerged. There were rules, it seemed, that defined a Record: four stanzas of four lines that rhymed A-B-A-B; some reference to each of the original spirit-mothers' domains of earth, air, water, and fire; and a key message that served to either warn, remind, or guide the Essen.

Like Malakai had mentioned, there were several Records that described the deadly consequences of speaking about Essen matters to non-Essen people. One of them impacted me more than the others:

> *3395 – The Cost*
> *We laid her on a pyre,*
> *Our daughter of the light,*
> *And we lit the wood with fire,*
> *Sending sparks into the night.*
>
> *Ashes, ashes, dust to dust,*
> *Her body once more earth,*
> *Then she left us in windy gust,*
> *Just six years from her birth.*
>
> *We beat our hearts and wailed,*
> *As she traveled out to sea,*
> *Since we knew that we had failed*
> *To train her properly.*
>
> *So no other child is lost,*
> *Her death must be a lesson:*
> *The whole Host must know the cost*
> *Of voicing secrets of the Essen.*

I stared at the tablet, reading it over and over, my heart breaking for the fallen child who had either unknowingly or accidentally "voiced secrets" that resulted in her death. In my mind, the little girl looked like Hannah, and I could see members of the Host carrying her lifeless body to a pyre for burning.

The disturbing image was still with me when Malakai met me at the Axis at 9:30.

"You're quieter than usual," he observed.

"Yeah," I said, looking out at the sea. Were flakes of the girl's charred remains still out there somewhere, floating on a breeze or drifting on distant waves? Or had they all settled somewhere on the ocean floor? Were the ashes of other fallen children lingering out there as well? I shuddered at the morbidity of my thoughts.

Who would choose to live like this? I wondered, not for the last time. *Who would choose to live in a world where children grew up parentless and parents often lost their children?*

It was a world of pain and loss, a world of restrictions and cages and running and death. I didn't need another reason to De-A, but now I had one.

Someday I might like to have a family of my own, but not here, and not like this. They could keep their tropical island, their mysterious bridges, their emerald tablets, their pool of healing, their elixirs, and their gold and cars and condos. I didn't need them. I didn't need my yet-to-be-solidified supernatural gifts. I didn't need the portens or the Host or *greatness*.

Eclipse was wrong. Not everyone wants to be somebody. Some of us just want to be happy, and if that means pursuing safety rather than greatness, then I guess I'd take my shadows.

CHAPTER 57

The overcast sky was the exact same shade of grayish-white as the snow-covered landscape. Everything looked bleak and dirty, trapped beneath the sunless dome. On days like this, there were no shadows. There was only the dreary, washed-out color of plaster as far as the eye could see.

I asked Malakai to pull into Jonny's driveway, rather than my own. As I got out of his car, he handed me an envelope.

"Puck gave it to me before we crossed the bridge," he said. "It's your bankcard, your PIN, and some extra cash." He eyed me evenly. "So I'll pick you up at four again, yeah?"

I put the envelope in my coat pocket, told him I'd be ready, and watched him back into the street and speed off.

Jonny was waiting at the door when I walked up. Holding it open as I entered the house, he said with an easy smile, "Hey, girl," and then wrapped me in a hug.

He looked and sounded exhausted. Though his face lit up at the sight of me, there were dark circles beneath his eyes, and his hair hung loose and messy about his cheeks. He was wearing his flannel pajama pants and a sweat-shirt, but they weren't wrinkled or creased from sleep.

"How was work?" He said through a yawn.

"Okay, I guess. Jonny… are you okay? You seem dead tired. Do you want me to come back later?"

"No!" he said quickly. "I want to spend the day with you. That's *why* I'm so tired."

"I'm not following. Didn't you sleep last night at all?"

He shook his head. "I didn't go to bed. I made myself stay up."

"So you've been up for more than twenty-four hours?" I put my hand on his cheek. "Why on earth would you do that? What did you do all night?"

Jonny tilted his head at me. "I kept myself awake because I thought... Well, I thought you'd be exhausted too." He took a step back and examined me. "But you look amazing, even more beautiful than you normally do. How do you do it, Gem? Look so gorgeous even after working all night? Aren't you tired?"

I was supposed to be tired. Of course I was supposed to be tired. According to the official story, I had been at work. I couldn't tell Jonny I'd actually slept for four hours and refreshed myself three times in a miraculous pool of healing.

"I'm completely beat," I lied.

"I knew you would be," he said, grabbing my hand and leading me to his bedroom. "I knew you'd want to sleep. And I knew if I wanted to spend the day with you, I should want to sleep too." He paused at his bedroom door and faced me. "Is that okay?"

I closed my eyes, overcome by his thoughtfulness and consideration.

"Hey," he said softly, lifting my chin with a finger. "If you'd rather... I mean, I understand if you want go home. I just thought... it would be nice to hold you for a while."

His dark blue eyes were fixed on mine, but his expression was tender. He really *would* understand if I decided to go home, despite the fact that he had stayed awake all night in the hopes of sleeping the day away together.

Who else in the world would ever value my company so much that they'd rather be with me as I sleep than not be with me at all? Who else in the world would be as accepting if I decided to leave? Who else but Jonny would give everything of himself without expecting anything in return?

It *would* be nice to be held, even if I wasn't tired. In Jonny's arms, I felt comfortable and content. In his arms, I felt the calming peace of long-standing and steadfast friendship. In his arms, I could temporarily forget that I was undergoing.

"I'll stay," I murmured, squeezing his hand.

He pushed the door open and guided me into his room. My letter was lying on his bed.

"That," he said, nodding to the paper as he shut the door, "was the best thing I've ever gotten from anybody. Ever."

I sat down on his bed and gathered up the pages, holding them in my lap. Unable to look at him, I stared at the letter and mumbled, "So you're not mad at me?"

"Mad at you?" Jonny said with a laugh in his voice. "How could I be mad at you?" He plopped down next to me and took the letter, flipping the pages over in his hands. "I've never been so in love with you."

The words sent a jolt through me. Sometime long ago, the phrase 'I love you' entered our friendship, but it had been platonic, almost familial. The words 'in love,' as Jonny used them now, had never been uttered.

I shook my head. "But yesterday—"

"Yesterday you were right," he said. "I was being insecure. And I'm sorry, Gem, I really am. I was hurt and confused, but I was never mad at you. I just wanted you to open up to me, and I didn't get why you wouldn't." He ran a hand through his disheveled hair. "But opening up... It's something you need to do when you're ready. I knew going into this that I'd need to be patient. You've always had your own pace for things. I can't force it, and I shouldn't have tried. ...Because I know that eventually, when you can, you'll find a way to tell me what's been going on."

Would I? Would I be able to find a way? He deserved to know the truth, and I wanted to give it to him... but at what cost?

I shivered and Jonny pulled me to him, setting my letter on his bedside table.

"What I really needed, Gemma—more than explanations for everything—was to know where we stood. Sometimes you can be so hard to read, even for me. And that's why it meant so much, what you wrote... I just needed to know how you felt."

"So you believe me?" I whispered against Jonny's shoulder. "About... Malakai?"

He kissed my head. "You said not to worry, so I'm not going to worry. I trust you. And if he's going to be your friend, I'll try to make him mine as well." He chuckled softly. "Just remember, I said *try*."

The knot of tension that had been tightening in my chest since Jonny left the previous day finally released. I took a deep breath, letting it out slowly, and settled against him.

"Come here," he said, reclining on the bed. He brought a blanket over us and we lay there, warm and close and relaxed. "Gemma?" he said, his voice husky with weariness.

"Hmm?" I tilted my head back to look at him, but his eyes were closed.

"I never want to face a future that you're not in, either."

Then his face went slack and the arm that was wrapped around me loosened, and I knew that sleep had taken him.

I wasn't tired, but I didn't want to move either. It felt *natural* to be tucked against Jonny, like our bodies were designed to fit each other. Though our relationship had not gotten particularly physical yet, the transition from friends to more-than-friends had not been awkward. I liked being with him. I liked his attention. It made me feel special that someone so sought-after would choose *me*, undeserving as I was.

He deserved better. He deserved a best friend who was worthy of his trust, one who wasn't lying to him at every turn. He deserved a girlfriend who felt more than devotion and affection, but passion and desire. He deserved a future filled with dreams and truths and intimacy and adventure.

Breathing him in, feeling his warmth, hearing his heart, I knew I was weak, far too weak to ever release him. I was committed. I hoped commitment would be enough.

I looked up at his face, at his smooth skin and angular jawline and straight nose. He really was so very handsome. I reached up to brush a few strands of hair away from his cheek, but as I did so, something else caught my eye.

Behind Jonny's head, inserted between the seams of his wooden headboard, was a tiny scrap of white paper. Though it was folded over, its shape was unmistakable: It was rectangular slip from a fortune cookie.

It was the fortune I'd asked him about, the one I'd seen in my memory—it had to be. I started to pull the slip from its hiding spot but hesitated. As curious as I was about what it said, I didn't feel right about reading it. *I can't show you*, Jonny had said. *Not yet. Not until it comes true.*

I shoved the paper back as it was. Jonny was willing to be patient with me, so I needed to be patient with him. …Because I knew that eventually, when the time was right, he'd find a way to tell me what it said.

The thought made me smile, and I closed my eyes against his chest, not needing sleep but finding rest.

CHAPTER 58

Kai owned my nights and Jonny ruled my days and the weeks bled by. The intense schedule became routine: An hour before sundown, Kai would collect me and bring me to Salvos for starlit combat training, recovery at the Mederium, dinner, and sleep. In the earliest hours of the morning, we'd do our fitness training, take another dip in the Mederium, and have breakfast. Then I'd work with Echo in the Tabularium until we could cross the bridge and Kai could bring me home.

My hours with Jonny were less structured, but only marginally so. Because we had such limited time together, a portion of which he insisted I be home "sleeping," we fell into a routine of our own, which started around lunchtime and consisted mostly of hanging out in his room, listening to music, talking, and laughing—until Kai arrived to pick me up for "work."

I saw very little of my aunt or Flash, and once spring semester began, I didn't get to see much of Jonny, either. Between working at the snowboard park, finishing his *summa cum laude* thesis, and completing his remaining credits, he had very few "daytime" hours available. Still, we tried to meet up on campus whenever possible, and since I was taking Professor Dagenais's "Storytelling in the Twenty-First Century" class, which met on Mondays, Wednesdays, and Fridays, at two o'clock, we got to see each other at least three times during the week.

It was pride more than anything that kept me from quitting school altogether. I was only taking the one course, but it was an honors-level course, and with everything else that was going on, I had no business attempting it—and it showed in my work. Professor Dagenais had on a few occasions now asked to speak with me after class, and in those conversations, I'd fallen from "Ms. Gemma Pointe" back to "young lady." And yet… I couldn't bring myself to drop the class. It was what kept me rooted in the "real world." It was my tie to normalcy.

Normalcy was a distant concept as my undergoing progressed, especially once my "gifts honing" sessions with Echo began yielding greater results. The conversations I started hearing in my mind as I moved from one imaginary radio station to the next were of a highly personal nature, personal to me, and I felt uncomfortable listening to the discussions others were having about me. It felt odd, hearing Aunt Sheri talking to God out loud, asking him to guard and guide both me and Flash; I didn't even know she prayed. Just as unsettling was the conversation I heard between Taeo, Rori, and Ren, in which they were arguing about whether or not I would one day replace Phoenix as the Augur of the Host. The worst dialogue I had the misfortune of hearing, though, was this:

"Come on, Jonny. You can't be that naïve." It was the gravelly voice of Devun Drake, one of Jonny's closest friends.

"She asked me to trust her, she told me I could, and I believe I can. That's all there is to it," Jonny responded.

"So you don't think it's just a little bit suspicious that she's gone—like every single night, man—for sixteen-plus hours. I mean, even the President takes a day off every once in a while."

"I'm not saying I think she's been completely straight with me, but Devun, it's Gemma. You know Gemma. She isn't exactly forthright. She'll tell me whatever it is when she's ready."

"So you really believe she's been working, even though some ogre in a fancy car brings her back home every morning?" Devun sounded incredulous.

"Here's what you don't know about Gemma, dude: She's loyal. She's a good person. She's honest. Besides that, she must be working—she bought me a piano for Valentine's Day. A piano! Do you know what those cost? I didn't want to accept it, but she insisted…

Said she's only been working so much because she wanted to earn enough to get me one. I've always talked about learning to play…"

"So she gave you a piano and then spent the evening with the other guy? Sounds like a gift of guilt, if you ask me," Devun muttered.

In a way, Devun was right. I had been feeling guilty, very guilty, *especially* on Valentine's Day. It had been the sweetest day, and Jonny had gone to such lengths to make "our first Valentine's Day as a bona fide couple" special. Not only had he snuck into my room while I was at "work" and filled it with my favorite flowers (where on earth had he gotten lilacs in February?), but he took me out to breakfast and then to Como Park, where he played a song on his guitar for me, his poor fingers turning blue as we sat on the frosty bench overlooking the frozen lake.

His song, called "Better Than Air," was like poetry. Afterwards, he gave me a copy, and I listened to it over and over again, memorizing the lyrics.

I never had the words
They didn't form in my mouth
I just waited and waited
For them to come

Every time I tried to say it
The breath caught in my throat
Some "Mr. Way-With-Words"
But here we are, finally

You're better than air,
And I can inhale you deeply
You're better than air
I can tell you now, my angel

I was never alone
But lonely without you
Suffocating slowly
But here we are, finally

You frustrated me, babe,
Then you resuscitated me, and

You're better than air,
And I can inhale you deeply
You're better than air
I can tell you now, my angel

They say love can leave you breathless
But it doesn't matter
Because, oh, you're so much better than air

Everything about the song, everything about the day, was romantic, and it was the romance, just as much as the leaving early, that left me feeling guilty. Jonny was *in love* with me; I simply *loved* him.

In the back of my mind, I clung to the belief that after Activation, when such things were supposed to happen, I would fall in love with Jonny. The slow burn of my commitment and loyalty would flare up, would ignite me from the inside out, and become that unquenchable *longing*.

But it hadn't yet, so I didn't have that type of love to give him. Instead, I gave him a piano.

Maggie was at a loss for where it could go in her house, something I'd neglected to consider, but she ultimately shifted everything in her living room to make room for it. "It's a little over the top, Gemma," she said to me when it was being delivered, but she smiled anyway.

All of my gifts were over the top. They had to be. I was "working" too steadily and for too many hours to give moderate gifts. Besides that, once I got used to using my Essen bankcard, which didn't take long after Puck assured me that more gold was constantly being manufactured (*"You're an Essen,"* he told me, *"Spend it. You're entitled."*), I enjoyed lavishing my aunt and cousin and boyfriend with presents. I even bought gifts for Paul and Lucy, too.

It was a delicate balance to strike, though. I needed to spend enough money to demonstrate I'd made some but not so much to arouse suspicion that I was acquiring it illegally. The last thing I needed was for my loved ones to stage some sort of intervention.

I drew the line at buying a car for myself. I still didn't have a license, and cars aren't a one-time expense. Once I became a De-A, I'd be cut off, and then I'd be stuck with the ongoing responsibility and upkeep.

This money situation is temporary, I told myself. *Just like being an Essen.*

"You're going to go through with it, aren't you?" Rori asked in a low voice during one of our combat training sessions. "You're really going to De-A."

I glanced at Kai and Taeo, who were arguing about the correct way to defend against a frontal knife attack. "What makes you think that?" I said quietly.

She rolled her eyes. "You're three weeks from Activation, and you've never been to your condo. Vivian told me you didn't bother to stop by, not even to check it out."

It was true. I hadn't been back to Riverview Estates since Gravitation had pulled me there the morning of Raela Celere's death. My reluctance to check out my new place stemmed from wanting to keep things simple and compartmentalized. I didn't want to introduce anything that might cloud my decision to De-A.

Or anything *else*, it would be more appropriate to say. Despite Kai's best efforts to keep me isolated, there were almost always a few others at the Mederium—people whom I suspected arrived at the same odd hours as us just to see me—and what started as amiable conversations began to turn into friendships. There was the slender-framed and stormy-eyed Ren, brother of the late Raela Celere; the flirtatious and charming Puck; his hilarious and sarcastic sister, Kelby; the brooding "walking tattoo" Alistair, and his equally-inked girlfriend, Jossi; the stalky, redheaded Shea; and of course, Taeo and Rori.

To Kai's great disappointment, Rori and I were becoming close, having truly bonded during combat training over jokes made at his expense. Though I was wary about getting too attached to anyone within the Host, my connection with Rori was strong, almost sisterly.

I was forming relationships with people and that worried me, particularly with regard to Echo, Eclipse, and Hannah. The three of them frequently hovered about, staying up into the wee hours of night, watching combat training or helping prepare "dinner." A fondness for each of them settled in me.

Fondness and friendships and familiarity were dangerous. They could grow in influence and possibly overshadow the future I envisioned with Jonny. I tried to distance myself, tried to make myself more remote, but it was hard.

It was hard to live two lives and be a liar in both of them.

As the days grew longer and my Activation approached, Kai could see the stress of my dual-existence weighing on me. During fitness training, about a week before my birthday, he said, "Just give me the portens, Gemma. Then you can stop pretending."

He'd been badgering me about the portens every day for months of course, but I still hadn't solved the riddle of Gate's message. There had been no more clues, nothing to help me understand whether I should or shouldn't entrust it to Kai, and I had already promised myself that I wouldn't give it to him in advance of my Activation unless there was new information. Additionally, I was still afraid to remove it from under my bed. There it had remained, a swirl of colors that mesmerized me every time I lifted my dust ruffle and stole a peak at it. There it remained, the enigma of my life.

"I can stop pretending in a week," I said as we ran our warm-up along the beach.

There was still a part of me that believed I'd figure out, before my Activation, how my mother had come to have the portens and how it worked. New memories surfaced every day now, rounding out my past, and I picked them apart, searching for some clue that would lead me to the answers.

But it was only a week, and whether I had my answers or not, I would De-A. Making it to Activation so I could De-A had been the goal all along. It was the understanding to which I had anchored myself, the reason I had endured my training, the ongoing, water-laden nightmares, and the constant and painful episodes of Affliction.

A thorough understanding of my gifts, like a thorough understanding of the portens, still eluded me. Sure, I was better able to manage the "brain buzz" and the pull of Gravitation, but to what end? And what was the mysterious second gift that Echo had referenced during my first visit on Salvos? We only ever worked on developing my 'gift of the mind.'

"In a week," Kai said evenly, setting the pace with his long strides, "you'll be twenty-one. You'll be twenty-one, and you'll have given up everything that made you special. Your gifts, your portens, your supernatural identity..." He shook his head. "I don't get it."

"In a week," I retorted breathlessly, "I'll be twenty-one and *free*. Free to be wherever I want whenever I want with whomever I want—"

"Jonny," Kai said, rolling his eyes.

"—and I won't have to lie or make up excuses or—"

"—Or be challenged or be bettered—"

"—Or be *divided*. I'll be able to—"

"—Finish a sentence without panting. Geez, you'd never know we'd been running forty minutes a day for ten weeks now. Maybe you should stop talking so you don't pass out."

One more week, I silently fumed. Then I could, to use Kai's words, take up the normal, boring life of a De-A. The life of a De-A may be boring, but at least it's *whole*. I would have one life, one circle, one world. It would all work out. It had to.

At least, that's what I thought before Taeo bolted towards us from further down the beach and stopped, bent and heaving, in our path.

"Kai," he said, his long honey-brown locks plastered to his sweaty face. "You need to come now."

"Where?" Kai said with an intensity I'd never heard before.

"The Hall of Records," Taeo said, standing upright but holding his side. "3629."

Kai's jaw dropped. "It can't be..."

Taeo nodded. "It is," he said. "Rori and I were on our way back from the Aerarium—having a nightcap—and I saw it. 3629. The first Record in eighteen years. I sprinted straight here to tell you."

"What kind is it?" Kai almost whispered.

"It's what you think," Taeo said. "A Vision. A Vision about the portens and the Link and the Host. Kai..." He put his hand on Kai's shoulder, his chest swelling as he tried to catch his breath. "Kai, it's bad. I'm not sure Gemma should..." He met my gaze and then looked quickly away.

Kai's body tensed and I caught the fiercest of looks in his too-green eyes. Then, without another word, he took off into the night, running faster than I'd ever seen anyone go.

CHAPTER 59

Taeo hadn't wanted me to see Record 3629, but he didn't try to keep me from it either. As I chased after Malakai, he kept pace with me, his concerned gray eyes sliding sideways to my face as we ran, as though he was trying to find the words to prepare me for what I would read.

We arrived at the Tabularium winded and sweaty and probably a good twenty minutes after Malakai. In the dimness of predawn, the great stone archway seemed almost foreboding. I hesitated at the threshold.

"Gemma…" Taeo began, placing a sympathetic hand on my shoulder. "The future isn't set yet. Remember that. The Records…"

I looked up into Taeo's face, his beard failing to hide lines of worry. "…Are never wrong," I said. "Echo told me. There isn't a single Vision recorded by an Augur, at least among the English Records, that hasn't come to pass."

His grip on my shoulder tightened. "But they aren't specific. They're vague, open to interpretation. We don't know exactly what Phoenix Saw, but things might not be as bad as they read. Phoenix can clarify. Rori went to get him while I came for you and Kai. Hopefully she's getting answers right now. If there's a way to help you… We'll find it."

He sounded so determined I gave him a small nod. Then I proceeded into the Tabularium, anxious to learn what he already knew.

I hurried through the maze of stone walls, awed once more by the majesty of the place. In the earliest hours of morning, I had expected to find the

Tabularium dark and hard to navigate. Instead, the green glass tablets seemed to glow as though backlit, illuminating the rows of Records.

As I neared the row of English tablets, I heard Malakai's raised voice carrying from the other side of a wall. His outrage was evident, and the very air seemed to shake as his deep bass became louder. I sprinted towards the shouting, but Taeo caught my arm before I rounded the corner.

"No," he said quietly, holding me back. He held a finger to his lips and raised his head, listening. A muffled, dispassionate voice carried over the wall. "He's with Phoenix. We shouldn't interrupt."

I met his slate-gray eyes and was about to respond when Kai erupted with anger.

"How can you say that? We still have two weeks! What we need now is a strategy and tactics and *direction*! *You* know peoples' gifts—who can help fortify the bridge? Who can place protections on the kids? Who can—"

"There is nothing anyone can do," Phoenix said, his voice flat and apathetic. "Evil is upon us, Malakai."

"So that's it then? You're just giving up? You're supposed to be our *leader*!" I heard a crunching noise and then the cascade of rubble, like Kai had punched or kicked the rock wall.

Genuine surprise colored Phoenix's words. "Giving up? No! Accepting fate! I have Seen what is to come. You know as well as I do that once a Vision has settled—"

"God *damn* you, Phoenix!" Kai yelled, drowning out Phoenix's words. "The Host will *panic*! Why the hell would you publish the blasted thing at all, if there's nothing—"

"Kai," the smoky alto voice of Rori broke in. "Calm down. You're being a hothead." Taeo's mouth quirked up a little as he heard her reproach. "Phoenix," she said, sounding both composed and assured, "what *exactly* have you Seen? What is certain and what is not yet fixed? Is there anything that *can* be done?"

Phoenix sighed heavily. "Everything I know is right there. You know the visions never come to Augurs in the greatest of detail."

"Can you at least specify what *part* of the past will be repeated?" Rori asked. "Is it just the attack itself, or will we lose thirteen again? How many of the Host will fall?"

"I—" Phoenix faltered. "In the Vision, only one death is clear. The fate of all others depends on whether or not we have the portens. But I don't know how *anyone* could possibly survive, not once the bridge is compromised..." He trailed off, sounding defeated.

"Pull yourself together," Kai demanded, his voice filled with disgust. "We *will* survive, every one of us will. I'll get the portens and on March 31st, we'll fight the Dothen and we'll *win*, even if it does have to happen this side of the bridge. *No one* will be lost."

"You can't save everyone, Malakai," Phoenix said resignedly. "Your Kept... she *is* going to die. That much I know for sure. I've Seen it. It makes no difference whether she decides to De-A—her choice is irrelevant. Gemma Pointe will not live to see April."

The world seemed to lurch beneath my feet and Taeo put out a steadying arm as I swayed. I clutched his elbow as Phoenix's words, spoken with such indifference, throbbed in my ears.

"Then I'm telling you again," Kai thundered. "Remove 3629 from the wall. You shouldn't have published it; it benefits no one. The Link—Gemma—is a symbol of hope. If people find out she's going to fall... they'll come apart. Take the tablet down."

"The Host deserves to know what's coming," Phoenix said. "They deserve this Record, this *prophecy*—"

"Even though there's nothing they can do to prepare for it? Why would you do that, induce that kind of panic among our people! Just to prove that you had one more Record in you? Just to prove you aren't as abysmal of an Augur as everyone thought? Don't make this about you and your shit! One Record can't redeem you from eighteen years' worth of failure!"

In the tension-filled silence following Kai's outburst, and I could picture him seething, jaw clenching and unclenching, his green eyes narrowed and looking almost black in the final moments before dawn.

"What would you have me do then?" Phoenix said in a dead voice.

This time Rori spoke. "Kai is right. There's no sense informing the Host of an impending doom that they can do nothing about. Either take down the Record—now, before anyone else, including Gemma, can see it—or leave it up and tell us what we *can* do about it."

At length, Phoenix said, "I will call an assembly for later this morning. I'll figure out how we might survive, and I'll... I'll assign tasks." His words lacked conviction.

"Make people believe you," Kai warned. "Make *me* believe you. Convince us with a *plan*. Give orders for preparation. Commit to standing with us. Inspire hope. Be a *leader*. Do everything in your power to ready us for the attack."

Phoenix grunted an acknowledgment.

"How much time do you need?" Rori asked.

"Give me until noon," Phoenix said.

"We'll spread the word, then. An assembly at noon at the Axis. What else do you want us to do?"

For a moment, nothing was said. Then in a weary voice Phoenix said, "You'll get your assignments with everyone else."

We heard Phoenix's slow and deflated-sounding shuffle as he departed. When we were sure he had gone, Taeo, on whose arm I still clung, led me around the corner. I stumbled ahead feeling like I was swimming rather than walking.

"I think she's in shock," Taeo said.

Rori rushed to us and searched my face, her forehead creased with concern. "How much did you hear?" she asked.

"Enough." Taeo said. He glanced at Kai, who was standing in front of the wall, trying to block the tablet from sight. "We need to let her read it."

Kai didn't respond, but there was a steely look in his eyes as he met Taeo's.

"Kai," he said gently. "You know she needs to read it. She's already heard..."

Kai's expression remained hard, but the Adam's apple worked up and down in his throat betraying some underlying emotion. As Taeo brought me forward along the tablet-lined wall, Kai refused to look at me. His lips tightened into a scowl and he turned away, walking quickly down the row and around the corner, disappearing from view.

Rori shook her head in disappointment. In a low voice she said to Taeo, "He should have stayed. He's her Keeper! If there was ever a time—"

Taeo silenced her with a look.

303

"Gemma," Taeo said stopping in front of Record 3629. "Do you want us to give you a minute?"

I'm not sure if I answered him, but I didn't release my hold of him either. Record 3629 was before me, the etched glass shiny and clean and untouched by the elements. A sudden shiver ran up my spine, and Rori came to stand next to me.

"It's okay, Gemma," she said. "We're here for you. Go ahead and read it."

And I did.

CHAPTER 60

In my daydreams, I am not afraid of the water.

In my daydreams, I am not afraid of anything.

But in my nightmares, like in real life, I am terrified of drowning, of getting pushed or pulled into the dark depths and not having the strength or the time to make my way back up to the surface.

It's a fear of dying, but why should I fear it? Hadn't I overcome Death once already? Hadn't I escaped his grasp that night I'd spent seventeen minutes submerged in the icy lake? Wasn't I convinced that I'd survived for a reason, that there was *purpose* to my life, that I had some work yet to complete?

Maybe not. Maybe I'd just been lucky, escaping the clutches of Death, and that his claim on me, like his claim on each of us, was still pending. Maybe, having experienced his power before, I was afraid of meeting him again. Because he *would* be coming for me again.

I just didn't think it would be this soon.

As fixated as my subconscious seemed to be on dying (based on the content of my nightmares), it hadn't crossed my conscious mind that my time was actually running out. My focus had been far too narrow to see Death coming. I had been consumed with preserving my relationship with Jonny and managing the lies of my dual-existence, and all the while, he'd been sneaking up on me.

What were the chances that I'd be able to thwart his efforts twice, especially when it was foreseen that I would fall? No, the universe did not hold me in such high esteem; I was not that favored. This time when Death came for me, I would surely go with him.

Which meant that I had less than two weeks to create my legacy. If my life was to mean something, to count for *anything*, it would be due to the choices I'd make between now and March 31st.

Maybe I hadn't been returned to life eight years ago by a greater power for a specific purpose. I had no way of knowing whether there was more I was *meant* to do. But there was something I *could* do, whether I was meant to do it or not, and maybe, just maybe, it would make a difference—even if it wouldn't save me.

PART THREE:
BROUGHT TO LIGHT

CHAPTER 61

Phoenix stood atop a transportable wooden platform on the beach in front of the Axis and gazed out at the Essen gathered before him. His eyes had an unfocused and glassy look to them, and his freckled skin looked exceedingly pale, almost translucent, beneath the noonday sun. He cleared his throat and wobbled a little as he stepped to the front of the box.

Rori narrowed her almond-shaped eyes. "You've *got* to be kidding me," she said beneath her breath. Shooting a look past me at Taeo, she said. "Is he really elevated right now?"

"He's an addict," Taeo responded quietly. "What did you expect?"

Apparently, she had expected the threat of annihilation to sober him up. Judging from the collective groan that ran through the crowd as he fumbled for his notes, that's what a lot of people had expected.

"Kai is going to kill him," Rori muttered, craning her neck to look for him in the crowd. She spotted him standing apart from the group at the edge of the woods. He *did* look murderous, leaning against a tree with clenched fists folded across his chest.

It was the first I'd seen of Kai since he'd stormed away hours earlier. I don't know where he'd gone, but he wasn't in the cave that he and Taeo had named 'the Nest,' because that's where Rori and Taeo had taken me.

They hadn't left my side since I'd read the Record, and while I was grateful for their support, I was bitter and resentful about Kai's abandonment. He was my Keeper, and after months of training together, I'd grown accustomed to his ever-present obstinacy. Why had he stalked off when I needed him most? Didn't he know I *did* need him? I needed his stubbornness, his refusal to accept fatalistic ways of thinking. I needed his sheer will and his unyielding belief that things would be okay. I needed him to remind me that, like him, I was *also* the master of my fate and the captain of my soul.

Instead, he'd ignored me. He'd deserted me as I tried to process the news of my imminent death. Even now, as I stood between the protective figures of Taeo and Rori, he avoided looking at me.

In that instant, I became furious.

If I'd been clear-headed enough to grasp that the Record foretold more than my demise but also the potential fall of the whole Host, I might have been better able to appreciate Kai's aloofness. I might have realized he was dealing with his own feelings—not that he'd ever admit to having them. But as it was, I saw only my pain and my need, and in those moments of self-pity, I was unforgiving. I was destined to die, and somehow, it was *his* fault.

I shifted my attention back to Phoenix, determined not to look at Kai again.

Phoenix cleared his throat loudly. "I'm not very good at this," he said, helplessly scanning the group.

The Host stared back at him, waiting for him to go on.

"You've all seen it, then?" he said solemnly, looking for nods of affirmation. He received little, if any, response. "The Vision," he said by way of an explanation, "came to me last night, and I—I recorded it immediately so we could... Well, there isn't much time. Quarter's end is less than two weeks away."

His voice sounded weak and his body was sagging and he was failing to be the leader Kai had commanded him to be. He blinked at his notes again.

"We need to be ready," he said lamely. "As ready as we can be for an attack of this nature. I will need everyone to—"

"An attack of *what* nature?" interrupted a female voice from the middle of the crowd. "You haven't even told us what you Saw yet!"

"Oh, I—"

"Read the Record, man! And then walk us through it, line by line," ordered someone from the same vicinity.

Clearly flustered, Phoenix shuffled his papers. "All right," he said. He cleared his throat again. "Record 3629. 'The End,' it's called." Then he began reciting his Vision:

"The end appears cold
Without the warmth of light,
The darkness now foretold,
Advances like the night.

The enemy draws near
Unseen and undetected,
And those who still dwell here
Will no longer be protected.

Time erodes, bridges fail;
The Link will be defeated.
Run and hide, to no avail—
The past will be repeated.

On this quarter's final day
All must be prepared.
The portens is the only way
Any might be spared."

A hush fell over the Host as they absorbed Phoenix's words.

"I've Seen the end," he said in a hopeless tone that suggested Kai's warning had been lost on him. "'On this quarter's final day'—March 31st—the enemy plans to attack. And like the attack of eighteen years ago, the Dothen will come at us en masse. They will cross the Wooded Bridge as Taken and... and strike at us *here*, on Salvos." He lifted his eyes to the sky. "May the cosmos help us."

Exclamations of disbelief and fear arose from the crowd.

"But non-Essen can't cross the bridge!" someone yelled. "Not without the *Dormit*! Even De-As can't cross unless they are accompanied by an Activated Essen! There's no way a Taken could—"

"What does it *mean*, 'bridges fail'?" another interjected. "If we lose the bridge—"

"The bridge is *secure!*" came a cry that sounded almost like a plea.

Phoenix's expression was doleful. "Is it, though?" he said in a quiet manner that recaptured the Host's attention better than if he had shouted. "Is it secure? What do we really know about the Wooded Bridge after all?" Sighing, he shook his head. "We all know the legends: There were once many bridges; the Essen of old were not so restricted as we are today. They traveled the shortcuts to faraway places, became fluent in exotic languages, and introduced much of the flora and fauna that surround us today. It was a time of prosperity for our race.

"The legends don't tell us why or how things changed. All we know is that about four hundred years ago, English became the sole language of the Record-keepers. We've all speculated about what happened. Were the bridges unstable in some way? Did they fall or collapse or break? Did the bridge-keepers die, and with them, the secrets of bridge operation? Were the approach locations lost?

"Or—this theory just occurred to me this morning—were they intentionally and permanently closed? Were our ancestors so concerned that bridge security was in jeopardy that they decided to destroy access altogether?"

Phoenix ran a shaky hand through his graying red hair. "I don't know what happened. But I do know that even if we *could* close it permanently—no one among us, not even Echo, is gifted with that ability—we wouldn't. The Wooded Bridge is all we have left. It's our only connection to the rest of the world, and we do need the rest of the world. While Salvos can shelter us, it cannot sustain us."

The collective spirit of the Host sank. I could almost feel the hope leaching from the air, replaced by a despondency that pressed in on us from all sides.

"So we leave," said Alistair resolutely. He was standing just behind Taeo, one tattooed arm slung across the shoulder of his petite girlfriend Jossi. "We abandon the island. Relocate to Riverview. Stay there at night."

Phoenix nodded slowly. "It's an option I've considered as well. The Estates have served us well over the years. But... the property was designed to be a secondary refuge, not a permanent nightly home for the entire Host.

The Dothen are smart, Alistair. If we left this place, if we were suddenly all concentrated in the Minneapolis condos... they would channel their energy into breaching our security there. And I believe it would take them little to no time to do it, even with the limitations of Taken bodies. The only reason Riverview is still viable, in my opinion, is because it's so seldom used; it hasn't been worth the effort for them.

"Our best chance for survival," Phoenix went on, "is to make a stand here, together." His eyes darted towards the edge of the woods and seemed to find Kai. I didn't follow his gaze, but when he continued, his voice held more courage. "At least on Salvos, supernatural energies surround us. The same forces that shield us from satellite detection and accidental discovery by ships or planes may aid us in our fight. And here we have the Mederium—" He stopped himself before saying what everyone knew he was thinking: *And here we have the Mederium, where we can attempt to heal our fallen.*

"I've developed a strategy for our defense," he said, "but executing it will require the help of all. There are things we can do to... improve our chances. Things like creating traps for the Taken and finding hideaways for the not-yet-Activated. To this end, I've assigned each of you a task. I will not share assignments here lest I compromise the secrecy of your gifts, but it is crucial that before sunrise tomorrow, you come to me, in private, to collect them."

He fell silent and shifted his weight between his legs, surveying the group. Then, satisfied that no objections had been raised, Phoenix made to lower himself off the platform.

"Wait," Ren said, rushing forward. "That can't be it. You haven't explained the most important parts yet—the Link—the portens—"

Phoenix straightened up once more, but whatever confidence he had gained from his glance at Kai seemed to be ebbing away already. It was obvious that these were the topics he had hoped to avoid. Shoulders slouching, he stepped to the front of the box once more. He wiped his palms on the front of his pants and looked back at Ren.

"The portens is... Well, it's the only thing that stands between us and complete decimation. It is the single most important tool for our survival, and its unavailability is the primary reason my Vision is clouded, why I can't see how many will fall. As you all know, it is Kai to whom the task of preparing the portens has been assigned, and he has assured me it will be ready for usage against the Dothen by the end of the month. But... until he or Gemma can demonstrate its potential, our future will remain uncertain.

"The only thing that *is* certain"—Phoenix closed his eyes briefly and swayed on the spot, looking as though he might be ill—"is the Link's death. I have Seen her passing from this world before the new quarter begins. I don't know exactly how or when or why, but she *will* die." He found me in the crowd, a regretful expression on his face. "I'm sorry, Gemma," he said softly.

He seemed to shrink as the words passed his lips, as though saying them released the last of the buoyancy in his spirit. There was such despair in his look I almost forgot my own sorrow in my pity of him.

Phoenix was no leader. He barely participated in his own culture—he was the only one I was aware of that didn't train, didn't cross the bridge, didn't interact with others—so how could he lead? It was clearly taking everything he had to even address the Essen, never mind rallying them in hope. As I stood there with the entire Host watching me, I fixed my eyes on Phoenix, silently imploring him to say more, hoping he wouldn't conclude his speech with such a demoralizing statement.

But Phoenix is not like Kai; there's not an ounce of fight in him. He was spent. He descended from the platform, the effects of his elevation slowing his progress, and parted the crowd to make his leave. Bewildered, every member of the Host turned and stared open-mouthed after him.

"That's it?" someone cried. "Where are you going?"

Phoenix paused and half-turned. "I'm going to the Aerarium. We have less than two weeks to complete our assignments, and the one I've given myself will require every minute of it: completing the invincibility elixir. I believe we're going to need it. We're going to need all your efforts too, so come get your tasks. You know where to find me."

And with that, he shuffled past Kai and into the woods. When he was out of sight, people looked at each other, dumbfounded. No one seemed quite sure what to do next. But I knew what I had to do. I'd made up my mind the instant I'd finished reading the Record.

"I'm going home," I said, turning to face Rori and Taeo.

Taeo nodded and Rori said, "You know you have less than six hours before you have to be back, right?"

"Yeah," I answered, stealing a glance at Kai. The crowd was breaking up, and several people, Shea and Puck included, approached him, undoubtedly to probe into his progress with the portens. I wondered if the person Echo had warned me about, the one who 'would seek to exploit me,' was among them. "I'm taking the bus, but I'll be okay. I have time."

Kai caught me looking at him, and I turned quickly back to Taeo and Rori, glowering.

"Don't be too angry with him, Gemma," Taeo said gently. "He just needs a little time to work through things. That's how Kai is. He doesn't like people to see him worry. And he's more than worried. He's downright terrified."

I let out a bitter laugh. "He's terrified? I don't believe it. Nothing scares him."

"Losing you does." Taeo cocked his head. "He's grown rather fond of you, you know. You're his Kept. And now, he's afraid he'll fail you like he failed... another. He's afraid of losing you to *them*, like he did her. It terrifies him, the idea of you dying. Honestly, I think that's why he was so keen to have you De-A—because even though you'd no longer be part of the Host, at least you'd be alive, and unhunted, and happy, and *safe*.

"It's difficult," Taeo went on, his gray eyes settling tenderly on Rori, "losing a Kept. I hope I never go through it. The bond that is formed when the *Consociare* takes hold... it's powerful. And the destruction of that bond, especially by a Dothen, is definitely something to fear. Look what it did to Phoenix—he became what he is now after he lost Kerithe. Yes, she was the Augur, but before that, she was simply his Kept. Losing her destroyed him. But he never had time to grieve because the gift of Sight flowed into him upon her passing, making him our next Augur.

"No one understands why Phoenix received the gift of Sight. He himself has said that he was unfit to be Kerithe's successor. He admits that he lacks the qualities required for leadership, but the choice was not his to make. All he could do was try to fulfill the role that fate gave him, in spite of his suffering. And I do think he's trying, Gemma. I believe he'll prove himself worthy before the end."

Taeo frowned so slightly it was barely visible from beneath his beard. "We all respond differently when faced with the things that scare us. Some of us lean on each other for support, some of us turn to elixirs, some of us take action, and some of us withdraw. Just don't judge too harshly those who respond differently than you."

His words stuck with me as I crossed the Wooded Bridge and began trekking along the East Bank. Though he had in no way reprimanded me, I left feeling ashamed of myself. There was so much more to Phoenix—and Malakai—than I had previously known. The next two weeks would show me just how much more.

CHAPTER 62

Given that winters in Minnesota typically extend well into April, the onset of spring so early in March made people very nearly euphoric. As I hurried along the riverside path that would take me across campus and to my bus, I saw that many students had traded their parkas for t-shirts and abandoned their boots for flip-flops. Some were even reclining across the wide and yawning stairs behind Coffman Union, attempting to catch a few midday rays.

The sun did feel warm and lovely, but I couldn't bring myself to find joy in it. I resented it, feeling as though its sole purpose was to taunt me with the prospect of a balmy and glorious summer that I wouldn't live to see.

I tried not to think like that, but I couldn't help myself. Though I kept redirecting my energy back to the task at hand, my mind continued to settle on the painfully plain prediction of Record 3629: *The Link will be defeated.*

Phoenix had made it clear that while the fate of the Host was uncertain, nothing could save *me*. With every step I took, with every minute that passed, I felt as though I was marching to my doom.

My heart was heavy, but also resolved. There was too little time left; I needed to make every moment count. I wouldn't squander the hours puzzling out the riddle of Gate's message any more than I would waste time going to class or doing homework. It was time for action. The Host needed the portens, and I intended to give it to them. Well, I intended to give it to *him.*

Malakai Zonn confused me. He was both passionate and cold, both serious and sarcastic. He was protective, but also belittling. I still didn't fully trust him, and yet I didn't entirely *distrust* him either. Rather, I'd come to appreciate him for who and how he was: sharp, disciplined, unsympathetic, and driving. If the mystery of the portens could be solved, he would be the one to do it. And once he did, I knew he'd use it resourcefully and for the good of all—especially the kids.

The only tenderness I'd ever seen in Kai was when he was interacting with Echo, Eclipse, or one of the orphaned children. He treated everyone else with a detached cynicism that made him hated at worst and tolerated at best. Taeo was the only one who really seemed to *like* Kai, maybe because he was the only one who seemed to *get* him.

It had come as a shock to me when Taeo said that Kai had grown fond of me. Kai had never shown any signs of affection at all, and his general treatment of me had caused me to think I was a wearisome burden he had to carry until my Activation. He had only become my Keeper in order to secure the portens, right? Whatever protectiveness he displayed was simply a manifestation of the *Consociare*; it was his duty to be as such. Wasn't it?

I wasn't attached to *him* either. He was arrogant and rude, and I certainly wouldn't miss him once I became a De-A. Or so I thought before that morning.

His behavior at the Tabularium had hurt me more than I wanted to admit. I knew he was hardened, but I hadn't expected him to be outright callous. How could he be so heartless as to just *leave*? I had been standing before the Record, ready to read it. My world was about to come crashing down around me, and, with a face like a wall, he just turned and walked away.

I had wanted him by my side. His presence made me feel secure. Even now, as I tramped along the path and stared out at the river, a small part of me hoped Kai was crossing the bridge behind me, trying to chase me down so he could put my mind at ease.

"Gemma!"

I jumped, startled to hear him calling out my name.

"Gemma, stop!" he said, his deep voice filled with urgency.

I spun around, scarcely daring to believe Kai was actually coming after me. He was running, covering the distance quickly with his long and easy strides. The mere sight of him, tall and dark and brawny, gave me comfort. He was coming, and he would have a plan.

But the initial relief I felt upon seeing him turned into uneasiness once I was close enough to see his eyes. They were a brighter green in the garish afternoon sun and they were flashing with intensity.

"I need the portens," he said coming to a stop in front of me.

I stepped away from him, taken aback.

"I'm done asking, Gemma." He advanced, closing the space between us until it felt like he was upon me. He bent down so his eyes were even with mine. "Give it to me."

He was so close I could smell the scent of ocean on his skin and hair. Feeling threatened, I stepped back again. "But I was going—"

"—To give it to me next week, I know," he said, interrupting what was going to be, *But I was going home to get it!* He let out a grim laugh. "That's not going to work for me. I need it now."

I looked at the ground so he wouldn't see the hurt in my eyes or the blush of embarrassment that I was sure was coloring my cheeks. How could I have been so foolish to think he had come to comfort me?

"I want the opal, Gemma," he said moving in once more.

Stunned, I raised my face.

"Yes, I know the portens is your opal," he said slyly.

"How—How did you…" I stammered.

"I've suspected it for a while now," he said, "but it was that shocked look on your face that just confirmed it. I didn't ask you sooner because I was waiting for you to be ready. I was trying to be patient. But things have changed. I can't afford to be patient anymore. The Host is counting on me. So hand it over, princess."

A sharp exhale of disbelief escaped my lips. My initial judgment of Kai had been right. He only cared about the portens. And to think I had started to become fond of *him*.

"You have five seconds," he said. "Four… three… two…" He shook his head. "You always have to make things harder than they need to be, don't you?"

He slid his finger beneath the chain at my throat and pulled, breaking my necklace. My pendant flew into the air and he rocked back and caught it. Pocketing it in his jeans, he said, "And now *I* am the portens-keeper."

I stood there dismayed, clutching at my naked collarbone, and watched him race back towards the Wooded Bridge. At length, I scooped up my broken chain from the ground, placed it in my pocket, and did the only thing I could do: I went on.

✳ ✳ ✳

At any given time, there are over fifty thousand students enrolled in undergraduate, graduate, or professional programs at the University of Minnesota's Twin Cities campus. Not all of them attend classes on the Minneapolis East Bank and only a portion of those who do were on campus that beautiful spring afternoon, but enough of them were buzzing about that the effect was dizzying.

I walked within the swarm, jostled between distracted professors and laughing coeds, all of them merrily oblivious to me and my misery. How was it possible to feel so lost and alone amidst thousands? Was there even one among them who would notice, let alone grieve, my death?

There *was* one, I knew, but when I unexpectedly caught sight of him as I fought the current on my way to the bus stop, my mood darkened. Surrounded once again by a slew of friends and admirers, Jonny was talking animatedly and gesturing broadly, and in that instant, I saw his future without me. He would grieve, yes, but once I was gone, he'd still be at the center of a wide and brimming circle, and eventually I would be forgotten.

The pain of the realization was too much, and for the first time since reading Record 3629, my sorrow overwhelmed me. My desire to leave a legacy was gone. My resolve was gone. As I stood there watching Jonny grinning, watching Jonny joking, watching Jonny running a hand through his loose-falling chestnut hair, I felt only the severe ache of crushing depression.

I wasn't ready to die.

The raven-haired beauty next to Jonny happened to glance my direction. Recognizing me as his girlfriend, she nudged him and pointed. He looked up, his whole face brightening with surprise and pleasure. He wasted no time parting with the group and sprinting across the lawn in my direction, his backpack swinging against his hip.

"Hey, pretty lady," he called cheerfully when he was still twenty feet off. "What brings you to campus on a Thursday? I didn't expect to see you today!"

I couldn't bring myself to move or speak or even breathe, for fear that my emotions would betray me.

"You aren't going to believe this," he said when he was closer. He wrapped me in a tight hug and said, "Paul and his girlfriend—Jeanette—they eloped yesterday. Just took a last minute flight to Vegas and got hitched. DJ and Mrs. McGregarious." He laughed and pulled away smiling, his arms still gripping my shoulders. "Crazy, huh? I never thought Paul would—"

He stopped short, his eyes drifting to my neckline. "Hey, where's your pendant?"

Leave it to Jonny to spot its absence immediately. Leave it to me to burst into tears at the question. With a strangled sob, I pulled the broken chain from my pocket.

"Oh no," Jonny said softly. "What happened?"

I shook my head, unable to form words. He wiped the tears from my cheeks and brought me into him, stroking my hair.

"It's okay, Gem." His voice was soothing. "We'll find it. I'll help you look. Where were you when it snapped?"

"Down by the river," I said. My words were muffled against his shoulder, but I felt him sag with understanding.

"Gone?" he said.

I shrugged weakly.

He held me tighter. "Well I guess I'll just have to replace it with something even better for your birthday."

I remained motionless against him, desperately wishing my biggest problem was my lost necklace.

"I've made plans for it, you know. You got the night off, right? They can't expect you to work on your big 2-1."

He was trying to cheer me up, but talk of what would be my final birthday, less than a week away, caused me to cry harder. Jonny steered me across the sidewalk and away from the people who had started to stare. He led me to the edge of the mall and sat on a patch of grass shaded by a large tree.

"Talk to me," he urged in a voice low enough that others nearby wouldn't overhear. When I didn't respond, he said, "Come on, Gem. I know something's up. I can't help you if you don't tell me what's going on."

With my head in my hands, I said through my tears, "You can't help me anyway."

"You don't know that. Try me." He tugged at my wrists, but my hands didn't budge from my face. "Please, Gemma... We've always told each other everything. Will you please just talk to me? Is it the stress? You've been working so much, taking an honors class, dating an annoyingly persistent boyfriend..." He chuckled quietly. "Not to mention finding time to do some sort of Pilates or something..." He rubbed at my arms, feeling the hardened muscle through my shirt. "How are you doing it? Don't get me wrong, your body's always been... but now... Well, whatever you're doing is working."

"You've noticed?" I croaked, lowering my hands.

Jonny's dark blue eyes sparkled appreciatively. "Everyone's noticed. You've changed so much. Not just on the outside, either. You seem... all of you seems... stronger. You're more independent, you're less appeasing..." His smile faltered slightly. "And I like it, I really do, but sometimes... sometimes I just wish it felt like you still needed me."

I *did* need him, of course I did; he was the main reason I was so anxious to De-A. If only I had told him that instead of what came out of my mouth next... But I was seeing red. Emotionally charged and mentally fatigued, I heard his words not as a plea for reassurance, but as confirmation of what Lucy had suggested months earlier: *You're exactly his type! You know... the kind of girl who has to be taken care of. One in need of rescuing. A perpetual 'damsel in distress...'*

My voice sounded cold even to my own ears when I said, "Is that why you wanted me as your girlfriend in the first place? Because I made you feel *needed?* Because you thought I was *weak* and I would be someone you could *save?*"

"What?" Jonny spluttered, looking thunderstruck. "You know I don't—I have never thought—You're the strongest person I know! After all you've been through—You're a survivor!"

"A survivor who's always leaned on you! That's what you want, isn't it? You want me to—"

"I just want you to *talk* to me," Jonny begged. "I feel like I don't even know you anymore. You're so distant. For the past few months, you haven't—"

"Revolved around you?" I supplied acidly.

He closed his eyes and swallowed. When he responded, it was in a strained whisper. "You haven't given *me* the chance to revolve around *you*. That's all I've wanted."

I drew in a sharp breath, shocked by his answer. All at once, my fury and resentment and self-pity faded away and were replaced with guilt. What was *wrong* with me? Why was I picking a fight with the one person I loved more than anybody? The one person who loved *me* more than anybody? If I truly did have less than two weeks left on earth, why was I pushing him away?

I launched myself at him and he fell back into the grass. "I'm so sorry, Jonny," I said, embracing him unabashedly despite the overt gawking of passersby. Burying my face in his neck, I said again, "I'm so sorry. I didn't mean it. I love you. You were right it's the stress of everything. I... I can't keep living like this. It's too much." I lifted my face to look into his eyes. "Next Tuesday, March 24th, will be my last night at work. I'll give notice tonight."

He seemed to sink deeper into the ground as a sigh of relief expelled the tension from his body. "Oh thank God," he said looking up at the sky. "I was starting to think... I was worried that if something didn't change soon... I didn't know if we were going to make it."

CHAPTER 63

I stayed on campus with Jonny until his next class started. Though I knew my time was dwindling, I didn't want to part with him. The dynamic between us had changed the moment I told him I was quitting my "job"—it had become as easy and relaxed as it used to be—and I was reluctant to shorten our afternoon together, knowing how few of them were left.

Nothing we talked about could make me forget the looming threat of March 31st, but it wasn't my sole focus anymore, either. Jonny distracted me with chatter about his upcoming graduation, the ongoing and (in his opinion) much-too-serious relationship between Lucy and Josh, Paul's nuptials, and the early close of Board Meeting due to the premature end of winter. He also told me, almost shyly, that Fervor Music Café had booked him for a couple more gigs in April and May (which, thankfully, he didn't make me promise to attend, or I might've started crying again).

Then, after a lingering goodbye, he entered Lind Hall and I resumed my journey to the bus stop feeling less upset than I was before. It had been an afternoon well spent, and as long as I caught the next bus, I'd still have enough time to get home, collect the portens, and return to Salvos before sunset at 7:25 PM.

"Good afternoon, Gemma Pointe," said Professor Dagenais in his thunderous voice, as he approached the steps of Lind Hall. He shifted his soft-sided leather briefcase to the opposite hand and began shrugging off his tweed jacket. "Beautiful day, isn't it?"

I nodded an assent without stopping.

"How's that novella coming? Don't forget, it's due Friday, May 8th. Worth eighty percent of your grade."

I gave him a tight smile as I passed him, fighting the urge to tell him where he could put his novella assignment. I really didn't give a damn about *Storytelling in the Twenty-First Century* anymore.

"Twenty-thousand-word novellas don't write themselves," he said. "Might I suggest you work on it next week? Put your spring break to good use."

I rolled my eyes and kept walking. Even if I wasn't turning twenty-one and hitting the final stage of undergoing next week, crafting a hundred-page story for his class was the *last* thing I would choose to do over spring break.

Undeterred by my blatant indifference to his advice, he bellowed after me, "Like I said in class: Everyone has a story to tell. If you get stuck, just write what you know!"

Write what I know, I thought scornfully. *Yeah, right. That's a good way to get—*

I stopped walking so suddenly, a petite blonde laden with books smacked into the back of me.

"What's your problem?" she grumbled, maneuvering around me.

But for once I didn't have a problem. I had a solution.

The accordion-style bus was packed with people on their way home from work or school. I squeezed into the only open spot, a back row seat next to the window, and tried to fend off the all-too-familiar vision migraine that always preceded episodes of Affliction. I'd become adept at staving off the initial symptoms before they worsened into full-blown torment, but as I leaned my head against the cool glass of the window, I feared it might be too late.

It takes concentration to block Affliction's strike, and though I tried to channel my energy into the management of my symptoms, my thoughts were wild and unfocused. I couldn't harness them as they ran through Record 3629, recalled my interactions with both Kai and Jonny, and reviewed the plan inspired by Professor Dagenais, the unlikely hero of my day.

Everyone has a story to tell, he'd said. *Just write what you know.*

I'd scoffed at his guidance. I couldn't write my story. It had been in-grained in me: sharing Essen information with a non-Essen results in death. But then it hit me—I was going to die anyway. Wouldn't I rather die honestly and on my own terms?

Jonny deserved the truth. He'd been patient, whole-heartedly believing that eventually, when the time was right, I would find a way to tell him what had been going on with me. In the back of my mind though, despite my desperate desire for the answer, I doubted ever being able to confide in him. It had taken a chance encounter with an English professor to help me realize that it was *that*—even more than dying—of which I was most afraid.

The idea of letting Jonny down, of passing from this world without having divulged the reasons for my mysterious behavior over the past several months, sickened me. I loved him too much to leave things unre-solved. Better to write everything down, beginning with my first brush with Malakai last fall in the woods, and present it to him, than to be depleted by the Dothen.

While the plan wouldn't save me, at least it could redeem me. It would be an honorable death, a death I could accept. A death Jonny would understand, though maybe not right away.

He would be grief-stricken at first, and possibly even angry and unforgiv-ing. But over time, he would come to appreciate my choice as the right one, the only one. Knowing the truth of my story, he'd be able to remember me not as evasive and troubled but as courageous and true. And he'd be able to see that to him, I'd always, *always* been committed.

Committed enough to De-A, an action I still intended to take. Though I knew the Host would view my decision as fear-driven, it was not. Phoenix had made clear that he'd Seen Death coming for me regardless of my choice. No, I wasn't Deactivating to try to avoid Death. I was doing it for love. I wanted to spend my last week alive with Jonny and my family, living as close to a normal life as possible.

And then, on March 31st, the day on which I was destined to die anyway, I'd give him my story.

The bus jolted to a stop and several more people climbed on, clogging up the aisle. I sighed, watching them shift their bags to grab the handholds. The spottiness in my vision was growing worse and I closed my eyes, trying to gain control of my thoughts, trying to reverse the progression of Affliction, but failing. Beads of sweat popped across my forehead and I cooled it against the glass once more.

I wondered how it would happen, my death. Would my heart stop beating immediately once Jonny accepted the story, or would it occur after he'd begun reading it? Or only after he'd finished? Would I feel anything? And would my soul leave my body right away, or perhaps linger, waiting for a revival, like it had once before? It wouldn't surprise me if it hung about for a while. I was a survivor after all, somehow miraculously programmed to persist against all odds. Jonny had reminded me of that.

You're the strongest person I know! Jonny had said. Was I? In what way? Why did he think that? Just because I was the only person he'd ever known to thwart Death? Just because once, eight years ago, a medical expert had called it, and I had proven him wrong? Just because I had survived?

I had survived.

My eyes flew open as adrenaline rushed through me. Eight years ago, an expert had called it, and I had proven him wrong. There was something in my spirit that *was* strong. I had fought my way through the brokenness and *survived.*

Who was to say it couldn't happen again?

This morning, an expert called it. Phoenix, the Augur of the Host, proclaimed my death. He said he'd Seen me passing from this world, and he probably had. But there was something he didn't know: *I was a survivor.* Even though he'd Seen me fall, how did he know I'd stay down?

I knew it wasn't something I could count on, surviving another would-be fatal experience, but I suddenly felt lighter. Jonny's reminder, once I really reflected on it, had been a gift to me. It did for me what the ongoing encouragements and consolations of Taeo and Rori hadn't. It gave me hope.

I had been wrong to despair, and I wouldn't any longer. I formed a new plan in my head: I would still write my story for Jonny, but I wouldn't give it to him as part of a premeditated plan to end myself before the Dothen could. Instead, it would be my contingency plan in the event that I did die. I'd give it to someone I could trust, someone who would deliver it to him if I didn't make it.

But for now I had to believe I *would* make it. Because if I believed that, then I could believe Jonny and I would make it, too.

A stabbing pain pierced my insides and I doubled up in the bus seat. Breathing slowly and deeply, I willed Affliction to retreat. I was almost home. I just needed to grab the portens, catch another bus back to campus, and cross the Wooded Bridge. I still had an hour and a half. I would make it.

CHAPTER 64

*A*ffliction was a winged beast writhing inside of me. It struggled against my organs, its razor-sharp talons shredding my insides to ribbons as it tried frantically to free its cramped self from my body. Its efforts were violent and frenzied; I could contain it no longer. It burst from my abdomen, expanding to its full and impressive height, and unfurled its mighty wings.

I screamed in agony, but the beast was not done torturing me. It chomped at me with its hooked beak and tore massive chunks of flesh from my bones, swallowing them while I was yet alive. I screamed again, and it seized my tongue and ripped it out of my mouth and ate that too, leaving a gaping and bleeding hole from which my terrified whimpers escaped. Then it descended upon me with its talons and picked me up, further slicing my beyond-mangled body, and took flight.

The sky had gone from an even blue to a dusky purple, and still it carried me on. But I was a heavy burden and we had covered a great distance. The beast was growing tired. I heard the beating of its wings slow, and then, finally, it released me.

I plummeted through the blackness of night for what seemed like hours but the ground came no nearer. And then... something snatched me from the air. With powerful arms, he lifted the ragged remnants of my body and placed me in the reclined front seat of his car. I knew who he was—the fiery glow of his amber ring lit his face—but how could he know me? I was surely unrecognizable, my skin and muscle and bone all damaged and deformed. I tried to tell him my name, but my tongue was still missing, and the only thing that came out was a mewling gurgle. Suddenly I was panicking, thrashing about, clawing at the air, and convulsing against the leather.

Malakai pressed down on me firmly, the full weight of his body restraining me as he buckled me into the seat. "Don't try to speak," he said, handing me a polished silver flask. "Just drink this. It will—"

But what it would do, I didn't find out. Malakai was yanked backwards by the pale hands of a wasted-looking thug, a scrawny man about half his size. The thug slammed Kai against the side of his car with Herculean force and gripped his neck.

"I've been—after you. For a long—time," the Taken said in an oddly staccato voice. He dug his fingers into Kai's caramel skin, but his sunken pupils seemed to be looking at me.

I unfastened the seatbelt and scrambled deeper into the car, clutching the flask. Uncorking it, I guzzled the liquid, madly hoping it was an invincibility elixir.

Kai's knees buckled as the Dothen began depleting him, but instead of clutching at the man's hands like instinct would have had him do, he reached down into the side pocket of his canvas combat pants and withdrew a black-handled knife with a wide, mean-looking blade, the edge of which was gleaming in the golden light of his ring. Without hesitation, he hacked at the Taken's right arm, slicing through it as easily as butter. The arm dropped to the ground, oozing fluid and twitching, but the Dothen paid it no mind. He continued to squeeze Kai's neck with the Taken's left hand, and Kai, losing oxygen and strength, dropped the knife. It clattered against the concrete.

"I have—you now," he said. I watched horrified as Kai's legs became limp and hung beneath him. If not for the hand around his throat holding him against the car, he would have fallen down. I let out a coarse wail of terror.

Upon hearing my cry, Kai seemed to revive. With a surge of power, he brought his legs up and planted both of his feet squarely against the Taken's chest and pushed. The Taken tumbled backwards, releasing its grip, but only for a second before it flung itself at Kai once more.

A second was all Kai needed. The instant the contact was severed, Kai's body became covered in miniature, diamond-like plates. Overlaid with iridescent reptilian scales, he looked more feral than ever before, like an antagonized dragon.

The Taken fixed its hand around Kai's neck once more, but its touch had no effect. Kai retrieved his knife from the ground and swiftly decapitated him with the fearsome proficiency of an embattled warrior. Blood splattered across his face and clothes as the man collapsed to the pavement.

Without a word, Kai sheathed his knife and reached inside the car and pulled me back into my seat. His touch was not gentle, but neither was it rough; it was precise and efficient. He fastened my belt once more and slammed the door. When he got into the driver's seat, his skin had returned to normal.

He threw the car into gear and sped off, his ring glowing more brightly than I'd ever seen it. It flooded the interior of the car, making the black leather appear orange.

"How do you feel?" he demanded, seeing the silver flask lying empty on the passenger's side floor.

I opened my mouth in a silent scream, my muscles contracting spasmodically.

Kai placed his hand across my chest and pushed me against the seat. "Lay back," he said. He rolled the window down, allowing the cool night air to rush over me. "Just relax. You're okay." His voice was even and controlled. "You're okay," he said again, but his green eyes flitted fretfully between me and the drained flask.

He turned his attention to the road, and I watched him shifting and turning and accelerating with wide, unblinking eyes. And then, through the windshield, I saw it circling above us. The great winged beast with the razor-sharp talons had found me. It swooped down, reached in through the window, and carried me away again.

✳ ✳ ✳

"Do you have any idea what time it is?"

The man spoke in hushed tones, but it was enough to rouse me from the dark, maelstrom-filled dreams in which I'd been trapped. His soft voice floated to me like a life preserver, freeing me from the whirlpool's arms. I let it pull me forward, away from the churning and malevolent waters that had been beating me to pieces of blue and black.

"You asked me to stay with her for a few minutes," he continued. "It's been *four hours*. You're not the only one who's had a rough night, you know."

"How is she?" came the reply. It was Malakai, but his deep voice, lowered to a whisper, sounded far away. I tried to open my eyes to see where he was, but I was too weak, far too weak, to move.

"How are *you*?" the other man asked. "You were a disaster when you got here."

"Like I said before: It wasn't my blood."

"Kai. Come on. No one gets *that* messy without using a weapon, and no one uses a weapon unless they've got no other choice."

"I'm fine," said Kai. "I just needed time to clean up. The car was a wreck."

"If you've been tagged—"

"Drop it, Ren." There was a note of finality in his statement, but his tone softened when he added, "I'll go to the Mederium at daybreak."

I heard him move across the floor and flop noisily into a chair, convincing me that I was not overhearing the conversation through any supernatural means. Ren and Kai were physically in the room with me.

"How is she?" Kai asked again. He sounded closer now.

"No change," Ren said. "Are you sure she drank it?"

"There wasn't a drop left in the flask. I checked because I needed some."

"Well, are you sure it was the *Indolentia*? Maybe the elixirs got—"

"I gave her the *Indolentia*," Kai said, his voice filled with exasperation. "I didn't mix anything up."

"All right man, easy. I've just never heard of it not working before."

There was a pause and then Kai, sounding very tired, said, "Me neither."

"So what now?" Ren asked. "If the most effective painkiller we have doesn't work on her, what do we do?"

"We wait," Kai said. "She'll come around."

"But what if she doesn't?"

"She will," he said. "She's okay. It was just a bad episode of Affliction."

Ren sounded doubtful. "Not like any episode I've ever seen."

"She's not like any Essen you've ever seen, either. She has a comprehensive notae, remember. She bears the mark of all four Affiliations. I think that's why her Affliction is worse. Probably four times worse."

They lapsed into silence and after a few minutes, I began to wonder if they'd fallen asleep in their respective chairs. Then Ren spoke again.

"Who is Jonny?"

I felt my heart lurch in my chest at the mention of Jonny's name. My eyes slid open involuntarily, as though hoping to see him in front of me. Instead, I saw the fair-haired and slender-built Ren Celere, his light gray eyes looking silver in the shadowy dimness of the room. He was stretched across a large, black leather couch, a mere twelve or so feet from the king-sized bed in which I was lying. On his forearm, the ash-colored circles of his notae, Affiliation Arith, were stark against his pale skin. Opposite him, reclining against a matching armchair, was Malakai, his feet up on an ottoman. Neither of them was looking at me.

"Jonny?" Kai repeated.

"She's been calling out for him to save her."

"From what?"

Ren hesitated. "From you. Her nightmares seem... intense. I know it's to be expected—she's only days from Activation—but they seem worse than average. She kept accusing you of trying to drown her, kept asking for Jonny to save her."

Kai examined his fingernails, looking subdued.

"Well? Who is he?"

Sighing, Kai lifted his face. Through the slits of my eyelids, I saw him glance at me before turning back to Ren. "Jonny is... the reason I went after her tonight. When I realized something was wrong, when I knew Gemma wasn't going to make it back in time, I had to go after her. Even though she's not yet Activated, even though the Dothen can't yet deplete her, I was afraid they'd try to communicate with her like they've done before. If that happened, and if she had been with Jonny, he would have been taken. That was a risk I couldn't take. Because if Jonny died... part of Gemma would too. And we need her whole if she's going to help us as the Link."

"This Jonny—he's her family?"

"She loves him like family, I think. Losing him would be like losing a sibling—it would devastate her, make her useless in the short term."

Ren stared at Kai, his expression shocked and affronted. He stood up abruptly. "I'm going to bed."

"Ren," Kai said, getting to his feet. "You know that's not what I meant. I wasn't implying that about *you*. She may have been your sister, but Raela's death devastated us all. I only meant that—"

"Grief hasn't rendered *me* ineffective," Ren said loudly. Kai winced and raised his hands, tilting his head in my direction. Ren glared at him but lowered his voice. "You want to know why I didn't make it across the bridge tonight? I was hot on the trail of Gate Dorsum, and I didn't turn back in time. Every day I pursue him; I won't leave it to the covenant-keepers. He murdered my sister and he *will* face justice. So don't tell me losing a sibling makes you useless."

"I know," Kai said, "I know. I'm sorry." He waited until the fire in Ren's eyes diminished and then asked, "Do you know where he is? Gate?"

Ren shook his head bitterly. "I'm so close, I can *feel* it. I'm using this"—he pulled something small and flat from the front pocket of his jeans—"to guide my Gravitation, but I haven't locked in yet." He paused. "What? What is it?"

Kai's face had taken on a strange and alarmed look. "Where… Where did you get that?" He took the item from Ren and held it up in the sliver of moonlight that fell through the gap in the curtains.

Ever so quietly, I shifted my position in the bed to get a better look at the object. It appeared to be an ordinary maple tree leaf—until the light flashed across it and I saw its color. The leaf was a brilliant shade of silver, shining as though it had been enameled with metallic paint.

Ren snatched the leaf from Kai's hands. "Why? What do you know about it?" he asked suspiciously. Kai blinked at him, his mouth agape.

After a moment, Ren shook his head, the anger appearing to dissolve from him. "Look man," he said, shoving the leaf back into his pocket. "I'm sorry. I'm just exhausted, and this leaf… It's like a taunt. They found it on Raela's body. The image of it plagues me. I can't stop seeing it in my head, her twisted form on the ground, blood pouring from her eyes, and Gate's leaf, his cruel calling card, resting on her body." He rubbed his face with both hands. "I just wish I could sleep, but she's stuck in my mind. I'm so tired, but even the *Dormit* elixir doesn't help…"

"She was bleeding from her eyes?" Kai asked, his brows furrowed quizzically.

"That's how they first knew she was poisoned, I guess. Diluted Necis juice has that effect. They confirmed it was in the wine Gate gave her." Ren moved to the door and opened it to leave, but turned to face Kai again. "What's really killing me though, is how he knew… How did Gate know that Raela, who had only just Activated, had received the gift of Hindsight? She'd told only me and I told no one. Well, until you just now, but it doesn't really matter anymore. Like her, the gift is gone forever."

Kai ran a hand through his short, dark hair. "Her gift… the gift of Hindsight… She would've been able to See and reveal secrets of the past." His voice held something like awe. "A gift like that—"

"—Would have been a real threat to people with something to hide." Ren pursed his lips. "People with sordid pasts. People like Gate."

As Ren and Kai said their goodnights, I stared at the ceiling, contemplating what I'd heard. So there *had* been a motive in the murder of Raela Celere. Someone had killed her to keep her from exposing certain truths that were hidden in the folds of time. But was that person Gate?

Kai closed the door. I shut my eyes once more, feigning sleep, and heard him cross the floor to the couch. The leather squeaked as he fell into it. Several moments passed, and then he spoke.

"I know you're awake, Gemma. You're far too still to be sleeping."

Startled, I opened my eyes to find him lying on the couch, which looked barely long enough to accommodate his large frame, peering at me through the darkness. I remained motionless and said nothing, though I'm sure he could hear my heart pounding.

"For what its worth," he said gruffly, "I'm glad you're okay."

I lifted my head off the pillow and started to respond, but he cut me off.

"Whatever you heard, we'll talk about it in the morning. For now, you need your rest. Try to sleep. And Gemma?" He drew in a deep breath. "If you can help it, don't dream that I'm the bad guy."

But as I melted into slumber, swirling waters surrounded me once more, and there was Kai, holding my head beneath them.

CHAPTER 65

"Wake up, Gemma," Kai said. "I have instructions for you before I leave."

My eyes fluttered open. He was looming over me, haloed by the colorful sunrise streaming through the window. He looked exactly as he had the first time I saw him: soldier-like in black utility pants, black boots, and a tight gray t-shirt. His eyes seemed weary but his expression was resolute.

I sat up quickly, drawing the covers up with me. At once, my head began to pound and nausea rolled through me, as though I'd spent the night single-handedly consuming a case of wine. I massaged my temples.

"Ugh," I groaned, thinking longingly of the days, only months ago, when hypnosis highs could abate the symptoms of undergoing.

Kai sat on the edge of the bed facing me. "Listen," he said, putting a hand on my shoulder. "Taeo and Rori will be here soon. They're bringing Supernovas, the flowers that help with Affliction. You should feel back to normal by mid-afternoon. When you do, go home or wherever you need to go—bring Taeo or Rori with you—and get the real portens." I tried to interject, but he held up a hand. "Yes, I realize I was mistaken. I'll give your silly little pendant back to you. Tonight, as a trade for the real portens."

"I had already planned to give it to you," I grumbled. "I was on my way home to get it when I…" I trailed off and looked down at the floor, unable to remember exactly what happened.

"...When Affliction struck," Kai said. "I felt it, your pain. It was severe. I knew you needed help." He rubbed his neck, his bicep swelling in my line of sight as he did. "I went to find you because I knew you weren't going to get back across the bridge before sundown. I had a hell of a time of it, though. Every time I locked in on you, you moved. I finally figured out you were on the bus. You'd ridden it way past your house. Unfortunately, I just had to follow it until you got off. There were Dothen about, Dothen that had locked on me, and it would've been too dangerous to board and collect you. Luckily you got off at a stop that was completely deserted so I was able to get you into the car without too much trouble."

"But there was trouble," I said, recalling the pasty-skinned thug. "I saw the Taken. You—You were tagged."

"Only for a second," Kai said dismissively. "I'm fine. Or I will be once I get to the Mederium. As soon as Taco and Rori get here, I'll go see Eclipse, and then I'll be off to—"

"You grew scales," I blurted. "When you were fighting the Taken."

Kai cocked his head at me, a perplexed look on his face.

"They were like diamonds, I saw them," I insisted.

He gave me a small half-smile. "It's okay, Gemma. You were very sick last night. It's not uncommon for delirium—"

"I wasn't delirious! I know what I saw. It's one of your gifts, isn't it? You can—"

"Gemma," Kai interrupted, "You *were* delirious. You kept babbling on about a giant bird that had eaten your tongue." I shuddered reflexively as the images flooded my mind. "Look, I don't have time to argue with you right now. I have to leave soon, and there're still some things I need to tell you."

I folded my arms grumpily and waited for him to go on.

"Most importantly, don't go anywhere today without bringing Taeo or Rori with you. You are too close to Activation. You could have an episode at any time, and the next one could be even worse. Stay with people who can help you, who can get you back to Salvos before the bridge closes.

"Secondly: Don't go in the Mederium if you have any residual Affliction pain at all. It doesn't heal symptoms of undergoing; it makes them worse. You might be tempted to try it, but I'm telling you, don't do it. You'll regret it.

"And finally, spend as much time as you can studying Record 3629. I need your help. There's something about it… It feels different to me. I can't put my finger on it, but you might be able to. Echo's told me you're pretty insightful at interpreting the Records."

"Not that insightful," I muttered. "I've read 3627 and 3628 each hundreds of times, and I still haven't been able to make sense of them. I still don't know how to work the portens."

"Which is exactly why it's time to give me a turn. Go get the portens today and bring it back to Salvos. I'll work on it tonight. I know I can figure it out." He stood up, pulled his phone off its belt holster, and checked the time. "We good, then? You're clear on what you need to do? Remember, stay with Taeo or Rori. That's the main thing. If you run into trouble today, you can be damn sure I'll feel it, but I won't be able to help you. I'll be too far away."

He spoke with complete composure, but his anxiousness was evident as he looked at his phone again.

"Where are you going?" I asked, fingering the ends of my tangled hair.

"To see Gate," he replied.

Gate? I threw off the covers, grateful to note I was still wearing yesterday's clothing, and jumped out of bed. My head was throbbing and my stomach was queasy, but I didn't care. "I'm going with you."

"No," he said, "you're not. You're in no condition to travel today. Besides, I'm already behind schedule. I can't afford to wait for you. As soon as Taeo and Rori get here, I'm leaving."

"But I need to see Gate! In the message he left me, before he disappeared, I think I missed something—"

Kai broke into a derisive laugh. "Of course you missed something! He never would have told you not to trust me! I could have had the portens worked out by now if he hadn't inadvertently set you against me from the beginning."

"Then you understand why I have to go! I need to find out what he—"

"You're not going, and that's final. You may not be Activated yet, but your notae seems to attract Dothen more strongly than average, and I'm not up to another night like last night. I can't worry about taking care of you *and* fending off more Dothen if it comes to that. Not when I'm weakened from yesterday's tag and on zero sleep and have such a long day ahead of me."

"Give me a break," I snapped. "You're just afraid of what Gate might say. If you take me with and he tells me—"

"Tells you what, Gemma? Not to trust me again? He's not going to say that. There's nothing he could say that I'd be opposed to you hearing. If I thought I could get you to Gate and back before the dusk, I'd say come along. But it's too far." He looked at his phone again and then holstered it once more on his belt. "Where the hell are they?"

He walked to the window and gazed down at the street below.

"If you're in such a damn hurry," I said bitterly, crossing the room and flopping onto the couch, "why don't you just leave already? Don't let me keep you. The sun is up. Feel free to get going."

Kai turned to stare at me. "You're unbelievable, you know that? I risk my neck, literally, to come after you last night, and then I arrange for your care today, and this is the gratitude I get?"

"My *care*?" I felt the heat rising in my face. "What am I, some invalid to be handed off at a shift change? Just go if you want to go! I'm sure I can handle the aftereffects of Affliction without you, just like I worked through the implications of 3629 without you. No need to have a sense of duty now, not after you ignored me yesterday."

Kai's mouth tightened into a scowl. "I didn't *ignore* you."

"No?" I scoffed. "I'd just been prophesized to die! The least you could have done was *talk* to me. You're my Keeper! Instead you stole my necklace—without even giving me a chance to speak—and then you abandoned me, just like your running off now—"

"You think I'm *running off*?" Kai demanded. "Like this is some joyride I'm going on? Let's get something straight, sister." He pulled an envelope from the back pocket of his jeans and withdrew its contents: a couple pieces of yellowing legal-sized paper and a shiny silver leaf, similar to the one Ren had shown him in the night. Then he strode across the room to me and unfolded the first paper, which looked to be a hand-drawn map, and flattened it on the arm of the couch.

"*This*," he said, pointing to a dot on the map, "is where we are. And *this*"—he made a sweeping circle with his hand—"is considered the Summer Safe Zone. It's the area in which Essen can move about freely and feel relatively confident about making it back to the Wooded Bridge before dark. And *here*"—he indicated a spot at the northern border of the Safe Zone—"is where Gate is. As you can see, it would be a risky journey even on the longest summer days. I've never even attempted it before. Yet here I go, fool that I am, trying to make the trip *today*, in twelve hours of daylight rather than sixteen. And *why* am I doing that? *Because* I'm your Keeper and *because* you were prophesized to die. I believe Gate has information that I need, information that can help protect you, and now that I know where he is…" He threw up his hands in frustration, releasing the pages, the envelope, and the leaf. "Don't you get it? I'm trying to figure out how to save you, you thankless harpy!" Turning away from me, he stalked back to the window.

The papers settled on the ground, but Kai kept his back to me, fuming. I gingerly picked everything up, careful not to tear the paper or the delicate leaf. One of the pages, I noticed, bore Gate's distinctive handwriting. I glanced over it and, realizing it was a personal letter that Gate must have sent Kai years ago, began refolding it.

"Go ahead and read it," Kai said flatly with his back still to me. "You might as well."

I hesitated, unconvinced that he really wanted me to read his personal mail. After a moment though, in which Kai continued to stare out the window, I bit my lip and opened the letter.

Dear Malakai,

Happy 16th birthday.
I know I'm not supposed to contact you, but given that it's your birthday, and a very important one at that, I needed to try.

I have been waiting for this day for more than a decade. I know uncles are supposed to say things like, "I can't believe you are sixteen already! It seems like only yesterday you were a toddler," but to be honest, the last eleven years have seemed like a hundred. Each passing day has felt like a month, but now, finally… You are sixteen.

I hope I'm not wrong in assuming that you've been granted your first car. Truthfully, it's the reason I waited until now to contact you. Desperate though

I've been to talk to you—my only remaining family—I knew you wouldn't have the freedom to visit me until you had a vehicle of your own.

But that's what I'm writing to ask for: a visit. I know it's forbidden, being in touch with a De-A, but I've set up a place at the edge of the Safe Zone where I daresay we can meet without being discovered.

I've included a map to the location. I know it's far, but I wanted you to feel comfortable that no one would stumble upon us accidentally. My place, which I've affectionately named The Lodge, is nestled deep in a forest, but you will find it easily enough if you use the enclosed leaf to guide you.

My phone number and local address are listed at the bottom, if you want to contact me with your response. I understand if you'd prefer not to formalize a meeting, though. Regardless of whether or not I hear from you, I will be at The Lodge starting next week and for the remainder of summer, until September 1. I hope you decide to come at some point.

Malakai, please know I'm not an evil person, no matter what you may have been told. Everything that happened that night my wife and children died, that night your parents died... It wasn't me. I think there's more to the story, and I think that because of you.

You may not remember this, but the morning after the attack, you told me something happened that you needed to tell me about. You said you saw something when you were stranded overnight on the wrong side of the bridge. You started to say it, but then Phoenix, who had just become the new Augur, called an assembly to debrief what had happened, and when I asked you about it afterwards, you couldn't remember what it was.

There is no doubt in my mind that you know something important about the events of that night, possibly something so traumatic that you blocked the memory of it as a form of self-preservation. But I need to know. I will never have peace until I can understand the full truth of what happened.

I would be remiss if I didn't tell you that I've been studying and practicing regression therapy as a certified hypnotherapist, helping people unearth repressed memories, for several years now. I did this so that if and when I ever got the opportunity to see you again, and if and when you were willing to let me... I'd be ready and able to help you remember.

Again, happy birthday. I know it's a lot to ask, but I hope to see you soon.
Your Uncle,
Gate

"You never went," I said quietly as I finished reading. "Did you?"

"Of course I didn't," Kai said, turning to look at me. "I was mortified that he'd even sought me out to deliver the letter. It was seven years ago, the evening of my birthday, and he'd been waiting at the Wooded Bridge to give it to me. I was with people, you know? It shamed me, being contacted by him. I didn't even read it, not right away." He shook his head. "When I did eventually read it, I didn't consider for a second going to see him. I put the letter, the map, and the leaf back in the envelope and hid them in the safe in my room. I forgot all about the place he called 'The Lodge.' ...Until last night."

"The leaf," I whispered. "The leaf that Gate placed on Raela's body..."

"He didn't leave it there as a calling card. It was intended as a clue for me. He wanted me to know exactly where he was going. I don't know whether he's still there—it's been months since Raela died—but I have to try. And I have to go *today* before Ren or others can find him. They don't believe he could be innocent, but after last night, after seeing that leaf... I don't see how he couldn't be. He wouldn't have left it for me if he had murdered her. There's something he needs to tell me, something I need to know. Maybe it's about Raela or her gift of Hindsight or the portens, but whatever it is, it's important."

"And you think... You think whatever he has to tell you, it could help me?" I asked, looking down at Gate's letter.

Kai rubbed his eyes, looking exhausted. "It's all connected, all of it, I just don't know how yet. The Dothen attack eighteen years ago, Raela's death, the portens, even Record 3629... They are all pieces to a puzzle. Anything

Gate can tell me will get me one step closer to fitting them together, one step closer to helping you and everyone."

"Are you going to let him hypnotize you then?"

"If I find Gate, and if we have time, I plan to explore any and all sources of information that might give me a better understanding of what happened eighteen years ago—even my own memories. Record 3629 says 'the past will be repeated' so I sure as hell need to find out everything I can about the past if I'm going to help anybody on March 31st."

"And what if you can't find him?"

He crossed the room, took the papers and the leaf from me, stuffed them back into the envelope, and shoved the envelope into his pocket once more. "Then I'll have wasted a whole day that I should have been working on the portens. There's a reason I wanted it yesterday. We're running out of time. With quarter's end only ten days away, I don't have *seconds* to squander, let alone days." He glanced at the time on his phone again just as the door swung open.

"What took you so long?" he growled at Taeo, who was carrying a large vase of Supernova flowers.

"What took us so long?" said Rori, filing into the room after him, a look of indignation on her face. "It's been less than thirty minutes since the bridge opened. We came straight here. Rethink your tone, asshole."

"Rori," Taeo chided. "You know what he's attempting to do today. Cut the guy some slack." He carried the flowers to the bedside table and set them down before turning to me with a sympathetic smile. "Hey Gemma. Doing all right?"

But before I could answer, Kai, who had already made his way to the open door, said, "I'm taking off then." And without so much as a glance back at any of us, he passed through the doorway and began his pursuit of Gate.

CHAPTER 66

I would not have admitted it, but Kai was right. I was in no condition to travel. I didn't realize it until after he left, until after the surge of adrenaline at learning Gate's whereabouts subsided, but I was in rough shape.

Taeo said it was the worst case of Affliction hangover he'd ever seen. He encouraged me to go back to bed for a few hours while the Supernovas did their thing. I didn't protest.

When I woke up just before noon, Taeo and Rori were cuddled up on the leather couch watching a movie displayed on a screen built into the wall. The volume was very low, probably as a courtesy to me, and Rori kept burying her face in Taeo's sleeve to muffle her giggling. Taeo was smiling down at her, obviously pleased by her amusement.

He stroked her hair and kissed the top of her head. "This is the stupidest movie I've ever seen," he said in a low voice. She elbowed him in the ribs. "No really," he went on, "I feel dumber for having watched it."

"Oh shut up," she said, still laughing. "You know it was my turn to pick." She lifted her chin and brought her lips to his in a kiss that seemed without end.

I yawned loudly. Rubbing my eyes, I sat up and swung my legs to the floor. Rori and Taeo sprang apart like teenagers caught parking.

"Gemma!" Taeo said in a tone that suggested he'd rather forgotten I was there. He rose from the couch and came to stand at the foot of the bed. "How ya feeling?"

"Hungry," I said, my stomach echoing the sentiment.

"That's a good sign," said Rori, coming to stand next to Taeo. "You're out of the woods then. What are you in the mood for? We have food here—they always keep the recovery rooms stocked with snacks and stuff—or we could go for pizza or something?" She raised her eyebrows in rapid succession, leaving no doubt as to her preference.

"We had pizza yesterday," Taeo said, wrapping his arms around Rori's waist. "You really want it again?"

"Hey," Rori said, "I'm told we may all die in a little over a week. Might as well eat what makes me happy until then."

"Whatever you say, woman."

Pizza did sound good. I took a hurried shower, anxious to get food in my system, and changed into the fresh clothes left for me by Rori.

"I grabbed them from my place," Rori said. "Up on twelve. I threw yours down the chute to be laundered. Hope you don't mind."

Laundry was only one of the services that the staff of Riverview Estates performed. As we took the clear glass elevator from ninth floor where the recovery rooms were down to the underground parking garage, Rori explained some of the operations of the property. The common areas of the premises, which included the grounds, garage, lobby, halls, bathrooms, gym, pool, spa, library, theater, game rooms, and recovery rooms (which were described to the non-Essen staff as "guest suites"), were maintained by a set of employees who worked between 9 AM and 3 PM each day. All of the staff members, including Vivian, the property manager, were paid handsomely in exchange for their dutiful and thorough completion of tasks, which included everything from cleaning and stocking supplies to logging and tracking visitors. There were only two rules for these employees: No fraternization with the Essen (known to them as "home owners") and no early arrival for work or lingering about after their shifts. The employees were expected to be present at precisely 9 AM and depart at exactly 3 PM. Violation of either of the rules would result in immediate dismissal.

"They don't have access to our condos, either," Rori said as she opened the passenger-side door of Taeo's burnt orange SUV. "Each 'home owner' is responsible for the upkeep of his or her own place. Which is why mine is immaculate, and Taeo's"—she gave him an exasperated look—"has been a pigsty since I've known him."

"You each have your own place?" I asked, climbing into the backseat. I don't know why, but I assumed they lived together.

Taeo found me in the rearview mirror. "Of course we do," he said as though the question was absurd. "Everyone gets their own place when they begin undergoing. Mine is on the twenty-third floor. I had my digs on the thirty-ninth, a unit next to Kai's, but this one"—he scrunched his face up at Rori—"doesn't like heights, so I moved."

He drove through the parking garage and up a spiral ramp, stopping in a strange holding-type room in which a garage door lowered behind us. He held a white plastic badge up to a card reader and then the door in front of us slowly rolled up.

We had just gotten on the road when Taeo's phone dinged. "Babe, check that for me, will you?" he said, turning onto the freeway.

"It's Kai," said Rori, reading the text. "He must have driven like he had a Dothen on his tail. He's there already."

Taeo let out a low whistle. "Six hours. Impressive. Did he say if he found Gate yet?"

Rori shook her head, typing a reply. After a minute, the phone dinged again. "He says he's close. He'll call when he's on his way back." She spun in her seat to face me, her coppery hair cascading across her shoulder. "He also wants to know how you are. You want me to respond?"

I shrugged. "I guess."

She flashed me a devious smile and then typed out another message. When the phone dinged a third time, she smirked slightly and showed the screen to Taeo, who read it aloud. "'Kiss my ass, Rori. I know that was you.' What did you say?"

"Just the truth," she said matter-of-factly. "That Gemma is doing better now. Mostly likely because she's not with *him*."

He groaned. "That wasn't called for. You know he's legitimately worried about her. He wouldn't even leave her alone for five minutes this morning."

"I think I'm entitled to be a little snappy," Rori retorted. "Given what's probably coming." Taeo kept his eyes on the road, his mouth in a thin line. Leaning towards him, her smoky alto voice sounding agitated, she said, "We both know he couldn't have made it up there already if he'd really gone to the Mederium first."

"That doesn't mean—"

"Come off it, Taeo. He's tired and he's been depleted to some extent, we don't know how much. He's driven to the border of the Safe Zone in that condition. And unless he's willing to head back within the next thirty minutes, he's going to run out of time. Or steam. Probably both. And then what? He's going to involve *you*."

Taeo scratched at his eyebrow, avoiding her gaze. "We'll worry about it when the time comes."

"Some of us are worried about it *now*," Rori said, her almond-shaped eyes wide and earnest. "Because some of us love you."

"Some of us love you too," Taeo said quietly. He pulled into a parking spot on the street and turned off the car. Then, giving her a playful smile, he added, "Which is why some of us are willing to have pizza two days in a row, even though some of us would rather have steak. The things people do for love."

Rori rolled her eyes, and the three of us clambered out of the SUV and into the restaurant for lunch.

✳ ✳ ✳

Across the street from the pizza parlor sat an adorable little hole-in-the-wall bookstore with its name, *Get A Spine*, hand-painted above the door. I spotted it through the window as we were eating and made a beeline for it when we were done. Taeo and Rori indulged me, following me across the street with interlocked hands.

I browsed the cramped aisles until I found the section I was seeking: journals and sketchbooks. I flipped through several blank-paged books, looking for the one that seemed right for my contingency plan. And then I found it—a leather-bound book in a shimmery sapphire blue color, debossed in the lower right-hand corner with the phrase, *My Life, My Words...* The pages were lined, and there were enough of them to hold my story, I thought.

I made my purchase discreetly, borrowing a pen from the frumpy woman who handled my transaction, while Taeo and Rori perused the store. Inside the front cover, I completed the sentiment begun by the debossed words: *...My Story. To Jonny, With Love, Gemma*

Handing the pen back to the shopkeeper, I tucked the book into the bag I'd been given and made my way to Rori, who would be as key to my plan as the book itself. If indeed I did die, I wanted her to be the one to give it to Jonny.

In the back of my mind, and for reasons unknown, I was convinced that Rori would come out of the March 31ˢᵗ Dothen attack unscathed. Maybe it was the strength that seemed to run through her, but I got the distinct sense that if she couldn't make it through that night... no one would.

"You ready?" Rori asked as I approached.

"Yeah," I said, holding up my bag. "I want to show you what I bought. Later," I added, as Taeo joined us by the door.

I don't know why I didn't want Taeo to see the journal. Chances were good Rori would tell him about it anyway. Somehow it just felt too personal though, and despite the fact that I liked and even trusted Taeo, I only wanted to share it with the one person essential to the plan.

"Where do we need to go now?" Taeo said, obviously implying the procurement of the portens.

"To my house," I said, exiting the store. "You'll need to help me with it. It's... stuck."

"All right..." Taeo said slowly, a question in his voice.

"I, uh... I haven't been able to pick it up," I admitted.

"Hmm," he said. "Interesting problem."

It was an interesting problem to say the least, and one, I thought with relief, that wouldn't be mine for much longer.

CHAPTER 67

I watched the flames dancing dreamily against the backdrop of the black nighttime sea. They licked at the inky star-filled sky, their citrine tongues moving lazily about, filling my eyes and blurring my vision. The heat of them drifted over me, but I felt cold inside. I dug my feet into the sand, the grains running silkily through my toes, and tried to hear only the soft crackling of the fire and the repetitive surging of the ocean, and not Hannah's quiet weeping.

A light breeze ruffled my hair and I tucked the loose strands behind my ears without taking my eyes from the blaze. I couldn't look away. If I did, I might see expressions of worry and fear and doubt on the faces of all those seated near me, and I didn't need that. It would make the dull nagging of nervousness that had settled in the pit of me grow into full-blown panic. So I stared at the glowing embers, the furling smoke, and the hypnotic, flickering light.

They told me I would feel something if Kai was in trouble, either a sharp stabbing sensation in my notae or a jolt throughout my body as though I'd been shocked. I'd felt neither, but there was a growing uneasiness in me that had nothing to do with the *Consociare* elixir and our Keeper-Kept relationship and everything to do with intuition.

Of course, we'd known Kai was going to be late. He'd called Taeo at 3 PM to say he was on his way back and that he hoped to reach the Twin Cities around 9 PM. As it would be a full hour and a half past sundown, Taeo urged him to go straight to Riverview, where he could drive directly into the secured underground parking of the facility, instead of coming to Salvos, which would require him to risk a run from the place he parked his car to the Wooded Bridge. Kai wouldn't hear of it, though. He said he needed the Mederium, and that the depletion he'd sustained the previous night had been worse than he'd let on. He was fading fast.

From what Taeo had been able to ascertain, it had, at least, been a worth-while trip. Kai was too fatigued to relay the details of his excursion, but he did say he had found Gate and that there was a lot he needed to share with us after he had been restored to full health.

At nine o'clock on the dot, Kai called Taeo again and told him he was twenty minutes outside of the Cities and that he'd be crossing the bridge within the hour. Taeo said he sounded exhausted but well enough. We built a fire on the beach by the Axis and waited.

With the exception of Taeo, Rori, and myself, no one knew where Kai had gone or why he was late getting back, but for the most part, the Host wasn't overly concerned about it. In fact, people seemed to expect this sort of reckless behavior from Kai; he was known for it, just like he was known for his narrow escapes. They went to bed, unperturbed that he wasn't yet accounted for. Even Ren, Shea, and Alistair, who were the closest thing Kai had to friends apart from Taeo, seemed untroubled. When they, along with Alistair's girlfriend Jossi, settled around the fire with us, it was with the air of a group anticipating tales of adventure.

Echo and Eclipse were another matter. They huddled together in the sand, their young faces twisted with worry. Trying their best to sound confi-dent, they consoled the increasingly-distraught Hannah, who had remained with our fireside group, refusing to go to sleep.

Ten o'clock rolled by, and then eleven. With each passing minute, ten-sion wound my body tighter until my breathing was shallow and labored. I stopped looking at the display on my phone, unwilling to acknowledge the time. I concentrated entirely on the leaping flames.

Out of the corner of my eye, I saw Taeo stand up and begin pacing. "Echo," he said, breaking the stillness of the night, "you still can't see him across the bridge?"

"Kai is not yet within range," Echo said somberly. "It is, at this point, unlikely he will be arriving on Salvos tonight." He patted Hannah's tiny seven-year-old hand, which was now trembling with dread.

Taeo called Kai's phone for what was probably the hundredth time, but still there was no answer. He closed his eyes for a fleeting moment, mumbling, "I'm so sorry, Rori."

"No," she said, springing to her feet, her brown eyes pleading with him. "Gemma hasn't felt anything yet. She's his Kept—she would *know* if he was in danger. He's not in trouble! Please don't go."

He touched her cheek, his face full of tenderness and apology. "You know I'm the only one who can. I'm sorry," he said again. "I love you. I'll be back before you know it." Without giving her a chance to answer, he took off towards the Axis, disappearing into it. Minutes later, he emerged wearing black combat gear. I couldn't see him very well, my pupils having contracted from staring at the fire, but he appeared to be carrying a wide- and long-barreled black gun, some sort of rifle. Then he was gone.

A steady stream of tears leaked from Rori's closed eyes. Our group fell silent once more, and I turned back to the fire, letting it burn golden streaks into my retinas.

CHAPTER 68

*U*nconquerable. That's what Hannah and the other kids called Kai. He'd said it was because of his amber ring, because they thought it protected him, but there was another reason they called him that, a reason perpetuated by Kai himself: Despite his repeated brushes with the Dothen, he'd always made it home.

It was his attitude, as much as his escapes, which allowed people to believe he was invincible. He was strong, not just of body but of spirit, and he displayed his strength of will in everything he did. It was the code he lived by. He had programmed himself to persist, and persist he would, until he either won or chose to quit. There was no third option, no alternate fate that could find him. This was *his* game; no Dothen would get him. He was unconquerable.

It was more than confidence; it was conviction. It led him to doing things others considered foolish—following his Gravitation to The Meet Lab on Halloween, for instance. And every time he did something like that and came out of it okay, it bolstered his belief in himself. Yes, he was fast and strong and agile, but more significant than those attributes was his unwavering discipline of the mind. He simply refused to acknowledge the possibility of failure.

But the possibility was there, whether he chose to acknowledge it or not. He was, after all, just a man. He was a giant of a man, conditioned and resilient and tough, but a man nonetheless. Whatever supernatural gifts he possessed, he was still mortal. And I feared for him.

Taeo had feared for him, too, which was why, after hours of waiting, he could be idle no longer. Other than Kai, he was the only time-keeper the Host had, the only other person privileged with the ability to travel the bridge after hours, and he'd made up his mind to go. He had the same steely look of determination in his eyes that Kai often had, and though Taeo's assuredness was less obtrusive than Kai's—he never came across as arrogant, just self-possessed—it was there. It made me wonder if it was that, as much as the presence of suitable gifts, that prompted Phoenix to award them the time-keeper jobs.

Or perhaps their high levels of confidence had resulted *from* their gifts. I guess I'd be pretty certain of myself too if I could sprout protective scales at will. Kai had denied it of course, dismissing what I'd seen as delusion, but I'd been lucid enough in that moment to differentiate fact from fantasy. He *had* covered himself in diamond-shaped plates, after which the Taken's hold had no effect. It was truly a remarkable corporeal gift, one I wanted to know more about, but I knew that the harder I pushed him, the less likely he'd be to tell me anything. Like all Essen, Kai was very protective of his gifts.

As he should be. If Raela's murder had taught me anything, it was that one person's gifts may be another person's undoing. You never knew who might feel threatened by them, or how desperately they'd want them gone. It was the very valid reason the Essen chose to keep their gifts secret. It was the reason I myself had not shared details of my gifts with anyone except with Echo, even though my understanding of them was increasing every day. It was increasing with each passing minute, as a matter of fact.

I hoped I was wrong about my second gift. I hoped that the dark suspicion that was swelling inside me was nothing more than the product of an overactive and worried mind. But as the night wore on and my fear for Kai intensified, I doubted it.

All the evidence, now that I was reflecting on it, was pointing to my corporeal gift becoming exactly what I thought. Maybe upon Activation it would take a different form than its developmental trajectory was suggesting, but with only four days until it settled, I didn't find that likely. Still, I *hoped* it would evolve into something else entirely—because if it shaped up like it seemed it was going to... how on earth was it a *gift?*

I felt Echo's eyes on me, studying me from across the fire. Did he somehow know what I was thinking? That I'd begun to see the clues?

The first one had come from him, after all. Last January. I had woken up on the beach after Kai had tackled me and injected serum into my neck.

How long was I out? I'd asked Echo.

Much less time than expected, he'd responded. *The serum typically affects people for a half-day or more. You were under its influence for less than twenty minutes. Kai asked me to keep an eye on you, but it was his intention to return to you before you awoke. I knew I should have told him to wait. It was only a matter of time before your second gift began developing…*

At the time, I'd had no idea what he was talking about. But then there was the *Restas*, the low-grade painkiller from Taeo that'd I'd drunk after my failed attempt to manipulate the portens, and also the *Restoration*, which I consumed every evening after my workouts. Neither elixir, to the confusion of Kai and Taeo, proved as beneficial to me as for others.

And then last night I'd been given the *Indolentia*. Ren had called it 'the most effective painkiller we have,' but it had done nothing for me. Nothing.

All of which was why, as I sat with the taciturn group gazing at the lambent flames, I feared for Kai. Through the *Consociare* elixir, we were bound to one another. As his Kept, I was supposed to be able to feel if he was hurt or in trouble. I was supposed to *know*. But I didn't know, I didn't feel anything, which meant one of two things: either Kai was really okay, or… the Essen concoctions—serums, elixirs, and the like—didn't have any effect on me.

I hoped it wasn't the latter. Not only was imperviousness to Essen formulas a crappy corporeal gift, one *no one* would mind losing in Deactivation, but it could also mean that Kai had been in danger—or worse—for *hours* before Taeo had gone after him. I put my head in my hands, overwrought with apprehension.

What if Kai had been depleted, his time stolen from him until his body had become dust? Would we know it only by his absence? Was there any other way to confirm his situation?

I tried reaching out to him with my mind. Without making any outward sign, I turned on my radio and brought the tuner dial up the FM band, searching for a frequency that might allow me to hear Kai's voice or Taeo's. All I got was static until I arrived at the end of the band, where I once again caught the ringing of mysterious and faraway wind chimes. Snarling in frustration, I stood abruptly, kicking at the sand, and stomped from the fire to the edge of the water, careful not to meet anyone's startled stares.

I have a gift of the mind and corporeal gift, both of which are just shit, I thought as I stared out at the sea. What the hell kind of job would Phoenix award to me, supposing I was to remain Activated? My gifts would be of no use to anybody. Why the hell *wouldn't* I De-A? I had nothing to offer anyone this side of the bridge, now that the portens was out of my hands.

But *shit*—

...*Was* it? *Was* it out of my hands?

If Kai and Taeo didn't make it back, then the only people who knew its current location were me and Rori, and Rori had already made it quite plain that she wanted nothing to do with it. What would I do *then*? Give it to someone else? Who? The hopeless addict Phoenix? One of the Anchored Set, Echo or Eclipse? The relentless charmer Puck? No one really sprang to mind as the right choice, but I couldn't keep it myself. I'd already tried to wield it and failed, and besides, I was Deactivating in a few days.

I would have to decide what to do with it before then. If I couldn't, I would be forced to leave it where it was and De-A anyway. Rori would have to figure it out. And as bad as I'd feel about doing that to her, I've already admitted the truth: I am selfish. My priority was Deactivation.

She would understand. She'd be pissed, but she'd understand because she'd met Jonny. She knew he was worth Deactivating for.

"I can see what you mean," she'd said appreciatively after meeting him that afternoon when we'd gone to my house to collect the portens. "Who *wouldn't* De-A for that?" Taeo arched an eyebrow at her. "I mean, apart from those of us who already *have* a perfect man," she amended, crinkling her nose at him.

It had been an odd convergence of my two worlds, a strange extended overlap between the different circles of my existence. In the hour we'd spent at my house, Taeo and Rori met not only Jonny, who had come by to see about hanging out, but also Aunt Sheri, Flash, and Paul, who had dropped by to tell Flash about his wedding. I'd told them all that Taeo and Rori were friends from work.

357

"Do we... know each other?" Flash asked, tilting his head and looking from Rori to Taeo. "You both look so familiar." He ran a hand through his blue-blonde hair, obviously trying to place their faces.

"I don't think so," Taeo said, acting perplexed and giving no indication that he'd once attacked Flash and stabbed him in the neck. "Like Gemma said, we just work with her."

"For four more nights," Jonny piped in, winking at me. "Right, Gem? Hey—if you guys don't have to work on Wednesday, you should come to the big twenty-first birthday party I'm planning for Gemma. Here, give me your numbers and I'll text you the details."

Rori played it cool, saying they might be able to drop by, as Jonny programmed their numbers into his phone.

"He really is something special, isn't he?" Rori said as we'd walked up the stairs to my bedroom after Jonny had left. Unfortunately, we didn't get to dwell on the topic of him for long. There was a portens to be secured, and none of us were exactly sure how to get it back into its plastic box without experiencing 'the effects that come to pass.' After what had happened to me last time, we weren't particularly anxious to touch it, even through a towel or a sheet.

We talked about it for a while, trying to come up with a strategy for retrieving it. Ultimately it was Taeo who, in a show of chivalry, demanded we stand back and reached, barehanded, under my bed. He grimaced as he withdrew the still-swirling rock from beneath the dust ruffle, and dropped it lightly in its box.

"Are you okay?" I asked, rushing to his side.

"I just tweaked my shoulder a bit." He rubbed at it vigorously. "I'll live."

My mouth fell open. "You mean you didn't... The portens didn't...?"

Rori, who had been watching Taeo closely, turned to me. "Don't trouble yourself over it," she said in a measured voice. "I'm sure I would have been affected the same way you were."

But as we left and made our way to the Wooded Bridge with the encased portens in Taeo's backpack, I wondered if that was true. *Would* Rori have been affected, or was I, the Link, the only one for whom touching the portens posed a real threat?

It didn't really matter, I told myself. It was out of my hands. Soon Kai would be back—he *would* be back, he was unconquerable—and he could deal with it. We'd left it for him in The Nest, hidden behind a loose boulder at the back of the cave. There it would wait for him, the object he'd sought for most of his life, and I would move on, forgetting about it and all of its troublesome properties.

He didn't want or need my help with it anyway, just like he didn't really need my help understanding Record 3629. He'd said there was something different about it, something he couldn't put his finger on, but he'd just wanted to keep me busy, right? So I'd stay out of trouble while he was on the road?

I'd had no problem staying busy once Taeo, Rori, and I had arrived at Salvos late that afternoon. Almost immediately, I'd begun writing my story for Jonny, recounting my first few interactions with Kai last fall, my accidental discovery of Gate Dorsum and his hypnotherapy practice, and my regular meetings with him in which I learned about the Essen, undergoing, and his process for recovering buried memories.

I felt a little guilty about choosing to write in the journal rather than work through the Record, but there was a lot to chronicle and not much time. I had my own plan to execute. Besides, Kai had so often reminded me that he'd spent *years* studying the Records. If there really was some mystery about it, he'd be far more likely to solve it than I would.

That's what I tried to tell myself. The truth of the matter was, I didn't *want* to study Record 3629. What if I worked on it and found nothing? I would have wasted precious time. Or what if I worked on it and discovered things I didn't want to know, for example the circumstances behind my own prophesized death? It might take away my newfound hope of survival. I had to be protective of my hope.

But as Hannah's soft whimpers, carried by the breeze, stirred in my ears, my guilt expanded and filled every inch of me. Who was I to hold onto my own hope if it meant depriving others from potentially having theirs? If there was more to Record 3629 than we currently knew, then I needed to try to puzzle it out. I'm no hero, but I can't turn my back on people either. Especially if Kai was no more.

I shuddered at the thought. Losing Kai would be horrible. The Essen needed him, even if they didn't like him. He was smart, enterprising, and dedicated to their cause. And when Taeo was there to balance him out, he wasn't altogether *un*likable… On a few occasions, he'd even been pleasant.

But it wasn't just the Essen that needed Kai. I did too. I needed him to return, and not just because if he didn't, I'd have to shoulder the responsibilities of solving the portens and Record 3629 on my own. I needed him to return because, in spite of myself, I had become attached. I hadn't realized it until he'd failed to turn up, but I was terrified of losing him, just like Taeo had said he was terrified of losing me. I hadn't believed Taeo at the time, but now I knew: Regardless of whether *Consociare* had truly taken hold, a bond had formed between Kai and me. It was a deep-seated concern for one another's well-being, an unspoken desire for each other's continued existence.

If Taeo was unable to bring him home… If, heaven forbid, neither of them returned to Salvos…

A scream pierced the air. I wheeled around and first saw Hannah leaping frantically to her feet, her long brown hair trailing behind her as she tore across the sand. All around the fire, commotion ensued as everyone vaulted up and hurried to the Axis.

My heart felt tight within my chest. I raced away from the water, straining to see into the blackness beyond the flames. Slowly, I began to make out the silhouettes of two people, one bearing the other over his shoulder. Drawing nearer, I saw the burdened man stumble to the ground, releasing the other gracelessly onto the beach. From his knees, he looked up at all of us as we came around him. His hair and beard were congealed with blood and dirt, his eyes filled with anguish.

"Help me get him to the Mederium," Taeo pleaded, his voice cracking. "I don't know how much time he has left."

My insides plummeted as I took in the motionless form of Kai lying in the sand, his body bent at odd angles from being dropped. His shirt was ripped, exposing the intricate tattoo that stretched across his back. The great ax-laden tree was unmoving, betraying no breath, no twitching of muscle. Ren, Alistair, and Shea hoisted him up, but Kai's eyelids did not flutter, nor did he give any other sign of life.

He hung limply in their arms, looking for all the world like he had been conquered.

CHAPTER 69

Once again, the young woman staring back at me did not look hopeful, but this time she looked forlorn rather than afraid. Tears glittered in her eyelashes and threatened to spill down her cheeks, but she clenched her jaw and swallowed hard, unwilling to admit defeat. Crying is for the bereft, for those whom despair has finally given way to grief. It is an act of acceptance. She would not allow herself to cry, because she had accepted nothing. She *would* accept nothing, not while there was life yet in him.

I looked away from my reflection in the glasslike surface of the emerald water to the behemoth sprawled out next to me at the edge of the pool. There *was* life in him; I sensed it rather than saw it.

Kai's normally golden-hued brown skin had a dull grayish undertone and his too-still body was positioned exactly as it had been hours ago. Even the telltale signs of respiration—the rise and fall of his broad chest, the airy sounds of exhaling—were missing. It was only through Eclipse's gift of perception, which she used to confirm he was in fact taking in oxygen, that we knew he was breathing at all.

But for how much longer he would continue, we didn't know. If the color of his complexion was any indication, he seemed to be waning. It was becoming ashier with every passing minute.

Apart from the night Uncle Dan died, it was the most helpless I'd ever felt. Kai was hanging by a thread, and there was nothing I could do for him. There was nothing any of us could do for him until the Mederium's energies shifted. Eclipse had been monitoring them since our arrival more than three hours prior, but they remained hostile, churning destructively deep below the placid surface.

Kai had warned me that the Mederium had the potential to harm rather than heal, but it was the first time I'd been present while it was cycling. It certainly didn't look any different than it normally did, but I realized quickly—after Rori, by way of demonstration, lowered a flower into it and brought up a shriveled and blackened petal-less stem—how dangerous it really was.

I wiped the unshed tears from my lashes and hugged my knees to my chest, leaning my head against them. Exhausted though I was, I dared not close my eyes. As soon as Eclipse gave the word, I had to get Kai into the pool.

Taeo and Rori would help me of course, but besides Eclipse, they were the only ones still there. Ren, Shea, Alistair, and Jossi, understanding there was nothing else they could do, had since gone to bed, taking Echo and Hannah back to the Somnus with them.

It was lonely, the waiting. Rori was dozing against the entrance boulder and Taeo was stretched out across the ground next to her with his still-begrimed head in her lap. Eclipse was the only other person still awake, and she didn't provide much in the way of company. Sitting cross-legged at the base of a tree a short distance from the water, she had a dreamy look about her. Her big brown eyes half-lidded, I got the impression she was worlds away, wholly absorbed in the reading of the Mederium's energies.

My heart ached as sorrow needled its way into me. I tried to fight it off, imagining Jonny next to me, comforting me, reassuring me that no loss had yet occurred. In my mind he was singing to me, repeating the same soothing melody over and over like he did the night my uncle died.

His voice, so clear and warm and perfect, filled my head. I hummed along with him, closing my eyes briefly to picture his nimble fingers sliding masterfully across the neck of his guitar. I envisioned him leaning forward, a curtain of dark hair swinging lightly into his face and him shaking it back impatiently, his dark blue eyes soulful.

God, I missed him.

"That's a beautiful tune," Rori said quietly. I opened my eyes to find her contemplating me from across the pool, still reclined sedately against the boulder. "Haunting, but beautiful." She tilted her head at me, a small frown forming on her face. "I didn't realize you loved him."

"Of course I love him," I answered automatically. "That's why I asked for your help with the journal. I love him too much to leave him wondering. If I die—"

"I wasn't talking about Jonny," Rori said. I followed her gaze to Kai's unconscious body and to my own hand, which I only then noticed was splayed in the short hair at his temple.

I retracted my arm quickly.

"You love him, don't you?" she pressed. He brows were knitted together in an expression of earnest bewilderment.

"He's a jerk," I answered, looking away.

"Agreed. But that doesn't really answer the question."

My eyes drifted over Kai, at his dull flesh that was looking deader by the minute, and began to well up again. "I just don't want him to *die*," I choked out. "Not because of me."

"It was *his* choice to go after Gate," Rori said gently. "Don't blame yourself. Kai knew it was risky and he went anyway."

"Only because he felt compelled to. Only because he's my Keeper." I tried to fight back the tears, but they rolled from my eyes and splashed onto my lips, tasting salty.

"He didn't go because he felt obligated, Gemma. He went because he *wanted* to. Because he loves you. And I don't think you're crying right now because you feel responsible for his current condition; you're crying because you're scared of losing him. Because you love him too."

I avoided her gaze, shaking my head faintly at the teal water, tears now falling freely down my cheeks.

"Taeo told me you had feelings for each other. I thought *maybe* he was right about Kai—pictures don't usually lie—but I didn't think there was any way he could be right about you. It wasn't until just now, when I heard you singing to him and saw you touching him, that I realized... you *do* love him."

"I just don't want him to die," I repeated in a whisper. "That doesn't mean I'm in love with him."

Rori sighed. "I never said you were *in* love with him. That might've come later, assuming—"

"He's *going* to live," I said sharply.

"—assuming *you* were to remain Activated," she finished pointedly. "But that's not what I meant. I was just talking about foundational love, the kind that starts with friendship, affection, and trust. Like the love you have for Jonny."

I felt my face flushing with indignation. "My feelings for Kai are *nothing* like my feelings for Jonny."

"But you do love him," Rori said.

"How could I love someone I don't even trust?"

"You've let him train you every single night for three months. There's obviously *some* trust there."

"That's—that's not the point," I spluttered. "With Kai, there's no friendship, there's no affection—"

"But there is affection," she stated simply. "From you, just now. And from Kai, too." She shifted her weight and reached into her pants pocket, careful not to disturb Taeo. Drawing out her cell phone, she tapped the screen several times and then looked over at me. "I just forwarded you the photo Taeo took a couple weeks ago. He sent it to me as 'proof' that his theory was right."

I wiped my eyes and reached for my phone, which was lying on the ground next to me. "When was this taken?" I asked, sniffling. The image was a picture of me in profile, sitting on the beach, stretching. To my left, standing over me and watching me with an expression of mingled tenderness and admiration, was Kai.

Rori shrugged. "Sunrise one morning. Taeo went to catch some early waves, and he spotted you guys finishing a workout."

My eyes flickered over the image again. In my months of knowing Kai, I had never caught him looking at me like that before. His features, lit by the sun's first rays, had a softness about them that seemed to stem from some internal emotion. I could see Taeo's point. Kai's expression did look suspiciously like love.

I set my phone back on the ground. "It was a fluke. Kai's never shown me affection. He's never shown me anything but contempt." Reflexively, I raised my hand to my throat and fingered my naked collarbone where my necklace should have rested.

"Shown you? Why would he show you? He's not one to show his feelings at all, but besides that, from the moment he met you, all you've ever talked about is Jonny. And then your desire to De-A."

"Why are you telling me this?" I snapped, growing angry. "Why now? What does it matter how I feel, how he feels? It's not going to change my mind. On Wednesday, I'm Deactivating so I can spend what'll probably be my last week alive with my family."

"I know, Gemma," she said gently. "I wasn't trying to change your mind." She stroked Taeo's gore-matted hair absently as she surveyed Kai. "I just thought that... If Kai is still hanging on, and if he can somehow hear us... It might help him stay, knowing you care."

I glared at Rori as more tears filled my eyes. They trailed down my face, hot and angry. I *did* care about Kai. Maybe it was even some version of *love*, like she was asserting, and maybe I *was* afraid of losing him... but how could admitting it keep him with us? He was dying; his flesh had turned the brownish-gray color of fetid meat.

And it was my fault.

Kai had gone after Gate *because* he was my Keeper and *because* I was prophesized to die. *Don't you get it?* he'd yelled at me. *I'm trying to save you, you thankless harpy!* He was right about me, too. I had been thankless as I watched him leave the Estates, risking his life for me for the second day in a row.

And then he'd failed to cross the bridge. We all waited, harboring our own silent misgivings about his whereabouts. Rori assured Taeo that Kai was okay. If he wasn't, I'd have felt something, she told him. But she was wrong. I'd felt nothing, and meanwhile, he'd fallen victim to the Dothen. Taeo's help had been delayed because I was somehow resistant to the effects of the *Consociare*.

Again, it was my fault.

Feelings of guilt and powerlessness overwhelmed me. It was all I could do to stay sitting there; I wanted to run. I wanted to take off along the beach until the fear and shame and sadness and anger and love—all of it—was done pouring from my eyes.

Taeo stirred on Rori's thighs. "Aurora?" he mumbled, his mouth moving tiredly from beneath his grimy beard.

"I'm here, babe," she said softly, looking down at him.

"They were just kids, Aurora," he said bleakly, opening his eyes.

"Shh," Rori said, her tone soothing. "Just rest. You don't have to talk about it right now."

"Eighteen, maybe. A boy and a girl, probably on a date. Out for a midnight stroll along the river."

"Shh," Rori said again. "Please, babe. Try to go back to sleep."

"I blew their heads off," Taeo went on roughly, "and I dumped their bodies in the river." Through my own blurred vision, I saw the pain sparkling in his eyes.

"Please, Taeo," Rori pleaded. "Just try to rest."

Taeo squeezed his eyes shut, a stream of tears issuing from beneath them and trickling into his beard. "He wasn't going to make it, Aurora. I saw him graying. I had to do it." Panic was rising in his voice.

"I know, it's all right, I know," she said consolingly, bending over him to kiss his forehead, her coppery hair dancing across his face.

He drew in a ragged breath. "I hope it wasn't for nothing."

"It wasn't for nothing," Rori said, her voice cracking. "Kai is... he's going to be fine. Gemma's with him. She's... helping him hold on. As soon as the Mederium is ready, we'll get him in. He'll be his obnoxious, conceited, reckless self again in no time." Taeo didn't open his eyes but pursed his lips into a weak smile. "And you'll be okay, too," she said, leaning her head against his.

"The *Oblivio*..." Taeo whispered.

"Soon," Rori said. "I'll get it for you once Kai's in the pool. But I need you with me until then."

I felt sick, hearing them, watching them... It was suffocating me, knowing that whatever had happened to Taeo was my fault, too. I couldn't stay there. I had to leave. I had to run. I would have, if Eclipse hadn't risen at that very moment and said, "It's time."

I shot up. "What do you need me to do?"

"Undress him," she instructed, "to his undershorts. For the degree of healing required, we have to minimize clothing interference. Then get in the water. You too, Rori. Taeo, can you lower him into the pool?"

The three of us hastily stripped off Kai's utility pants and his torn shirt. Rori and I jumped in the water and helped guide Kai's cadaverous body into the pool as Taeo lowered him from the edge. We kept him upright, each clutching a bicep, until Taeo joined us in the water and tipped Kai back so everything but his mouth and nose was submerged.

Pearly clouds of talc-like minerals surrounded us. I felt the familiar tingling sensation as they settled on me. Tension seeped from my muscles, swept away by the rolling pressure of the kneading particles. I sank deeper into the water, relaxing against the side of the rocky basin, still holding one of Kai's gray-brown arms.

It didn't register right away, what I was seeing: Rori and Taeo and me, each blanketed by the floury substance, and Kai's corpselike body, stretched out between us like a morbid version of da Vinci's 'Vitruvian Man,' looking even more leaden beneath the green-blue water.

Looking even more leaden...

I was still holding his gray-brown arms...

He was uncoated. None of the powdery minerals had attached themselves to his skin. Taeo was staring down at him, the look of dread in his eyes confirming the terrible truth: Kai wasn't healing. There may have been life yet in him, but it was continuing to wither.

CHAPTER 70

Rori, Taeo, and I, we didn't let go. We held Kai in the water for hours, long after our own recoveries were complete, scanning the depths for some stirring of opaque minerals around his flesh. None appeared.

We got discouraged in turns. Eclipse begged us not to abandon the effort. Kai's deterioration, she told us, was slowing. Soon, she promised, it would be stopped. And only then, after the downward spiral had ended, could the damage be reversed. That's when the particles would begin the rebuilding process.

Dawn approached. Alistair and Jossi came to relieve us, slipping into the pool around Kai. When they arrived, Rori dashed off to the Aerarium to retrieve the *Oblivio* elixir for Taeo. He consumed the entire bottle in three great swallows before they left together for the Somnus.

I did not go to bed. I went to the beach. The sun rose and I stared at it, dropping to my knees with all upon my shoulders.

✳ ✳ ✳

Sunday passed, and Monday, and Kai continued to hover somewhere between no-longer-deteriorating and not-yet-healing. The Host was devastated. They lined up at the Mederium, sharing in the rotation of his care. Their concern, Taeo assured me with bitterness in his voice, was less about Kai himself, unpopular as he was, and more about the portens. After all, he said, they hadn't bothered to help with his recovery last November, when he'd been nearly as bad off as he was now. No, they wanted him well because *he* was the one Phoenix had tasked with preparing the portens.

There was resentment among them. Why had Phoenix given such an important assignment to *Malakai*, a known risk? Surely he would reassign the task, now that Kai was... as he was. Each of them claimed to be the right choice as the next portens-keeper.

But Phoenix could not reassign the task, namely because as far as he knew, there were only two people who were privy to the portens' current location, and while one of them was unconscious and battling for his life, the other had gone missing.

Where is she? the Essen demanded of Taeo and Rori with increasing agitation. *She is the Link, she has the portens, she must bring it forward!* Taeo and Rori told them they did not know where I had gone. Taeo and Rori were lying.

They knew that I, in the manner of a coward, had secluded myself in the Nest. I had been there since early Sunday morning, following my complete breakdown on the beach.

"You can't stay here forever," Rori admonished, finding me tucked against the cave wall later that day.

"I'm working," I snapped, wild-eyed and frantic. Lines from various Records ran through my head unceasingly, but they were jumbled and confusing.

"You're *hiding*," she said flatly.

"I need to figure this damn thing out!" I shrieked, shaking the clear plastic box in which the portens resided. Even to my own ears, my voice sounded hysterical.

"You need to sleep," she said. "And then you need to tend to your Keeper, Gemma. Eclipse thinks your presence... Well, she says Kai displayed other colors when you were with him last night... like he can sense you. Please, go to him. Let Taeo and I work with the portens for a while."

But I couldn't go to him, not while there was so much to do, so much riding on *me*. I remained dutifully out of sight, fretting over the portens and Record 3629.

There exists a colored spire, nestled in the sand...

Taeo and Rori came to me at regular intervals, bringing me food that I never touched and pillows that I never rested on. They exchanged uneasy looks with one another as I slid further and further from reality.

For the war cannot be ended until the portens is revealed...

They cast about for the right words to hook me and reel me back to them, but nothing they said could steal my focus from the Records. With Malakai unconscious, it was on me, all of it was. *I* was the Link, the one to whom the portens had come.

The forces of the four reside inside the stolen mass...

They tried to help. Taeo frequently took the portens out of the box and held it, sometimes tossing it back and forth between hands, meditating on its properties. At one point he dropped it and it rolled to the entrance of the cave. To stop it from falling off the ledge and out of our possession, Rori lunged at it, snatching it up. She was instantly affected, much like I had been. Taeo wrestled the stone, which was freezing to her skin, out of her hands. He dropped it in the box, taking a trembling and shocked Rori to the Mederium, leaving me alone with my thoughts once more.

Seductive is the might the portens shield contains...

Rori entered the Nest, announcing it to be Monday evening. Kai's condition, she told me, was unchanged. She implored me to go to the Mederium, for my own benefit as well as his. I still didn't go.

Yet earth and fire, air and water, were all for life designed—

I didn't go because I couldn't bear to face the Host. Interspersed with the random Record lines, Echo's and Rori's warnings, given to me my first day on Salvos, sounded in my mind. *There is one who would seek to exploit you...* Echo had told me with solemnity in his clear blue eyes. But who? The only person he said I could trust was Kai, and Kai was the one person Gate had told me not to trust. So I should trust... nobody? And still try to help everyone? I *wanted* to help them, I did, but I was running out of time. Activation was nearing, and along with it, my sole opportunity to De-A. Yet Rori's words rang in my ears: *If you can't or won't help them... I fear they will turn on you.*

"Gemma, *please* go to the Mederium," Rori urged when she returned to the Nest a few hours later. I don't think I even acknowledged that she had spoken.

It wasn't just the Host I couldn't bear to face. It was Kai, too. The memory of his skin, sick and muddy-looking, and of his motionless body, floating corpselike in the water, preyed upon me. I could not stand to see him like that. It was bad enough that I had to see him every time I had the misfortune to drift into slumber. There he was, starring in my darkest and most Afflicted nightmares, an undead version of himself, his cold hands pressing my head below the water.

Don't dream that I'm the bad guy, he had said. Deep down, I don't believe I ever really thought he was the bad guy, but I couldn't keep myself from dreaming it, from waking up shivering and haunted and gasping for air.

That's how Tuesday greeted me: with uncontrollable shivering, with the ghost of Kai's lifeless body lingering in my mind, with a shortage of air. Choking and coughing, I crawled to the entrance of the cave and saw that the day was dawning gray and lusterless.

A portens for a full release, to which the power's bound...

I wanted to create a legacy, to do something noble and honorable, to make a difference... but it was now Tuesday, the day before my twenty-first birthday and exactly a week until quarter's end. I'd been holed up in the cliffside cave for the better part of three days, and still no epiphanies had struck.

Tempting hearts of right to launch evil campaigns...

By Tuesday afternoon, Kai still showed no signs of recovery, and I was in ruins. I had failed. Activation was upon me. Sometime after midnight, just six hours from now, it would start. With mounting panic, I realized how little I'd accomplished: I hadn't solved the mystery of the portens, I hadn't figured out what was different about Record 3629, I hadn't helped with Kai's care at the Mederium, and I hadn't finished writing my story for Jonny.

Jonny.

The thought of him swept down on me, bringing both clarity and pain. It was the first I'd thought of him since Saturday night, when I'd hummed his song to Kai. I hadn't communicated with him or my aunt since introducing them both to Rori and Taeo on Saturday afternoon. I was a horrible, wretched human being. I reached for my phone. It was dead.

The Link will be defeated.

If I had destroyed my relationship with Jonny during my three-day journey into madness, then I was already defeated. I just hoped that when I saw him tomorrow, when I presented him with whatever excuse I could think of for my disappearance, he would be forgiving.

The sky outside grew darker. At the Nest's opening, where Taeo and Rori had placed vases of Supernovas, a pale purple glow lit the walls.

"Gemma?" Taeo said faintly.

I started. Though he had been with me since late afternoon, when he brought the news of Kai's still unchanged condition, we'd sat in silence for so long that I'd forgotten he was there.

He blinked at me, his gray eyes looking sooty in the dimness of the cave. "You can't stay here for Activation. You know that don't you?"

I nodded grudgingly, remembering what Kai had once told me about the final stage of undergoing. 'It's like Affliction, but a hundred time worse,' he'd said. 'You'll need to be by the Mederium. You can't go in it while you're Activating, it would make the process even more agonizing, but as soon its over, you'll want to take a swim. Believe me.' I met Taeo's eyes, a knot of anxiety tightening in my stomach.

"When it's time," Taeo said, "I'll go with you. As your sort of... substitute Keeper. Most Kepts, they don't want to go through it alone. Activation is excruciating, most people black out for hours at a time. It will be later in the afternoon when your gifts finally settle. And after they have..." He looked down at his hands. "I'll take you to the Deactivation Bridge."

"The Deactivation Bridge?" I whispered.

"It's the one-way bridge, open to every Essen on their birthday—post-Activation, I mean. It's so charged with supernatural energy that to cross it is... well, damaging. It has the power to fry out whatever gifts you might end up with, thus ending your stint as a supernatural. That's what you want, isn't it?"

I opened my mouth to speak, but no words came out.

"It's okay, Gemma," Taeo said, still avoiding my eyes. "You don't have to worry about us. Rori and I, we'll make sure the portens is ready for next week, I promise. As soon as Kai is conscious again, as soon as he can tell us whatever it was he learned from Gate..."

He trailed off, turning to gaze out the entrance of the cave.

"Has anyone ever taken this long to heal before?" I asked quietly.

Taeo shook his head and unscrewed the top of his hipflask, taking a large draught before facing me. "Last November when Kai was tagged, he was unconscious for several days, but the healing process began immediately. But I think this time"—he offered the flask to me—"he'd been holding on much longer by the time I finally got to him."

I took the flask, knowing it was the *Oblivio*, the elixir Taeo had been drinking nonstop since Sunday morning, and took a swig, also knowing it would do nothing for me.

"His gift—he told me you know what it is—it's difficult to maintain," Taeo said. "It offers him protection, but it also drains him. It's painful to use. His efforts were... intermittent, I guess, when I found the Taken depleting him." His lips disappeared beneath his beard as he pursed him. "If I'd only gotten there faster..."

"I'm so sorry, Taeo. I didn't know—"

"It's not your fault, Gemma. There was no way we could have known you wouldn't feel anything."

"But I failed him," I said glumly. "I failed you both."

"You didn't fail anyone. Not Kai, and certainly not me. I know I haven't been myself lately"—he reached out to get his flask back—"but it's not from anything you did."

"If I hadn't... detained you..." I wrapped my arms around myself, suddenly feeling cold. "You might not have been..."

"What—hurt? Look, Gemma, you should know: I've never been tagged. I've never been physically injured in any way. The blood you saw on me, it was from the Taken. I had to, um,"—he closed his eyes and swallowed—"obliterate them. It was the only way. Breaking a Taken's body, damaging it so it's no longer usable to a Dothen... It forces the Dothen out to look for another resource. But it's against the Essen code. We never dismember a Taken unless it's absolutely necessary." He shuddered.

I hesitated, unsure of whether I should say what I was thinking. Finally, after a moment's silence in which Taeo seemed to collect himself, I decided to ask. "But why? They were dead anyway, weren't they? Kai told me that once a Dothen takes a body, once a person's soul had been displaced... It's over. What difference does it make if you have to, you know, destroy the shell?"

Taeo eyed me evenly. "It makes a huge difference: to the victims' families, to the community, to the law enforcement agencies who are now looking for a perpetrator... And to the new victims the Dothen take to replace the ones that were destroyed… It's devastating for everyone when it looks like there've been murders versus natural deaths—not least of all for me. It makes me look like a killer."

"But you're not—"

"It makes me *feel* like a killer."

For a while neither of us spoke. The first star of evening, low in the ever-darkening sky, twinkled through the opening in the cave.

"I'm sorry," Taeo said at length. "I'm always a little off after I…" He cleared his throat. "After I use a weapon. I've done it more than everyone else in the Host combined, and I don't regret it because it's necessary in order to rescue people, but it… affects me. I'd just as soon forget." He raised the flask. "Cheers."

Draining the container, he tossed it to the side. Then he leaned back against the stony wall and closed his eyes.

"That elixir—*Oblivio*—it makes you forget?"

"Not really," he said, without opening his eyes. "But it dulls the memories at least. Makes them less burdensome for me."

"And you offered it to me to… help relieve my burdens?"

"Did it work?" he asked.

"Well… no."

"No, I thought not. How could it, when you're immune to the effects of elixirs?" Through the slit in his eyelids, I saw him watching me for a reaction.

"I don't know what you're talking about," I said feebly.

"Relax," he said, waving an airy hand at me. "I'm not going to tell anyone about your gift. Besides, you'll have it for less than a day before you De-A anyway."

"What makes you think—"

"I put two and two together," he interrupted, shrugging. "Plus, it's shaping up like one of mine did—as more of a curse than a gift—so it was easy to recognize." He raised his head, squinting at me through the violet flower-light that was now emanating deep into the cave. "But if it makes you feel any better, I don't think anyone else has figured it out yet."

I chewed on a fingernail, saying nothing.

"Look, Gemma. I know you don't trust easily, but you have to trust someone, and I'm telling you, you can trust me." Taeo cocked his head at me, his long, sand-colored hair showering to the side. "Would it help if I told you my gift? The corporeal one, the one that's like yours?"

Before I could reply, he said simply, "I'm immune to Gravitation. And apparently"—he eyed the portens, which was swirling colorfully in its box—"other such forces.

"It seemed like such a stupid *non*-gift when it began developing that I was tempted to De-A on principle. I wasn't able to lock in on people or places. I couldn't make discoveries, like Kai did in finding that amber ring. I was actually *angry*, especially when Phoenix made me a time-keeper, emphasizing that my main responsibility would be for rescue missions. I was like, 'How in the cosmos am I supposed to *find* people to save them if I have no Gravitation?' But what I couldn't see at the time was, absence of Gravitation was just that: Absence of Gravitation. It wasn't good, it wasn't bad; it just *was*. Though I couldn't use it for my benefit, neither could it be used to my detriment. No Dothen has ever locked on me. I am the only Essen alive, at least that I'm aware of, that has the ability to *sneak up* on a Dothen. And unlike other gifts, it's not painful to use."

He stopped speaking abruptly, taking stock of the rising moon, which was framed evenly in the cave's opening.

"So you're saying that my elixir immunity—"

"I'm not saying anything, Gemma. I was just telling you about my gift. It's not forbidden, telling other people about your gifts, but it is a demonstration of trust. Take it for what it is."

I sighed, looking at the café-au-lait symbol on the inside of my wrist that I'd always believed to be my birthmark. Tracing the light brown lines of my notae, remembering how Jonny liked to call it my compass, I murmured, "That's why Rori hates Kai, isn't it? Because she thinks he takes advantage of your gift. Because he gets himself into trouble without regard for you."

Taeo sighed. "That's the thing about Kai, Gemma. He doesn't get himself in trouble *without* regard for me. He does it *because* it's me. He knows that even if everyone else in the world is against him, I am for him. No matter how brash he is or how dangerous the situation, I'll be there. *That's* what Rori can't stand: *my* stupidity, as much as Kai's."

"Some might call that loyalty, not stupidity, always going after a friend…"

"The two aren't mutually exclusive," Taeo said, cracking a small smile. He stood up, walked to the front of the cave, and peered out into the night. "It's almost time, Gemma. Let's get to the top." His smile faded as a grim expression took over his features. "The worst hours of your life are about to begin."

CHAPTER 71

The final stage of undergoing seized me sometime after I had clambered to the top of the cliff but before Taeo and I had arrived at the Mederium. The force of it struck me down like lightning. I collapsed against the earth, burning, burning, burning from the inside out.

"Happy twenty-first birthday," Taeo said soberly, lifting me as though I was weightless. His face swam above me, blocking out the stars, as he moved lithely through the woods. The lightning struck again and again, and I writhed in his arms, the jolt of each electrocution searing every nerve. He held me tight against him, whispering that he was there, that he'd stay with me until the end.

Then I was on a thatched, makeshift bed at the edge of the woods surrounding the Mederium. Taeo was cradling my head, and Rori was bent over me, stroking my hair. Vaguely, I knew there were others there as well. I heard them muttering about my three-day disappearance and grumbling about the absence of the portens. Taeo and Rori ignored them, cooling my feverish skin with wet cloths.

Between shocks, my organs sizzled with electrical charge. When the shocks came, my muscles contracted so violently I thought my bones would snap or my heart would give out, or both. The current ran through my body, crushing my nerves, as if with pliers. I screamed out in agony, thrashing my head from side to side.

Everything went dark. When I came to, the sky had lightened. Rori had gone, but Taeo was still with me, and he tipped water into my mouth. It amplified the pain, making the sparks within me leap and sing as they sought not-yet-cauterized nerves. I wailed into my hands and melted away again.

A loose collection of disjointed images, viewed in a detached way, as though from outside my body, gathered in my mind: the repeated movement of the sun across the sky; the constant presence of Taeo; the comings and goings of Rori and others; my body, twisted and convulsing with the immutable and excruciating pain…

At one point I glimpsed, as though through a haze, the still-unconscious Kai in the pool, held afloat by Essen I couldn't identify. Was I delusional, or was the faintest coating of milky particles now lining his skin?

My gifts were settling. Through the torturous pulses of electricity, I felt them, as much a part of me as my limbs. I knew what they were. A blistering sensation, like a brand, fiery and stinging, stabbed at my wrist and scorched my notae. The voices in my head, though many, were clear and distinct; no longer did I hear the obscure "buzzing" that had accompanied them before. And the wind chimes, ringing ominously through the raging storm inside me—I knew about them and their otherworldliness, too.

Lightning struck once more. The blow landed squarely in my chest, and I faded into nothingness.

✳ ✳ ✳

A cheer erupted in a faraway place, waking me. I listened; no further sounds met my ears. I rubbed my eyes and scanned the scene in front of me, but I was quite alone, save one person.

Silhouetted by the emerald water under the dusky sky, Kai was lying on his back, draped in a towel, at the edge of the pool. Another towel had been rolled up and placed under his head. His skin appeared dry, as though he'd been there for some time, and it had lost its ghostly grayish undertone. I couldn't tell whether he was still unconscious or now just asleep.

"Kai?" I said weakly. My voice rang through the otherwise-silence eerily. I pushed myself upright, my aching muscles protesting the movement, loose grass and leaves falling off my nature-provisioned cot as I did. The world spun and I covered my mouth, anticipating sickness. The exertion of sitting was too much; I wanted to flop back down and close my eyes again.

Kai didn't respond, nor did anyone else at hearing my voice. Where was everybody? Where was Taeo? Didn't he say he would stay with me until the end? Surely this was the end; it was evening after all, and though I felt frail, I was no longer in pain. Activation was over. Why wasn't he there to help me cross the impossible distance to the pool? And then bring me to the Deactivation Bridge?

The thought of the Deactivation Bridge heartened me. Today was my twenty-first birthday, and within a few hours, I would be celebrating it with Jonny, Flash, Lucy, Paul, and others, but most importantly Jonny. Beginning tonight, I would be unAfflicted and unhunted and whole. Marked for death maybe, but for one full week, *whole*. I staggered to my feet and hobbled determinedly to the rocky basin.

"Eclipse?" I called out. No answer came, so I lowered a broken tree branch into the water. I raised it out and gasped, dropping it as though I'd been scalded. The stick appeared unscathed; that's not what startled me. I'd noticed something else, something unexpected.

My birthmark had changed. Not the shape of it—it was the same "comprehensive notae" it had always been—but the general appearance. It was like the process of Activation had burnt it into my skin, coloring the lines of it and inflaming the flesh surrounding it. It looked like a tattoo, a new one, all red and puffy around the design.

The core of the symbol, the larger circle, was now a deep blue, as was the horizontal wavy line within it. The vertical line was forest green, and the smaller circle that surrounded the intersecting lines was gray. A dark red, almost crimson, colored the diamond that encompassed it all.

It was that, more than the knowledge of my gifts, which confirmed my undergoing was complete. I was now an Activated Essen. It freaked me the hell out. I jumped in the pool, anxious to feel the peace of recovery.

The water was warm and silky, and immediately the pearly clouds of fine white powder swirled around me, landing on my clothes and skin. The tingling sensation that I'd come to associate with the Mederium rippled pleasantly through me.

...Except at my wrist, which stung. My notae throbbed under the pressure of the bandage-like minerals that rolled across it. I gripped my arm, refusing to lift it out of the water.

Time passed, probably only twenty minutes though it seemed longer in the strange quiet, and I began to regain my strength. The particles fell away indicating my return to physical health, but a cold stone of uneasiness was now forming inside of me.

Where was Taeo to take me to the bridge?

I scrambled out of the pool just as another burst of cheering broke the silence. This time the yells and applause carried on, and I placed them in the vicinity of the Tabularium. Dripping wet but fully rejuvenated, I dashed towards the noise, where I hoped I'd find Taeo.

I found him rather quicker than anticipated. Before I'd even gotten to the woods that surrounded the Mederium, I smacked into him, dampening his shirt with my soaking clothes.

"Gemma!" he exclaimed, releasing Rori's hand and grabbing my shoulders. "We were on our way back to check on you! You scared us! I wasn't sure you—I mean I wasn't sure *when* you were going to come around!" A broad smile split his face and he drew me into a crushing hug, disregarding that I was drenching him.

Rori hugged me too, a short but impassioned embrace, dropping the backpack she was carrying to one side. She pulled away and turned to Taeo. "It figures, doesn't it? That the *one time* we leave her is when she wakes up? Good thing we left the assembly when we did." She let out a throaty laugh, tears springing to her eyes. "You had a swim, I see. That's good! How do you feel now?"

Their emotion confused me. While I was flattered they were so happy to see me, I knew I was missing something. I looked between them, trying to make sense of their jubilant and expectant expressions. "I'm all right," I said slowly. "Is there some reason you thought I wouldn't be?"

They shared a glance before Taeo spoke. "It's just... your Activation. It was different than normal. It was rougher, longer. We thought that maybe—well, that it might be too much for you. You were in and out of consciousness, mostly out, and we worried—we *feared*—it was the end... that Phoenix's vision—'The Link will be defeated'—was coming to pass."

"But you're okay now, that's what matters," Rori concluded in a rush. "And you'll be thrilled to know"—her face flushed—"that Taeo and I, we solved the portens! We just told the Host!"

So this was the real reason behind their barely-contained excitement. "Wow," I said, nodding my congratulations. "That's really great." The weight on my shoulders, the guilt that had burdened me when I thought of Deactivating, lightened. Now at least I could De-A without feeling like I, the famed Link in whom the Host had trusted to deliver a weapon, was abandoning them.

"It's pretty ingenious how it works, actually," Rori gushed, stooping to dig in her pack. She pulled out a set of clean, dry clothes and tossed them to me—"Here, you can wear these," she said—before resuming her search. From the bottom of the bag, she drew out the encased boulder opal. "Stand back," she said, removing the lid.

I set the clothes aside and addressed Taeo. "Take me to the Deactivation Bridge," I said with enough force that I surprised even myself. Rori looked crestfallen. "I'm sorry, but I really don't want a demonstration. I'm glad you know how it works, but I don't need to. I just want to go home. Please," I added emphatically.

Taeo sighed heavily, taking my hands in his. "Gemma…" he said, his eyes settling on my notae, which, despite my dip in the Mederium, was still red and puffy. "There's something you need to know."

I stared at him, bewildered. Why was his expression, his voice, his very demeanor, suddenly so grave?

"Maybe she should sit down," Rori said, guiding me by the elbow to a flat boulder on the opposite end of the pool. Taeo trailed, still holding my right hand.

"What is it?" I croaked as Rori and Taeo settled on either side of me, Taeo clasping my fingers, Rori resting an arm over my shoulder. "My family? Jonny?"

Rori shook her head. "No, Gemma, they're okay."

"Then what?" I squeaked in a voice that didn't sound like my own.

"Your undergoing has been different from the start," Taeo said. "We should have known… In the first stage, your Gravitation was stronger, pulling Dothen to you even though your birthday was still months away.

And when Affliction began, your episodes, they were more frequent, more disturbing…"

Where was he going with his? What had happened during Activation that made them both look at me like that, with such sad, sympathetic eyes?

"We should have known," Taeo said again. "Based on the evidence we had, we should have known your Activation would be worse in some way. But we didn't… we didn't put it together, so we couldn't tell you in advance." He squeezed my hand. "Gemma… your Activation took much longer than expected, longer than it's ever taken before. Like I said, we didn't even know if you were going to pull through…"

"What are you saying?" I challenged, lifting my face to the sky. Above us, wispy clouds were sweeping across the colorful canvas of sunset. "It's barely nightfall!"

"Gemma," Rori said, her eyes level with mine, "listen to me. It's *Saturday.*" I looked at her blankly. "It's Saturday, March 28th"—she glanced at the phone holstered on her hip—"just after seven o'clock in the evening. You've been in Activation for nearly four days. Your birthday, your annual chance to De-A, it's come and gone." She tucked a loose clump of damp hair behind my ear. "I'm sorry."

The world was closing in on me. The sky, the trees, the ground, they were all coming nearer, pressing into me, making it hard to move, hard to speak, hard to breathe. Taeo and Rori were watching me, but they had slid out of focus.

"There's something else," Rori said quickly, following a sharp intake of air. I sat there mutely, numbly, sure that nothing could be worse than the hunted Essen life to which I was now condemned.

She nodded at Taeo, who took my cell phone out of his pocket and placed it in my palm. The screen was glowing with an incomprehensible number of messages.

"I charged it for you," Rori said. "I didn't know it was dead until Jonny called me to ask if I'd… well, if I'd heard from you. Your aunt, your cousin, Jonny… they were worried. They said they hadn't seen or talked to you in days. Gemma, they were filing a Missing Persons Report! I had to tell them something." Her voice was pleading.

I blinked at her, stupefied.

"I told them you'd gone out of town and forgotten your phone. You'd taken a spur-of-the-moment vacation with a friend, I said. They asked who you'd gone with, and I—I had to say the only other person I knew they'd met: Malakai. I told them I didn't know when you'd be getting back, but Gemma, I wasn't even sure you would be 'getting back.'

"They didn't buy it. They said you'd *never* leave town like that, so suddenly and without telling anyone. Especially not on your birthday, not when you knew Jonny had planned something. And then Jonny showed up at Riverview demanding to talk to me. I panicked! I needed him to believe me, so I... I showed him the picture of you and Kai on the beach."

Rori hung her head, her long copper locks falling forward and veiling her face. Taeo reached across me and rubbed her arm consolingly.

A loud and indecent cheer shattered the moment. Several Essen emerged from the forest, yelling and whooping and talking animatedly. The eyes of a tawny-skinned brunette, who I recognized but didn't really know, fell on me.

"Could this day get any better?" she exclaimed. "The Link hasn't been defeated after all! And she *won't* be defeated!" she added, stripping down to her bikini and cannon-balling into the water. She popped back up as others from her group began jumping in around her, one of them stark naked, all of them ready to party. "So you've told her the good news, have you?" she went on, oblivious to the conversation she'd interrupted.

"We told her about the portens," Rori acknowledged quietly.

"And Phoenix's announcement?" the girl prodded. "Did you tell her about that?" She was positively bursting with glee.

"Invincibility!" shouted a man lumbering forward with an armful of glass bottles. "The best defense!" He collapsed onto the ground in a fit of giggles, the elixirs dropping all around him and rolling across the ground.

"Yes, *that*," said the girl, raising her fist out of the water. "Invincibility!" Everyone else raised their fists too, a chorus of *"Invincibility!"* echoing across the Mederium. She tossed her sleek hair and added with a tone of incredulity, "I can't believe he's really figured out the formula. Just think, once he's finished producing the solution—by Tuesday he told us—we'll all have..."

Her last word was drowned out by a second rowdy chorus of *"Invincibility!"* which was shouted in unison and met with several more punches to the air.

An icy wave ran through me. So Phoenix had been able to create an invincibility elixir to defend the Essen against the impending Dothen attack. I met Taeo's eyes. He looked away quickly, and I knew it was true.

I stood, needing to leave, needing to be alone. Despite the calls that echoed after me, I was in the woods, running from everyone, running from the truth: that though an invincibility elixir would be able to save the entire Host, it wouldn't help *me*, newly Activated with the unique and worthless gift of elixir immunity. It was now abundantly clear to me why Phoenix had Seen "the Link" as the one who would surely be defeated.

CHAPTER 72

My life is not my own.

I fell into the trap of black thinking, succumbing to the notion that no one, not even Malakai Zonn, was the master of his fate or the captain of his soul.

My life is not my own.

I let the mantra fill me up, the rhythm of it matching my footfalls as I raced along the edge of the moonlit ocean, tears streaming down my tiny, insignificant face, my heartbreak lost to the star-speckled expanse above me.

My life is not my own.

It belonged to Circumstance, that uncaring entity of which I was a victim. I'd been a fool to think the choices were mine to make. The outcome—my continued Activation, my destroyed relationship with Jonny, my impending death—were all predestined. Any semblance of control I thought I'd had was an illusion.

My life is not my own.

Providence had dealt me losing cards; it hadn't mattered how I'd played them. The ultimate authority rested, as it always had, outside of me. My life—and my death—was out of my hands.

My life is not my own.

"Gemma, stop!" Rori called after me, chasing me down the beach. "Please—just talk to me!" Her voice sounded higher than normal, pinched within her throat.

I kept running. I didn't even turn to look at her. I went faster, the shadowed world a blur.

"Gemma!" she cried. "Gemma, I'm so sorry! I shouldn't have shown Jonny—"

I shook her off, darting across the sand and into the woods. I wasn't mad at her, even though Jonny now believed I'd betrayed him. She'd done what she thought she had to do. I was mad at the *universe*, the true culprit of my devastation. Still, I had no desire to talk to Rori. I had no desire to talk to anyone.

I flew between the trees barely feeling my legs, months of conditioning leading them to operate automatically.

My life is not my own.

Deep down I knew my thinking was wrong. Deep down I knew that even now, in the darkest moments of my life, there were always choices. I didn't have to lie down and submit to Death. I could fight. I could strategize. I could *try*. But I didn't want to think that way; it was too hard. Thinking that way would mean acknowledging my own mistakes—my actions and my failures to act—and accepting responsibility for them. It would mean applying energy to the search for solutions, and I just didn't have any. It was easier to blame Providence, even though I knew that Gate, wherever he was, would be ashamed of me.

'The human mind is mighty,' he'd once told me. 'It has power over the body, over the environment, over reality. Don't forget that. You have untapped potential and fortitude beyond your own understanding. You *will* be able to master this.'

But my mind didn't feel mighty—it was overwrought with grief and bitterness—and my situation was no longer one I could hope to master. All I could do was run, let my body take over, and push myself physically until I was completely spent.

Kai had given me running, just like Jonny had given me writing, and I used it the same way: to cope with the pain of loss. Through the hours and through the night I ran, distancing myself from the cacophonous groups of celebrating Essen, from the things Rori and Taeo had told me, and even from conscious thought.

When I finally collapsed to the ground sometime in the earliest hours of morning, I was alone at the cove, that circular recess in which swayed countless Supernova flowers, their faint purplish glows glimmering across the surface of the sloshing inlet.

My life is not my own, I repeated to myself, though with less conviction now as fatigue set in. The tears had stopped flowing long ago; I was wrung out. I flung myself back into the sand, closing my tired eyes to the world. Through my lids, I saw the light of the blossoms and the corresponding fluorescence of the strobe-like tree sap as a patchwork of violets and greens against the black. In the stillness, thoughts crept back into my head.

I'd been deprived of my opportunity to De-A, I'd undoubtedly lost my best friend and the future I'd hoped to have with him, and I'd received an Essen gift that would nullify the only protection that might have helped me survive past Tuesday, March 31st.

And now I had given up. I faulted Fate for my plight and retreated into the shadows, unwilling to come forward and fight. I was behaving exactly as Eclipse had known I would.

'I see fern green, Gemma,' she'd said, 'the color of terror. I see an over-whelming fear and a longing for safety. I see a desire to hide in the shadows. ... But know this: In the shadows, you can never be great. Only safe.'

I'd resented her comment, assuming she was referring to my unspoken decision to De-A. *How can I possibly be hiding in the shadows,* I'd wondered, *when I'm standing next to the light?* For that was what Jonny was to me: the light. In wanting to Deactivate, I never saw myself choosing shadows and safety over supernatural-ness and greatness. I saw only a world with Jonny, the light, and a world without him, a world in darkness.

But Eclipse wasn't referring to Deactivation at all. Here, stuck on this side of Activation, I realized what she was really talking about: *Courage.* She spoke of greatness, of being somebody, of leaving a mark on the world... not in the absence of fear, but in spite of it.

I've never aspired to greatness, but I've never imagined myself a coward either. Yet that's how I was behaving. Cowardly. I had yielded to the philosophy that things-happen-to-people, instead of believing that people-make-things-happen.

It wasn't just Gate, whose name had yet to be cleared, that I was letting down by thinking that way. It was also Kai, my Keeper and the one who had risked everything to try to get answers, and who, for all I knew, was still unconscious. And it was Jonny, too. Jonny, to whom I'd promised to be committed, and to whom I would remain committed, even if he couldn't know it until after my death.

They needed me to not give up, to persevere through the disappointment, and to maintain the attitude of a survivor. I needed to try to be great for them. I *wanted* to be great for them, to make them proud, to live my final days courageously.

Silently, I battled the black thoughts that would defeat me before the Dothen had the chance to. I let Jonny's exclamation—'You're the strongest person I know!'—ring in my ears. I forced myself to believe his words, even though he might not believe them himself anymore. And I pushed rage and resignation out of me, ousting the enemy within so I could prepare for the one without.

I opened my eyes and sat up, the brightness of the cove filling my vision. It was Sunday, March 29th, and soon the glow of the Supernovas would fade into the light of day. Though my heart still ached, a new thought occurred to me, a thought that lent me mettle:

My life is not my own.

It belonged to others, to all those who had invested in me and still believed in me. It belonged to my family and friends and those in the Host, who deserved the best of whatever I had to give. It belonged to Uncle Dan, whose death I could still avenge, and to all of the Taken, whose lives were ended abruptly by those wretched *sub*natural beings. It belonged to whomever I could help, either with my gifts or my wits or my courage.

My own hopes for the future had been dashed, but my life, I knew now, could still have meaning. However much of it there was left would be given in service to others. And my mantra, revived with new meaning, repeated in my head:

My life is not my own.

CHAPTER 73

I n the darkness, spurred on by the decisions I'd made, I set out from the cove. There were several things that needed to be done, but my priority was, and will always be, Jonny.

I made my way to the cliffs, and, emboldened by my mantra and feeling rushed, dropped from them to the ledge below. I landed easily on the rocky platform and hurried along it to the Nest, from which I took the sapphire-blue journal and the pen I'd stowed over a week ago, the day Kai had gone after Gate.

A thin line of pale orange was forming at the horizon. I sat at the mouth of the cave, my legs extended across the ledge, and began writing furiously. The time for eloquence had passed; it was now a matter of haste. I kept scribbling, recording the essential facts and dates and impressions of my undergoing, the pale orange of first light growing into the golden pink of sunrise. And then the sun was up properly, its radiance reflecting garishly off every moving swell, and still I wrote.

I finished my story with an account of my Activation—including a description of my gifts—and an apology for the incomplete ending, which for obvious reasons, could not be written. Then I tucked the book into my pocket, withdrew my cellphone from the other one, and typed the following text message:

Jonny, I didn't want to call you and put you on the spot—I know you probably don't want to talk to me—but I wanted to tell you I'm sorry. I don't know what I can say at this point to make things right, but I would like to see you. There's something I need to give you. I'll be at Como Park at noon, at the spot we went to on Valentine's Day. I'll understand if you choose not to come, but please know I do love you. Right now, all along, forevermore.

I felt my heart lurch as I read over what I'd typed. The thought of meeting Jonny sickened me. For the first time in my life, I didn't want to see him. I didn't want to look into his dark blue eyes and know our friendship was over. But not seeing him, or at least not attempting to see him, was cowardly, and I owed him my courage. After everything I'd put him through, he deserved that much.

A lump rose in my throat as I hit 'send.' I knew he wouldn't write back. He'd either show up to meet me or he wouldn't. With a heavy heart, I tucked the phone back into my pocket, climbed the rock face, and made my way to the Mederium where there was another apology to make, and a recipient who was just as unlikely to respond.

✳ ✳ ✳

Seven days had passed since Taeo had rescued Kai from depletion, but despite the efforts of many, and despite the long hours of healing in the miraculous pool, Kai remained out of reach.

I knew he was yet unconscious before I even saw him; his signal was still very weak. I felt my shoulders sag as I approached him through the entrance boulders.

He was slumped against the base of one of the waxy-looking trees, and his head had fallen forward so that I could see nothing of his face. His arms hung limp at his sides, his fingers brushing the fabric of his navy-colored board shorts, and his legs were outstretched. He appeared to be alone, but he was also dripping wet, apparently freshly removed from the pool. Teal droplets clung to the ends of his hair and glinted on his skin, which had returned to its normal caramel color.

"Hello?" I called out. "Is anyone here?" I twisted around, searching.

A jolt of surprise shot through me even as I spoke. Kai's signal, which I'd continued monitoring though he was now within my sight to observe, had spiked the moment my voice rang through the Mederium.

"Kai?" I said, crouching down beside him. "Kai, can you hear me?"

The signal flared a second time, but did not maintain an increased strength. I glanced around again, surprised but also grateful that we were alone.

"Kai," I repeated, noting the ongoing effect my speech seemed to be having on him. "Kai, I'm here."

I settled down beside him, resting against the base of the tree as well, and sighed. I had come with the intention of owning up to a few things, of expressing them out loud in an attempt to make amends, but self-consciousness made me mute. Though I was relieved to have found him alone—I had anticipated an audience of at least Eclipse—I was thrown by his responsiveness. Granted, he was most likely responding to my voice only and not my actual words, and granted, his responsiveness was all the more reason to keep talking, but... I suddenly felt awkward.

Closing my eyes briefly, feeling the warmth of the leaves-filtered midmorning sun on my cheeks, I said simply, "Kai, I'm sorry."

I fidgeted with a lock of hair, twirling it around my finger before going on. "You've been...like this...for over a week now, and I—I know it's my fault. I'm the reason you went to find Gate... I'm the reason Taeo was late coming for you... and I'm the reason it's taking you so long to heal. Eclipse said I should come; she believed it would help. And as I sit here now feeling your signal getting stronger, I know she was right. But I couldn't do it, Kai, and I'm sorry. I guess I thought you'd come around soon enough without me.

"The truth is... I was afraid. I was afraid to come to you because of what might happen and what it might mean. I didn't want to know that I had an effect on you, like the one I'm seeing right now. And I—"

I fell silent, listening for anyone approaching, but the only sound was the rustle of wind through the trees and the faint echoing calls of exotic birds.

"And I didn't want to admit that you also have an effect on me," I finished in a whisper. "I didn't want to admit that I've gotten... accustomed to you. Or that I've become attached, despite the fact that I'm immune to the *Consociare*. It felt like a disrespect of Jonny. But... you're my Keeper—well you were until I Activated—and it's my responsibility to be here, helping you find your way forward.

"You need to make your way forward, Kai. Today. Quarter's end is thirty-six hours from now, and if you're still out…" I trailed off, a shiver running up my spine. "Besides, Rori's worked out the portens, and I… I've figured out what's different about Record 3629. I know what it is, Kai, but I don't know what it *means*. If I could just talk to you about it… If you could just tell me what you learned from Gate…"

I reached over and touched Kai's shoulder, imploring him to wake up, but the only movement was the barely perceptible motion of his breathing. After a minute, discouraged, I released him. "You were right, you know. The morning you left to find Gate, you called me a 'thankless harpy,' and you were right; I never appreciated you. I was so busy pushing you away, so consumed with keeping my guard up around you, that I didn't see that you were trying to help me, that you've been trying to help me all along. So… if you can hear me… thank you."

I stood, watching the water drip from Kai's hair onto his chest and abdomen, leaving tracks across the curved muscles. "I have to go, but I'll be back tonight. I know I should stay, that you need me to stay, but it's just—there're some things I need to do, and I'm not sure… Well, I don't know how much time I have left." I dipped my head and turned to leave, only to find several sets of feet before me.

"You don't know how much time you have left?" Taeo repeated in disbelief. "Are you… You're not saying your *goodbyes* already, are you?"

I looked from Taeo, who was carrying several vials of liquid in varying shades of orange, to Rori, who had an armful of syringes, to Eclipse, who was offset from them and focused on Kai. All three of them looked as though they'd slept as much as I had last night.

"I—I was just—" I stammered, but I was stopped short by Rori, who had dropped her load and was hugging me.

"I'm so sorry, Gemma," she said into my hair, holding me tight. "I knew what Jonny meant to you, what he means to you. If there was any way for me to change what happened, I would, but the picture was the only thing—"

"It's fine," I responded quickly, though it came out rather cooler than I'd intended. "It's done." I pulled away, taking the journal from my pocket. "I'm giving this to him today—"

"What? Are you sure that's—"

"—With the instructions that *you* will let him know when to read it." I met her eyes, which were big and brown and filled with remorse. "Rori, I need you to do this for me. If something happens to me, I need you to call Jonny I need you to call him and tell him—in whatever way you can—what became of me, and tell him that it's okay to read it."

"But the *Invincibility* elixir..." she argued. "Nothing's going to happen. You're going to be fine, we're all going to be fine." I shot a look at Taeo, but though his face was impassive, his eyes were somber. "We just came from Phoenix, he's working on the elixir right now. There'll be enough for everyone, and it'll last for a full day, long enough for us to use the portens, to eradicate the Dothen once and for all..."

She trailed off, searching my face, but I was watching Taeo, who had bent for a syringe and was filling it with liquid from one of the vials.

"What's that?" I asked as he stuck the needle into Kai's arm.

"Part of the regimen," Taeo responded, "to keep Kai's body from weakening while he's unconscious." He began filling a second syringe with a different fluid and then injected that into Kai as well.

"It gives him strength," Eclipse said, not taking her eyes off of Kai, "but not as much as the presence of his Kept does."

"I know," I said quietly, noting the continued spikes in his signal whenever I spoke. "But I still have to go."

"Jonny?" Rori asked. "The book?" A hint of disapproval colored her words.

"Yes. By way of Phoenix. You said he's in the Aerarium?"

Rori nodded. "You're going to request keepership?"

"It's what's done, isn't it? I'm Activated, aren't I?" There was an unintentional edge to my voice. "I'm part of this now. I'm supposed to be assigned a job, one that aligns with my gifts... Though what job Phoenix could name for me with *these* gifts is hard to imagine." I huffed. "Tell me he's lucid at least."

Rori opened her mouth, but it was Eclipse who answered. "Remarkably so." She turned to face me, her sightless eyes scanning the world around me. "In the six years I've known him, Phoenix has always appeared the gray, dingy color of an elixir-induced stupor. I've never been able to read anything in him beyond the charcoal mask of his constant elevations. But today, for the first time ever, he's not murky. He's a bright lemon-yellow, the color of unadulterated happiness."

"It's the elixir," Rori commented. "I suppose I'd feel the same way—and proud, too—if I'd developed the best defensive elixir the Host had ever known, one that no one believed could be made." Her eyes drifted over Taeo, who was squeezing the sixth and final syringe into Kai's arm.

"Well go on, then," she said with a half-shrug. "Collect your keepership. See Jonny. Do whatever you have to do." She looked at the book I was clutching. "And I'll do whatever you need me to do, too. I said I'd deliver the book to Jonny after, I mean *if*, you... you know... but if you really think it's best to do it yourself today... I'm not going to try to stop you."

I nodded gratefully and, with a last look at Kai, left the Mederium.

CHAPTER 74

I cut through the maze of green glass tablets and exited the Tabularium on the opposite side, stopping at the wide and rocky hole in the ground that served as the entrance to the Aerarium. Like before, a yellow-orange light flickered up through the opening from the cavern below.

Climbing down the wooden ladder until my feet were solidly on the earthen platform, I stood briefly at the mouth of the massive room, scanning the overwhelming goldenness for Phoenix. I spotted him in the deepest part of the cave next to the elevated worktable, where he'd been the last time I saw him in the Aerarium, except this time he was bent over the worktable rather than slumped against it.

I walked toward him, squinting as my eyes adjusted to the brightness of the room. From the glass vials of yellow-orange liquid that lined the walls, a rich, buttery glow emanated, setting every gilded surface—walls, ceiling, floor, shelving—ablaze with reflected light.

Phoenix had his back to me, but I could see him pouring some sort of fluid into the large ceramic bowl that rested in the surface of the table. As I got closer, I heard him humming cheerfully, immersed completely in his task.

He was a different person from the one I'd previously met. Gone was the crumpled-looking, older-than-his-years man I'd first encountered passed out across a boulder. He was clean now, his clothes fresh and neat, his rust-colored hair combed. He even smelled better, the combined stench of his elixir habit and his poor hygiene replaced by a mild spice scent. When he turned from the table, intent on grabbing another bottle from the nearest shelf, there was deftness to his movements, as though sobriety had lent him grace.

"Gemma," he stated, stopping short as he saw me, his mud-colored eyes widening slightly with surprise. "They told me you were finally done with Activation, but... I wasn't expecting you." The tone of his voice was apologetic.

"I'm here to collect my keepership," I said, "now that my gifts have settled. Isn't that what I'm supposed to do?"

Phoenix gave a small shrug. "Yes, I suppose it is. I just thought that, given your, um, *situation*... you might prefer not to be named keeper of anything." He began fussing with the buttons of his shirt.

"So you still think I'm going to die?" I asked, keeping my voice even.

He looked down and away, still fidgeting. Here again was the squirmy, non-confrontational Phoenix, his newfound happiness momentarily displaced by the topic of my future. "I don't know how it will happen—your life will be protected by the elixir and the portens, just like everyone else's—but I believe it will happen. Based on my experience, Gemma, visions do not change."

"But this Vision is different," I said. "It isn't like the others. Maybe it's... Maybe there's a chance it *will* change."

Phoenix looked up abruptly, alarm crossing his face. "What do you mean it isn't like the others?" he asked defensively. "It came to me like they're supposed to. I recorded it exactly. It may have been eighteen years since my last Record, but I know I did it right." But he suddenly seemed nervous and uncertain, edging towards panic. "What's wrong with it?"

I blushed under the intensity of his gaze. "It's the domains," I said meekly. "The original spirit-mother's domains: earth, air, water, and fire. The Records always mention all four of them—sometimes by another name, like calling water 'sea' or 'rain'—but 3629 doesn't. It only references fire, and that only by the label 'light.'"

His brows furrowed and his eyes darted back and forth, like he was wracking his brain for some example of a Record in which that was not the case.

"I don't know what it means," I said gently. "All I know is that three of the four elemental domains are missing from this Record, which makes it different. Which makes me, for obvious reasons, hopeful." I gave him what I thought was an encouraging smile.

"I don't know what it means, either," he whispered, "but if the Host finds out, they could lose faith in me." He started pacing, his posture hunched; he was deflating into the Phoenix of before.

He was right, of course. If the Host became aware that Record 3629 was an anomaly, they would probably consider it a further deterioration of the role of the Augur. I remembered the first time I'd laid eyes on Phoenix, and Kai's words on that occasion, spoken with such contempt: *Our fearless leader*, he'd said. *The first and only Augur to fail at Record-keeping.* And he wasn't alone in that opinion. From what I could tell, the majority of Essen felt the same way. It was only Taeo, who tried to see the best in everyone, that seemed to think of Phoenix as something other than a failure: *I do think he's trying, Gemma*, he'd said to me. *I believe he'll prove himself worthy before the end.*

And hadn't he proven himself worthy? With the formulation of the *Invincibility* elixir? As I watched him anxiously crossing the floor in front of me, I couldn't help but pity him. I stepped forward, placing my hand on his arm.

"I don't think anyone else knows," I said. "At least, I haven't said anything."

He halted and met my eyes. "And you won't say anything? I don't want the Host's confidence undermined... Not when victory is so near."

"I won't say anything."

Phoenix's whole body seemed to loosen with relief. His shoulders relaxed, his arms fell to his sides, and a small, grateful smile emerged on his pale, freckled face.

"I know I haven't been the best Augur," he said. "My foremost gift has always been the development of elixirs." He stole a glance at the bowl within the worktable.

"Is that it?" I asked. "The *Invincibility* elixir?" I peered around him at the eggplant-purple liquid within the bowl.

"It *was*," he said ruefully. "But I'll have to start over. The elixir's temperamental. The ingredients need to be added in precisely the right order and mixed at precisely the right times. It's complicated to make and just as complicated to administer. One wrong move, one unexpected interruption, one extra stir... and everything is ruined."

"You're sure it'll work?"

My question made him grin; it seemed that some of the cheerfulness I'd witnessed when I first entered the Aerarium was returning to him. His chest swelled with pride when he answered, "Every elixir I've ever created has done exactly what I've designed it to do. This one was especially difficult to develop—the circumstances had to be just right—but when it's done, it'll certainly work." His smile faltered slightly. "As long as it's consumed *exactly* according to my instructions."

The question hadn't yet passed my lips before Phoenix answered it. "The *Invincibility* elixir, like the *Consociare*, like many of our elixirs in fact, must be drunk in a certain manner to be effective. With the *Consociare*, the Keeper drinks, and then the Kept, both from the same glass. With the *Invincibility*, everyone must drink simultaneously, each from his or her own glass. If everything goes according to plan, we'll all have twenty-four hours of invincibility."

Talking about the elixir was restoring Phoenix's exuberance. I looked at my fingernails, unwilling to voice the concern I was thinking, unwilling to puncture his spirit yet again.

"What is it?" he asked. "What's the matter?"

How could I tell him that the elixir of which he was most proud would *not* work as intended, at least not for me? That the reason he'd Seen me fall, the reason the Link would ultimately be defeated, was due to my 'gift,' an immunity to elixirs?

I shook my head, remaining silent.

"It's Malakai, isn't it?" Phoenix pressed. "You're worried about him."

My jaw fell open. How could I have forgotten Kai in this?

"It's natural to fear for a Keeper or a Kept," he said. "The bond is powerful. Kerithe, my Kept, was my best friend. We told each other everything, and when I lost her... Well anyway, I'll make sure Kai is taken care of. If he's still unconscious tomorrow evening, he'll receive an injection of the formula instead. As long as it occurs at the same time the rest of us drink, it will still work. But I hardly think it's worth worrying about. The battle won't take place anywhere near the Mederium. The Dothen will be destroyed the moment they cross the bridge, thanks to you bringing us the portens."

Phoenix was positively beaming now, a boyish wonder taking over his face as he said the word *portens*.

"Who's keeping it?" I asked. "Who'll be responsible for using it?" I thought I knew, but I wanted confirmation.

"Rori has it. She demonstrated its capabilities yesterday; she clearly understands it. Maybe in the future, after quarter's end, it will be transitioned to someone else for keeping, but… not before the attack. We need someone with already-established proficiency to manage it."

A seed of uneasiness planted itself in my stomach. Rori would be in the most dangerous position, leading the offense, once the battle with the Dothen began. And as much as he would want to help her, there was nothing Taeo would be able to do to share her burden.

Was there anything *I* could do to share her burden? Was there anything I could do at all? I wanted to help destroy the Dothen, but what use could I possibly be to the Host?

I closed my eyes and repeated my request to Phoenix. "I want you to assign me keepership."

"But—"

"Hear me out. Even if I've got less than two days to live, shouldn't I have the chance to make those two days count? Shouldn't I have a role that could help make a difference? Please. There must be something I can keep."

"Okay, Gemma," Phoenix said resignedly. "Tell me about your gifts."

CHAPTER 75

I was a statue, a stationary figure on the south-facing park bench that over-looked Lake Como. My shadow danced around me as the world turned, but I stayed motionless, frozen in place by the hope that he might yet come.

It had been foolish to think he would, and even more foolish to remain there, fixed to the bench hours later. The sun began its descent, my shadow elongating with its slow trajectory to the horizon, and I knew that before long I would have to leave.

I felt squeezed, as though I was in a vise. With each minute that passed, the vise cranked tighter, compressing me, crushing me, until my lungs could scarcely expand and my heart ached to beat. And there could be no release, not without Jonny.

All around me, people came and went, enjoying the unseasonal warmth of the Sunday afternoon. Mothers pushed strollers, dogs trotted ahead of owners, and old men cast lines into the ice-free water, but amidst the activity, I was entirely still, entirely silent, and entirely alone.

A light wind, still cool with memory of winter, grazed my skin, leaving goosebumps across my bare arms. I had no jacket to throw over my t-shirt; I'd left Salvos in a hurry following my meeting with Phoenix. Our discussion had taken longer than I'd anticipated, and I had been worried about arriving late and missing Jonny.

I hadn't been late though, so there was no chance that I'd missed him. I looked down at my hands, at the leather journal clutched within them. Light bounced off the shimmery sapphire-blue of the cover, and I was forced to acknowledge the truth: He wasn't coming.

He wasn't coming, and yet I couldn't bring myself to leave. A tiny fragment of hope, however ill-advised, still bobbed inside of me, hovering like a candle above the growing sea of disappointment. I pressed my eyes closed, mentally shielding the hope against the black waves of doubt and dispiritedness that threatened to extinguish it.

That hope, the reason I remained anchored to the park bench, was also the reason I'd resisted using my gift to determine whether Jonny was coming. I was tempted, and it probably would have worked, but a part of me didn't want to know—the part of me that was protecting hope from being engulfed by disappointment. That and I didn't want to use my gift on Jonny; it felt like supernatural spying. It was a slippery slope from supernatural spying to supernatural stalking, and that wasn't the type of relationship I wanted to have with him. Wouldn't no relationship at all be better than one in which I maintained a secret and one-sided connection? An unscrupulous one that would rob him both of privacy and… choice?

Regarding any aspect of our relationship, I wanted Jonny to have a choice. It was why I'd asked him to meet me at the park, rather than showing up at his house or even just going to mine. I didn't want to force my presence on him. As much as it was killing me to wait, he needed to have a choice.

In the text message I sent, I told him I'd understand if he chose not to come. He'd chosen not to come, and I did understand. Who *would* show up to meet the person they believed had betrayed them? Not me, if the tables had been turned.

I tucked the book in my back pocket, trying to muster the will to leave. Instead, I leaned forward on my knees and buried my face in hands, blocking out the world and all of its signals, opting to remain ignorant and hopeful.

It was difficult, blocking signals, though I'd told Phoenix it wasn't. It was far easier to detect them—I was a Receiver after all—than to shut them out, despite the fact the detection was uncomfortable. But I'd lied to him about that, just like I'd lied to him about having a second gift.

"Tell me about your gifts," he'd said.

"Gift," I'd corrected. "Just one, though it does have a couple facets."

I'd chosen not to tell Phoenix about my elixir immunity because the knowledge was a burden, and it was for me alone to bear.

His brows had drawn together in puzzlement. "That's... unusual. In the entire time I've been Augur, no one has had just one. There've always been two, or sometimes three. But I suppose... Yes, that would make sense after all," he said, nodding to himself. "You're the Link. I suppose your other gift was simply the portens. Go on, then."

I'd proceeded to tell him about my primary gift.

"It's a gift of the mind," I said, relieved that he'd supplied his own justification for the fact that I was sharing but a single gift.

He looked at my wrist. "Gifts of the mind are not altogether uncommon for those of Affiliation Merla. You *are* Affiliation Merla, I see—the core of your notae is blue. A daughter of the sea, then, even though your mark combines the symbols of all four." He raised his eyes to mine. "So what is your gift of the mind? Electrolocation? Dream manipulation? Pyschometry? Astral projection?"

I looked down at my feet, feeling a little sheepish. I didn't know what any of those things were. "What I can do is... Well, it's strange."

"You're dissatisfied with your gift, I take it?"

My eyes shifted around the Aerarium, searching for an answer that wouldn't make me sound like an ingrate. "It's just not what I expected. My gift is a bit limited, and also, um... shady." I felt my cheeks flush.

"What is it you can do?" Phoenix asked again, this time warily.

"I can detect communication signals... signals put out by others through their thoughts and words. And if the circumstances are right, I can... understand them."

He blinked at me. Then, in a lowered voice, he said: "You—you can read minds? But that's impossible. I was given to understand—Echo once told me—telepaths don't exist, that there's no such thing..."

I couldn't help but feel let down by Phoenix's response. He obviously had no familiarity with my gift. How would he be able to assign me keepership?

"No," I said. "You misunderstand—it's not like that. Echo was right, there's no such thing as a telepath... People who use that term are... misguided."

Slowly, almost suspiciously, he asked, "What do you mean?"

"'Telepath' is an ambiguous term," I began, "used by people who don't understand the true nature of telepathy, though at first that's what I thought I was going to be, too. During my undergoing, I was already picking up *spoken* communication signals, and I thought, once Activation was over, I'd be able to understand *thought* signals, too. I believed I'd be able to reach out with my mind and communicate with anyone, anywhere. It wasn't until my gift had settled that I realized how erroneous my notion of telepathy really was.

"Telepathy is just a form of communication, that's all, and like every form of communication, it's only effective if there are message *transmitters* and message *receivers*. The thing is, everyone in the world, supernatural or not, is a transmitter. With every thought we think and every word we say, we are broadcasting communication signals out into the universe and transmitting messages. *Everyone* is a transmitter. But the thing called *telepathy*—unspoken communication over distances—can only be achieved if there's someone who can *receive* the messages. *That's* what's uncommon, what's extraordinary, what's *supernatural*: being able to *receive* messages. And that's my gift: Psionic Reception." I exhaled fully. "I'm a Receiver."

Phoenix took a step back, his mind obviously reeling. "But... if you can receive communication signals from peoples' thoughts... *How* exactly is that different from mind reading?"

I was getting frustrated by my own inability to make things clear. "Okay, let me break it down for you. There are two types of communication signals a Receiver can pick up: thought signals and spoken signals, signals that come from spoken words.

"Regarding the first, I can only detect the presence of thoughts, the volume of thoughts, and the speed of thoughts, all of which translates into the strength of an individual's thought 'signal'... But I have no way of knowing *what* a person is actually thinking, namely because peoples' thoughts are layered, multi-directional, and unfocused. The signal is comprised of too many competing thoughts, all occurring simultaneously, for a Receiver to make sense of it.

"I suppose I *could*, theoretically, understand specific thought signals from people if they sent them to me directly, with intention, in a focused way, having cleared their minds of all other 'noise.' But in order for that to happen, I'd have to share my gift, right? So they'd know to do it? And besides that, what purpose would it serve? The communication would be one-sided… unless of course, my counterpart was also a Receiver. But based on your reaction to my description so far, there's no one else within the Host gifted with this same ability. Is there?"

Phoenix pursed his lips, shaking his head. "I see what you mean," he said. "Your gift is rather… limited. The only benefit I could see for the Reception of thought signals is… in cases like Kai's, to determine how close to consciousness a person is."

"Exactly," I said. "And as for the other type of signal a Receiver can pick up—those derived from spoken messages—well, those are much easier to understand. I can 'hear' those messages without a problem. It doesn't matter whether I know the people transmitting them or how far the signal has to travel… Spoken signals are readily available to me, mainly because by the time thoughts are spoken, they are singular, directed, and focused."

"And you can do this anytime, anywhere, to anyone?" He frowned in a contemplative way, as though weighing the benefits of such a gift against the drawbacks.

"I know," I said, sighing. "It's just… *shady*. It's essentially supernatural eavesdropping, and I don't think I'll ever feel right about doing it."

Neither of us spoke for a moment. Then Phoenix said quietly, "Does it hurt?"

"What, you mean Receiving?"

"Some of the gifts, most of them actually, are painful to use. I would imagine that something as intense as Receiving—you said everyone in the world is transmitting communication signals all the time—would be agonizing at worst and overwhelming at best."

I shook my head. "No, Ga—" I caught myself before I said Gate's name—"No, Echo taught me how to manage the gift early on. I have a… psychological tool I can use to turn it on and off, and to find the right signal. So it's not painful, not overwhelming."

That wasn't precisely true. It *was* uncomfortable to use my gift, to Receive signals, but only because it left me feeling morally conflicted, not because I was in genuine pain. And it *was* difficult to block signals, to turn them off all together, especially with regard to people with whom I was very familiar or in cases of immediate physical proximity.

My answer had satisfied him, though, and with a thoughtful nod, he'd gone on to ask about other aspects of my gift—including whether it was only the communication signals of *people* that I could Receive. He wasn't referring to squirrels.

I told him I didn't know. I *did* know the answer to some extent—I knew the kind of unorthodox communications that would come through the wind chimes eventually—but I wasn't sure whether I'd be able to listen in on the Dothen. *That's* what he really wanted to know.

By the end of the conversation, at which time I think Phoenix had fully grasped the concept of Psionic Reception, I had been given the job of intelligence-keeper. As the first ever Essen in the role, it was my duty to gather information—remotely, from Salvos—that would enable us to better understand the enemy.

Somehow I doubted I would be able to Receive signals, spoken or otherwise, from the Dothen, but I'd left the Aerarium having accepted the charge. And once night fell, I intended to give everything I had to the task.

For now, though, I was having enough trouble just blocking out the unwanted signals of passersby, not to mention Jonny's, whose signal I was sorely tempted to Receive.

As the hour grew later and my time at Como Park continued to dwindle, the temptation to use my gift on Jonny became harder and harder to resist.

And then I knew why.

Immediate physical proximity. He was near me.

I raised my head from my hands and spotted him at the edge of the park, coming towards me with his head down, his hands shoved into the front pocket of his navy blue hoodie. His chestnut hair had fallen forward and was screening his face, but his posture, if not his expression, was subdued.

I knew then what Rori had meant when she'd use the word *explosive*.

It was like Activation all over again. The force of it struck my heart like lightning, and I was burning, burning, burning from the inside out, staring at a Jonny I'd never seen before. I leapt up, entranced by him, longing for him, *needing* him. And still he advanced, each step bringing him closer to where I stood, feverish and hard-breathing and terrified.

Then he was in front of me. He looked up, his eyes the dark blue color of the ocean at dusk, and I fell into them, lost myself completely in their depths, and wanted to drown—because only that could quench the fire within me.

I *wanted* him. In the whole of my remembered life, and surely in whatever of my life I couldn't remember, there was never anything I'd ever wanted as badly. He was all there was. Nothing else in all of creation mattered except for him. And with the desire, there was the horrible, sickening, devastating knowledge:

I had fallen instantly, desperately, and fiercely *in love* with Jonny.

CHAPTER 76

Before I could stop myself, I launched myself at Jonny, throwing my arms around him, covering his mouth with mine, and pressing myself against him in the most passionate and unabashed display of emotion I'd ever shown anyone.

I knew it was wrong. I knew he was brokenhearted and confused and angry, despite the composure he'd shown as he'd walked to me. I knew it wasn't what he needed, not now, not like this, but I had to show him, to prove to him, that it had always been *him*, would always be him. He had to *know*.

He'd gone rigid at my touch, but I kept my lips to his anyway, my fingers moving up his back and into his hair, twisting the strands of it, pulling him into me.

"I can't," he murmured, barely a whisper. He started to turn his head, but I brought a hand down his neck, tracing the line of his jaw until I caught his chin. He groaned a little, a low sound of protest in his throat, but he let me keep kissing him.

And then the stiffness in his posture melted away. Relenting, his hands rose to my waist as his lips, soft and familiar, moved under mine. He tilted his head forward and several strands of satiny hair lighted upon my cheek.

I wanted to be even closer to him, despite the gawking of onlookers, and I crushed myself against him, flattening my chest against his. I slid my hands down to his shoulders, and I held him there against me, electricity coursing through my veins, whether a natural or supernatural sensation I didn't know.

"I can't," he moaned again, seemingly in conflict with himself, because his mouth was still against mine. But then he drew me tighter, his palms firm against my lower back, and began kissing me faster, even hungrily.

This was what he'd wanted from me. From the moment he'd confessed his feelings for me, that night on the snowboard hill, *this* was what he'd wanted. Not the touching and the moving and my lips stretched over his, all in this very public space, but the heat and the intensity and the *yearning*. For longer than I probably even realized, that's what he'd wanted, what he'd hoped for: a love as maddeningly consuming on my end as it was on his.

And now I could give it to him. I was desperate for him. Though the day was diminishing and with it the warmth, I did not feel cold. Tucked against Jonny, tasting the sweetness of his lips, arching into his touch as his callused fingers found their way beneath my shirt and into the waistband of my pants, I felt only the devouring flames of desire.

It made me reckless. I leaned into him fully, feeling my hips rub against his. He objected with another muffled groan, but his fingers curled into my skin, clawing at my flesh. He kept kissing me, harder and more passionately than before, kissing me with his whole body, kissing me with abandon.

Without meaning to, I let out a small moan as well. My hands slipped from Jonny's shoulders to his back and I gripped his sweatshirt, wishing we could go somewhere. Then his hands were traveling forward, around my waist, coming to rest on my hips. He held me tightly, the strength of his arms binding me against him, while his thumbs stroked gently over my hipbones. My heart thundering, I kissed him even longer and more sensually. It was fervent. It was rough. It was immodest.

And then it was over.

With both hands, Jonny pushed against my hips, thrusting me away from him. "I can't," he panted, his head bent forward. "I can't do this."

His voice sounded anguished. I rushed forward wanting to comfort him, but he backed up, shaking his head. "Don't—don't do this to me, Gemma."

I was only feet from him, but he might as well have been on the other side of the lake if he wouldn't let me hold him.

"Don't look at me like that, either," he said quietly. "You... You made your choice. And it wasn't me."

"But it *is* you," I pleaded. "It's always *been* you. I love you! I'm in love with—"

"Don't you dare say you're in love with me," Jonny said. "Not after last week." He shoved his hands into the front pocket of his hoodie and looked at the ground. "It's true, isn't it? What Rori told me? You were with Malakai on some tropical island?"

Technically it *was* true, but not in the way Jonny feared. Still, I lowered my head in shame and nodded.

A strained noise escaped Jonny's throat. "I just needed to"—his voice hitched and he looked at the lake and then up at the sky, anywhere but at me—"I just needed to hear it from you. That's why I came."

He turned to go, but I dashed forward and seized his arm. "Wait. Please. There's something I need to give you." I peered into his face, waiting for some sign that he wouldn't take off the moment I released him.

But he didn't seem to have the energy to run. Instead, he closed his eyes and said, "How could you, Gemma? How could you do what you did, not just to me, but to your aunt and to Flash?" His voice sounded hoarse with emotion. "How could you leave us all to worry while you were off with him? How could you come back into town and not even show up at your own house?" He swallowed but his voice was still husky. "How could you ask me to meet you *here*, where we had our Valentine's, and then kiss me like that, and touch me like that, and make it seem real…" He trailed off, gazing at the lake.

"It is real," I whispered. "I love—"

"Did you sleep with him?" Jonny blurted.

"No!" I almost yelled. "I swear! Please believe me. I would never—"

"I can't really know what you would never do, can I? There's nothing you can say that I feel I can believe anymore. You *lied* to me, Gemma, over and over again." He didn't raise his voice. He didn't even sound angry. He just sounded hurt. It was the worst.

I let go of his arm and grabbed the blue leather journal from my back pocket. I flipped through the book, exposing pages and pages of handwritten entries. "I know this can't make up for anything that's happened… but I want you to have it. It explains… everything. I just need you to promise that you'll wait to read it until—"

"I'm not reading that at all," he said flatly, eyeing it. "I won't."

"What do you mean?" I squeaked, my tone verging on panic. I hadn't seen this coming. He *had* to take the journal; he *had* to promise to read it once the time came.

"I mean I'm not interested in your reasons. I don't want to know why you picked him over me. I don't want to read line after line of justifications. For months I asked you to talk to me, but you wouldn't. Now it's too late—I don't want any explanations." He met my eyes, and for the first time, they looked cold. "I just want to move on."

"Jonny…" I begged, extending the book to him. "Take it. I need you to know…"

"You might need me to know, but I don't need to know," he said, backing away again. "I don't need—" But what he didn't need, I'd never find out, because he stopped speaking abruptly and was staring at my outstretched hand as though it was a poisonous snake.

"What is that?" he breathed. He looked up into my face. I bit my lip, unable to respond. His eyes bulged and his face contorted into an expression of outrage. He grabbed my wrist and held it up in front of me. "*What is this?*"

It was my notae, still a little red and puffy, the colored lines of which looked like a brand new tattoo. I hiccupped slightly, scared to answer. I'd never seen Jonny so mad. I'd never seen Jonny mad at all.

"You got it inked to match *his*?" He shook his head in fuming disbelief. "You guys have matching tattoos?" He opened his hand like touching me now repulsed him and my wrist fell from it, the journal slipping from my fingers to the ground.

He stepped forward to the lake and seethed; the muscles in his jaw kept tightening as he struggled to control himself. But he couldn't anymore, and I caught the first tears rolling silently down his cheeks. He sunk to the ground and let them fall freely for several minutes before wiping them away with the sleeve of his sweatshirt.

I wanted to sit next to him on the bank of the lake and just be with him, even if nothing was said, even if he refused to acknowledge me. But that wasn't what I was supposed to do. I knew what I was supposed to do.

Gate had urged me, back in November, to let Jonny go. "Your path will lead you away from him," he'd said. "Best that you leave him behind now."

But I couldn't. I *wouldn't*. Instead, convincing myself that everything would be okay in the end, I'd hung onto him, knowing that I was less than he deserved.

In the past few months, I hadn't been able to give him anything: not the time our relationship needed, not the kind of love he was looking for, not the answers he was due. And now, even though I could finally love him the same way he loved me—more, even—it was too late. He'd rejected my attempt to give him answers, and I still couldn't give him the time. All I had left to give him was… closure.

I didn't approach him. I stayed where I stood, looking at his back, trying to gather the courage to do what needed to be done. After a while, I said softly, "I never meant to hurt you, Jonny. I'm so sorry I did." I took a steadying breath and willed my voice to stay even. "I know we can't be anything to each other anymore, I understand that. But I…"

I wanted to tell him that I loved him, that I'd always love him, but I knew that wasn't what he needed me to say. "But I wish you the best, Jonny," I finished lamely. I leaned forward and placed my hand lightly on his shoulder in farewell. And then he reached up and put his hand over mine—only he wasn't putting his hand over mine, he was tucking something between my fingers. A small black piece of cloth.

My heart stopped because I knew what it was before I even looked at it. My Christmas present to Jonny, the guitar polishing cloth. I held it up, saw the little blue forget-me-not flowers embroidered in the edge of the microfiber, and choked back the sob that was rising in my chest.

He didn't face me when he spoke. He continued to stare across the lake, at the last rays of sun reflecting off the water. His voice was apathetic.

"Consider yourself forgotten," he said.

I stumbled backwards gasping for breath, like I'd been punched in the stomach and had the wind knocked out of me. I stood there, sucking air, looking at the back of him, and for a moment I was a statue again, unable to move, frozen in place by shock and horror. But Jonny didn't turn around; he ignored me completely.

There was nothing left to say, nothing left to do. My legs felt like stone as I slowly walked away, leaving Jonny at the edge of the lake, his static outline making him look like the statue now. And then, before I left the park, I stole one last look at him.

He had looked to the ground, his eyes fixed to the journal I'd left lying there. Picking it up, he glanced at the front cover, on which was stamped the phrase, *My life, My Words...*, and then opened it to the first page where I'd written, *...My Story. To Jonny, With Love, Gemma.* He thumbed through the pages like it was a flipbook, and then closed the cover, holding the journal between his hands.

He looked from the book up to the sky, his shoulders falling visibly, like he had heaved a great sigh. And then he raised his arm back, the journal tight within his fingers, and flung it from them. The book soared through the air, the pages fluttering; with a *plunk*, it landed in the middle of the lake, disappeared from sight, and was gone forever.

I shouldn't have seen it. I don't think Jonny meant for me to. I don't think he would have done it if he'd known I was still there watching. I wish I hadn't been there watching. I wish I had left the park without turning back, without that final look. Because now that was my most acute memory of Jonny and my most painful memory of all time, rolled into one.

Affliction was over. The nightmares, the episodes of sickness, the development of my gifts—it was all over. But the worst suffering of my life had just begun.

CHAPTER 77

The world had ended. I knew it had because the sky was on fire, and the ground had dissolved from beneath my feet.

"Gemma," Rori called to me. I turned towards the sound of her voice. "Where are you going? Hurry up, get in the car." She opened the passenger's side door of a lime-green Mustang and beckoned me urgently with her head.

Where was I going? All around me Como Park was teeming with life. Even the parking lot, where her car sat idling, was busy: people were loading up their dogs and children, leaving the lake, and driving away. But that was impossible, because the world had ended. Why did it matter where I went?

Rori scanned the parking lot anxiously and, leaving the car door open, darted over to me. "Come on," she said, grabbing my arm.

She guided me to her car and waited for me to get in before slamming the door and sliding into the driver's seat. Silently, she threw the car into gear and raced down Lexington Parkway, squinting into the persimmon sky. I was in a zombie-like trance watching the trees bleed into one another through the window.

"You weren't going to make it back," Rori said at length. "It's your first night off Salvos as an Activated Essen, and you weren't going to make it back." She spoke without looking at me.

Gravitation had compelled her to come for me. Even in my detached state, I knew that much. Rori had never cut her return to the island this close. She was prudent and disciplined and shrewd. She left nothing to chance.

"Thank you… I guess." I kept gazing out the window.

"Hey," she said sternly. "Don't go there."

"I'm not going anywhere," I mumbled, staring numbly into the fiery sunset.

"You know what I mean. Don't go disengaging from everything. Don't deaden yourself. I don't know what happened back there, but you can't shut down now."

But the world has ended, I thought. *At least, my world has ended. What else is there to do?*

"Whatever it is you're going through," Rori said, "you have to *go through it.* You have to let yourself think about it and be affected by it and *deal* with it if you're going to recover from it. You won't *get* through it if you don't *go* through it."

I dropped my eyes to my lap. She kept talking, kept lecturing me about the dangers of detachment, and though I nodded at the right times, I was barely listening to her. Her smoky alto voice was far away, somewhere outside of the barricade in my mind.

It had been hastily constructed, the barricade, but it served its purpose: defense. Few of her comments went by it. I didn't have to talk about Jonny if I didn't hear her questions. For the remainder of the car ride, I heard the rhythm of her voice without registering her words.

I didn't let myself think. I didn't let myself feel. I knew she was right, that I would have to go through it to get through it, but it was too soon. Detachment was my drug, my morphine for the pain. It was all I had, all that stood between me and unbearable, paralyzing heartache.

Getting through it—not recovery, I'd never be recovered—could come later, if there was a later. For now, I just had to stay remote, keep my senses numb, and appear to be functioning. For now, I just had to exist.

✳ ✳ ✳

Rori jumped out of her car. "Run!" she shouted at me. I blinked at her and then I was running.

She raced ahead of me on the path. I couldn't see the sun through the trees, but it was in the final moments of setting, if it hadn't set already. It hadn't set already—Rori glanced at her wristwatch and then sprinted faster. I tore after her, dodging cyclists and skaters and couples holding hands, all relishing the final remnants of daytime.

"Get out of the way!" Rori hollered at them sounding maniacal, and the people parted for her, giving her a wide berth through which to run. Her long coppery hair streamed behind her and I tried to keep up, but though I was normally as fast or even faster than her, my legs felt lethargic and disconnected.

The world was a blur, and from a distant place, a thought came to me: My world hadn't ended. It was in the process of ending. Right now. On the East Bank of the Mississippi. Surrounded by all these innocents. Under the pale red sky that some people, non-Essen people, might call *rosy*. But it wasn't rosy—it was bloodstained. Foreboding. Evil.

Rori left the path and was running into the woods. I shot left to follow her but stumbled into something solid, something I hadn't seen with my eyes so fixed on Rori, something tall and dark and smiling.

"What's your hurry, sugar?" Paul said, catching me before I tumbled to the ground. "Where's the fire?"

"Paul?" I said, disoriented, my eyes flickering between him and the exotic-looking woman next to him. *Paul*. Flash's best friend. My second brousin. "What're you doing here?"

He shrugged. "Going for a walk. With my beautiful, new"—he paused dramatically—"*wife*." He beamed at her. "I don't think I'm ever gonna get used to saying that."

But even as he told me her name was Jeannette, and even as Jeannette extended her hand, I was backing away from them, getting as far from them as I could, my feet moving of their own accord, hurtling me towards Rori and the Wooded Bridge.

I scrambled across logs and dodged bushes and wove through the trees, but we were still so far from the circle of oaks, from that place I'd once thought of as *my spot*. And though I still ran, I knew the truth: We were too late. Sun had set. The Wooded Bridge had closed. Rori knew it too because her running slowed and I caught up to her.

"It's okay," Rori said reassuringly, even though I knew it wasn't, even though I knew she'd never been on the wrong side of the bridge after hours and that she was terrified. "Taeo will come for us."

But it wasn't Taeo I sensed coming for us.

I detected their signals at the very moment of nightfall. All twenty-eight of them. Awakening, conspiring, moving. All twenty-eight of them, thinking the same focused thought, making their intentions as plain to me as though they'd said them out loud. They were coming for *me*, the most offensive existence on earth, the worst of God's enemies, the one stamped with *all four* domain symbols. They were drawn to me with four times the pull; Gravitation was making me easy to find.

"The Dothen are almost upon us," I whispered. "Are we deep enough in the woods?" Rori peered into my face, understanding my real question: *Are we far enough from the people on the path, the ones who could be Taken?*

"We need to keep moving," Rori said, but she didn't move. Her eyes had fallen on Paul, who was hastening through the woods, trailed by his wife.

"Gemma?" he said as he spotted me. He rushed forward, but I held up my hands.

"Get away from me, Paul! Take your wife and go! NOW!"

"What's going on? Are you okay?" he asked earnestly, advancing several steps.

I screamed at him, a menacing growl of a scream. "LEAVE US! YOU DON'T BELONG HERE!"

Paul recoiled, as though my words had physically struck him. He looked dumbfounded, angry, and worst of all, humiliated. He glanced toward Jeannette, but she was focused on her shoes, avidly pretending she hadn't heard anything.

"Are you in some kind of trouble?" he whispered. "We're like family, Gemma. You're the only sister I've ever had. Let me help you."

"*Please, Paul*," I begged. "*Go.*"

He came closer and lowered his voice. "Who're you running from, Gem? Who's after you?"

But I didn't have the chance to answer him. Rori, looking wild and fierce and tougher than I'd ever seen her look, had drawn a black-bladed machete and was holding it to Paul's throat.

"Are you *deaf*? She said get lost!"

Jeannette whimpered and scuttled backwards. Paul, holding his hands up in surrender, swallowed. His Adam's apple moved beneath the edge of the knife. Rori lowered it, and he rushed to his new bride's side.

And then they attacked us, both of them at once, in a motion so quick even Rori was caught off guard. The machete fell to the ground in the commotion, and then Jeannette's fingers were laced around Rori's neck; Paul's around mine.

There were defensive moves, things I'd been taught to do, but I couldn't think, couldn't breathe, couldn't stand. All I could do was scratch at Paul's arms, at his hands, at his face, my legs flailing violently beneath me, and try to make sense of the fact that this was *Paul*. Paul McGregor. DJ McGregarious. Flash's best friend. My second brousin. The guy I'd known since I could remember knowing things. The one who always called me 'sugar.'

But it was not Paul, and I knew it. Paul was gone, taken, as evidenced by the sunken pupils within his chocolate-brown irises. I closed my eyes, wanting to shut out the sight of his, and felt myself growing weaker, my thoughts fuzzier.

I heard movement and tried to look left. Through the black spots in my vision, I saw Rori struggling against Jeannette, trying to pull something from the side pocket of her utility pants. Her face was wet with tears, and a gurgling noise came from deep in her throat. Somehow her fingers found their way into her pocket, and then she was holding something small, something swirling.

The portens.

There was a rush of energy all around me, like a storm building in the air, accompanied by a high-pitched keening. Then, with a surge of power like nothing I'd ever experienced, Paul and I were blown apart. So were Jeannette and Rori. I flew through the air, my shoulder cracking against the thick branch of an oak, and I crashed to the ground. Coughing, choking, gulping air, I forced my eyes open. I couldn't see Rori, but Paul and Jeannette, now more than twenty feet away, were hovering midair. Then they exploded, their bodies bursting into millions of fragments, scattering across the woods like gruesome confetti.

I got hit; tiny bits of their pulverized remains, wet and sticky, splattered me. I convulsed, sickened, and excruciating pain wrenched my shoulder. But before I passed out, I detected the signals.

Now there were twenty-six.

CHAPTER 78

The tinkling sound of wind chimes woke me up. There were words too, carrying over the gentle music, spoken in a murmured voice. It was a soothing sound, but my eyes flew open, and I clamped my hands over my ears, trying to make it stop.

A bolt of pain shot through my shoulder with the sudden movement, but it was nothing compared to the agony in my chest, the tightness in my throat, and the throbbing in my head that came with the knowledge that Paul had been taken. He and his bride, taken. Newlyweds, destroyed. Both of them, gone.

The wind chimes grew louder, as though the imaginary breeze in my mind had increased intensity, and the words became clearer. They rang in my ears, the same words repeating over and over, and I squirmed, not wanting to hear them. Not wanting to hear *him*.

Carefully, still covered in gore, I pushed myself to sitting position and rested against the base of a tree, scanning the woods for Rori. I felt drained and weak, like my strength had been depleted.

Depleted. So this was what it felt like to be tagged. I closed my eyes and leaned my head against the bark, knowing I had to get up, find Rori, and get us both to the Wooded Bridge where we would be easier to rescue.

I couldn't concentrate, couldn't channel my energy into moving, couldn't stop Receiving. I tried to shut off my gift, tried to block the message he was transmitting, but it was no use. He was broadcasting a communication signal

419

specifically to me, specifically *for* me, and it was the one type of signal I was powerless to control: an egress signal.

Egress signals, different from thought signals and spoken signals, came to me unbidden. They were another type of communication signal, one I hadn't told Phoenix about, and they scared me, not just because I couldn't turn them on or off. They scared me because they came from the recently dead. They were an individual's last opportunity, in that 'in between' space after dying but before moving on, to communicate with the living. Correction: to communicate with *me*. And I was obligated to Receive them whether I wanted to or not.

I didn't want to. I didn't want to hear Paul's voice in my head, the proof that he was really gone. I'd known when I Activated that egress signals would come to me, but I never expected one to arrive this *soon*, and never from Paul. But there it was, his voice in my head, his last transmission playing again and again, his words drifting to me over the wind chimes:

Be at peace, Gemma. Jeannette and I, we've gained. Know that: To die is gain.

I didn't realize I was crying until I felt the tears, hot and salty, land on my lips. How could I be at peace? Paul and his wife were dead because of me, and they couldn't even be given a proper burial. I squeezed my eyes shut, but forced them open again immediately, trying to unsee the scene that was burned in my mind, the one where their bodies hung in the air before erupting into tiny pieces.

Slowly, the sound of the wind chimes waned and Paul's voice began to fade, echoing distantly until all I heard were isolated words …*peace…know…gain…* and the only thing left was the musical rise and fall of the wind chimes themselves, tinkling gently once more. Then they were gone too, and I heard something else, something chilling: shuffling feet and ragged breathing to my right.

I started as Rori came into view. Her shirt was ripped, a strip of it torn from the bottom and tied around her thigh as a tourniquet. She limped forward, the long slash in her pants spreading open to expose a massive wound above her knee. She extended a shaky hand and pulled me up. "Let's… go," Rori said between breaths. "Before someone comes… to investigate… the noise."

Before the Dothen find others to take.

420

We hurried forward, Rori gritting her teeth and dragging her injured leg, and then I felt him. Taeo was nearby. I wanted to call out to him and let him know where we were, but I was afraid to attract others to us as well. Instead, I grabbed Rori's hand and pulled her through the trees, leading her on.

He saw us before we saw him; he was already running towards us, his footfalls silent, his eyes locked on Rori. Without a word, he scooped her up, motioned for me to follow him, and brought us the remaining distance to the Wooded Bridge. Then he shifted Rori so he was holding her with one arm, grabbed my hand with his other one, and took us across the bridge and back to Salvos.

✳ ✳ ✳

The air at the Mederium was heavy, humid. I walked between the entrance boulders after Taeo, who was still carrying Rori, and saw that the pool was busy. More than a dozen Essen were splashing about in the water, enjoying their evening post-workout swims. Floating among them was Kai, still unconscious, held up by Alistair, Jossi, and Shea.

Taeo strode to the edge of the teal water without setting Rori down. He got in the pool gingerly, handling her as though she was fragile. Ignoring the open-mouthed stares of other Mederium-goers, he untied the shred of fabric that was serving as a tourniquet and, with deft but gentle fingers, removed all of Rori's clothing except her undergarments, placing them on the side of the pool. She buried her face in his neck as the swirling clouds of minerals began attaching themselves to every bit of bare skin, mending her leg, her muscles, her depletion.

It was no time for modesty; I had been tagged, too. I undid my pants and kicked them off, but struggled to pull off my shirt. Every time I tried, searing pain burst through my shoulder. Wordlessly, Puck hoisted himself from the pool and approached me, his boyish face solemn, his golden hair dripping. He gathered my shirt in his hands and lifted it over my head, leaving me standing in front of him in just my bra and underwear. He never took his blue eyes off mine, though, and, in the manner of a gentleman, offered me his hand. I took it and lowered myself into the water next to Taeo and Rori.

For a while, no one said anything. Everyone just gawked at Rori and me, their mouths agape. Then, unable to contain his questions any longer, Alistair blurted, "What the hell happened to you two? Why were you both covered in blood?" He zeroed in on Rori. "You've never not crossed before sunset."

Rori didn't answer right away. When she did, she spoke quietly and without looking at him. "It works."

"Wha—?" Alistair began.

"You mean the portens?" Puck exclaimed, swimming closer to Rori. "You stayed out intentionally? To test it? *Holy shit.*" A look of admiration took over his features.

The smallest of smiles crept across Rori's lips. "It works," she repeated. "We got two of them."

Suddenly everyone was talking at once, talking enthusiastically, asking for details, praising Rori and me for our daring. Their reaction unsettled me.

Kelby, Puck's sister, asked, "How can you be sure? How do you know they've really been defeated?"

"Because," Rori answered simply, "the Dothen are made of energy— energy that I was able to bind to their Taken." She made an explosion gesture with her hands. "And then I dispersed it."

"Wow," Jossi breathed, her eyes wide. "Just like that, two of them gone."

Then Ren spoke, sounding eager. "So what's stopping us from getting more? From hunting *them*? Let's go after them! Tonight, now!"

The unsettled feeling inside me grew. It was the hint of pride in Rori's voice, the outright awe in Jossi's, the bloodlust in Ren's... It *bothered* me. It was one thing to use portens against a Taken in defense. It was quite another to create a Taken as the strategy for offense. As far as I was concerned, luring Dothen into innocents and then detonating them like bombs was reprehensible, the worst kind of wickedness. It was nothing to get excited about, to be *proud* of.

"We can't," Rori said. "The portens isn't ready. We need to make more deposits, all of us do, so it's available when we need it. Tomorrow night."

Ren nodded, approving. "And then"—he imitated the explosion Rori had made with her hands—"*Boom.*"

The thought of it *exhilarated* them, all of them; I could tell. Like blowing up twenty-six Taken was an acceptable price to pay for freedom. Like it was a damn *bargain*—the lives of twenty-six unknown others in exchange for their own.

I felt my chin quiver as the image of Paul and Jeannette, the exploding newlyweds, flooded into my mind once more. Would anyone else I loved be destroyed right in front of me?

I jumped out of the pool, too upset to feel embarrassed by my uncovered body, and gathered up my clothes.

"Wait—Gemma. Where are you going?" Taeo said. "You've been tagged. Even if it was only for a second, you're depleted. Full recovery takes at least—"

But I didn't care. I had to get away from them. The numbness and detachment were gone, leaving me with a swelling ache in my heart that was threatening to overcome me. I stalked through the woods heading towards the Somnus, where, with any luck, I'd drift into a dreamless sleep from which I'd never waken.

CHAPTER 79

I was unlucky on both accounts. I woke up just before dawn following a night of Jonny-filled dreams that left me feeling both raw and hollow. It was Monday, March 30th, the day before quarter's end. The day before *my* end, according to Phoenix. I stared up through the sheer material of the tent but didn't get out of bed. I couldn't. The weight of the world was pressing in on me from all sides, making it hard to breathe, let alone move.

I cried. The tears poured from me freely in the semi-privacy of my tent, spilling down my face, into my hair, across my pillow. I cried out of grief, out of loss, and out of fear. It was easy for me to believe, as darkness became light, that Paul had spoken the truth. To die really would be gain. Only death could relieve the strangled feeling inside me. I wanted that relief.

I wept for Jonny, for Paul and Jeannette, for all the innocents yet to be taken, but most of all for myself, because I knew that in spite of the pain, I had to go on. My life was not my own.

I got dressed and left the tent.

✳ ✳ ✳

The healing process took most of the morning. I needed to be there, I knew I did, so I stayed at the Mederium until Eclipse judged me as 'whole,' even though I would have preferred not to be in the company of so many others.

There really were *so many* others. Nearly the entire Host showed up at the pool during the course of the morning, though no one had done any training and they all looked to be in perfect health. They wanted Eclipse's 'blessing'— her assessment of them as entirely well—before the battle with the Dothen.

Phoenix believed it would begin just after midnight. In an assembly that took place midafternoon, he told the Host that the enemy would cross the Wooded Bridge as Taken, and that everyone should gather at the Axis by 11:30 that evening so he could administer the *Invincibility* elixir. Then everyone would get into position and wait.

The idea of waiting seemed to terrify people as much as the idea of the battle itself. People looked at one another without speaking, their expressions apprehensive, their postures tense. And though Phoenix spoke more confidently than I'd ever heard him speak before, and though he appeared to have genuine faith in elixir, the portens, and the plan, he was also afraid. His eyes swept over the Host and I saw a flicker behind the assuredness; he was worried about what could go wrong.

I wondered that myself. I looked over at Rori, who was standing between Taeo and me, rolling the portens unaffectedly in her hands. Her attention was focused on Phoenix but her face was impassive.

Rori and I hadn't talked about what had happened the previous night. We hadn't talked much at all. Then again, no one had. People were unwilling to speak, like breaking the silence would somehow break Salvos' protections. When people did talk, it was in hushed tones and whispers, as though the Dothen might hear them and find their way across the bridge sooner.

The bridge was closed, which everyone hoped would help. Echo had left it closed after no one expressed any desire to leave the island that morning. Why would we? There was nowhere to go, nothing to do. Better to stay put and review the plan and try to believe in it.

People were trying to believe in it. They *wanted* to believe in it. But the happiness and excitement that had led to Saturday night's celebrations were gone. The plan was solid, all the preparations were complete, but the future was still uncertain.

Phoenix concluded his address with a reminder to meet back at the Axis at 11:30. The crowd dissipated; I wandered to the edge of the water.

Gemma, a voice said in my head. *What intelligence have you gained?*

I whirled around. Phoenix stood at a distance, watching me.

Nod if you are hearing me, he said.

I nodded.

He walked across the beach and stopped in front of me. The silver in his rust-colored hair glinted in the sunlight as he cocked his head to the side. "So. Turns out it's a practical matter, not a theoretical one."

"Um... Huh?"

"Yesterday when we met, you said that it was *theoretically* possible to understand thought signals if someone sent them to you directly, with intention, in a focused way. That you could make sense of them, rather than just detect them, if there was no other 'noise.' You said you could, in theory." He gave me a half-smile. "But I've just proven you can, in practice." The smile faded and his pale, freckled face grew serious. "I understand you and Rori were attacked last night."

I pressed my lips together and nodded again, hoping he wouldn't ask for specifics. I was okay right now, in this moment. I wouldn't be if I had to relive the ordeal, describing every detail for his benefit.

"Can you confirm two Dothen were destroyed?"

"Yes. At first I detected twenty-eight signals. After Rori used the portens, there were twenty-six."

"Twenty-six..." Phoenix said with unrestrained excitement blazing in his dark eyes. "No one's ever known how many of them there are. We've all imagined the worst, thinking them to be in the thousands. But twenty-six... Twenty-six we can handle."

I closed my eyes and swallowed, trying to think of something, anything, other than twenty-six faceless, exploding Taken.

A silent moment passed, and then Phoenix spoke again, his tone suddenly laced with uncertainty. "What if there are more of them, but you were only able to *detect* twenty-six?"

"There are only twenty-six Dothen, Phoenix. Twenty-six Dothen that are bent on killing Essen... especially me."

He clasped my hand between both of his, a desperate move that belied the confidence he was trying so hard to project. His palms felt clammy and cold around my fingers, making me wonder if he was elevated. "Where are they now?"

I blinked at Phoenix. "I have no idea."

"What do you mean? You can only detect them at night?"

"Well there's that, but also… My gift doesn't work that way. I can't sense location, just presence."

"I don't understand. I thought communication signals—"

"Listen," I said, withdrawing my hand from Phoenix's. "When you turn on a radio, can you pinpoint the location of the broadcast tower that's transmitting the signal? No. It's like that with me. When I Receive, I'm not certain about the sender's location. All I know is that the signal is stronger when I am in close physical proximity. I mean *close* physical proximity, like within earshot."

Phoenix dropped his hands, which had remained suspended in front of him, and sighed. "So you won't be able to tell us when they're coming tonight. You won't be able to give us any advance warning."

"Not unless they think it. Plainly, in a focused way, as clearly as if they were saying it out loud."

He sighed again, looking past me at the sea. "Then let's hope that's exactly what they do."

✳ ✳ ✳

By sunset, nearly every Essen in the Host had already gathered at the Axis. With nothing left to do, we sat there in silence, watching the heavens and the earth grow darker. The first star appeared in the sky, blinking low on the horizon like some faraway firefly. Many more emerged, and the moon too, casting dim white light across the landscape.

Phoenix sat apart from us, his flaccid-looking body hunched against the wooden beach house. He was within himself; his eyes were closed as though he was meditating, but he seemed far from calm. The rapid movement of his chest evidenced his anxiety.

I waited for Rori and Taeo, but when ten-thirty arrived and they had not, I let Gravitation pull me to them. It brought me through the woods to the south side of the island.

Rori had her back to me. She was perched on the broad tree stump at the shoreline, the one that sat lonely before the wide expanse of ocean, watching a solitary surfer.

She looked up as I approached, her features looking sharp in the white light of the moon, but then turned back to the water. I stopped next to her without sitting, my eyes drawn to the figure cutting through the perfectly tunneled starlit waves.

"He needed to ride," Rori said without taking her eyes off Taeo. "It's what he does when he's…" She trailed off with a half-hearted shrug.

"I know," I said. "I feel the same way." I sat next to her on the tree stump and noticed she was holding the portens, rolling it between her hands like she'd done earlier.

"He misses Kai," she said. "We really thought he'd be conscious by now."

I gazed out at the water and said nothing. I was acutely aware of Kai's absence at the Axis. Though I'd spent time with him during the day, though I talked to him and pleaded with him to wake up, he was barely stirring, not yet responding. The decision had been made to leave him at the Mederium, where Taeo would, upon hearing Phoenix's count over the phone, administer the *Invincibility* injection at the same time he drank his own elixir. Then Taeo would leave him to join Rori and the rest of us at the Axis where we planned to ambush the Taken.

"I miss him, too," Rori admitted with a sideways glance at me. "He's a jerk, but he's a jerk with tenacity. We could have used him this past week. We could have used someone better than Phoenix, at least. Someone to rally us, someone with strength…"

I studied my fingernails, avoiding Rori's eyes.

"What's it like at the Axis?" she asked.

"Quiet."

"I would've thought everyone would be there by now."

"Everyone is. But it's still scary quiet. Which is partly why I came here."

Her brows furrowed. "Partly?"

"I wanted to get away from there, but more than that, I wanted to be… here."

Rori looked down at the portens, at the array of colors curling around one another in its surface. "I know, Gemma," she said softly. "I'm scared too."

"It's not just that," I said, digging my toes into the sand. "You and Taeo are basically the only friends I have le—"

"Don't," Rori said gently. "Don't do that. It's not like we're going to die. Besides"—she met my eyes, a solemn expression on her face—"I'm the one that destroyed your other friends."

"You're the one that saved my life," I said, my voice catching a little. "We both know they were already gone. You did the right thing. There are two less Dothen in the world."

For a while, neither of us spoke. We stared at Taeo, at his tiny form carving distant waves. The only sound was the repetitive *whoosh, crash,* of the sea, retreating and advancing loudly in the otherwise noiseless night.

"Gemma?" Rori said hesitantly. "What happened with Jonny?"

Unconsciously, my fingers rose to my collarbone to trace the chain of the necklace I was no longer wearing. "The journal is gone," I answered vaguely. "Just tell him I loved him," I added, my voice sounding husky. "If something happens to me, just tell him and my aunt and my cousin I loved them."

"Nothing's going to happen. We have the elixir, we have this"—she held up the portens—"and we have a plan. Everything's going to be okay, nothing's going to happen."

"Rori." I touched her shoulder. "Just in case something *does*. Please tell them."

She pursed her lips and brushed a wisp of long, copper hair from her face. Sighing, she nodded. "But assuming you *are* okay, assuming we all make it through this whole thing fine... then I need you to do something for me."

"What?"

"Take this back," she said, indicating the boulder opal. "Take it back and find a way to destroy it."

CHAPTER 80

I followed Rori's gaze to the vibrant whirling of colors that was the portens. Clouds of blues, greens, and reds, curled around each other, giving the illusion that Rori had lighted smoke trapped between her palms, rather than a boulder opal.

"It's dangerous," Rori said, "and not just in the way you think."

I knew it was dangerous. After I'd touched it, Eclipse assessed the damage. It was like various aspects of my health had been *consumed*, she'd said. Like my cells had been deprived of adequate levels of water, salt, and oxygen, not to mention heat. I recalled only too well the feeling of panic as the stone froze to my hand, robbing me of my breath, leaving me gasping and choking and desperate to get it off. I fought the urge to shrink away from it, even as Rori held it unconcernedly in her lap.

"The portens is a... capacitor, for lack of a better word. It takes and stores energy—elemental energy, specifically—so it can be released at the desired time. It pulls this energy from human sources, taking the water, earth, air, and fire from our very flesh. But it only does it *automatically* when it's completely empty... which it was the first time you touched it."

"So that's why Taeo could handle it when we went to my house? Because it wasn't empty anymore?"

"Not... exactly," she said slowly. "It was still empty after you held it; you must have severed the connection before the deposit was made. Because when *I* accidentally touched it—last week in the Nest—it had the same effect on me. Taeo wasn't affected because of his gift; he told me he told you about it. His immunity to Gravitation extends, apparently, to other forces as well. But anyway, that's not the danger I was referring to."

I thought of the Records, 3627 and 3628, written eighteen years ago, just after Phoenix became Augur. They ran through my mind, line by line, until I came to the familiar words: *And all who use it shall abide / Effects that come to pass.* The automatic transfer of elemental energy from a person to the portens—that's what those lines were referring to. What other dangers could there be? What could be worse than an empty portens?

She must have read the thought on my face because she said, "The energy flow isn't really that difficult to manage. I described it to the Host using a banking analogy, telling them that an account like this one can *never* be allowed to go dry. Without sharing specifics about what would happen, I made it clear that energy levels must at all times remain in the black. So every day, each of us has been making small but intentional deposits of energy. The Mederium restores us immediately after, so it's not really that big of a deal, but the efforts have helped our 'account' grow rapidly. Which means that tonight, when the time comes for me to make a very large withdrawal in binding the Dothen to their Taken, I won't run the risk of emptying it."

"And there's enough in there to do that? To take out all twenty-six Dothen? You're sure?"

A small crease lined Rori's forehead. "Twenty-six? How do you know there're twenty-six?"

"What? I—Didn't Phoenix tell you? He's made me intelligence-keeper. I found out there are twenty-six—"

"It must have slipped his drug-addled mind," Rori said with a grunt of annoyance. "It doesn't matter, though. There's enough juice in here to handle hundreds of Dothen. Thousands, even. Enough for a goddamn apocalypse, a decimation of the world."

"What are you saying?" I asked, shaking my head. "That it's not just the Dothen the portens could—"

"That's what I'm trying to tell you," Rori said, growing exasperated. "We don't *know* everything the portens can do. But it's more powerful than any of us imagined, and it's a *dangerous* kind of power—because it's easy to use, it's effective, and it's... fun." I saw a look of shame cross Rori's face before she turned away from me. "It was *fun* to waste those Taken. Don't get me wrong—I don't regret doing it; it enabled us to destroy two of our enemies. But I do regret *liking* it." She lowered her voice. "Just like I'm going to regret liking what I get to do tonight."

I don't know if she deliberately chose to say 'get to' versus 'have to,' but the unmistakable excitement in her whisper was enough for me to take her seriously.

Rori went on. "I'll do whatever I can to destroy every last Dothen that comes across our bridge—and I'll be able to do it, too, because that's what this portens was designed to do: end the slaughter, end the war, it's all there in Record 3628—but once that's done, the portens itself needs to be destroyed. ...Or it will destroy *us*."

"What do you mean, us? How?" I asked, failing to understand.

She hung her head. "I made a mistake, Gemma. When I figured out what the portens could do... I was pumped. I told everybody. I *showed* everybody. But now everywhere I turn, I can see the greed in their eyes. They all want it for themselves. They want to try it, to use it. Just for fun, but it'll turn into more. This kind of power... it will lead to a different war. A war within the Host."

"Rori..." I said quietly. "What exactly can the portens do?"

She glanced at her watch, which displayed a time of 11:10. "I told Taeo I'd give him a sign when it was time to go back to the Axis."

Suddenly a fire erupted on the beach, not far from where we were sitting. Its flames rose into the sky, a giant tower of blinding light. I jumped up and stumbled backwards, away form the heat.

"You wanted to know what the portens can do," Rori said simply, still sitting. "It allows me to release elemental energy. I can use it, direct it, *rule* it. As long as I'm holding the portens, as long as I'm mindful of my intentions, I can control elemental energy—air, earth, water, and *fire*." On the word 'fire,' her voice became reverent, awed. She stared at the blaze, and I saw the red streaks reflected in her eyes, giving her an almost demonic appearance.

I tore my gaze away from her and tried to find Taeo in the water between the orange starbursts burned into my retinas. He was in the middle of a barrel wave, gliding swiftly through the almond-shaped center.

"He'll head in after this ride," Rori said quietly. "I just had to give him one more flawless tube."

My jaw dropped open. "You... used the portens for that?"

"We've never had waves like that before," Rori said. "Not on Salvos. But surprisingly, they weren't that hard to make. A slight increase in the wind speed, some small changes in the ocean floor topography... And voilà, tube waves." She grinned at me, looking pleased with herself. "It was my gift to him, the one thing I wanted to give him before..." Her smile faded.

"...Before you gave it back to me to destroy," I finished, my mind reeling. An unlikely memory popped into my head, the memory of Professor Dagenais' scrawled response to my American Nature Writing final. He had called my argument 'more fantasy than philosophy,' but here it was: proof that it *was* possible for 'Man'—at least in an individual sense—to command Nature.

Rori gave a single nod. "The portens needs to be destroyed, Gemma. I don't know where it came from, how you came to have it, and I'm not even entirely sure why it works against the Dothen, but once they're gone, it doesn't need to exist anymore. The power is too great, too dangerous, too *fun*. Especially if the regret never comes until later... or worse, if it never comes at all."

She frowned, watching Taeo swim towards shore, and murmured, *"Seductive is the might / The portens shield contains / Tempting hearts of right / To launch evil campaigns."*

"Record 3628," I said automatically.

"The portens isn't harmless, Gemma. It wouldn't be difficult to abuse its power, to cause a cataclysm of epic proportions." She took a deep breath. "Or a tragedy infinitely more subtle."

I opened my mouth to ask, but she continued without waiting for the question.

"Think about it. If you were my enemy, or my rival, or just in my way, I could deal with you. I could deal with you, and I could make it look innocent. It's a delicate balance, the amount of water in the human body. If I pulled enough of yours away, you'd die of dehydration. If I added a little, you'd die of dilutional hyponatremia—water poisoning."

Rori stood up as Taeo waded through the shallower water. She let the fire burn out and walked across the beach towards him. I chased after her, feeling dazed.

"But why me? Why should I be the one to destroy it?"

"Because," she said, stopping to look at me. "You're the Link. The original portens-keeper. Whether you like it or not, the portens was given to you. For reasons we don't yet know, it's supposed to be your responsibility."

"But—"

"I'm not saying you'll be on your own. You don't even know the *Pactem Orbis* legends. It was the legends, as much as the Records, that helped me understand how the portens worked. Maybe the clue to figuring out how to destroy it is in the legends, too. And if that's the case, you'll need me—I know them better than anybody. But I'll only help you. I won't do it for you."

I looked away from her, feeling overwhelmed, and watched Taeo emerge from the water and plod through the sand in our direction. Rori lowered her voice. "Look, the truth is—I *can't* do it for you, Gemma. I'm too attached. I wouldn't be able to destroy the portens because I don't *want* to destroy the portens. I *like* energy bending, manipulating the elements, refining nature. But that doesn't mean we should keep it. I'm no Augur, but I know what's going to happen, and I'm *afraid* of what's going to happen. The Dothen don't scare me anymore, Gemma. *This* does. We're going to make it through the next twenty-four hours just fine. It's the aftermath we need to fear."

Taeo arrived next to Rori and, still dripping, swept her into his arms. "*That,*" he said, "was freaking awesome." He kissed her vigorously before releasing her. "Kinda makes me want to rethink our discussion about—"

"We can't keep it," Rori said firmly. "No one can." She turned to me, her eyes full of warning. "Never use it, Gemma. Because once you do"—a thrilled type of shudder ran through her body—"there's no going back."

The three of us left the beach together. Taeo was focused on Rori, his expression trusting and relaxed. Rori's arm was looped through his, but her eyes were on the swirling colors of the opal. I trailed behind them slightly, wondering whether Rori would really be able to part with the stone, assuming we both survived quarter's end.

✳ ✳ ✳

I observed the activity at the Axis with a disconnected sort of awareness, as though I was having an out of body experience. Every Essen in the Host, with the exception of Taeo and Kai, was at the Axis, but the air was heavy with silence. Spherical paper lanterns, like the ones that hung above the clearing where I had combat training, decorated the beach house and swayed in the ocean breeze, giving off pastel-colored light. Some of the children, Hannah among them, were huddled against Keepers, their faces pale and frightened. Echo and Eclipse looked equally fearful, but they were moving through the crowd handing out the small magenta Amaranth flowers. I took one and stuck the stem in my pocket, copying my neighbors, as Rori muttered something about an Essen superstition.

Phoenix ushered us into a large circle so that we could all see each other, all make sure to swallow our drinks at precisely the same moment. He lifted an enormous decanter and began pouring the elixir into small plastic cups. It looked like red wine. People passed the cups.

There was no speech, no pre-battle pep talk. Phoenix dialed Taeo's phone number and confirmed that he was with Kai, and that he had found the cup that had been left for him and the syringe that had been left to inject into Kai.

When everyone was holding their drinks, a countdown began. After 'one,' we would drink the *Invincibility* elixir, and then designated Keepers would bring the children to a hiding spot while the rest of us waited as Dothen bait.

I gripped my cup, but it wasn't enough to keep me from floating away. I felt disassociated from everything. Distantly, I knew that fear was untethering me from reality. It was a coping mechanism, an act of self-preservation. But I couldn't drift away. I needed to be here, present, in the moment, ready to do whatever needed to be done. My life was not my own.

Unexpectedly, Gemma-with-the-lantern appeared in my head. She began running through the tunnels of my mind, raking frantically through my memories to find something, anything, to keep me from slipping further into remoteness. She stumbled upon a scene and latched onto it, attempting to keep me grounded.

"Five," Phoenix said solemnly.

In the memory, I was very young. My father and I were playing, his hands, rough and large, encasing my own. We spun around, reciting a simple nursery rhyme. I remembered the words, the melody, and the laughter. It was a time of innocence and of love, and it rooted me in myself, taking away the fear. I held the memory firmly in my mind.

"Four," Phoenix said, his dark eyes sweeping across the Host.

Ring around the rosie…

I whispered the song in my head, scanning the faces in the circle. Some of them looked terrified, some of them looked numb, and some of them looked resolute. No one looked exhilarated anymore.

"Three." He glanced at his cell phone to make sure he was still connected to Taeo.

Pockets full of posies…

The little purplish flowers protruded from my pocket and the pockets of everyone around me. I wondered what it was they were believed to do.

"Two," Phoenix said, raising his cup.

Ashes, Ashes…

I tried not to think about Kai, about the gray undertone of his skin after Taeo had rescued him from the Dothen. I tried not to think about how my own skin would look if they began to deplete me, or how it would feel if my time was stolen, or whether I'd know it once all that was left of me was dust.

"One." All of us watched each other as we lifted our cups and drank.

We all fall down.

There was a commotion. I stepped back reactively, removing myself from the circle. My heart raced as I tried to understand what was happening. I heard howling, wailing, screeching. And then, one by one, people dropped to the ground. But we didn't *all* fall down.

Two of us remained standing.

CHAPTER 81

P hoenix stood at the opposite side of the circle, his pale face becoming even whiter with shock. He stared at me, his eyes bulging. Both hands found their way into his hair and were twisting it violently in disbelief and horror. He surveyed the Host, all of them writhing in the sand, and raised his gaze back to me. "Why didn't you *drink* it?" he shrieked.

I was shaking all over. At my feet, Rori was convulsing, a gurgling noise coming from her mouth as blood trickled down its side. It dripped onto her shirt, leaving a crimson stain at her neckline. Her eyes were wide, terrified, and locked on me, imploring me to do something to help her.

"I—I *did* drink, I swear I did!" My voice sounded octaves higher than normal.

"You lie!" he screamed, his face now contorted with fury. "Didn't I tell you this elixir's temperamental? That *everyone* needed to drink it at *exactly* the same time?"

"I did, I did!" I cried. "I have a second gift, an elixir immunity! I didn't tell you because I didn't want you burdened with knowing it wouldn't work on me!"

"Then this is *your* fault!" His face, so pale just moments ago, was turning bright red. "Your *gift* has altered the elixir's functionality!"

My body grew cold, my shaking uncontrollable. I saw Echo squirming, his crippled leg trapped beneath him, and Alistair, the blood pouring from his ears, obscuring the tattoos on his neck. All around me in the collapsed

437

circle, Essen were straining, bleeding. "How? Why? Oh my God, oh my God, what's happening?"

"Nothing we can stop now!" Phoenix bellowed. "Their muscles are seizing, their organs rupturing! Because of *you!*"

"Please—there must be something we can do to help them!" I said between sobs. I scrambled to my knees and pulled Rori across my shoulder. Her breathing was sharp and sporadic, like hiccups. "Their thought signals are getting weaker, but I can still feel them. We haven't lost anyone yet. We need to get them to the Mederium!" I heaved myself up, nearly losing my balance under Rori's weight.

Phoenix didn't move. He glared at me, his dark eyes flashing with rage. "Don't you get it? They're *dying!* All of them, every Essen left in the world! You've done the Dothen's work for them!"

"Please…" I said as tears streamed down my cheeks. "We have to at least *try* to heal them… Before the Dothen—"

I couldn't finish the sentence. My eyes had just found the delicate form of Hannah—sweet, seven-year-old Hannah, who reminded me of a child-version of myself—slumped at Phoenix's feet. She was staring at me blankly, blood pouring from the corners of her glazed-over turquoise eyes. And still Phoenix just stood there.

He just *stood* there.

And in that instant, it all made sense. It was the final clue, the one that made all the others click. I fell to my knees, the enormous impact of my realization forcing me down. "No-no-no-no-no," I moaned, but it was too late; I had solved the riddle too late.

Rori slid off my shoulder, the portens slipping from her twitching fingers as she hit the ground. It rolled away, coming to rest outside the circle in the sand behind me. I raised my eyes to Phoenix. "The Dothen aren't coming," I whispered, aghast. "Are they?"

He froze, but not before I saw his eyes dart to the boulder opal, much further from him than it was from me.

"*You* did this," I said, covering my mouth. "*Intentionally.*"

He didn't respond, but his jaw clenched and his expression hardened. Between us, the air was thick with the Host's whimpers.

"There's no *Invincibility* elixir," I said. "There never was. It's always just been poison—a death-inducing elixir laced with Necis berry juice. And *you* were the one who didn't drink it, which is why you're just *standing* there while everyone else is—"

My voice broke and gave out. At Phoenix's feet, Hannah trembled, blinking at me slowly, rivers of red tracking down her cheeks. I choked on a sob and continued. "You poisoned the Host just like you poisoned Racla Celere. You killed her with the same elixir you used on us—she was found with blood coming out her eyes."

The world swam before me but I didn't take my eyes off Phoenix. "This was your plan all along, wasn't it? Record 3629 was a fraud—the lie you invented to orchestrate this moment! That's why there's no reference to the elemental domains; you didn't know to put them in! The Record was never *real*. There was never going to be a bridge failure or a Dothen attack. 'The Link will be defeated' wasn't a *prophecy*—it was your plan!"

Phoenix looked past me, and I could see the wheels turning behind his mud-colored eyes. He was trying to figure out how to get to the portens. I shot to my feet at once and lunged towards it, Phoenix racing through the sand at my heels. My fingers closed around the stone and I held it firmly, mustering every ounce of will in my body to command it.

A huge gust of wind came forth and blew Phoenix back. He landed on his ass, once again on the opposite side of the circle.

"What are you going to do, Gemma?" he said coldly as he got up. "Let the wind defend you forever? We both know you're not going to kill me. So you're just going to—what? Wait until I die on my own?"

He spoke without looking at me. Even at a distance, I could see his eyes on the portens, drawn in by its swirling colors. In the pastel glow of the paper lanterns, his freckled face appeared manic.

I wiped at my tear-streaked face and lifted the portens in front of me. "It was all for *this*?" I spat. "You've plotted for months just for—"

"*Months?*" He shifted his gaze abruptly; there was a demented look in his eyes when he met mine. "And here I thought you were clever! Try *years*, you stupid girl. Since I first learned the portens existed—twenty-two years ago! Since before you were even born! You think it was easy getting all the pieces to fall into place, playing a role in my own life for more than two decades? After all that work, I wasn't going to let anyone—least of all some newly-Activated Affiliation Arith—mess it up."

Raela, I realized. He was referring to Raela Celere, who, in keeping with Essen practices, had divulged her gift of Hindsight to him once it had settled. But her gift was a threat to him, a threat to the plan he'd been executing for so long. With her gift, Raela stood to unearth every secret he'd been burying on his journey to obtaining the portens. And one of those secrets, I knew in my heart, was his responsibility for all the deaths that took place eighteen years ago.

"She was on to you…" I said. "Raela was on to you. She knew you had something to do with it, with what happened the night Kai's parents died."

"She wasn't on to me yet," Phoenix corrected, "but what *was* revealed to her was a little too close for comfort."

"But you admit it, it was you! You're the reason Kai's family is dead, and Gate's. You're the reason the last Augur, Kerithe—" I stopped talking, my eyes growing wide with revelation. Outrage swept through me, my knuckles whitening as I gripped the portens tighter.

"That was the *point*, wasn't it?" I said through gritted teeth. "That was your whole sorry objective in closing the bridge that night—or at least in drugging Gate so he failed to open it. It was to kill *Kerithe*, your own Kept! The other twelve just happened to be there, the casualties of your plot! *She* was the one you really wanted dead—because she was Augur, and as long as she was alive, you couldn't be!" I was screaming now, my anger spilling from me, drowning out the gagging and wheezing noises of the dying Host.

"Well I couldn't very well publish Records about the portens without being the Augur, now could I?" He laughed, which infuriated me more. "It was phase one of the plan! How else was I going to get everyone looking for it?"

I called on the wind again. It lifted him from his feet and he hung there, suspended in midair, until I made it slam him into the ground.

He was hurt, but his cough turned into a laugh as he lay there. He pushed himself up to sitting position. "It's been eighteen years since I published those Records, since I ordered the Host to search for the portens," Phoenix said through his laughter. "And I always thought Malakai would be the one to find it, or to find *the Link* anyway, but I didn't know it would take him *so long*.

So I waited. I waited for it, or you, to turn up so I could act on phase two of my plan: the phase that would bring me the portens and rid me of all my competition in one blissful moment."

His laughter died instantly, and he got to his feet. "Tonight was my moment," he snarled, taking a step forward. "And you took it away." He took another step towards me, and I raised the portens threateningly. His advancing stopped. "You think it was *easy* developing a plan to obtain the portens without arousing suspicion from a hundred supernaturals? You think it was *easy* trying to come up with a way to kill them all simultaneously, in spite of their gifts? Everything had to be done at once, in a single moment, or someone would've caught on, would've overpowered me. The Record was the only way, my only chance. I needed them scared; I needed whatever hope they had in *you*, their precious *Link*, dashed. I needed them desperate enough to trust me, desperate enough to believe in an *Invincibility* elixir—which any fool with half a brain knows could never actually exist!"

He was laughing again, a deranged and chilling sort of laughter that echoed into the night.

"But *why*? Why take the portens for yourself? Why kill the Host? The others, they would have used it against the Dothen, would have ensured every Essen the freedom they—"

He straightened himself, still chuckling. "You don't get it, do you? It's not about the Dothen, not for me. You think my plan ended here, tonight? The portens wasn't the *end*, Gemma, it was the *means*. And I had to kill anyone who might get in the way of what was still to come! I didn't need them, any of them, for phase three. Just like I don't need *you!*"

He dove at me, a motion so swift and reckless that it caught me completely by surprise. But he never stood a chance. I was conditioned—fast and strong and agile—while he was an addict and soft. I dodged away from him across the sand, running through the circle to the—

I fell to the ground, struck down midstride by a powerful blow to the back of the head. Next to my face in the sand—Phoenix's black combat boot. I blinked rapidly, trying to clear the stars in my vision. I staggered to my feet just as Phoenix tackled me back down. The portens flew from my hand, and we both clawed at each other to get to it. We reached it at the same time. I clamped my hands around it, palming it so tightly I knew he'd never shake me off. But his hands were on the opposite sides, gripping it just as hard. We wrestled across the sand, kicking, biting, thrashing, everything, but neither of us let go.

I focused my intentions, tried to employ all of the four elements, but none of them came to my aid. With Phoenix also clutching the stone, commanding it differently, the energy just flowed out undirected. I could actually *feel* the portens emptying, the stored energy of many peoples' and many days' worth of deposits gushing into the void. It bled out quickly while we fought. And then, when the whole supply was nearly exhausted, I caught a glimpse of the star-strewn sky, exhaled fully into the night—and I let go.

CHAPTER 82

It was a split-second decision, one I might've been too scared to make if I'd really thought about it: the decision to let Phoenix kill me.

And he would, too. There was enough energy left in the portens for him to do it—just enough, a fact I'm sure he knew. But what he didn't know, what I was counting on him not knowing, was what would happen after that.

I had survived the empty portens by accident. The sudden impact of my fall to the hardwood floor of my bedroom had knocked the stone from my hand. Rori had survived it with Taeo's help. From her flesh, the stone had stolen an initial deposit. It would have taken more—it had frozen to her hand, after all—if Taeo hadn't wrested it away. But Phoenix had neither a hard surface nor a friend's assistance with which to break the portens' connection. The automatic transfer of energy would kill him shortly after he killed me.

My life wasn't a sacrifice. It was a gift—the last and only thing I had left to give. It was too late to save the Essen, but it was not too late to save humanity. And though I didn't know what phase three of Phoenix's plan was, I knew it would be abominable. There would be more lies, more destruction, and more murder—not in this world, but in the non-Essen one. In Jonny's world. The world that had only me and my split-second decision to protect it.

I had expected Death to greet me instantaneously. Instead, the moment I released my grip on the stone, it responded to Phoenix's unspoken behest—which was not, apparently, to manipulate the elements within me. It was to control those around him. He rose thirty feet above me, riding a thermal of air. He cackled loudly, held aloft by the current.

"Ready to die, are you?" he jeered at me from above. "But then again, you've made your peace with dying, haven't you? You've been expecting tonight to be the end for a while now."

I got to my feet and stared up at him. I didn't know how he planned to kill me, but I wasn't going to die on my knees.

"That's right, Gemma! Stand up and face your fate!" He threw his head back in mad laughter. Then he smiled and spread his arms wide, letting the wind rush over his body, reveling in the power of the portens.

He rose higher into the sky, forty feet, fifty feet, then sixty, become a moving speck against the starry backdrop.

I couldn't fathom what he was doing, but I didn't stand there and wait for it. I took off towards the circle, desperate to save whomever I could while I still could.

I know what you're doing, Gemma, Phoenix said into my head. *I know what you're doing, but it's too late. Everyone's dead. Well, almost.*

I didn't know whether his 'almost' applied to the word 'everyone'—meaning me, that I was still alive—or to the word 'dead,' in that the dying Essen weren't dead *yet*. Either way, I knew time was running out, both for them and for me.

It's coming for you, he said.

Instinctively I turned around and faced the ocean. In the darkness, I could distinguish nothing.

It's coming for you, he said again, *and it's a fitting end for a* Merla.

I heard it before I saw it: a thunderous rushing sound that filled up my ears.

You see it now, don't you? It's a small sample of what I'll unleash in phase three!

I didn't see it. I saw nothing at all—just a black ocean and a starry sky.

Once I destroy the Dothen, I'll have free rein in the world. And with every tool at my disposal—my money, my elixirs, my control over the elements, the Mederium—I will make the world mine.

Stars started disappearing. At the horizon, one by one, they began to vanish.

Impossible.

It was impossible. The amount of energy required to cause stars to burn out—

The rushing noise grew louder. More stars disappeared. Now there was a barren field in the night, a blank spot just above the skyline.

This is just a taste, Gemma. There'll be more, much more. Everyone on earth will see what I can do. In fear and amazement, they'll ask one another, 'Who is this? He commands even the winds and the water, and they obey him?' His raucous laughter rang into my mind. *And then they will either worship me… or perish, like you are about to.*

And then I saw it. The stars hadn't disappeared from the sky. They'd been eclipsed by a rising swell of water. I had no concept of its distance, but it was increasing in height… which meant it was approaching land.

I screamed and ran, knowing there would be no outrunning it. The wave was moving too fast. It would catch me on the beach and kill me on contact, crushing my body and everyone else's, washing away all the evidence of Phoenix's treachery.

How could I have so grossly miscalculated the amount of energy left in the portens? It had felt empty, like there was just enough power left for some subtle manipulations of the elements. And yet Phoenix had created a monster wave, one that was building speed as it raced across the water, all while he maintained his position of safety high above everything.

The roar of the water was deafening. *Get to higher ground!* I shouted at myself, remembering what I'd once heard about tsunamis. But there *was* no higher ground, just the cliffs at the north side of the island, so distant! I ran anyway, my feet moving independently, flying across the sand away from the water.

…And then I was almost flattened by Phoenix, who had plummeted from the sky, landing with a crunch on the beach mere feet in front of me. He was dead, whether from the impact of the fall or from the portens' replenishment of energy from his flesh, I didn't know. I stared down at him, at his open and shocked-looking eyes, feeling at once victorious and revolted. His body shriveled and crystalized before my eyes as the portens stole the last of the elemental energy from his very cells.

I kicked the portens from his frozen hands, praying to the cosmos that a deposit had been made, and picked it up without effect. I turned with it to the sea.

It was no longer where it had been. In the moment I'd faced away, it had receded dramatically, exposing hundreds of feet of usually-submerged seabed. For a second, I thought the wave was gone, that it had shrugged back into the sea with Phoenix's demise.

But I could still hear it. And then I looked up.

Surging forward, advancing on me with incomprehensible speed, was my worst and most terrifying nightmare come true: No longer a giant swell out in the ocean, but a towering wave, a wave like none I'd ever seen, coming towards shore. For an instant it appeared to hover out there, a stories-tall wall of water in the distance that appeared to stretch heavenward rather than forward. Dark and endless as space, solid as steel, it seemed suspended in time. It yawned before me, its enormous mouth impatient to swallow me up.

But it hadn't paused or even slowed, and I stood there, locked into place by sheer terror, clinging to the portens, without a single conscious thought. I blinked, holding my salvation but somehow helpless to use it.

The portens is dangerous.

Not only because it automatically steals energy when it's empty and because it has the potential to corrupt minds and hearts with its greed-inducing power. Its greatest danger, insofar as I can understand it, is its *responsiveness*.

But its responsiveness is also what saved my life. It responded to my *intentions*—not my conscious thoughts or decisions, absent as they then were under that speeding, looming mountain of water—but my *intentions*. And my *intentions* had been to save whomever I could and to get to higher ground. So the portens responded, releasing elemental energy to enable me to do just that.

It released *a lot* of energy. From beneath me, the land shot up like a rocket. Just like that, without even meaning to, I had summoned the earth. The sand shifted under my feet and I fell backwards, landing across Phoenix's cold, lifeless body, pinned there by the acceleration. I turned my head, straining to see through the blowing sand. A huge chunk of the beach the size of a football field was soaring into the sky, riding a vast and unseen pillar of stone. The collapsed circle of Essen was on it, too; I could see them lying unmoving, all ninety of them, a short distance away. We flew upward, my eyes level with the crest of the breaking wave as it toppled over, but still we rose, bolting past it. I squeezed my eyes shut, bracing myself for the wave's impact. An instant later, I felt it: it crashed into the monolith with a shuddering rumble, but the rock, still rising, withstood its force. The thundering rush of water continued, but I was safe above it, safe at the top of my earthen elevator. Then the movement stopped like it began: suddenly, and with a jolt.

I rolled off of Phoenix, retching. It was several minutes before I could crawl, slowly and shakily and with the portens still in my hand, to the edge. I glanced at the motionless Essen, whose signals were all terribly weak but still present, and then over the side.

We were on a giant column, almost perfectly cylindrical and maybe eight stories high. It appeared to consist of a single block of stone, a continuous slab of the same grayish-white rock as the cliffs to the north. Below, the sea was still violent. Subsequent waves, though much smaller than the first, flung themselves against the structure.

I pulled back from the edge and surveyed the Host. Across from me, at the opposite side of the column's circular top, they continued dying.

…And then they were dead.

Their thought signals were dropping off, one by one. Then the wind chimes began, a tinkling sound in my mind, and I jumped to my feet, howling with misery, because I knew what was coming.

When the egress signals began, I couldn't understand them. There were so many of them, all jumbled together, playing at once. I heard their voices, so many Essen voices, none of them distinguishable, transmitting their final messages, also indistinguishable.

Was anyone still left? I was too distraught; I couldn't Receive thought signals through the egress signals. It was too late for those who'd relayed final messages, those who'd transmitted egress signals, but which ones were they? I ran from Essen to Essen, looking for but failing to find any signs of life.

I would have to take them all. I couldn't know if it would work, or for whom it might work, without attempting it on everyone. In haste, I held out the portens and commanded the air to lift us up and carry us across the island to the Mederium. If only we could get to the Mederium… maybe some could be saved.

Because if there was one thing of which I was convinced, it was this: Death is *both* a process *and* an event. The process relates to the body, and the event relates to the spirit. And the death process can be reversed as long as the death event has not yet occurred. The body can, if the conditions are right, be brought back—as long as the spirit has not yet departed.

I knew that for many it was too late; their spirits had already departed. I had their egress signals still echoing in my head as proof. But there were still some, there *had* to still be some, for whom the death process could yet be reversed. I owed it to them to try.

CHAPTER 83

We were about ten feet above the Mederium grounds when I lost command of the air. Everyone fell to the earth, landing roughly in various places around the pool, but not because the portens had run out of power. No, we fell because, at some subconscious level, my intentions had faltered.

I couldn't help it—the moment the two of them came into view, I just lost it. It wasn't that I'd forgotten that Taeo and Kai would be at the Mederium, but the knowledge had been pushed back into a corner of my mind. And then as we approached the pool, as I prepared to set the Host down gently, I saw them, the gray light of predawn illuminating their faces, and the sight of them broke me. All of the sudden it was *them* I needed to help, *them* I wanted to save.

I fell out of the air with the rest of the Host, my ankle rolling painfully as I hit the ground, but it didn't stop me from running to them. They were sprawled out next to each other, the syringe that Taeo had used to inject Kai now lying empty near Kai's arm. The cup from which Taeo had drunk had been flung away; it was prostrate at the base of one of the entrance boulders.

They were very near the edge of water, and Taeo's hand was against Kai's shoulder. It was like Taeo, upon realizing the elixir's true nature, had attempted to push Kai into the pool. But between the muscle spasms and the internal bleeding, he'd been unable. Now he was motionless, like Kai had been for ten days, and his face was streaked with bloody tears.

In fury and anguish and desperation, I tried to Receive them. I sensed nothing—no thought signals, no egress signals, nothing.

"No!" I cried, my knees buckling. But then, like had happened before, Kai responded to the sound of my voice. His signal was briefly and faintly but distinctly present following my utterance.

"Kai!" Tears of relief prickled in my eyes and I closed them. Still clutching the portens, I released energy, commanding the air to lift Kai and Taeo into the pool and ordering the water to stir beneath them and keep them afloat.

With newfound resolve, I did this for the rest of the Host, all ninety of them, refusing to believe that it was too late for some, even though I knew it was. Though the egress signals had faded away, they still echoed in my mind, a confused mess of words and voices, the evidence that several of the floating bodies were already corpses.

It took all of my focus to keep the currents circulating evenly beneath the Host—all of my focus, and a significant amount of energy—but I was able to keep their heads above the water as the powdery substance began coating them. I tried not to notice where it wasn't working, to which individuals the minerals weren't clinging. Instead, I watched them with an almost clinical detachment and tried to minimize the bumping that occurred between bodies as they floated at the surface.

The bumping was inevitable; the pool was very full. At one point, I lowered myself into the water between the reaching arms of two nameless victims—I was badly in need of healing as well—but though I flattened my body against the side of the rocky basin and though no one's limbs actually touched me, my concentration wavered. The current subsided, and slowly, people began to sink. I jumped out of the pool and refocused my intentions. The current stabilized.

Time passed. I settled myself against one of the entrance boulders and maintained the current's flow. Eventually, the gray light of early morning gave way to an amber sunrise that trickled through the tree branches. The patchwork of light felt warm on my face and I began to tire. Vaguely, I wondered what would happen if I fell asleep. Would the portens continue to expend energy, guided by the intentions I'd had prior to falling asleep? Or would the current melt away, leaving the Essen to sink beneath the calm water? And then another question: What if they did go under—was it even possible to drown in a pool of healing?

At the thought, I jerked upright. My adrenaline from the night's events was gone, but none of us were out of danger. The most immediate one, I knew, was the same for the Host as it was for me: an empty portens.

How much energy could possibly be left? Truthfully, I'd expected it to be drained hours ago. The automatic transfer that had occurred after Phoenix had drained it—well, that was only one person's deposit. And I'd made some substantial withdrawals since then: enough to raise a column of earth into the sky, transport ninety-one people across the island on the wind, and circulate currents of water to uphold the entire Host. Soon it would be empty. The problem was, I didn't know how soon; the portens' energy levels felt full.

This was a deception, I realized, a protection established to deter abuse of the power. It was the reason Phoenix had, to his own demise, overestimated the available energy. Though we'd both felt the portens' true balance upon touching it together, he had believed it was once again full. To an individual holding it alone, it would always feel such. But was that really my primary problem?

Suppose I did have the ability to know the portens' fullness level... would it really help me? After all, there's no standard unit by which one can measure elemental energy. Even if there was, could anyone say with any certainty how far a unit of that energy would go, in terms of work? I doubted it was even consistent—maybe air bending takes less energy than fire bending, for example. Or maybe the amount of work that released elemental energy can do depends on other factors such as weather, time of day, geography, or perhaps certain attributes of the wielder.

What I really needed to know was how much "work" Phoenix's energy deposit had bought me, and how much of that work was left. Not much, I was sure, but *how* much?

I tried to make a deposit of my own—something small to pad the balance—but it wasn't possible to contribute energy while simultaneously releasing it, and as long as I was holding the portens, it was releasing energy. Apparently, my intention to keep the Host alive overrode any intention I had to replenish the portens. I told myself this was okay. For now it was okay, because if I *did* stop releasing the energy, the current would stop circulating and the Essen would sink.

So instead of supplementing the portens' energy with my own, I just tried to use it sparingly. I focused my intentions on maintaining the current in the pool while using as little power as possible to do it. It was a matter of efficiency. The better I managed the energy, the longer the Host would have to heal.

My efforts were working. An hour past sunrise, I detected thought signals. From several people, thought signals. Kai's was the strongest, the one I detected most easily. And as the morning progressed, the signals got stronger. I continued releasing energy slowly, my eyelids drooping with exhaustion, but their collective improvement gave me the strength to keep going.

By mid-morning, I saw twitching. Peoples' bodies were responding, thank the cosmos, because mine was giving out. I was so tired. After twenty-nine straight hours of being awake, I wasn't sure how much longer I could last. I wasn't sure how much longer the portens would, either.

There was a splash, and my eyes snapped open. How much time had passed since they'd closed? The sun was higher in the sky... I blinked at the pool, looking for the sound that had roused me. Had someone gone under? I leapt to my feet too quickly and swayed...

I needed to get in the pool. I wouldn't be able to continue to care for their healing if I didn't start my own. And if I couldn't maintain the current while I was in the water, and if people started to sink—

What could I do? Let them go under until I finished refreshing myself, and then bring them back up? I leaned against a tree, weighing my options.

That's when it happened. That's when the portens ran out of energy.

I'd had a plan for that moment, which was why I'd positioned myself by the tree closest to the water. Once the automatic transfer of energy had begun, I'd let it take a deposit or two. Then I'd knock the portens from my hands by banging it against the trunk of the tree and, once I was free of it, throw myself into the pool.

It was a decent plan, but for one overlooked detail: I was already weak with weariness, and I grew weaker as soon as the portens began taking my energy.

From my cells, the stone stole water, earth, air, and fire. Within seconds, I was unable to stand, let alone fight. I was too dehydrated, too suffocated, too cold, too *tired*.

So this is how it ends.

Phoenix had been right after all—I wouldn't live to see April. But that didn't mean he'd won. No, the splash that had awoken me came again. Someone was alive and moving within the pool. And whoever that was would finish what I'd started. They would. They *would*.

I relaxed against the ground, surrendering myself to the portens, letting it take deposit after deposit from my flesh, letting it take everything I had. And it did take everything—even the brick wall that for so long had blocked my memories. I couldn't breathe, I couldn't cry, I couldn't move, but I could still *feel*, and what I felt was indescribable joy. I was moments from dying, but it didn't matter—I could finally *remember*. The smile that formed on my lips would freeze there, and people would know that I'd died without regret. I'd done what I could for them, I'd done what I could for me, and I was at peace.

Another splash, bigger and louder than the others, filled my ears, but I couldn't turn my head to the pool. It sounded like someone had gotten out of the water. In my peripheral vision, I caught movement. There were feet coming towards me.

Then he was hovering over me, dripping teal water onto me, peering down at me with those unnaturally green eyes. They'd been closed for so long, I'd forgotten just how green they were. But his eye color was less remarkable than the fact that his eyes were finally open and that he was standing there above me, very much alive.

I thought of Jonny and how he'd said I was the strongest person he knew. 'A survivor,' he'd called me. But the strongest person *I* knew was looking down at me now, wearing the same grim expression of determination he always wore. *He* was the real survivor, the unconquerable one.

I wanted to ask him his secret, how he managed to persevere all the time, but there was too little of me left to form words. What came out instead was a wheeze-like cough.

"Stop being so dramatic," Kai said, his voice sounding even deeper than I'd remembered it but just as calm. He twisted the portens from my hands—I heard my frozen flesh crack where it broke—and tossed it aside.

He scooped me up into his arms. "You're going to be fine." I felt my head jerk, a minute shake of dissent. "Yes you are," he said firmly.

He walked to the edge of the pool and stepped into it, still holding me. "You're going to be fine," he said again. "You are, because I say so." Then he thrust me into the water, pushing my entire body beneath the surface, and held me there. I was powerless to resist, powerless even to close my eyes. Through the blue-green water, his face rippled above me, as serious and resolute as ever. I saw his mouth move, and I thought I heard him mutter, "…And my will is stronger than yours."

But then I was gone, and all the world, black.

CHAPTER 84

L ike "The Day of the Bouquet" eight years ago, it was the scent of flowers that awakened me. I inhaled the heady, musky scent, and saw the small magenta Amaranth flowers in my mind before I saw them in real life. Opening my eyes, the blossoms filled my vision. They were lying on the ornately carved table next to my bed, along with a glass of water and some snacks.

Past the table, at the opposite side of the tent was Rori, sitting cross-legged on the bed where Flash once slept. She was holding the portens, her brows furrowed in concentration as she considered it.

I sat up slowly, blinking against the sun that shone through the sheer fabric of the tent. Rori looked up, pressing her lips together in a sad smile. I saw the truth in her eyes and glanced away, focusing instead on the Amaranths.

"Eclipse asked me to place them there," she said of the flowers, "to help restore your spirit." She shrugged. "They're said to be from Terran, one of her *Pactem Orbis* gifts to the Alchemists. They're supposed to fortify the soul."

They weren't working. My spirit felt damaged, like it had been ripped apart and would never be whole again. "How many?" I asked dully, staring at the blossoms.

She didn't answer.

"Rori, tell me. How many have we lost?"

I knew the number, probably better than she did, but I didn't trust my gift. There were too few signals. I was Receiving too few... The rest, they couldn't all be gone. Could they?

Rori sighed heavily. "Fifteen... so far. But there are others that I don't think... The count will probably be in the twenties."

My throat tightened. I couldn't look at her. "Who?"

"Gemma, now's not the time to—"

"Who?" I demanded.

I heard her swallow. When she spoke, her voice was choked. "They were my family, my friends... And some of them, just kids..." She fell silent, and for several minutes, her ragged breathing was all there was.

Not Taeo! I thought, *Please, please, not Taeo. For Rori's sake, and mine, and Kai's. Don't let it be Taeo...*

"Not Taeo?" I burst out, my head snapping up.

Rori shook her head weakly. "Not Taeo. He's with Kai. They've been working all night to... do what they can." She wiped her eyes, sniffling. "Kai asked me to bring you here and stay with you until you woke up. He said the Mederium had done as much as it could do for you and that you... that you just needed real sleep and real food and..." She trailed off, gazing into space.

"Rori," I said gently. "Who?"

She closed her eyes. "Shea," she said. "Kelby... Ren... Hannah..." She listed others, but I'd stopped listening after I heard Hannah's name. My heart sank, and I felt hot tears roll down my cheeks.

Why did it have to be Hannah? Why did it have to be anyone? I stood up too quickly and swayed. Rori leapt to her feet to steady me.

"When was the last time you ate anything?" she asked.

I waved her off. "I need to go—"

"You don't need to go anywhere. There are enough people at the Mederium right now. The ones who are well are helping everyone who's not. Or they will be once the pool is done cycling again."

"But we can help, too," I said, eyeing the portens, reaching for it.

"No," Rori said flatly. "I recovered from the poison just after Kai, and so did Taeo; we saw what it did to you. No one needs to use this portens. Not now, not ever again." Then, softening, she added, "Besides, we really *don't* need it. No one's died as a result of our not using it. Even before, when Kai was trying to save you, there were enough of us reviving to grab those who were sinking."

She braced my shoulder. "You've done what you could do, Gemma. Now you need to sleep."

"I've been asleep," I argued.

"For three hours, that's it," she said. "That's not enough. Eat something. Drink that water. Then try to rest some more."

Starting to feel lightheaded, I slumped onto the bed and obeyed. Rori sat back down across from me. "Just one question," she said, her expression and tone suddenly flinty. "What became of Phoenix?"

✳ ✳ ✳

I think I told Rori everything before I succumbed once more to sleep. When I awoke again, it was nighttime and I was alone. But I hadn't been for long. A whitish haze obscured my view of the stars, and the smell of cigarette smoke still hung in the air.

Kai.

I rolled to my side and saw my boulder opal pendant, my Christmas gift from Jonny, hanging from the corner of the table on a new chain. Fresh heartache stirred inside me on seeing it, but I clasped it around my neck nonetheless. On top of the table, beside the Amaranths, were two sheets of paper. The first was a letter written in Kai's familiar scrawl.

Gemma— it began,

> *There's too much to say, too much to hear you say. We'll talk, but for now you need your sleep.*

> *I've got to get back, but here are two things I wanted you to have right away... two things that might give you the strength to face the days ahead.*

> *1) Your pendant. It must mean a lot to you since you never took it off. I put it on a sturdier chain than that flimsy one it was on before.*

2) My poem. It means a lot to me, which is why it's tattooed, at least in part, on my back. I'm sharing it with you because it keeps me going, and maybe it will do the same for you.

"INVICTUS" by William Ernest Henley

Out of the night that covers me,
Black as the Pit from pole to pole,
I thank whatever gods may be
For my unconquerable soul.

In the fell clutch of circumstance
I have not winced nor cried aloud.
Under the bludgeonings of chance
My head is bloody, but unbowed.

Beyond this place of wrath and tears
Looms but the Horror of the shade,
And yet the menace of the years
Finds and shall find me unafraid.

It matters not how straight the gate,
How charged with punishments the scroll,
I am the master of my fate:
I am the captain of my soul.

I thank whatever gods may be, Gemma, for your unconquerable soul.

Stay strong.

—Kai

My eyes prickled with emotion, and I set the letter aside quickly and picked up the other piece of paper. It was a note from Taeo, a short scribble of a note, but it touched me just as deeply. Across the top of the paper, he had written:

Greater love has no one than this: to lay down one's life for one's friends.

And beneath that:

Gemma,

Rori told me… told everyone… what you said to her about last night. She told us what you did and what you were prepared to do.

Thank you.

Thank you for saving us, thank you for loving us.

We love you, too.
Taeo

I cried myself back to sleep.

CHAPTER 85

My dreams of Jonny were punctuated with voices and wind chimes, voices and wind chimes. I heard them, wondered if they were real, and then made my way back to Jonny. All night long, the same pattern: Jonny, egress signals, bleary interest, Jonny. But the pattern ended a few hours before dawn with a message I couldn't ignore.

"Go to him," Echo was saying. "Now, at this very moment. He despairs, but he need not mourn. Amaza will take care of me. Tell Kai, Gemma. He needs to know. And tell Eclipse—tell her she was right. She was right all along."

His words echoed in my head and then faded away, leaving me with the gentle sound of wind chimes until those too had faded.

I got up and left my tent, letting Gravitation guide me to Kai. When I arrived at the Tabularium some time later, the sky was still dark and star-filled. I walked beneath the great stone arch—*Solve et Coagula*, destroy and recreate—and through the maze of glass plaques, that seemed, once again, to glow as if backlit.

Kai was sitting on the ground, knees up, with his back against the slab of rock opposite Record 3629. He glanced my direction as I approached, and then turned back to the Record without comment.

I sat down next to him and stared at the Record, too. A mere two weeks had passed since Phoenix had published it, but everything had changed. Nothing would ever be the same again.

After a long silence, Kai said, "We did everything we could. We fought and they fought and everyone tried *so hard*, but in the end... We lost them. And now it's finished and we have the final count: twenty-two dead, eight of them kids."

He sounded so exhausted, so defeated. Tears gathered in my eyes as much for his pain as my own. I wanted to console him, but no words came. I looked at my hands.

"Echo was the last one... Eclipse just wouldn't let him go..." He sighed and looked heavenward. "I promised him mountains. He'd never seen any, not in real life. And I told him I'd take him, that we'd see them for the first time together... once we were free."

"I'm so sorry," I whispered. "I know you felt responsible for him." I paused, unsure of how to go on. "But Echo... he's okay. He wanted me to tell you—"

"He's not okay," Kai said, suddenly angry. "He's dead!"

I nodded, blinking, willing myself not to cry. "I know. But he wanted you to know... Amaza will take care of him. He said not to mourn for him."

At the name, Kai's anger broke. His head bent forward and he closed his eyes, overcome with grief.

"Who's Amaza, Kai?" I asked quietly.

His voice was thick when he replied. "My Kept. Another Terran. She died a year ago, just after Activating."

We sat there, shoulder to shoulder, his words hanging in the air. Eventually I said, "They'll take care of each other, then."

"Yeah," he responded bitterly. "They'll *all* be able to take care of each other. My parents, my Kept, my friends, and my... Echo." He shook his head, wiped at his eyes, and then turned to me, his face angry once more. "So—what?" he said, his tone accusing. "He came to you in a dream or something?"

I met his gaze, saw the hurt behind his eyes, and decided. "No, Kai. Echo didn't choose me over you. He didn't seek me out at all. It's just... my gift. My gift of the mind. I'm a Receiver. I can... well, sometimes I get messages."

He didn't say anything at first. Then understanding dawned in his green eyes. "Like the one from Gate."

"Yes. Like the one from Gate."

"The one that made you think you shouldn't trust me."

I felt my cheeks redden and I looked down, tugging at a strand of hair. He reached over and lifted my chin, forcing me to meet his eyes. "But you just told me about your gift. You decided to trust me now?"

"Yes," I said softly.

"What about Gate's message, then?" Kai challenged, dropping his hand from my face.

I shook my head slightly. "He told me, 'Malakai, he is not to be trusted. I don't know what he has planned.' And so I guarded myself… But then you said something that made me think… When you were telling me about the *Pactem Orbis*, you said the omission of certain details—it can distort meaning. And I realized… there was a section of static in my message from Gate. My gift was still developing, so my Reception wasn't always clear, and… words were lost, words that might have been important, words that might've changed how I understood what I heard. Only…"

"Only you never got the chance to find out for sure," he finished, subdued. He dug his cell phone from his pocket, tapped on the screen a few times, and handed it to me. "Here, press play. It's a voice memo from Gate. I asked him to record it when I was with him." He shrugged half-heartedly. "Not that it really matters anymore."

I played the message.

"Hi Gemma. This is Gate, but I suppose you know that already. Malakai told me there's been some confusion about my message from a couple months ago. He asked me to repeat it so he could give it to you. I will, but first let me apologize for giving you such a cryptic message to begin with. I did that for the same reason I've refrained from contacting you again. You see, it occurred to me that there might be others out there who… Well, let's just say I was afraid my message might be overheard, or worse, intercepted. It never crossed my mind that there was another risk—that it would come through incompletely. Forgive me.

"I never meant to imply that Malakai could not or should not be trusted. In fact, now that Raela's gone… he's my only hope. *Please* trust him. Please *help* him. It's the only way I'll ever know if Éoin…

"Let me back up. What I'm about to tell you, I've already shared with Malakai today. I asked him to relay the information to you, but he preferred…

this. He wanted you to hear it directly from me, said you would find it more credible. So here it is, I guess.

"On New Year's Day, early in the morning, I got a call from a woman named Raela Celere. I knew who she was at once... I had been close with her parents years ago, before..." He cleared his throat. "Anyway, she said she'd just Activated and that one of her gifts was very special. She said it was imperative that I come to Riverview Estates at nine AM sharp so she could tell me about it.

"I was leery, of course. 'What about the rule?' I asked her. 'The one that forbids Essen from interacting with De-A's?' But she promised me every-thing was okay—she'd gotten permission from the Augur before extending the invitation. Not just permission, she told me, but a *blessing*. Phoenix was *supportive* of the meeting, she said.

"Raela was waiting in the lobby when I arrived. We went up to her condo, and she told me about her gift. Hindsight, she called it. The ability to See into the past. I understood it to be like the Augur's gift of Foresight—limited to glimpses. But she'd had one Sight that was more than a glimpse, one that she knew to be important, particularly to me. It was from the night my family died.

"I told her to stop, that I didn't want to relive those horrors, but she pressed on, almost enthusiastically. 'You don't understand,' she said. 'Éoin—he didn't die that night! He escaped! I saw him disappear across the bridge just before the attack!'

"And all at once, tears flooded my eyes and I thought, *Oh Éoin! I knew it. I've always known it*. And I asked Raela if she'd Seen him after that, if she knew whether he was still alive today—he'd be twenty-seven now!—and where I could find him if he *was* still alive...

"Raela held up a bottle of wine. 'It's a gift from Phoenix,' she said, 'a *Gaudium* elixir.' I knew the *Gaudium*—it's a celebration elixir, used mostly at weddings. But Raela said it would work differently if we both drank it together, at exactly the same time. Phoenix told her that if we did it that way, Éoin's current whereabouts would be revealed to us.' So Raela poured the glasses."

There was a pause in the recording and I glanced over at Kai. He had his elbows on his knees, his head in his hands. Gate coughed a little and continued.

"We were both about to drink the wine—the cups were to our lips—when intuition nudged me. Something didn't feel right. 'Stop!' I yelled, but too late. Raela had already drunk. And fallen.

"I wanted so desperately to help her, but there was nothing I could do, nothing, and it was then that I realized Phoenix had given the bottle to Raela with the intention of killing us both. But why? *Why?* Why would he want us dead?

"There was only one answer I could come up with: We were the only two people, other than himself, who knew Éoin had survived the attack of eighteen years ago. And for some reason, that threatened him. He wanted to get rid of us, the only ones who could expose the truth. But his plan didn't work; I was still alive. I knew I wouldn't be for long, though, if I was found next to Raela's dead body. I started to panic.

"I didn't know what to do or who to tell or even how to tell them—I don't have anyone's phone numbers—but I knew I had to warn Malakai at least. So I took the silver leaf from my wallet, the one I've carried since Tathra gave it to me on our wedding day, and I left it on Raela's body, hoping Malakai would see it or hear about it and realize it was message for him. Then I fled.

"I went to the Lodge and waited, even though I knew Malakai wouldn't come until the summer months, if at all... But there was nowhere else for me to go and no other way for me to reach anyone... Except...

"And that's when I thought of you, Gemma. I thought that maybe, just maybe, if you could hear me the way you sometimes heard others—forgive me for alluding to your gift—then maybe I could warn Malakai that way. So I developed a message. I wrote it down and read it out loud, focusing every ounce of my will on conveying it to you. And this is what it said:"

I heard a crinkle, as though Gate was unfolding a piece of paper. When he spoke again, his tone had changed slightly, like he was reading rather than speaking extemporaneously.

"Malakai knows you have the portens. He will try to bring you to Phoenix by way of the Wooded Bridge. When you see him, ask him about that night eighteen years ago. I need to know what he saw. You must do this for me. And tell him I did not kill Raela Celere. Given my history with the Host, he may not believe it, but it is critical you tell him that I didn't do it. Phoenix did, and he tried to kill me as well. I don't know what he's up to, but protect the portens. Phoenix is not to be trusted, especially not with the portens. Tell Malakai, he is *not* to be trusted. I don't know what he has planned, but do not part with it willingly. Hide it, keep it safe. One more thing… There is more to all of this than I have been able to piece together yet. Do not tell anyone about your gift of the mind. I hope you get this message."

The tears I'd been holding back spilled forth, and I buried my face in my elbow. Kai reached over, took his phone from me, and clicked it off.

"He knew," Kai said. "As soon as I told him about Record 3629, he told me not to trust it. He said it couldn't be trusted because Phoenix himself couldn't be trusted. I don't think he knew it was a fraud, but he knew to be suspicious of it…"

I felt Kai's hand, warm and heavy, on my shoulder. "I should've told you right away. I should've called you on my drive back and told you over the phone. But I… I knew you didn't trust me and I didn't think you'd believe it unless you heard it directly from Gate. And I never thought I wouldn't make it back… not with you being able to sense whether I was in danger and Taeo being able to come rescue me…"

I cried harder. "It's my fault," I said into my arm. "The *Consociare*—it didn't work on me. None of the elixirs do. It's my other gift, how I survived Phoenix's poison. It wasn't because I didn't drink it, it was because it didn't affect me. Just like the *Consociare*. I didn't know you were in trouble, because I'm not really your Kept."

"Hey," Kai said gently, squeezing my shoulder. "Look at me." He waited for me to raise my face. "It's not your fault. You didn't know that was your gift… Besides, without it we'd all be dead right now." Then he smiled faintly and tilted his head at me. "And just because the *Consociare* didn't work on you doesn't mean you aren't my Kept. It worked on *me* after all. It just means *I'm* not *your* Keeper. But you'll always be my Kept."

I couldn't hold his gaze and looked down, embarrassed. "Always? I thought that after Activation…"

"Upon Activation, the bond created by the elixir disintegrates. But in most case, and in mine, a different one takes its place…" He started to say something else, but stopped himself and stared back up at the Records instead.

The sky was lightening; as dawn approached, the glow of the tablets began to fade. We sat in silence, the two of us looking at the Records, thinking.

"It's funny," Kai said sometime later, scanning the row in front of us. "I've spent my whole life studying these things, and it never occurred to me that some of them might be false. How much time have I wasted examining Records that aren't even real? And which ones are they? Will they be obvious to me at some point in the future, like it happened with 3629?" He pointed at it. "Look at those lines. The stupid, arrogant bastard gave us every clue, and still I didn't see it until tonight. 'The enemy, unseen and undetected'—he was referring to himself—and 'the past will be repeated'—he meant his own treachery!" He shook his head. "I'm such a fool."

"You're not," I said. "You're brilliant and decisive and courageous... if a little rough around the edges." I tried to smile. "I think you might even be the next Augur."

Kai laughed scornfully. "Believe me, that would never happen. Anyway, the next Augur's already been chosen, and it wasn't me. Whoever it was received the gift of Foresight the moment Phoenix passed, like our own little 'mandate of heaven.' Now we just have to wait for him or her to come forward."

He leaned his head against the stone wall and closed his eyes. He looked so tired; I doubted he'd slept at all since rescuing me from the portens.

"Kai?" I murmured. "Can I ask you a question?"

"Yeah," he said.

"What are you going to do now?"

He opened his eyes and squinted at his phone. "I guess it's probably time for bed." He stood up, held a hand out to me. I let him pull me up.

"That's not what I meant," I said, as he led the way out of the Tabularium.

"I know what you meant," he said solemnly, "but I just don't know... I was looking for the portens, for you, for so long... I always thought the next step would be to go after the Dothen, but now... I just don't know." He shrugged. "Today's April first, right? Maybe I'll just Deactivate."

I stopped walking. "What?"

"It's my birthday," he said. "I'm twenty-four today. And for the first time, I'm really considering Deactivating."

466

He watched me splutter for a moment before breaking into a grin. "Kidding, princess. It is my birthday, but I'm not going to De-A. The way I look at it, you're my Kept as long as your Activated. I'm not going anywhere. Except now, to sleep."

I shoved him hard in the chest but he just laughed.

CHAPTER 86

Kai slept his entire birthday away, and most of the subsequent days as well. His recovery, Eclipse informed me when I finally sought her out to relay Echo's message, was yet unfinished. Not only had the Dothen attack been the most severe he'd ever sustained, but Kai's healing, I learned, was unlike that of other Essen. It was slower, much slower. And though he was conscious now, it would take at least two more months of a carefully followed recovery regimen to restore him to full health. She estimated that she'd be able to 'release' him from her care at the beginning of June.

"Let him sleep," she told me. "He may look as strong as ever, but he needs the rest to truly become so. Now—you said you had a message from Echo?"

I told her what Echo had said: that she'd been right, that she'd been right all along. She didn't ask me how I'd gotten the message, but instead just smiled a Mona Lisa smile.

"Do you know what it means?" I asked.

She searched the space around me, reading me, like a seeing person would search another's face. "Of course I know what it means. My brother wouldn't give me a message I couldn't understand, would he?"

I flushed, and I'm sure Eclipse somehow noticed. "Oh. No, I guess not. What were you right about?"

"About Echo and me. Where we came from, why we are the way we are..." She smiled that same mysterious smile and then, as though reading my mind, said, "A tale for another day, perhaps. But now I believe it's time to go, isn't it?"

It was time, but though I let Eclipse lead the way from the Mederium, I dragged my feet, silently thinking that Kai had the right idea. It would be far better to sleep through days like today.

The south side of Salvos had been razed by Phoenix's wave. Where Echo's beach cabin once stood, a heap of debris now waited to be burned. But the place still was, and would always be, the Axis—the location of the bridge and the center around which the Essen world rotated. So the burning was practical, but also symbolic: a way to reconcile ourselves with what had happened and ready ourselves to rebuild. But that wasn't the burning I was dreading.

At the edge of the beach, on the southernmost tip of the island, was a collection of wood more than forty feet long. It stood four feet high and was about seven feet wide, and laid across the top of it were the bodies of twenty-two Essen.

It was the only pyre I'd ever seen, and the largest one the Essen had ever built. And when the 'passing ritual' began with each of the seventy-one living Essen—including Kai, who had arisen in time to participate—lowering a lit torch to the wood, there wasn't a dry eye to be seen. But unlike non-Essen funerals, no one spoke and no one sang and no one even wept audibly. Our fallen friends were honored with silence, which the Essen believed was the most dignified way to pay tribute to them.

Of course, the ritual was overshadowed, figuratively and to some extent literally, by the presence of the enormous monolith, at the top of which lay another dead Essen. No attempt was made to retrieve Phoenix's body, though, and as far as I knew, no one ever referred to the death count as twenty-three. He was dishonored by this neglect. Letting his body rot where the cosmos could witness it but where we didn't have to was the most fitting end for Phoenix, the Essen thought.

Once or twice, members of the Host asked in hushed voices—to each other, not to me—what had become of the portens. The general understanding was that it had been somehow lost or destroyed during the events of the night. Otherwise, whoever had it would surely have used it to help restructure the south end of the island. Right? Or they'd be out hunting Dothen with it, according to its intended purpose. Wouldn't they?

The truth was, there were only four of us who knew that the portens was once again with me. After Kai had rescued me from it and tossed it to the side, Rori was the one to recover it, probably because she was the first one to seek it. She stashed it away in the Nest, and sometime later, Taeo returned it to me. I think Rori was either unable or unwilling to do it herself.

My relationship with Kai, once I'd confessed my trust of him, had changed completely. Maybe he wasn't my Keeper, but he was now without a doubt my friend. He could still be a bit of an ass—he was still Kai, after all—but we tended to see eye-to-eye on things. Well, *most* things. He disagreed with my decision to hide the portens.

He *understood* the decision, but he didn't *accept* it. He knew about Paul and Jeannette and their horrific deaths, and he knew how it had killed Phoenix and nearly killed me. He'd seen the effect it'd had on Rori, her obsession with it, so he could appreciate the risks involved if the Host became aware of it. ...But he still wanted to *see* it. He'd been searching for it his whole life, he said. Didn't he at least deserve to *try* it?

His fixation on it concerned me, and *trying* it was akin to *liking* it, which I told him I knew from experience. Rori was right. It needed to be destroyed. The problem was, none of the four of us knew how to do that. So while we were trying to figure it out, the stone would have to stay hidden.

I'd put it back in its clear plastic encasement and hid it in a shoe box on the closet shelf of my bedroom. Well, on the closet shelf of what *had been* my bedroom.

My aunt and Flash were both in the living room that day I first returned home. Without a word, Aunt Sheri marched over to me and slapped me across the face. I stood there stunned, and then she burst into tears. Flash pursed his lips and tried to comfort her while also rebuking me.

It had been twelve days, *twelve days*, he told me, since I'd been home, and how could I let them worry like that? How could I just leave town with that-Malakai-guy and not tell anybody? Didn't I know how stupid and dangerous that was, not to mention how hurtful to Jonny? The three of them had spent my entire birthday scared to death I was lying in a ditch somewhere but reassuring each other that I wasn't. Just to find out from that-Rori-girl—

Aunt Sheri interrupted, her cherub-like features blotchy and tear-streaked. "Maybe it's time," she said through her angry sobs, "for you to move out. Since you appear to have both the money and the inclination."

There was nothing I could do but nod, ashamed, and climb the stairs to my room to collect my things.

When I opened my bedroom door, I saw the pile of birthday gifts that'd been left for me. They sat on my dresser like a little shrine. I looked at them but didn't touch them or take them with me. I knew I didn't deserve them. Still, I lingered over them, especially the one I was sure was from Jonny, a tiny box with a folded slip of paper taped to the top.

I wanted to know what the fortune said, but I didn't want to find out like that. Not like that. I left it alone, along with everything else, and returned downstairs with just a small backpack of essentials.

"I'm sorry," I told my aunt. "I'm so sorry for hurting you. And you, Flash," I said, inclining my head. "I love you both."

"Wait," Flash said as I turned to leave. "You should know"—his face tightened with emotion and he had to force himself to go on—"Paul was murdered. He and his new wife. They were found yesterday... on the East Bank... in pieces. They were hard to identify because they'd been"—he choked on the words—"blown up. There's an investigation, but we really don't know anything yet, nothing about why or how or when... But I knew you'd want to know. I'll call you when I hear what they're doing for a memorial."

I started trembling, the horror of Paul's and Jeannette's deaths filling my mind once more. Flash hugged me and even Aunt Sheri did too, both of them moved by my immediate and almost fearful response to the news, but eventually I left with my bag over my shoulder, tormented and anguished and guilt-ridden. And homeless.

I went to Riverview Estates, met with Vivian, and got established in a condo. Thirty-ninth floor, in the unit that was once Taeo's, next to Kai's. It was clean but cold-looking, decorated without color, all blacks and chromes. I didn't care. I dropped my things to the floor and I slept.

Paul's memorial service was the following Monday and I arrived alone. During the visitation, I made my way to Aunt Sheri and Flash... and the girl attached to Flash's elbow. He introduced her as Velixa, Vex for short, his girlfriend since early February. She was a petite twenty-something woman with super short bleach-blonde hair and a sleeveless black dress that exposed the large, swirling tattoos covering both of her arms. She looked familiar to me, but I couldn't place her. Flash smiled and said he'd seen her in a dream before they'd ever met. That's how he knew they were meant to be.

I'd seen the person with whom I was meant to be in my dreams, too. I'd seen him every night since I'd fallen desperately in love with him. But my dreams weren't foreshadowing our future happiness; they were a reminder of our permanent separation.

I wasn't prepared to see Jonny in person, not after the way things had ended between us. Still, when I spotted him at the service, his eyes all red and puffy with grief, my heart fluttered. He was wearing a dark suit and a blue tie, one that brought out the color of his eyes, and his hair was neat and combed, not hanging in his face like it usually was.

He saw me watching him, and I looked down, blushing, fidgeting with my handbag and smoothing out my skirt. I wanted to run to him, touch him, kiss him, hold him, but when I raised my eyes again, he was disappearing into the crowd. I didn't even glimpse him again.

Instead I saw Maggie, his mother, glowering at me with disapproval, and Lucy, as beautiful and assured as ever, looking torn between familial loyalty and genuine curiosity. Eventually curiosity won out, and she dragged—wow, it was still Joshua after all this time—over to me to get the gossip.

I disappointed her with my unwillingness to discuss my 'vacation' with Kai, but to my relief, we were asked to be seated for the service before she could press for anything more.

Paul's and Jeannette's deaths, someone said, were the result of a terrible but random act of violence, unrelated, they believed, to the murders of the previous week. For though both sets of murders had taken place along the East Bank, the young couple that had been retrieved from the river were gunshot victims—no explosives had been involved. And as we all sat on hard wooden benches honoring and remembering them, we were assured that justice would be had. Investigators wouldn't rest until they could give Paul's and Jeannette's family and friends, and our community, the answers.

I felt numb as I left the memorial. Numb and afraid and penitent. I went home, either to Riverview or Salvos, depending on how late it had gotten. I honestly don't remember what time it was when everything was over. I can only remember the rain.

It rained for days, and then weeks. Life rolled on, and I went through the motions. Rori and I studied the Records and the *Pactem Orbis* legends, Taeo began teaching me to surf, and Kai continued my training. But I wasn't really living.

I couldn't. I was empty, like a zombie version of myself, able to perform functions but not have experiences. My new life, my life of unlimited money and endless health and supernatural gifts, seemed meaningless without my family, without Jonny.

I missed Jonny terribly. I swore I'd never use my Reception gift on him, but I was just so lonely... I wanted so badly to hear his voice...

It doesn't excuse what I did, but maybe it explains it. Either way, I did it. In a moment of weakness, on Saturday, April twenty-fifth, the night of Jonny's show at Fervor, I tuned in.

It was nice at first, eavesdropping on his performance. Like my own private listening party. It was nice to hear his voice, so smooth, so familiar. It was nice to hear his songs too, all the ones I'd heard a million times before...

But then he announced a new song, one he'd written the previous month when he was "dealing with some stuff." He called the song "Forgotten." The song had a grittier sound than most of his other music, a sort of angst-like vibe. I didn't like it, but I didn't *hate* it until I heard the lyrics. I don't remember all of them, but I do remember the bridge and the chorus:

> *I'm forgetting you, no matter what you say,*
> *My fight for you is over now, so please just go away.*
> *You've always owned me, maybe you always will,*
> *But I can't watch you moving on*
> *While I'm stuck here standing still.*
>
> *That's why you are forgotten,*
> *Why I've shut the goddamned door—*
> *That's why you are forgotten:*
> *Right now, all along, forevermore.*

My stomach dropped right out of me when I heard it. I stopped Receiving immediately, but it was too late, the damage had been done. The little life that I'd retained following our breakup in Como Park began to wither away. It was then that I knew it was really over—the circles of our Venn diagrams were now completely detached, never to intersect again. I hid in the Nest and bawled the entire night.

Kai and Taeo and Rori all tried to coax it out of me, but no, I didn't want company, and no, I didn't want to talk. I cried into my hands, refusing to meet their eyes. By morning, only Rori was left, and she got tough with me.

"Dammit, Gemma," she said, "You're behaving like a child, not an Activated Essen. You're a *super* for heaven's sake. Pull yourself together! You can't *behave* like this! There are only seventy-one left in the Host, and I'll not have even one of them, especially not you—*the Link*—acting so helpless!"

I raised my face, and when she saw the heartbreak etched on it, she softened. "Look," she said, "I've told you once before: You need to *go* through it if you're ever going to *get* through it. It's painful and horrible and it sucks, but you can't just push everyone away. You have to let yourself talk about it and feel it and *deal* with it if you're ever going to recover. And I won't push you to do it a certain way, but I need you to promise me—promise me, Gemma—that you aren't going to bury everything you're feeling and hope it just goes away. Promise me you'll find a way to go through it."

I promised her I would.

CHAPTER 87

Today is Saturday, June thirteenth—seven weeks since I made the promise to Rori. And though I am nowhere near *through* it, I guess I'm on my way.

'Going through it' has been hard for me. Everything has changed: my home, my family, my priorities, my body, my beliefs, my *life*. Emotionally, I've been all over the board—something Eclipse has not failed to notice—but I've been pressing on, taking each day as it comes, working through the pain and the loss and the guilt and the loneliness.

Rori let me work through it my way, like she said she would, and *this* was the result: this book. It's an account of my whole story, chronicled on paper. A living record of everything I went through over the course of the past seven months.

It took me four full weeks to write this, and I never intended to share it. I did it for me, as part of the healing process I adopted after my Uncle Dan died and Jonny gave me that leather-bound journal.

The soul would have no rainbow, he'd written on the inside cover, *if the eye had no tear. May writing be your therapy, as it is for me.*

My rainbow hasn't appeared yet, probably because the tears still sometimes flow, but Jonny was right about one thing: writing is therapeutic. And so I wrote and I wrote, hoping that maybe one day, I'd be able to fulfill my commitment to Jonny, the commitment that eventually, when I figured out how, I would tell him the truth about everything.

'One day' arrived two weeks ago, exactly four days after I finished writing this book. It was dusk, and I was in the Tabularium with Kai, Taeo, and Rori. We were studying Records, looking for anything that might help us destroy portens, when I solved a different riddle.

"Look at this," I called to Rori, sweeping my hand across Record 3395. *"The whole Host must know the cost / Of voicing secrets of the Essen."*

She arched an eyebrow at me. "How exactly is that supposed to help us?"

"It may not be help *us*," I said, "but it might help *me*. Don't you see? It says *voicing* secrets of the Essen. Not 'sharing,' not 'writing,' not 'disclosing' or 'revealing,' but *voicing*." I locked eyes with Kai. "It's the reason Hannah didn't die after Jonny read the note she'd given me, the one that called me the 'Hero of the Essen.'"

Kai looked skeptical. "I don't think so, Gemma. I'm pretty sure other Records use different words for 'communicate,' ones that make it clear that information should in *no way* be transferred to non-Essen."

But he was wrong. We spent the rest of the evening reviewing dozens of Records pertaining to the rule, and they all used verbs like 'tell,' 'speak,' 'utter,' and 'proclaim'—words that indicated a *vocal* conveyance of information.

They were doubtful, but I was convinced. So convinced, in fact, that I saw no risk in printing a copy of my story to share. I was positively gleeful knowing that at last I could give Jonny the truth without suffering the 'deadly consequences' I'd learned about so long ago.

I added a cover page to the printout. On it, I wrote a dedication:

> *To Jonny,*
> *the Keeper of my heart,*
> *and my one true rock—*
> *more valuable to me than the portens ever was.*

Then I packaged the document and mailed it, too afraid of rejection to deliver it to him personally.

And reject it he did. The unopened package was forwarded back to Riverview Estates with these two words written in Jonny's hand: *Sender Unknown.*

I was crushed, but for the first time, not completely forlorn. A tiny flame of hope had reignited within me. *One day*, I thought. *One day, Jonny will know the truth.*

But in the meantime, there was something else I could do with the print-out. I opened the package, and added a new note below the dedication:

Dear Professor Dagenais,

This is no novella. I think I passed twenty thousand words sometime around my description of that first hypnotherapy session with Gate.

However—
You encouraged me to write what I know, and that's what I've done.
I know I've missed almost the entire semester's worth of classes, and I don't expect you to award me a passing grade given my attendance record, but I do hope that reading this helps explain why.

Thank you for inviting me to take your honors course. I'm sorry if I disappointed you.

Sincerely,
Gemma Pointe

With that, I resealed the package and mailed it to my professor's office on campus. And just this morning, it came back to me at Riverview Estates with the following response:

Gemma Pointe,

What a fantastic story, and by 'fantastic,' I mean 'of or relating to fantasy,' not 'wonderful,' and by 'story,' I mean 'a collection of lies' and not 'a tale.'

You correctly inferred my disappointment at your regular, and then expected, absences throughout the course of the semester. Regrettably, I did not find your outlandish and fanciful account of how you spent your time to be entertaining.

Rather, it simply displeased me that someone with such creativity and talent would squander her gift by creating a five hundred-plus page excuse for missing a semester's worth of classes. You certainly took "Storytelling in the Twenty-First Century" to a whole new level. That was not intended as a compliment.

Additionally, I would encourage you to seek professional counseling. Your attempt to rationalize the unfortunate deaths of those closest to you as supernatural phenomena, not to mention your passive claim of responsibility for those deaths, suggests an inability to cope beyond which I could ever hope to help.

Regardless, the syllabus clearly outlines the final project as constituting eighty percent of the overall grade. As such, I have no choice but to give you a B- for your final project (quantity doesn't make up for quality, my dear) and a C for the course.

—Professor Dagenais

I sat in my condo, lounging across the black leather couch, musing over his letter. My professor's response to my story was harsh, but I couldn't help smiling. After all, my theory had panned out. I wasn't dead.

A knock came at my door.

"Kai!" I exclaimed upon opening it. "You've been released!"

"Twelve weeks later," he grumbled, pushing past me into my living room. "Listen, princess. We need to talk."

There was an intensity in his green eyes that I hadn't seen in months. "What is it? What's wrong? Has the new Augur—"

"No," Kai interrupted. "No Augur has come forward yet."

"What then? And don't even *think* about lighting up in here." I slapped the cigarette pack from his hand.

Sighing, he picked up the pack and tucked it back into his jeans. "It's about this," he said, taking a folded paper from his pocket and handing it to me.

I opened the note and read it. "I don't understand. Where did you get this?"

Kai rolled his eyes. "Don't be obtuse."

"You *didn't*," I whispered. "You *wouldn't*."

"I only wanted to *see* it," Kai said. "I wasn't going to *do* anything with it."

"YOU BROKE INTO MY AUNT'S HOUSE!" I shrieked.

"Settle down. My God, you're like a banshee."

"Let me get this straight: The *first* thing you did after getting released from recovery was break into my aunt's house and look for the portens!"

"Is it really breaking in if all the doors were unlocked?"

"YOU SNUCK IN WHILE THEY WERE *HOME*?"

"Shh! Seriously! Stop yelling! And you're really missing the point here. Yes, I snuck into your aunt's house—you should've hid it someplace more secure—but that's not the issue. Gemma, focus. It's *gone*. The portens is gone."

I felt my face blanche. "I don't understand…"

Kai snatched the paper from my hands. "*This* was on the shelf in your closet, where I'm assuming the portens used to be." He proceeded to read it aloud.

> *"Gemma:*
>
> *You are not yet my enemy, but I daresay, with the portens in your possession, you were en route to become so. Best to relieve you of it before then.*
> *—GOD"*

He ran a hand through his short, dark hair. "God?" he said. "God, Gemma? You know who that is, don't you?" I started to respond, and he blurted, "G-O-D. Gate Dorsum, middle name Obidiah."

"Gate?" I said, shaking my head in disbelief. "Why would Gate take the portens? How would he even know it was there? Gravitation?"

Kai scoffed. "De-A's don't have gifts like Gravitation, remember? And if Gravitation worked on the portens, do you really think it would've taken me eighteen years to find it? As for *why* Gate would want it… That I think I know. You said yourself we don't know everything the portens can do. Maybe he thinks he can use it to find Éoin. He's a father, Gemma. He just discovered his son's alive after nearly two decades of believing he was dead. He'll try anything to find him."

I sat down on the couch. It didn't make sense to me, Gate taking the portens. The note didn't sound like him, and he'd been used as a scapegoat too many times before.

"I'm going to the Lodge again."

I stared at Kai. "But you were just released! And it's already after noon—you'll never make it in time!"

"Don't be ridiculous. I'm not going today. I'll go tomorrow."

"You think he's still even there?"

"No," he admitted. "I'm betting he left once he was able to warn me about Phoenix. It's safer for him to stay on the move. He doesn't know yet that his name's been cleared, that no one's pursuing him anymore."

"Then why go to the Lodge?"

"It's a place to start, Gemma. Maybe there'll be some clue as to where he's gone. Besides, on the off chance he *is* there… I can propose a trade. My memory for the portens. He wants it desperately. He begged me for it when I saw him in March, but there wasn't enough time for him to take me under." Then he flashed me a crooked grin. "So… are you in?"

"What?" I asked, bewildered. "You want me to go with you?"

He shrugged. "Your gift might be useful."

"Gee, thanks."

"And if Gate is there, maybe he'll take you under, too. You know… so you can continue… reconstructing your past." He eyed me evenly with crossed arms and waited.

I lowered my gaze and mumbled, "You know?"

"I didn't know, but I suspected. You've been a different person these past few months, like you've come to terms with who you really are. I figured the only explanation was that your memory is back—that you realized you were one of us all along." He came to sit next to me on the couch. "Why didn't you tell me?"

His green eyes were penetrating; I could feel them boring into my face. "I don't know. I guess I just wasn't ready. There's so much more to the night my father and I—the night our car went into the lake. I'm still processing it."

"Tell me about it. Maybe I can help you."

Maybe he could, but I needed to keep it to myself a little while longer. "I will, Kai. Just not yet."

"Tomorrow, then. We'll have *lots* of time in the car." He winked at me and told me we'd leave at sunrise.

I sat on my couch for a long time after he left, thinking, remembering, processing. But there was too much and my thoughts were too jumbled, which is why I switched to writing.

I'm looking out the window of my condo now, watching the sun sink lower in the sky. Soon I'll have to leave for Salvos, I know, and then I'll log one more night in what Echo called my 'beautiful, tropical cage.' And tomorrow I'll go with Kai to the Lodge.

Who knows, maybe I will be ready to tell him what I remembered about the night my father died on our way to find Gate. He's smart and insightful and could probably shed some light on things...

Things like who she might have been, that dark-haired, green-eyed woman that came to our house and interrupted our dinner that snowy November evening eight years ago. I didn't know it at the time, but she was an Essen or a De-A for sure, and probably Affiliation Terran—she had Kai's height and coloring.

I remembered my father opening the door and hearing her say, "It's about Eliana."

"Lia?" my father asked, confusion coloring his words.

At my mother's name, I got up from my place at the kitchen table and ran to his side. The woman surveyed me appraisingly. "And this must be her daughter," she said. "You look just like her." Her eyes landed on my birthmark. "You are destined for greatness, you know. But there is another like you, another with a mark like that. Together, the two of you could be unstoppable."

My father put his arm around me. "What is this about? Who *are* you?"

She smiled and extended her hand. "My name is Haddie, David, and there's something I need to show you."

My father reluctantly invited her in, and I was sent to my room so the two of them could talk. It didn't take long for her to convince him that we needed to go and that there was urgency in going, because soon the three of us were in the car and on the way to whatever it was we needed to see.

The *three* of us. The three of us were in the car when it went into the lake. Only two of us were pulled out. So what ever happened to Haddie?

I don't have all the answers. But for the first time in my life, I believe that I *will have* all the answers. Maybe not right away, but I'll find them. I know

I will, because I'm the Link. The one capable of connecting the seemingly unconnected.

Gate doesn't have the portens, of that I'm sure, and I don't think we're going to find him at the Lodge. But Kai was right about one thing: It's a place to start.

I need a place to start. There are too many riddles to be solved, and I can't puzzle them out all at once. So I'll work with Kai to find the portens first, and maybe along the way I'll get more clues—clues about who my mother really was, why I bear 'the mark of the four,' whether there really is another with my same notae, and *why* the ocean still calls to me.

Despite my comprehensive notae, I'm Affiliation Merla. Yet even among Merlas, the pull I feel seems to be unique. The sea beckons me, promising a prize that waits always beyond the next swell…

I can't worry about that right now. My first priority *has* to be the portens because I've seen what it can do, and worse, I've seen what it can do in the wrong hands.

It was stupid, hiding the portens in my aunt's house, thinking no one but the four of us would know to look for it there. I made it so easy to get, a mistake I won't make again once I've recovered it.

And I *will* recover it—before anyone else dies as a result of it. Because that's my job. I'm the portens-keeper. I will seek it, obtain it, and then hide it once more, until such time that I can destroy it. It's the cause to which I'm dedicating my life.

It's the only cause that matters, because it's the one that can protect Jonny's world. And though I've lost him, though he's out there somewhere actively forgetting me, I remain here, committed to him. I'll position myself between him and anything that threatens him.

My life is not my own. It belongs to Jonny. He said I'm the strongest person he knows—a survivor—but if I am, it's because of him. Because he's worth surviving for.

I don't know where my story will go from here, but I'll persevere until the end of it. I'll fight the enemies I'm bound to fight, though I'm starting to wonder if there really are no good guys and bad guys, no heroes and villians, no supernatural and subnatural. I think there's a bit of both in all of us.

Regardless, the Dothen still want me, want all of the Essen, dead. Kai believes it's "hunt or be hunted," but I think there's more to that riddle, too—and maybe an answer that doesn't require the sacrifice of Taken.

I'll figure it out. I'm the Link: a light in the dark, a destroyer of evil, a conqueror of enemies, and a beacon of hope in a desolate world.

My name is Gemma Alexandra Pointe.

ACKNOWLEDGMENTS

Writing a story is a solitary endeavor. *Righting* a story is
not. My sincerest thanks to everyone who helped me get it
right—before, during, and after the writing process:

My husband, *Michael Seymour*, for his complete faith in both me and
this project: I love you, babe. Thank you for your support, your ideas,
and for indulging me each day by participating in "story time."

My mom, *Carol Cocchiarella*, for encouraging me to follow my dreams
and for finding manuscript mistakes that eluded everyone else.

My dad, *Archie DuCharme*, for believing in me before he'd read a single
page and for his ongoing enthusiasm once he'd read them all.

My twin, *Kevin DuCharme*, who suffered through the first (and
worst) drafts but still kept reading what I sent his way.

My sister, *Megan DuCharme*, for loving my characters
from the very beginning and for keeping me on task with
her perpetual eagerness for the next chapter.

My friends and family, for heartening and helping me
along the way, both on the page and off:
*Jamie Bales, Annette Cocchiarella, Mark Cocchiarella, Denise DuCharme,
Diane Fay, Dan Gallop, Randi Gallop, Jeni Goodenow, Carol Green, Jason Hannah,
Anna Lawrence, Mary Lecy, Johnetta Paye, Katherine Pittman, Keith Pittman,
Bonnie Seymour, Hannah Sjogren, Luke Sjogren, Leedjia Svec,
Julie TenBarge, and Misty Williams.*

My teachers and mentors, who contributed to this book without
even knowing it, having influenced me long after class had ended:
*Dan Butler, Nina Buzzell, Ray Gonzalez, Edward Griffin, Rebecca Hauth-Schmid,
Gordon Hirsch, Glenn Karwoski, Bruce Moskowitz, Jim Otto, Dan Philippon,
John Watkins, and Donna Whitney.*

And finally, my muses—my favorite artists, musicians, and writers, without
whose craft and creativity my work would have been uninspired:
*Anthony Bell and Chris Underwood;
Atreyu, Francesca Battistelli, Blue October, Breaking Benjamin, Cedar Avenue,
Citizen Cope, Counting Crows, Deep Dish, Gavin DeGraw, Eric Hutchinson,
Imagine Dragons, Matchbox Twenty, James Morrison, Matt Nathanson, Parachute,
Damien Rice, Scars on 45, Taxiride, Thousand Foot Krutch, and Trapt;
Jim Butcher, Cassandra Clare, Charles Dickens, Jen Hatmaker, Dean Koontz,
Madeleine L'Engle, Tim O'Brien, Christopher Paolini, and J.K. Rowling.*

Karen Seymour began her writing career drafting technical manuals for a medical device company's neurology division, a job she facetiously describes as "writing 'how-to' manuals for brain surgeons." She held various communications positions in Corporate America, writing everything from marketing plans to advertising copy, before returning to her native Twin Cities to work full time as a novelist.

Seymour enjoys reading (whatever she can get her hands on), traveling (to remote and high-adventure places), working out (because physical exertion stimulates creativity), and writing (everything, even the occasional limerick). She also relishes time at home with her husband and her two feisty American Eskimo dogs. She can be contacted via e-mail at EssenFans@gmx.com.

Made in the USA
Charleston, SC
22 December 2013